WITHDRAWN

MARY CRAWFORD

Love Seasoned

HIDDEN BEAUTY BOOK 5

COPYRIGHT

© 2015 All rights reserved. No portion of this book may be reproduced in any form or by any electronic or mechanical means including information storage and retrieval systems – except in the case of brief quotations in articles or reviews – without permission in writing from its publisher, Mary Crawford and Diversity Ink Press.

This novel is a work of fiction. Names, characters, businesses, places, events and incidents are either the products of the author's imagination or used in a fictitious manner. Any resemblance to actual persons, living or dead, or actual events is purely coincidental.

All brand names and product names used in this book are trademarks, registered trademarks, or trade names of their respective holders. I'm not associated with any product or vendor in this book.

Published on November 1, 2015 by Diversity Ink Press and Mary Crawford.

ISBN: 978-1-945637-43-8 (Diversity Ink Press)

Cover by Covers Unbound

Hidden Beauty Series

Until the Stars Fall from the Sky
So the Heart Can Dance
Joy and Tiers
Love Naturally
Love Seasoned
Love Claimed
If You Knew Me (and other silent musings) (novella)
Jude's Song
The Price of Freedom (novella)
Paths Not Taken
Dreams Change (novella)
Heart Wish
Tempting Fate
The Letter
The Power of Will

Hidden Hearts Series

Identity of the Heart

Sheltered Hearts

Hearts of Jade

Port in the Storm (novella)

Love is More Than Skin Deep

Tough

Rectify

Pieces (a crossover novel)

Hearts Set Free

Freedom (a crossover novel)

The Long Road to Love (novella)

Love and Injustice (Protection Unit)

Out of Thin Air (Protection Unit)

Soul Scars (Protection Unit)

OTHER WORKS:

The Power of Dictation

Use Your Voice

Vision of the Heart

#AmWriting: A Collection of Letters to Benefit The Wayne Foundation

Dedication

Whether you are someone's
first love or their last,
celebrate the fact that
you are loved each and every day,
for it can be gone in an instant.

CHAPTER ONE

DENNY

As I open the door to Gwen the Flower Petal'r, the bright Mother's Day's bouquets make me smile. Gwendolyn's creativity is amazing. Her arrangements are not your run-of-the-mill, cookie-cutter type, although, you can get those here if you choose. It's her custom touch which sets her apart. Miraculously, her flowers still smell like real flowers. I'm rather old-fashioned that way; I appreciate roses that still smell like roses from my mom's garden.

The fact that Gwendolyn works around flowers all day and loves to make delicious goodies makes it incredibly hard to find gifts that she truly finds original and useful. It's been challenging, but not impossible. When she first remodeled her floral shop, I had great fun getting her all sorts of coordinated gardening tools. Still, there's a limit to how many of those I could get. I moved on to fun kitchen gadgets. However, I have to be careful, because I'm not technically her boyfriend. As far as she knows, I'm just the father of her daughter-in-law.

I don't think she has any idea I would like to change

the nature of our relationship. For all intents and purposes, I've been doing an old-fashioned version of courting her for about a year now. I've been purposely taking it very slow for a good reason. To say she was married to the world's nastiest Neanderthal is the biggest understatement of the year. The man beat her and abused her children for years. To make matters worse, he didn't even try to hide it. In fact, he flat out bragged about it in front of a law enforcement officer and the rest of her family and friends with absolutely no compunction.

I know that there's more to the story with her daughter, but I don't have the type of relationship with Donda that would allow her to feel free enough to share the story with me. I really wish I did. That girl has some serious demons in her soul and Kevin Buckhold put them there.

Gwendolyn has her own scars from the battle. I know that she's not ready for another relationship yet. I'm biding my time until she's got some distance from the situation and can gain some perspective. I need her to be able to trust that not every man is evil.

I've got my own ghosts to put to rest. It's been a quarter of a century since I buried my wife. That does not mean that I don't miss Karen every single day. Some days, it seems like it was a whole lifetime ago that we met and fell in love, yet other days, when I see the light in my daughter, Kiera's, eyes or the tilt of her smile, it seems just like yesterday. I still hate the cancer that took my wife far too early.

I set my packages down on an out-of-the-way crafting table and I'm still looking around the store when

Love Seasoned

from the back room, I see Gwendolyn struggling with a huge arrangement of daffodils and ferns. The arrangement is almost larger than Gwendolyn's petite frame. I set my gift down and rush to take the flowers from her. She starts to cough violently.

"Are you okay?" I ask as I set the arrangement on her workbench.

Gwendolyn takes a drink of water and pops a cough drop into her mouth. "I don't know what's going on. There must be a lot of unusual pollen in the air. My allergies don't usually bother me this much, but I can't stop coughing. It's so annoying. I have to talk to customers on the phone and they think I'm going to hack up a lung or something. I feel so rude."

"I'm not worried about that, I'm worried about you." I place today's present in front of her.

"Oh my gosh! You are just the sweetest thing. How in the world do you always know what I want before I want it? Maybe a peach smoothie will help me stop coughing."

"Well, it couldn't hurt. However, that's not why I brought it. It's a prop to help persuade you to go on a road trip with me for your birthday."

"Oh, I can't possibly go anywhere. Madison and Kiera are both planning big baby showers. Not to mention that we're coming up on wedding season and graduation. I can't leave right now. There's just no way."

"Gwen, you've been working yourself to the bone. You need to take at least a weekend off. Turning seventy-one is a big deal. You need to celebrate it and be adventurous. If you're not going to celebrate turning seventy-one, when are you gonna celebrate? A road trip is the perfect way to mark such a great milestone."

"That's ridiculous, Denny. Who celebrates turning seventy-one? It's not even a milestone birthday. Who would I get to cover the shop for me? I'm usually the busiest on the weekends, you know that —"

"Well, I would've celebrated your seventieth birthday, but you went on that book lovers cruise with your sorority sisters, so I couldn't last year. Consider this a rain check. Don't worry about your shop, I'll ask Isobel to cover for you. She used to work at the hospital gift shop. They make bouquets and balloon arrangements there. It's not perfect, but she could fill in for a bit. I'm not talking about going on a month-long cruise — although that does sound fun. I'm just talking about going away for the weekend."

"Are you sure she wouldn't mind?" Gwendolyn asks skeptically.

"I'm positive. William and Isobel have been my friends forever. Kiera is their goddaughter; they would be delighted to help out, I'm sure."

"Where are we going and how would we get there?" Her brows furrow.

I'm trying to look very composed, but inside I'm doing a version of John Travolta's disco in *Saturday Night Fever*. She is not saying yes, but she's definitely not saying no. It looks very much to me like she's leaning toward yes. I take a deep breath to compose myself so I don't lose it. I feel more like fifteen than sixty-five.

Gwendolyn looks at me and taps her foot. "Please tell me we are not going to take that rattletrap of a thing

Love Seasoned

you call a truck."

I can't help myself as I attempt to hide a rather smug smile. "Oh, I forgot you haven't been out to my place in a while so you haven't seen my newest little project. I affectionately like to call her Betty — as in Betty Boop."

Gwendolyn raises a single eyebrow at me in a gesture that reminds me she was raised several echelons above my humble beginnings,. "I'm sure there's a reasonable explanation for that remark."

"You bet your bippy there is," I respond with a wide grin.

"Don't keep a girl waiting," she prompts.

"Hmm, maybe I should do just that. It'll be part of your birthday surprise. I won't tell you your mode of transportation. It'll all be a big mystery," I tease.

"Dennis Allen Ashley! If you want me to step one foot out of this shop, you better tell me what's going on. I'm as adventurous as the next girl, but even I have my limits."

"All right, all right. I didn't mean to offend your sensibilities. I was just teasing. Little Miss Betty Boop is a prime little vintage motorcycle and sidecar I've been restorin'. She runs like a dream. I took her for a spin with Mindy the other day and she is as stable as they come. I thought we'd run up to Hood River and run through the orchards and take some pictures of blossoms on the fruit trees. I've got a friend who has a cabin up there. Actually, he runs a yuppie dude ranch and the guy that was supposed to rent it broke his leg in a biking accident so it's free this weekend," I blurt all this in one long breath, like a kid whose reading Scripture in church for the first time. By the time I'm done, I'm ready to pass out.

Gwendolyn notices this and gives me a crooked grin. "Oh my, that was quite an offer. I'm not quite sure what to make of it. I'll have to think it over."

I'm a bit deflated. I'm not sure what I was expecting her to say, but I guess that wasn't it. I was hoping that she would say she was delighted by my offer and would be ecstatic to go with me. I guess I knew better, because if anything, Gwendolyn has become cautious. Life has taught her that people and situations cannot be trusted. I've got my work cut out for me if I'm going to convince her otherwise.

I hand my daughter and my granddaughter cans of Pepsi as we sit on my front porch. "How did it go?" I probe impatiently.

"Well, I'm fine, the baby's growing nicely and kicking up a storm, Mindy made The Honor Society at school and Becca's got a loose tooth, thanks for asking," Kiera teases as she strokes her ever-growing belly.

"Never mind then, maybe I should take back this Pepsi — it has too much caffeine and sugar in it anyway," I joke as I take a playful swipe at her drink.

"That's what I keep telling her. It isn't good for the baby. I read all about it in the pregnancy books but she won't listen because I'm only a kid," Mindy complains with a huff.

"Mindy Mouse, it's not that I'm not listening. The cravings are just insane. I've already given up Nantucket

Nectar because it gives me indigestion and chocolate because it makes me constipated. I can't afford to give up any more vices. You have to leave me at least one. It feels like I've been pregnant forever. I can't even sleep anymore. This baby is breaking my ribs."

"Nuh-uh, it just feels that way because you sit down. Charlie Dennis wouldn't do that to you."

"Oh, you not only know that it's a boy — now you know what we're planning to name him?" Kiera asks with a laugh.

Mindy just stares at Kiera and shakes her head. "Really, Mom? How long have you known me? Since I was like, six? Did you really just ask me that question?"

I laugh out loud as I glance at Kiera. "Your daughter has a point, her accuracy rate is near one hundred percent."

"No, Dad, Mindy is frighteningly similar to Tara. When it comes to predicting things in other people's lives, her accuracy rate is one hundred percent. She's a little sketchier when forecasting things in her own life. Since Jeff is in charge of naming the baby if it's a boy, I can pretty much have the whole nursery monogrammed based on Mindy's prediction."

"Not that I'm not a proud grandfather or anything, but can we get back to my original question? How did it go with Gwendolyn? Did you take her my other gift?"

"She seemed charmed, for sure. Gwendolyn thought the apple cider was a sweet touch and she gave you points for sticking with the theme of Hood River. She seems stressed about our baby showers. I told her that Madison and I wouldn't be particular and that we were flexible on the dates, but she still seemed a little off. I don't know how to explain it, but she doesn't seem to be her efficient self. Usually, she seems like she can conquer the whole world. Something seems a little off kilter. She appears a little run down. I haven't seen her this way since she escaped from Kevin."

"Papa, I'm afraid Grummy is very sick and isn't telling anyone," Mindy adds. "She was coughing a lot. It was like she couldn't stop."

I kneel down to where Mindy is playing with Lincoln Logs with her sister on the porch, I meet her gaze directly and ask her somberly, "Princess, is this something you *think* or you *know*?"

Mindy looks up at me with the saddest eyes I've seen her display in years. I haven't seen that expression on her face since Kiera and Jeff rescued her from her abusive family. "Papa, for once, I just don't know, but thinking about it gives me a terrible stomach ache. Don't let Grummy too far out of your sight, okay?"

"I never planned to, Princess Pumpkin," I reply, using the nickname I gave her years ago.

Mindy dives into my arms like a small child instead of the pre-teen she is.

I unceremoniously plop a pear tart and a cup of steaming orange spice tea on to the counter of the flower shop. Gwendolyn looks a little taken aback. "What's this?"

"Gwendolyn, what's your business structure here?" I ask abruptly.

"I'm a sole proprietor. I already filed my taxes. Why?"

"As a sole proprietor, aren't you completely responsible for your business?"

"Of course. You know I set it up that way so that Kevin couldn't get to my assets."

"Well, there's a downside to it, isn't there?"

"What do you mean?" she asks, perplexed.

I try to surreptitiously wipe my hands on my jeans. I don't think I've been this nervous since I stuck Mary Beth Anderson in the bosom with the corsage pin at the prom in front of her dad and made her bleed. It didn't help any that she was the pastor's daughter. I clear my throat and try to pretend my mouth doesn't feel like I've been sucking on cotton balls, as I try for a tone that spells utter nonchalance. "You know, if you get worn down, it starts to impact the way you deal with your customers."

I meet her gaze steadily as I suggest firmly, "You need to take a break now and then to refresh yourself. When you're a sole proprietor, it's harder to take those kinds of breaks. I've taken the liberty to talk to Isobel. Did you know she's also worked at Michael's Craft Store and is handy with other forms of design? Your store will be in great hands. I promise that I will have you back here no later than eleven o'clock on Monday morning."

I grip her hand lightly. "Gwendolyn Whitaker, what do you say, for your health and the health of your business — will you take a walk on the wild side and celebrate your birthday with me?"

Chapter Two

Gwendolyn

That's the oddest question I've been asked in a while. Sure, Denny and I have lots of fun together. The reason I like Denny so much is because he's totally nonthreatening. He's very careful with me. He doesn't cross any lines. He's a complete gentleman and very respectful. He is loads of fun and applies no pressure of any kind. Therefore, I'm a little confused by this new, intense Denny. It's a little out of character for him.

I can't say it's *completely* out of character for him because I got a glimpse of it just once. I saw the fierce side of Denny on the day Kevin Buckhold, my ex-husband showed himself to be the asshole he truly is — or, as Denny likes to say — asterisk. When I was first introduced to his family, I did not understand their secret cuss words, but they've grown on me over the years and I understand their appeal now — especially as my granddaughter, Becca, has grown up to repeat everything her parents and Papa say. It's funny how age makes us forget the tendencies of our kids. I now remember Jeff

Love Seasoned

and Donda repeating everything Don, and then Kevin, used to say. Don, my first husband and the kids' dad, was a firefighter who was going to get his shot at joining the Air Force before he was killed in a boating accident. Then there was Kevin — there is just no excuse for what Kevin was. My second husband was a dentist who liked to appear perfect but he was far from it. To the outside world, he appeared to be the ideal husband and father.

Behind closed doors, Kevin Buckhold was a sick, power-hungry son of a gun. I'm not sure I even know the full extent of his perversion. I thought I was protecting my children from his dark side by staying with him, but what I was really doing was victimizing them further. I didn't know it at the time. In the meantime, he was beating me senseless, raping Donda and convincing Jeff it was all his fault. What a prince I married. How I could've fallen for such a man, I will never know. He seemed so normal at the time. Kevin was like every girl's dream. The stupid thing was, if I had any doubts, he made me think I was crazy. Now, I wonder if my judgment is solid or if I'm off in fantasyland somewhere like I was when I was married to what I thought was the perfect guy.

Which brings me to the situation in front of me: here is a seemingly charming, wonderful, warm, loving, personable, caring guy and the only thing I can think is, *what am I missing?* Does that make me extremely cautious or crazy? Am I being prudent or unfair? After all, I have now known the man for years. He's never done anything to harm me. In fact, he's done nothing but look out for my well-being. Kiera and Jeff, Heather and Tyler and Aidan and Tara all think he's the best thing since sliced bread — not to mention Mindy and Becca, who worship the ground he walks on. All those people cannot be wrong. Perhaps I need to get over my fear of judging people inaccurately and trust that maybe, just maybe, he has good intentions. However, his recent change in behavior has thrown me for a loop. Why has he all of a sudden become more possessive and bossy? It's not like him to be so — how are the women saying these days — Alpha? It's very odd. I'm not sure how I feel about it. I'm not sure I like it and yet I'm not sure I truly dislike it. I know it makes me feel discombobulated.

I have a huge decision to make. Am I going to go on a trip, alone, with Dennis Allen Ashley? This is not a decision I thought I would be making at seventy. But then again, I never thought I would be single at seventy. I thought I was done making these awkward choices after the first time I got married. After I was widowed and got married again, I certainly figured I was finished. When my Prince Charming turned into a frog, I never anticipated ever — and I do mean ever — wanting to be in the company of another man in my lifetime. So, now what?

I look over at Denny who has taken up residence in his usual spot by the water feature in the store I affectionately call 'the pond'. What it is, more precisely, is a large fountain I had built into the wall. My daughter, Donda helped install it and one of Tyler's Army buddies, Matt, who is a computer genius helped sync it to a soothing soundtrack that plays throughout the store. There are nifty colored lights which play with different pieces of music. It's very calming. It's like entering some sort of enchanted wonderland in the corner of the store.

Love Seasoned

I summon up my nerve and walk over to him.

"Can we go to coffee before we jump to an overnight date?" I propose, as I trip over my tongue. A woman my age just isn't used to asking for a date. In my day, we didn't do the asking. We may have done a lot of hinting, but we'd never come right out and ask. It just wasn't done. Oh, I'm sure some women did, but not anyone I knew. It was considered unseemly. People in my social circle would never have been caught doing anything of the sort. For one thing, my dad would have given me the silent treatment for weeks and weeks on end if I would've ever done anything to embarrass him among his friends. Lord knows, I was a daddy's little girl.

I lived to make my daddy proud. Of course, in those days, it was much more difficult for little girls to make their daddies proud. Children, of any gender were meant to be seen and not heard. Little girls especially were meant to be nothing but decoration. You weren't supposed to be smart and good with numbers. My daddy, bless his soul, tried his best to break the barriers of his time. He used to sit me on his lap when he read the paper and talk about the headlines. He would explain what each and every story meant. He didn't try to dumb down the headlines for me because I was a girl. I was one of the few girls who knew what the stock market meant and how to invest. There were some real perks to being the daughter of a banker. I did some very interesting things with my allowance throughout the years. I am forever grateful for his advice.

My dad had long ago given up on trying to find an appropriate governess for my brother and me — he just allowed the housekeeping staff to watch over us. He figured we were old enough to fend for ourselves. My mother had died from what they thought at the time was pleurisy, but nobody really knew. My dad was so busy trying to keep our household afloat, that he left us to our own devices. I fell in love with one of the older housekeepers, Althea, who took me under her wing. She made our very sterile house seem warm and inviting. She taught me a wide variety of Southern cooking. It made my Washington Beltway strict, regimented almost-formal upbringing seem normal and fun. I learned to fix my dad and brother food worthy of a restaurant run by Norman Rockwell. I could fix them anything from fluffy biscuits and gravy, to a Thanksgiving dinner with all the fixins' including cornbread stuffing and homemade cranberry sauce; strangely, my dad's favorite was giblet gravy. My dad was an upper crust Easterner with a taste for cognac and caviar, but his favorite Thanksgiving dish was something made with turkey necks.

I try to bring my mind back to the present and remember what I was thinking about … Oh yes, I was thinking about the money I saved by handling things on my own. That money helped me escape from Kevin Buckhold.

Denny is looking at me expectantly and I realize I must have missed something.

"What?" I ask, sounding as dazed and confused as I feel. I don't know what's with me recently; I can't seem to get it together. I never used to have this much difficulty concentrating. I used to be so much better at focusing on things. I feel like I'm slogging through mud these days. I am so tired and I can't stop this stupid cough. I cough all night and through the day. It's never ending. I guess I should go see an allergist or something. Maybe I've got that crazy black mold growing in my house. Lord knows it rains enough in Oregon. Perhaps that's the problem — maybe I should be like other retirees and go to Arizona or Hawaii. It would be fun to retire in Hawaii. They have cool trees and flowers in there — it would be like a florist's dream. Except, I went to a flower convention one year and talked to a florist from Hawaii, she said importing the flowers onto the island was so hellaciously expensive she was having difficulty keeping her business afloat. I don't know if I would want that part of the business. It would be wonderful to grow orchids and other tropical flowers without hot houses though.

Crap! I realize my thoughts have wandered off again when I see Denny regarding me with an amused look on his face. He's standing there watching me as my thoughts are taking their own little field trip to a completely different state.

I shake my head to clear it. "You were saying?"

"I was saying, I would meet you any time, any place. Just name it, I'll be there."

"Well, I received a notice from the city. They're going to be tearing up the road in front of the shop with heavy machinery today. I planned to close up at two o'clock."

Then he smiles widely. "That works for me, I adore Luigi's chicken parmesan."

"Hey, I thought we were just going for coffee?" I protest.

"No way! You can't expect me to go to a restaurant where they make amazing Italian food with handmade noodles and not eat while we're at it. Sorry Gwen, I'm going to make sure you eat properly while we're there. No main-lining caffeine for you. You have to eat good quality food while we're at Luigi's. It's a prerequisite for me. If we're going to talk about serious stuff, you need to do it on a full stomach. Those are the rules."

As much as I resent being directly handled, I appreciate Denny's efforts to make sure I'm properly fed and taken care of. It's been a long time since someone's cared about me. It's wonderful to have someone be concerned, even if it seems a little bothersome and controlling. I know he's got good intentions, or at least I hope so.

"Well, I guess it wouldn't hurt me to pick up some lunch while I'm there. Personally, I love their spinach ravioli."

"Okay, I'll pick you up later then." He waves goodbye and straightens my sign as he walks out the door.

It's been an insanely busy afternoon. It seems everyone and their cousin has forgotten their loved one's birthday or anniversary today and needs last-minute flowers. To make matters worse, I cut my finger on the ribbon cutter earlier this morning, making it difficult for me to handle the floral tape. I'm not even paying attention to the clock, so when Denny shows up at the counter, I'm thrown for a loop. At first, I ask, "What are you doing here?"

Denny looks surprised by my question as he stammers, "Did I misunderstand? I thought we had plans for this afternoon."

I take a moment to take a deep breath and pause to look around. Just then, the whimsical cuckoo clock in the store chimes to indicate it's thirty minutes after the hour. Startled, I look down at my cell phone and notice it's two-thirty in the afternoon. I am absolutely mortified. I haven't even wiped the dirt off my face. I was replanting a bunch of geraniums I had purchased in bulk and the bag of potting soil collapsed, sending a cloud of dirt up into my face. I'm sure I must look like a disaster area. Yet, Denny hasn't said anything to me. Suddenly, I break out into a violent coughing fit. By the time I'm done, I have tears streaming down my face. I must look like something from a horror film.

Denny digs in his leather jacket and pulls out a soft white cotton handkerchief, reminiscent of the ones my father used to use. Gently, he wipes under my eye. I hear him mutter, "Hold still, *Amasa*, you're about to get some mud in your eye." As he says it, the corner of his mouth hitches up in a funny smile as he recognizes the inadvertent movie reference.

"Wait, what did you call me?"

"I guess I didn't realize I said that out loud. It's what I always call you in my mind. Tara taught me the word one day when I told her you are one of the sweetest people I've ever met. *Amasa* is the Japanese word for sweetness. I guess, that's my mental nickname for you because it's what I think of when I think of you."

I look at him in stunned silence. It's hard for me to believe men like him actually exist in the world any more. I thought they disappeared the day my husband died. I examine his face closely to see if he's pulling my leg and trying to gain some sort of favor with me by feeding me a line. But, all I see is a vague sense of embarrassment that he'd been caught calling me by a private endearment. As I'm examining him, I notice he's taken his usual wardrobe up several notches. He looks very nice this afternoon. He is wearing a dress shirt. He doesn't have a tie on, of course, because we're just going to the local Italian place. It's a family restaurant with no tablecloths, candles or any romantic atmosphere to speak of. Still, it's clear Denny has put some effort into today's outing. He is wearing a blue striped shirt which brings out the wonderful color of his eyes and freshly pressed jeans.

That's not to say Denny is a slob, because he's not. He's always clean and shaved with a relatively fresh haircut. Although, his hair can sometimes be unruly, his red hair has turned gray recently. You can still see the occasional red highlights in it, but he has definitely turned into a silver fox. He is a handsome man, although quite different from Don's devastatingly dashing looks. Don was a strong and strapping firefighter. But Don knew he was handsome and he wanted everyone else to acknowledge his looks too.

Denny's attractiveness is much more understated. In fact, Denny doesn't even seem to know he's at all good-looking. I once commented I thought freckles were sexy on a man. I swear he blushed for an entire week. He couldn't look me in the eye for a whole month after we had that conversation. I have never met a man quite so shy. My son, Jeff, is known for being a tad awkward around women, but even he isn't that bashful. Although, the funny part is, Denny is not reserved about handing out compliments. He will tell me quite often if he likes my outfit or my new haircut and will notice immediately if I've tried a new perfume or lotion. It's an interesting paradox to say the least.

Speaking of cologne, whatever he's wearing today smells delicious. I miss men's cologne. Whenever Donald had to go work at the firehouse for several days straight, he would douse one of his shirts with his cologne and place it inside his pillowcase. At night, I would cuddle with his pillow to keep me company. I remember after he passed away, I was devastated when his pillow lost the scent of his cologne. Yet, I couldn't bring myself to spray the bottle on my own; it didn't feel right for me to be the one to apply the scent. That was Donald's ritual. I never knew when he was going to refresh it. Sometimes, he would even leave me little love notes tucked inside. It was like our own little secret treasure hunt.

Denny's voice brings me back to the present. "All right, I think I've gotten the worst of it, but there are still some pieces left. You should probably go rinse your face before more of it gets in your eyes."

For the moment, I'm lost in the intoxicating web of the rough texture of Denny's fingers against my cheek and timbre of his voice interwoven with my memories of the love of my life.

"*Amasa*? Are you okay? You look a little pale."

The unfamiliar word brings me right back to the present. I shake my head as if to clear an unpleasant design from a kaleidoscope.

"I'm all right, just too tired. I don't sleep well at night because of all the coughing,"

"I think you should go to the doctor. It's not normal

to cough for as long as you have been."

"I might at some point. There are still some over-the-counter remedies I haven't tried yet. I'd feel really stupid if I go to the doctor and they say I have a weird case of allergies. After all the time we spent with Donda in doctor's waiting rooms, hospitals and in outpatient care, the last thing I ever want to do is spend one more minute at the doctor's office if I don't need to. I think sometimes doctors do more harm than good. I'll never forget the horror. We thought Donda would die from her drug addiction and eating disorder. So, you'll forgive me if I don't immediately seek out the opinion of a doctor in a white coat. They're not my favorite people on the planet."

"I hear you there. It took me nearly two years to go back to the doctor after Karen died. It was the hardest thing ever to sit in the hospital with Kiera and help her get better knowing the doctors had failed to save Karen. How do you stay hopeful about a profession which has so profoundly let you down? It was the most difficult thing I had ever been through, aside from the court proceedings where they tried to indict my critically ill wife for murder. I had to put on a happy face for my toddler — when inside I was shattered in a million pieces."

I can't keep from gasping when I hear him matter-of-factly describe that time in his life. I can't imagine what it was like for him to learn Kiera would never walk again and that his wife caused it. I know Karen was technically not responsible for her actions because of the brain tumor, but I wonder if he ever doubted in a corner of his mind whether she did it on purpose. I think it would be human nature to be skeptical about that kind of thing.

Love Seasoned

Especially if he wasn't there when the accident occurred. I reach up to scratch my nose and realize my face is still dirty.

Denny watches me do this and suggests, "You go freshen up. Is there anything you need me to do?"

I look around the workbench and I spot a box of brand-new ribbon I haven't even unpacked. It got set aside when I had a surge of customers. I hold up my injured hand and show him my injury from the ribbon cutter. "I am operating at about half speed today because I'm a klutz. I didn't quite get to these. Do you remember how to use my antiquated inventory system? I need these organized so I can use them for a wedding reception early in the morning."

He shrugs. "As I recall, it's not exactly rocket science; I think I can handle it. You go ahead and clean up before you get any more dirt in your eye. I'll call ahead and make sure we've got a table at the restaurant. Then I'll start organizing this stuff. What gorgeous colors — let me guess, the couple is having their wedding at the medieval theme park?"

"Ohh, you're good! Someone should hire you as their wedding planner if you can tell all that by the color of the ribbon."

"You forget I raised a daughter through her high school years. She didn't go to a lot of dances, but she loved to be on the planning committees. We scouted a lot of locations for prom, homecoming and senior nights to make sure they were wheelchair accessible," he explains. "I restore a lot of vintage vehicles so, I have an eye for color."

I smile at him. "I can tell. You were apparently a pretty tip-top dad."

Our waitress looks like she would rather be any place on the planet except serving us. Granted, 2:50 on a Wednesday afternoon is not your prime tip-generating shift, but lady, it might work a little better if you look us in the eye. I know I don't look like much in my work uniform. Unlike Denny, I didn't have a chance to dress up much. I'm wearing a crisp — or at this point, not so crisp — peach Oxford shirt and khaki pants. There is a little butterfly resting on a flower which says **Gwen the Flower Petal'r**. Yes, I'm aware it's kitschy, but I thought it was cute.

I think Denny senses my rising frustration as I try to get the waitress's attention. I'm coughing again and I need ice water. Much to my dismay, I can't seem to tear her away from her riveting conversation about her hot date with seemingly half of the senior graduating class.

I start to cough uncontrollably and I'm so embarrassed. I don't want my stupid coughing to ruin our time together. Denny has been so generous with his time recently. It would be good to be able to sit and relax for a change. I feel like I have been running and running and running. I'm like a deflated mylar balloon which doesn't have the air to be able to float one-second longer. I need to find my gust of wind to be able to even function. Denny lays his hand on my shoulder. "Do you mind if I handle this?"

I shake my head now in relief. "No, please do. It's

been a long day. I don't feel like fighting."

"It would be my pleasure, Gwen." He flashes a small smile.

Without causing any fuss, he walks over to a busboy who has been working diligently to clean the tables and booths. He has a brief conversation with him and they both walk back over to our table. Denny sits back down and places his napkin on his lap. He looks up at the very startled busboy. "Is your memory pretty good, young man?"

"Yes sir. My mother doesn't speak any English and I have to interpret for her all the time."

"Great! Then you won't have any trouble with this."

"Yes sir," the young man replies nervously. I can see his bottom lip tremble slightly. I wonder what in the world he and Denny talked about back at the other table.

Denny gestures in my direction. "The lovely lady will have the spinach ravioli with a house salad, light on the house dressing with no sunflower seeds. To drink, she would like orange spiced tea with lots of honey. Please bring extra hot water and more honey."

I have to remember to close my mouth because it is gaping wide open with shock. Denny and I have known each other for quite a few years now since our children fell in love and got married, but we haven't eaten out much. That he would know my preferences — right down to my absolute dislike for sunflower seeds is shocking. I don't even eat granola because I can't stand sunflower seeds. It's not something I advertise. It's such a weird food aversion, that I don't go around telling people. No one knows about it except for Jeff and

Donda. It's not like saying I don't like spinach or liver and onions. Denny orders for himself and the busboy heads to the kitchen.

"Is he going to get in trouble for taking the waitress's job?" I ask in a hushed tone.

"Well, first she'd have to notice he took over her station. Secondly, in order to complain about it, she'd have to admit she wasn't doing her job. If she does complain, I will totally have his back since I'm the one who asked him to take over. If I'm on my mark, I believe he is the son of the long-term janitor here. He's also one of Luigi's hardest workers. I believe he has some hard-earned credibility. If he doesn't, I'll have words with the owner. I eat here often enough I can give him an education on the inner workings of his staff if he needs to be enlightened."

"You would do that? It's incredibly generous; most people wouldn't want to get involved. How do you even know all of this stuff?"

"Of course I would do that to save this young man's job. It's only right to step in if the boss is making faulty assumptions. Look, I've been the low man on the totem pole more times than I can count. Most people believe to be a long-haul trucker, you must be dumb as a rock and can't find any other type of position. The reality is actually much the opposite. You have to be an excellent mathematician, strategist, social mediator, navigator, negotiator and businessperson to make it all work. If you're not, you'll be off the road in no time flat. Being a trucker is a very complicated business. It's not as glamorous as they make it seem on TV and in the movies.

Let me tell you, before I met Aidan, I had never been to any television or Hollywood premiere in my life. Being a trucker does not make you an instant celebrity or famous. It makes your back, your knees, your neck and your eyes hurt. It does *not* give you any celebrity or political influence. It makes you sleepy and tired and prone to pain."

"I can only imagine that it would make you lonely and homesick, too. How in the world did you manage it with Kiera? You had to be Mom and Dad both."

"Well, when her grandparents were still alive, they helped out a little. But after they passed, it was just Kiera and me. During the summers and school vacations, I took her with me. Other times, generous classmates' parents took her in two or three days a week."

"That must have been hard."

"It was. But, in some ways, it gave her an education she would have never gotten in a classroom. She learned a lot about human nature and relationships. I think part of the reason she became a social worker is because she learned so much from observing people while we were on the road. I'm so proud of the generous spirit she became."

"It's true, your daughter is a gem. When my son fell in love with her, his whole world changed. Jeff became a better person because of Kiera. He was able to let go of the pain in his past and learn to forgive himself for things he never should've blamed himself for in the first place. Your daughter and those beautiful girls they adopted have performed miracles in my son's life."

Denny blushes. "Well, I can't claim all the credit.

Kiera is a lot like her mom. Even though Kiera was tiny when Karen passed away, Karen's genes are strong in my child. The gentle spirit which seems to understand all of your problems just by looking at you comes straight from Karen."

"It's so hard to see our spouses in our children, isn't it? I look at Jeff and he is the spitting image of Don. His long athletic body is Donald all over the place. Don would've been thrilled to know Jeff competed in track and field in college. Donda's sassy attitude is Don to a T. Don was a supreme smart aleck and was so proud of it. If he could get the burn on someone, it made his whole week."

"He certainly sounds… interesting," Denny comments carefully.

"Oh, I'm probably painting Donald in a way that sounds unflattering; he had his flaws, but he was an incredibly generous person. He would literally give you the shirt off his back and his shoes and probably his underwear. He was so amazing. He was larger-than-life. Everyone wanted to be him. He was a natural leader. He was like the Pied Piper. Everyone was drawn to him. He could cross racial barriers in a time when it was not accepted. We were an interracial couple in a day and age when people still looked upon it like it was a disgusting thing. There are still people in my family who won't even talk to me because I married a black man even though, God rest his soul, he's dead.

It mattered not to them he saved lives for a living or that he was willing to go serve his country. He was willing to go enlist in the Air Force when we were going to war in Iraq. War was not just a philosophical thing. Men and women were going over and being killed. But that was not enough for my family just because of the color of his skin. I am still shunned because I let the man I love touch me and give me children and somehow, it poisoned me. I'm not okay with that." I have to catch my breath after my rant.

Denny pours me some tea and doctors it with honey. He levels his gaze at me and states somberly, "You should never have to be okay with that attitude and anyone who is asking you to be is dead wrong. Do you hear what I'm saying? I traveled all over this country from end to end and side to side. I've encountered all sorts of people from rich to poor from black to white and every color in between. I saw smart people and I saw people who were not very smart. You know what I figured out? There were rich people who were stupid and dirt-poor people who were geniuses. Money doesn't make you smart and being poor doesn't make you dumb."

I chuckle out loud at the blunt way he neatly summed up my whole existence.

Denny unexpectedly reaches across the table and grabs my hand. "Gwendolyn, I'm so sorry you lost the love of your life. No one ever deserves that. It's so painful. It's the kind of pain you feel in every cell of your body. I know, because I've been there. I hope someday you'll find something or someone to make the pain better. I'm here to tell you that it's okay to feel pain. It's also okay to let it go. The people who loved us wouldn't want us to hurt this much."

I sit silently as I absorb his words. Much to my

horror, a tear slides down my face. I don't want him to see the pain leaking out of my soul. Then again, I suppose he's seen me in much worse situations.

Quietly, Denny hands me a napkin. I wipe my eyes and raise my gaze to meet his as I whisper hoarsely, "I wish I could believe those words. But I feel like if I let go of the pain, I let go of what I have left of Don. I loved him so much. He was the happiest part of me. He was the strongest part of me. He was the part of me that mattered. If I had been the kind of person I was when I was with Don, I would've never fallen for a monster like Kevin Buckhold and my kids would've remained untouched."

Denny looks like one of Tyler's horses kicked him in the chest. "Gwendolyn, you can't take all that on yourself. Kevin Buckhold was his own kind of sick and twisted. He was a master at hiding his true nature. He had it long before he ever met you. He hid it from his high school counselors, his college professors, his doctors, his dental school advisor, the people who administered the dental boards, the other women he dated, the people in his church and even you and the kids for the first few years of your marriage. He was a master of disguise."

"Yes, that may be true. Still, I should've known something was up."

"If we could look at our lives through the lens of hindsight, we could find all sorts of clues about what would happen in the future, but you know what? We can't."

"But, shouldn't my instincts as a mother have kicked in?"

"I think they did. You knew something was up. You told me you took Donda to the doctor repeatedly for her eating issues and then for her drug problems. If the medical professionals couldn't figure it out, why should you have had that responsibility?"

My shoulders sag as the truth of his statements sinks in. He's right; Donda was seeing doctors of many types the whole time. None of them said anything about what was going on.

"I struggled too. I had to get over the fact I'd missed Karen's illness and not fully protected Kiera. For a long time, the simple act of touching her wheelchair felt like it was scorching my skin because I felt the guilt so acutely. Finally, another father whose daughter was injured in a drunk driving accident he caused said if I continued to wallow in my own guilt, I would be compounding her injury. Those words haunted me for months."

"What did you do?" I ask, riveted by the story.

Denny looks lost and thought. "Finally, one day in the hospital, we were watching Sesame Street — my daughter was giggling as if nothing had changed in her life, even though she was immobilized from head to toe. I finally realized I was the only one who hadn't found the strength to move on."

I wipe tears from my eyes as I confess, "Denny, I feel stuck. I don't know what I want. Some days, the past feels so heavy I can barely lift it. I want to set it down and run free like a child who's never visited the beach. Other times, it feels warm and comforting like an old down comforter that's soft and well worn. I don't know which is the true reality or which is the one in my imagination.

I don't know which one gives me permission to move forward. My grandmother lived to be one hundred and three — which means I've likely got many, many more years to live. I don't want to live in this weird state of suspension for the rest of my life. I don't know how to get unstuck. What do I do?"

I swear I see Denny flick away a tear as he shifts his grip on my hands and strokes my wrists with his thumbs. His hands are gnarled with arthritis and bumps and scrapes from all of his years doing mechanical work and home repair projects.

"*Amasa*, I don't have all the answers, I wish I did. But as near as I can tell, You don't have to hold onto those bad memories any more. I think you can keep as many of the good ones as possible and try to destroy the bad ones by replacing them with good memories. Treat your memory like a big scrapbook. Throw away the bad pictures and put in good ones. That's all I can suggest. From what I can tell, it sounds like you have lots of good pictures to put in there. So, why don't you start telling me some of the good memories? Maybe they will drown out the bad ones. Perhaps that will free up space to put some new pictures in."

I give up trying to disguise my tears; they are freely flowing down my face. It's a good thing I put on waterproof makeup when I fixed my face earlier. Otherwise, I would look like a complete clown.

A few minutes later, our busboy comes over with a big tray of food. He is carrying the tray like a professional. I notice he now has a service apron on and a tablet of tickets. It makes me very curious about what happened behind the scenes because, I no longer see our inattentive waitress anywhere in the restaurant. He efficiently serves us and refills our water glasses. When he is done distributing dishes, there is an extra bowl of fresh pineapple. I glance at him with a befuddled expression.

When he sees my confusion, he addresses me, "My grandmother swears fresh pineapple is the best thing for coughing. It's okay with me if you don't want to try it, but I thought it was worth a shot. I know when I had pneumonia a couple years ago, my ribs hurt bad and I would've done anything to stop coughing."

"Yes, that's exactly how I feel," I agree with a sigh of relief. "I love pineapple anyway, so this won't be any problem at all to eat. I just didn't realize it had any medicinal value."

"I don't know, it might be an old-wives-tale, but my grandma swears by it. My grandma is usually right about most stuff. So, I guess it couldn't hurt."

"Thank you —" I pause for his name.

"Eduardo," he supplies.

"Well, Eduardo you've been most helpful. I really appreciate you. You made this dining experience great for us."

"No ma'am, it's you and your husband who have changed my life. Because of his kindness, I received a promotion and a raise today. He sent my boss a text message. I have been working here since I was old enough to hold a broom, and no one has ever done anything nice for me."

I watch as Denny blushes deeply. "It was no

problem, son. You deserve it. I have watched you for several years. You are a very hard worker. I'm a truck driver. I have been in thousands of restaurants across this nation, I've seen many busboys and you are one of the hardest working ones I've ever seen. So, it's about time you got promoted."

After Eduardo leaves the table, I study Denny. "So, when did you manage to pull off that little miracle?"

"Oh, remember the century and a half we had while we were waiting for our former waitress to seat us in the almost empty restaurant and I excused myself to go wash my hands? It doesn't really take me all that long to wash my hands, but, it does take me a while to send a text message on those confounded smart phones. You know, they're not really so smart. If they were truly smart, they'd make the buttons bigger. My poor old fingers and thumbs aren't made for pushin' those itty-bitty buttons," he explains with a note of frustration.

I have to giggle at his exasperation. "You know, you can make your text messages with your voice?" I suggest.

"Really?" he asks his eyebrows climbing up his forehead in surprise.

His exaggerated response makes me laugh out loud. "Yes, most phones will allow you to operate them completely hands-free if you wish. You wouldn't even have to touch your phone."

"No soufflé!" he exclaims incredulously, using one of his faux cuss words.

This makes me laugh even harder, but unfortunately laughing makes me cough. When I finally settle down, Denny looks at me intently and asks, "What do you think about what Eduardo said?"

"I thought it was extremely sweet of him to be so grateful for your intervention. You don't usually see such politeness out of kids these days. Although, I have to say we've gotten pretty lucky with Gabriel and Mindy. Mindy sometimes forgets, but I think that's because her brain works about a thousand times faster than all the rest of us," I respond with a wry chuckle.

Denny nods and smiles. "I don't disagree. I wasn't asking about your grandkids. I asking about what our waiter said."

My gaze widens as I try to replay the conversation with Eduardo in my head.

"Gwen, I was talking about when he referred to us as husband and wife. What do you think about that concept?"

Of all the things I was expecting Denny to say, this was not one of them. This is Denny. I'm practically related to him in some weird way. Well, not really. But it would make for a very strange family tree, that's for sure. More importantly, Denny represents safe for me. He's the guy who's not interested in me. He never pressures me. He doesn't view me as a conquest. That's why I feel so comfortable around him. Why is he changing the rules now?

I finally muster up my courage. "Denny, of all the women in the whole wide world, why me and why now?"

Chapter Three

Denny

"Gwendolyn, have I not made it clear how special you are to me? You're not the only person who has to live down an epic love story. I have one in my past too. I fell in love with Karen the very first time I saw her. She was the most beautiful thing I had ever seen. She had the grace and poise of Princess Grace or Jackie Kennedy. She was like an exotic creature and I was scared to look at her for fear I might somehow sully her. As she put it, she thought I was nice enough, but she didn't exactly see fireworks when she first saw me. She said my hair was nice enough to catch her eye though. I don't blame her for her doubts. Yet, somehow through all that we still found love."

"That's a sweet story, Denny," Gwendolyn's eyes immediately mist up. She clearly was not expecting this wave of emotion. "But, love doesn't always work out so well for me. I'm not sure I'm worth the gamble."

"But, that's the thing, Gwendolyn — we never know how the story will turn out. What started out as our perfect fairytale, complete with our little fiery-haired cherub turned into every family's worst nightmare. I don't know how much of the story the kids have told you, but it was horrific."

"I'm so sorry," she whispers as if she can't stop herself.

I shrug. "One of the things I learned the hard way is that whatever happens, happens. There isn't anything we can do to stop it. It just is. We live our lives the best way we possibly can and things happen. In this case, I was away on a short-haul two towns away. As nearly as I can remember the events of that day, nothing seemed out of the ordinary except Kiera was getting a set of molars in. That's it. She was doing what every eighteen-month-old kid does; she wasn't even abnormally cranky. She had a bit of a runny nose and she was drooling and trying to stick every weirdly shaped object like pencils, remote controls and calculators into her mouth, so we had to be careful to make sure she didn't inadvertently swallow a battery."

Gwendolyn nods as if she's recalling those days with her kids. "You have to be so watchful when they're that age."

"We had this silly cocker spaniel puppy named Snickers who thought he was a human being. Anyway, he kept leaving milk bones around the house. Kiera kept trying to stick them in her mouth. I was raised around dogs, so I wasn't particularly worried about it. I knew there wasn't anything in the milk bones which would kill her. Yet, for some reason, this particularly agitated Karen."

Gwendolyn's eyebrows raise surprise.

I hasten to explain, "Of course, we didn't know how sick Karen was at the time. She had been having some headaches; but she had a history of migraines, so no one was overly alarmed. She had changed medicines and we were waiting for the new medicine to become effective. This was supposed to be the newest, latest, greatest remedy. The doctors were sure it would cure her migraines. She was so sick of headaches she was willing to try anything. I went on my delivery circuit thinking everything was relatively normal. Sure, Karen had a headache — but sadly, that was nothing new. She had one so regularly, we'd gotten used to it."

"I imagine you would get into a routine. We got used to Don's crazy sleeping schedules even though the rest of the world thought we were nuts."

I nod. "Yeah, it's crazy what becomes normal in your family. Kiera is such a naturally helpful kid. Even as a small child, she was willing to help her mom in any way she possibly could. Even as young as Kiera was, she knew to bring her mom an ice pack if Karen said she had a headache. Kiera already knew what the word meant. She would climb up on her little step stool and turn the bedroom lights off for Karen. Little did I know it would be the last day she would ever be able to do that."

Gwendolyn shivers as if a chill just traveled down her spine. I take a drink of my Italian soda and I have to swallow hard before I can continue. Even nearly thirty years later, this story is still devastating for me to retell. "As nearly as I can piece together from what the evidence at the scene showed and what Karen told me, my wife got angry at my daughter and at the puppy for sharing dog bones and she decided to teach them both a lesson by throwing them into the basement as if it was a dog kennel."

"Oh no —" Gwendolyn breathes as she sways a bit.

I reach out to catch her as I nod and confirm, "Yes, we'll never know exactly because Kiera was too young to have more than a few words of language and there were no other witnesses. This was several years before there were nanny cams all over creation. Therefore, we don't really have a reliable record of what happened. According to Karen, she had a brief moment of lucidity in the moments after it happened. She tried to go down the basement steps, but there was blood on them from a cut on Kiera's scalp so Karen slipped and fell. Karen had a deep gash on her temple. Ironically it's fortunate she had a head injury. As a result, she had to get an MRI or CT scan and they found a golf ball sized tumor in her frontal lobe. The tumor in the decision-making portion of the brain meant she was incapable of making the proper choice between right and wrong."

"Wow! That's the most bizarre story I have ever heard in my whole life."

I can't hide the sad look on my face. "You know, that's almost word for word what the District Attorney told us when he threatened to charge Karen with attempted murder because he didn't believe her diminished capacity claim based on medical defect. The DA thought we were making the whole thing up. He was about to cart her off to jail even though she was dying from cancer. The jerk wouldn't even believe the hospital's oncologists. He thought we had doctored the medical results to get my wife off on child abuse and attempted murder charges."

I shake my head in disgust as I remember the pious look of superiority on the DA's face as he visited me in the hospital chapel to tell me he was planning to challenge the medical findings.

"My wife had weeks to live. The tumor had wrapped itself around crucial blood supplies in her brain and there was no way to remove it. While I was trying to keep my wife alive on one floor and my daughter alive on another— some rich, entitled lawyer was trying to make a name for himself by plastering my wife all over the front pages of the newspaper by making her out like she was some baby killer."

"Denny, I have no idea how you made it through that."

"I'm going to tell you something I've never told anybody else in my whole life — because you need to know this," I admit.

Gwendolyn grips my hands tightly between hers and presses softly, "It's all right Denny, we've both been through the wringer. You can tell me anything."

A single tear falls off of the tips of my lashes as I swallow hard; I have to clear my throat twice before I can actually speak, "When the police officer questioned me about Kiera's injuries — basically demanding to know if I had anything to do with the accident while they showed me each and every step Kiera hit on the way down those cold, damp cement stairs and showed me the puddle of blood where she laid crumpled at the bottom for God knows how long before Snickers got out of the basement and a helpful neighbor stumbled on the gruesome scene

— for the first time, I fell out of love with my wife. It was something I promised before God, my family, her parents and her baby sister with leukemia I would never ever do. Yet in that moment — in the grungy, stinky interrogation room with those cops believing I somehow hurt my baby daughter — I started to hate my wife."

"Oh, Denny —" she whispers, but I abruptly interrupt her.

"Don't you see? I am a disgusting human being. My wife was upstairs fighting for her life and I'm downtown in some dingy police station and I loathed her so much I was having a hard time stomaching my lunch. I was trying to decide if I wanted to pay to have Kiera transferred to another hospital so I could hop in my truck and get the Hershey out of Dodge and never look back. Do you understand? That's how bad it was. I had promised to love this woman forever, and I didn't ever want to see her again. What kind of degenerate slime ball does it make me?"

"It makes you a dad who has been horribly betrayed by the actions of his wife. I understand those actions were not of her own volition, but they were by her hand. You were put in an untenable position of having to choose between being loyal to your daughter or loyal to your wife. There was no way to be loyal to the both because by supporting one, you were inherently being disloyal to the other. You were in a true no win situation. So, if you felt strongly aligned with one side over the other, that was exactly what you were supposed to feel. You did nothing wrong," she argues passionately.

By the time she's done with her impromptu speech,

she's shaking from head to toe. I'm not sure why she feels so strongly about the subject. Perhaps it's because she knows Kiera so well and she's never met Karen. Or maybe it's because she's the mother of two children and I can't imagine she would physically harm them. Maybe it's her own guilt over the fact that even in her own home, her children were harmed by someone she trusted. I bet she understands my anger and fear. I suspect she has the same mixed emotions about her ex. As soon as I notice she's trembling, my body is on full alert. I am studying her like a hawk. I pour her another glass of hot tea and wrap my leather jacket around her shoulders. "*Amasa*, you good?" I ask, my eyes full of concern.

To make matters worse, instead of being able to assure me she's fine, she breaks out into another round of coughing. To add to her embarrassment, Gwendolyn just realizes we've been talking for so long the restaurant has started to fill up with the dinner guests. Now I fully take notice of this as well, so I put in an order for appetizers and another round of drinks. Taking Eduardo's advice to heart, I order Gwen a piña colada with an extra garnishment of fresh pineapple. I tell the bartender my girl weighs about a buck-twenty soaking wet and to take it easy on the booze. I am being charitable because she looks as if she has lost even more weight recently.

She takes a drink of the hot tea in order to try to stop coughing. Finally, she answers my question. "Yes, I think I'm fine. It's been a long day. Actually, it's been a long week. Okay, who am I kidding? It's been a long year."

"I hear you. I really do. Having Tyler away has been hard on Jeff. To hear Kiera tell it, Tyler was his best friend in college and not much has changed. Those two are like brothers."

"Yes, it's been hard. But it's so wonderful to have him back. It is so sweet to see them back together. Heather treats him so well. That child is so interesting. She reminds me a little of myself. She's got so much sass, but she can be such a traditional perfect little 50s housewife. My home economics teacher would have been proud. It's a fascinating mix."

"Oh, I know. Tyler loves that girl to pieces. We all went out to lunch the other day to celebrate an accomplishment of Mindy's. It was a pretty big group of us. Aidan happens to be on a tour break, so they were there too. Some complete loser thought it would be funny to make pig noises when Heather stepped up to the buffet line. The look of rage on Tyler's face was so extreme you could hear a pin drop in the restaurant. The whole place went eerily silent. Trevor grabbed Tyler and escorted him out one door and Tara went and had 'words' with the jerk out in the parking lot in the other direction. I don't know what she said to him or how it was resolved. But, the guy left a full set of ribs untouched on his table and never came back."

"I had my doubts in the beginning, but those two were meant to be together. God knew what he was doing when those two found each other," Gwendolyn comments with a laugh. "That Tyler is one fine gentleman under all his bluster and humor."

"The other one who surprised me is Aidan. I watched Tara for several years because she was Kiera's friend, she was always the quiet, strange one and I wondered if anyone would be able to tough it out with her. She seemed unreachable, but Aidan has sort of cracked her reserved shell. I've been pleasantly surprised about how much they're connected. He seems to be able to fill all of the cracks in her soul. It's wonderful to see them together. They blossomed into this wonderful couple. It's a pleasure to see them together. It makes me so happy to see her joyful and see a smile on her face. I wasn't even sure she was capable of actually smiling."

"When I first met Tara, she seemed to have so much pain buried deep inside, but you're right, I see less of that these days. More often than not when I see her now, she has a smile on her face. She has such a gentle beauty about her. Yet, there's an inner strength there too. I'm so glad Tara and Donda struck up a friendship. I think it will be helpful for Donda to have some women friends. I never realized it when we were going through it, but Kevin kept us all quite isolated. He monitored who we could see and interact with. In retrospect, I understand how controlling he was. I feel stupid for not realizing it when it was happening."

"I know what you mean though. When I look back on my time with Karen, I realize she was probably getting sick for a couple of years before the tragic incident, but I never noticed because I lived with her day in and day out. The changes were so gradual I didn't see them. In retrospect, her personality was changing and her physical appearance was a little different. I mean, even she noticed her eye was drooping. Karen kept asking me about it. She was saying that she couldn't get her eye makeup on straight and felt like she couldn't get her eye all the way open. Personally, I didn't notice a lot of difference. I thought she was being silly."

I take a long sip of my soda before I admit, "Now, I wonder what would've happened if we'd paid attention to those subtle little differences. Karen had never been a particularly cranky person. Then suddenly every little thing bothered her. I mean *everything*, from the sound of my bare feet walking across the room to the smell of the peanut butter on my toast in the morning. She was annoyed by what I watched or didn't watch on television or even if I chose to read a book. After Kiera was born, her annoyance level grew exponentially. It seemed that even though she was ecstatic to become pregnant, she could barely tolerate Pip's existence. Back in those days, no one talked about postpartum depression. I happened to read a little about it in some of her pregnancy books. It seemed like maybe her symptoms were similar. Her family doctor gave her some pills to deal with what might be depression, but they didn't do her any good. The doctor chalked it up to being a complication of her headaches and didn't think another thing about it."

"It's too bad they didn't know enough to find a brain tumor. But, I'm confused — to hear Kiera tell the story, you were madly in love with Karen until the day she died," Gwendolyn says as she fiddles with the napkin in front of her.

"What do you say we get these appetizers to go and go back to my place and I'll tell you the rest of the story? These chairs look more comfortable than they really are."

Gwendolyn's eyes light up. "Okay, I know this will sound weird because it's the middle of summer, but can you light a fire in your stone fireplace? I love it. Your place is so homey."

"*Amasa*, for you, I'll do anything you wish. Let me go track down Eduardo and pay the bill. I'll be right back," I reply as I run my fingers across her shoulder blades on my way to the cash register.

"I can't believe Eduardo made me a virgin piña colada so we could take it with us," Gwendolyn comments as she curls up in my big recliner.

"I know. Somehow I'm not surprised. He is very dedicated to the job. There is something a little strange about curling up to a fire to drink a piña colada in the middle of summer. Yet, oddly it works."

"It does, doesn't it?" She smiles with contentment.

I sit down in the recliner chair across from Gwendolyn and place my steaming mug of coffee on a NASCAR coaster. I might be dressed up today, but there's a limit to my sophistication. I clear my throat as I begin to speak in a quiet voice, "I promised to tell you the rest of the story. You might wanna settle in, this could take a bit."

"Didn't I tell you my favorite books are the really long ones?"

I flash her a grin. "Well, it's a little ironic you mention books because they're part of the reason my Pip doesn't really know the whole story of Karen and me."

"Oh, that's right!" exclaims Gwendolyn. "I forgot you call her Pip as well. Although, you don't call her Pip for the same reason Jeff calls her Pip, right?"

"Honestly, I think it's a little of both. I started calling her Pip because she was such a little pipsqueak. She was so small when she was born. I could almost hold her in the palm of my hand. But it wasn't too long before she grew her long beautiful red hair. She loved wearing it in pigtails just like the character, Pippi Longstocking. She was a voracious reader and loved the Pippi Longstocking books. I can't count the number of Halloweens she dressed up as her favorite character. Her life was often intertwined with those books."

"She definitely resembles Pippi, for sure," Gwendolyn observes.

"That's one of the reasons I knew your son was absolutely perfect for my daughter. Well, that and the first time I saw them together, I inadvertently overheard a private conversation they were having when he told her they were going to go slay dragons together — then I knew for sure."

Gwendolyn dabs at her eyes with the Kleenex she's been holding. "That sounds so much like my Jeff. He's so very quiet, but he's always been a knight in shining armor and he naturally stands up for everyone who needs a champion. I think it's why he became a lawyer and a lifeguard."

"It's true. Your son is a fine young man and just the type of man I hoped my daughter would end up with. Even as a young girl, Kiera always had stars in her eyes. She was sure all men were solid, strong and perfect. It might've been weak of me, but I didn't want to shatter her illusions. I wanted to be her hero. I perpetuated the myth I continued to love Karen to the bitter end, through thick and thin — like I was supposed to. Kiera had no idea about my abandonment fantasies. I was too weak to tell her the real truth."

"Denny, I think sometimes as parents it's our job to shelter our kids from the ugliest side of life. I think your gut reaction to the situation was one of those ugly sides she just didn't need to see. You are entitled to have a bad reaction to the worst nightmare in your life. You weren't required to share every bad thought you've ever had."

"Don't you think I did her a disfavor by presenting her with the illusion that every marriage is totally perfect? What happens when she and Jeff have a fight? Is she going to think her marriage is over because it doesn't measure up to the perfect ideal I presented to her?"

"Actually I think you helped her by not destroying her hope. Think what a powerful message you sent to her by standing by Karen. You may not think you stood by Karen, but you did. You fought the DA to make sure she stayed in the hospital and got treatment and you refused to buy into the media hype surrounding your wife. As mad as you were, you did not throw her to the dogs."

I shoot daggers at Gwendolyn as I snap, "Of course I didn't; I loved my wife. There's no way I could've betrayed Karen. She was like the oxygen I breathed."

Agitated, I pause to take a breath and drink some coffee. My reaction was a tad touchy — considering my wife has been dead almost three decades. Feeling a bit disconcerted, I look over at Gwendolyn and I notice she is softly smiling at me with a look of approval.

"What's that look for?" I ask, a little exasperated now that I've worked up a good head of steam.

She grins slyly. "Oh, nothing. You just told me what I already knew."

I raise an eyebrow at her and motion for her to continue. "Please, enlighten me."

"Well, you, Dennis Allen Ashley have given yourself permission to forgive yourself for all the shame you've been caring around for decades," she replies gently.

I'm unable to cover my surprise. "What do you mean?"

"For years, you've been under the assumption you fell out of love with your wife and broke your wedding vows and then compounded the problem by not telling your daughter what happened. You just told me that you never fell out of love with your Karen. Sure, you were mad — there isn't a soul on the planet who wouldn't be furious if they found out their spouse threw their toddler down the stairs and caused a permanent disability. You would be inhuman if you didn't rage about it. Despite that, the one thing you didn't do was betray your wife. So, Denny — you can set your burden down."

It's like time stops. I can hear my heartbeat in the room. The sound of my pulse behind my eardrums is almost deafening. It sounds as if I've run a marathon I sink back into the leather recliner and feel the cool leather on the back of my neck. The sensation is disconcerting in contrast to the heat of the fire on my face. I can barely breathe. It feels like the whole world is shifting on its axis.

I don't know how much time passes as I sit there waiting for this alternate truth to sink through my pores. What if she's right? What if everything I thought to be true about myself — isn't? Could I see myself again as a whole human being? Could I put the past behind me and move on? What would that mean for me? What would it mean for *us*? The thoughts swirling in my head are overwhelming.

Gwendolyn gets up and lays her hand on my shoulder, concern dimming her crystal blue eyes. "Denny, are you all right?"

My voice is a little shakier than I'd like. "Eventually, I'm sure I'll be fine. Right now I'm not sure what I feel. It's been an earth-shattering day to say the least. It's like I just found out the earth is round after believing it was flat my whole life. I need a little while to adjust. I don't know what this means going forward."

She pats me on the shoulder. "I think it means you get to be a little less hard on yourself. It sounds to me like you've always been a really great guy. It appears perhaps Kiera didn't get all of her stellar qualities from her mom. I think she got many of them from you. Your epic love story appears to be intact and you can honor your wife's memory."

"Speaking of epic love stories, you never told me yours. How did you meet Don?" I prod, suddenly eager to get the focus off of me. It's gotten a little too emotionally intense for my comfort level. I'm starting to feel like this is an episode of *Dr. Phil*.

Gwendolyn gives a low husky laugh as she goes back to her chair and takes a long sip on her piña colada. "Are you sure you want to hear this? It's like the most clichéd story you ever heard and not all that interesting."

"Yes, course I want to hear. Otherwise I wouldn't

have asked. I spilled my guts, it's your turn now."

"Okay, you might be sorry, because this is not riveting storytelling."

"Remember I told you about how Althea taught me to cook delicious food?"

I nod. "Yeah, it makes me hungry just thinking about it."

She smiles. "I know what you mean; I have the same response every time I think about Althea myself. Anyway, she had this cat she totally adored. Puss-in-Boots was a very spoiled indoor cat. However, one day he escaped. Somehow he managed to get himself stranded up a tree. Althea called her grandson over to help get him out of the tree. I thought it was funny. How was her grandson going to get the cat out of a giant tree? Of course, Althea neglected to mention her grandson was actually a firefighter."

"That's funny. What did you do?"

"I've already mentioned I was more than a little bit like Heather in my younger days and a tad boy crazy. Donald came waltzing in the house in all of his firefighting gear and — pardon the pun — I about melted on the spot. He was the single most handsome man I'd ever seen in all of my life. He had this southern accent because Althea's family was from Tuskegee, Alabama and he turned on the charm. He could tell in a heartbeat I was completely smitten. Still, I tried to play it like I was cool, calm and sophisticated."

"You are the epitome of all those things."

"Not really. In truth, I was none of those things. I

was tripping over my tongue like an old basset hound with no teeth. We flirted shamelessly for a few days, but that was brought to an abrupt end when I left for college. Althea had to go home for a while to take care of her sister who had a stroke and I lost touch with Donald. I finished my business degree at Brown. Then I was faced with a startling realization — the 'good old boys club' wasn't really interested in having somebody like me as a stockbroker. They saw my diminutive size, blond hair and blue eyes and told me to go home and have babies. I was devastated because I'd always planned to conquer the business world in honor of my dad's memory. Luckily for me, a former colleague of my dad remembered me hanging around my dad's office when I was little and decided to take me under his wing and allow me to work in his bank."

"Good for him. The guys on Wall Street don't know what they were missing. You would've a made a heck of a stockbroker. You're sharp."

"Thanks, Fred thought so too," Gwendolyn replies.

"But, this doesn't explain how you married Donald."

"I'm getting there! I told you this wasn't a very riveting story —"

"Okay, I'm just checking."

"Anyway, as I was saying … Althea's sister got worse. When she was placed in a nursing home, Althea eventually came back to work for us. Things were going smoothly for a couple of years but then Althea slipped on our icy back step one day and she broke her ankle. The doctor was really concerned she might need surgery, so they asked us to contact her family. Althea wanted me to call Donald."

"Well, that was bad for Althea, but good for you."

"Let me tell you, I was petrified. I was sure he had gone out and changed the world and here I was working as a bank teller. The last time we met, I'd had all these glorious plans about how I was going to storm Wall Street and change the way things were done. I was planning to be the Gloria Steinem of business. Sadly it's not the way things turned out. Even in the booming computer age where so much progress was supposed to be taking place, the workplace was not so kind to women like me. We were supposed to be able to have it all, but the opportunities to succeed in big business might've been there on paper, but in real life, they were much less common. I got to the point where I couldn't even pick up a magazine anymore because they were all telling me about this perfect work life balance I was supposed to have and I couldn't even get a date — let alone find a husband and have babies and conquer the workplace. Heck, I couldn't even land the perfect job. They all decided I was a bimbo — despite the fact that I have a degree from Brown. I learned to hide that I went to college at all."

"That's a dandelion shame! No one should have to do that," I blurt, shaking my head. "If you've been able to get an education, you should be able to put it on a billboard in the middle of the freeway."

The corners of Gwendolyn's eyes crinkle up with laughter as she hears my funny cuss word. I know I don't have to use them any longer, but it's become such a habit with me that it's hard to stop; so, I keep using them.

"Well, what happened when you guys saw each other for the first time?" I ask, unable to contain my curiosity.

Much to my amusement, Gwendolyn blushes as she answers, "I almost hate to admit this because it's so cheesy." She grimaces.

"Come on," I cajole, "you promised to tell the whole story."

"Okay, by that time, Donald had moved back to Tuskegee, so his accent was even more pronounced. I had to meet him at the airport, so when he saw me at the terminal he let out a long wolf whistle. When he finished, he announced to the crowd, 'Can you believe this gorgeous creature is here to pick me up? How in the world did I get so lucky?'"

"As you can imagine, I almost fell through the floor with embarrassment. You know how tall Jeff is? Well, add about two more inches and about twenty pounds of muscle and that's what his dad looked like. You have to understand — by the time he came back in my life, *Miami Vice* was all the rage across the country. So here he was with his rich, gorgeous dark skin and beautiful brown eyes with those lashes which wouldn't quit — wearing a baby blue suit jacket with white pants and big boat shoes with no socks — the man was a sight to behold. He was staring at me waiting for an answer. I hadn't been notified that this would be fashion show, so I was wearing the clothes I typically wore when I worked at the bank. I had one of those god-awful plaid skirts from the eighties and a cream colored blouse which had lace up the front and a high collar. I think my hair was even back in one of those banana clips. I was no vision of sexiness, trust me I'm not sure how he came up with the adjective gorgeous — frumpy would've been more appropriate."

"I'm sure that's not true, I bet you were stunning. I can't ever imagine you not looking amazing. Your eyes alone are phenomenal. It wouldn't matter what you wore. I'm sure he recognized that too. He doesn't sound like a stupid man," I offer.

Gwendolyn gives me the kind of look a teacher gives a small child who has no chance of ever understanding the material. "Spoken like a man who was decades away from ever meeting me. You can afford to be nice. The eighties was not a very kind decade. Somewhere, I'm sure Gabriel has taken it upon himself to restore the old VHS tapes if you really want to see visual proof. I wouldn't watch them anytime close to your bedtime because it might give you nightmares," she says with a self-deprecating laugh.

"Oh come on — they can't possibly be worse than pictures of me. You're talking to the guy who has self-multiplying freckles and vibrant red hair that can't be controlled with any hair product. I have to be the only person on the planet who actively rooted for male pattern baldness and for my hair to turn gray," I reply as I take off my ever-present hat and show her my hair.

Gwendolyn shrugs. "Actually, I kind of like your hair both ways. I like guys with wavy hair and whatever fragrance Heather makes for you makes you smell amazing."

I grin at her. "I know, it's nice, isn't it? I don't even

ask her what's in it, I just tell her when I'm out of it and she makes me more. I didn't tell her much about what I like. She asked me about what makes me happy and what I like to eat. I told her a story about how my grandpa and I used to walk to the corner store and buy red-hot candies and the next thing I know she brought over a bottle of this shampoo and body lotion; she made a little label for them, which was a cute little guy on a motorcycle and it says, 'Red Hot Dad'. It's the neatest gift I've ever gotten."

"I tried to get her to sell her stuff in the gift section of my store, but she says she only does it for friends and family. It's too bad because her products are amazing."

"You never told me what you did after he saw you in the airport," I prompt.

"Well, I don't know if you know me well enough yet to know I'm incredibly stubborn. I was not going to allow him to embarrass me. So I showed more bravado than common sense. I just stood there and stared at him without moving for the longest time. One of the many people in the audience surrounding us finally commented, 'Hey man, I don't think she's so impressed.' Donald came back with, 'Really? You're going to just drop a compliment like that?' It seemed like the whole airport started cheering him on."

"I was scared to death about offending him, but I also didn't want to lose the war of words, so I replied, 'When I actually see a compliment, I'll pick it up.' Then I blushed as red as a field of poppies."

"Donald later told me he was so impressed by my moxie, he fell in love with me that very day. He said he was so used to girls falling all over themselves to get his attention, he was completely bored by them. He was very grateful for all the love and support I had given his grandmother over the years. I treated Althea like family because she was family to me. I had done nothing heroic, but apparently Donald disagreed."

"Heroes come in all shapes and sizes. I know I considered all of those families who took care of Kiera when I was on the road to be superheroes. I would've never been able to support us if they hadn't stepped up to give us a hand. I know many of them thought they hadn't really done much, but their contributions meant the world."

"Maybe so," she replies, "but I always thought Donald tended to exaggerate a bit. Tyler reminds me a lot of Don. You know how he makes over Heather because she cooks for him? Well, I used to plant flowers in our yard. By the way Donald reacted, you would think I was the one who had the power to make them grow. He would be sooty and exhausted from fighting fires, but he would still stop and smell each and every flower I planted. He was especially partial to pansies. I got as many flower catalogs as I could find and try to get a wide variety so I could surprise him with different colors. The wide smile on his face would always make my day."

"Karen used to do something similar. Only, her thing was finding me different kinds of tomatoes. My favorite sandwich when I was home was a bacon, lettuce and tomato sandwich. She would try to get different kinds of tomatoes to make the sandwich taste a little different. She went so far as to write to gardening clubs to get different strains of tomato plants. It was a lot harder back then; there weren't very many Internet chat groups or Facebook. I always thought it was the sweetest thing."

"That was inventive. I don't know if Karen was this way, but if Don was over-the-top with me, you should've seen him with the kids. I wish we had the technology then we have now. It would have been so much fun to be able to catch those every day moments. He was teaching Donda how to pitch a softball. It was the most amazing thing you ever saw in your life. He was so patient with her. She blossomed under his tutelage. He would praise all of those intricate little drawings Jeff used to do. Not surprisingly, Jeffrey was never a fan of coloring outside the lines. Even as a kid, his drawings were so neat. Donald always found a way to complement his use of contrasting colors, his neat work or his diligence. Jeffrey ate it right up. Both kids were so devastated when he passed away. It was like they lost their compass in life."

"I bet. I guess if you can interpret it that way, I was blessed Karen passed away when Kiera was so young. She didn't have a chance to know what she was missing yet. Along those lines, I'd like to thank you for stepping up into the role of mom for Kiera. I know she appreciates it a lot."

"*Pfft*, Denny, if you think that's been any struggle at all, you need to think again. Your daughter has done more for me then I've ever done for her."

I grin at her. sounding like the proud dad I am, "I hate to be biased, but she is special isn't she?"

"You have every right to brag, you silly man," Gwendolyn adds with a light chuckle.

"Okay, we've settled lots of things tonight. We've

decided our kids are awesome and they have amazing friends. We agree our grandkids are phenomenal. We've established we both had epic love stories worthy of a *Hallmark Movies of the Week* and that our spouses died far too early. We both heartily agree your second husband deserves any mistreatment he might inadvertently get while he's in prison. I may even buy the premise that I can stop flogging myself for being mad at Karen for hurting Kiera. But, the one thing we didn't establish is whether you'll go on vacation with me," I say as I pin Gwendolyn with a direct glance. I hold my breath. I'm well aware I've taken the biggest gamble I've taken in quite some time. I also know I'm asking her to take even a bigger jump.

Her hands shake a little as she sets down her cup. She slowly blinks and takes in a breath. "You know, Don was the life of the party. He wouldn't want me to be alone the rest of my life. He would want me to be out in the world exploring. He would also get a kick out of the idea that I'm going somewhere on a motorcycle, especially at my age. So in honor of our past loves, I'd love to take Betty Boop for a spin."

Chapter Four

Gwendolyn

"Heather Colton! Why in the world would I need a cocktail dress if I'm going on a motorcycle ride with Dennis Ashley? You have met the man — formal attire is not exactly his thing," I remind her as I look around at the pile of clothes she has laid out for me.

"Well, you never know with these men of ours. They've all been hanging around each other a bit too much and they are a bunch of romantics at heart. It's hard to predict what might tickle his fancy. He might want to take you out to dinner and dancing ... or something," Heather advises.

"Are you serious? We'll be all grimy and sweaty from the road. We have about two square feet to pack all of our stuff for the whole trip. There's no way to be prepared for all possible contingencies. That's ridiculous. I think he said we are staying at some dude ranch. What in the world could we do at a dude ranch which would require a cocktail dress," I argue.

Heather shrugs. "Well, we have reinforcements

coming. Tara will be here any minute. With all of her dance experience and the life on the road with Aidan, she has become a commando packer. She can pack anything and make it fit into a microscopic space. She could probably fit your entire wardrobe into one suitcase. She'll figure it all out. I'll tell you a secret about Tara, she likes to say she's not interested in fashion, but she's got an excellent eye for this kind of stuff. She's got casual chic down to an art form. If anyone can figure out how to dress correctly for a dude ranch, it's Tara."

"Did someone say my name?" Tara peeks her head around the corner.

"Well, as Althea used to say, 'Your ears must be burning, child' because we were just talking about you. Heather says you have spectacular packing skills. Apparently I'm going to need them."

Tara holds my hands between hers and gently squeezes them as she quietly advises in a calm soothing voice, "Gwendolyn, honey, the first thing I need you to do is breathe. Denny has only good intentions. I promise."

"Tara, in my heart, I know. A man who calls me the Japanese equivalent of sweetness and really means it, probably doesn't have a mean bone in his body."

Tara smiles serenely. "Oh, I'm so glad he told you about that. I melted inside just a little when he told me how he sees you. He took such great pains to learn how to pronounce *Amasa* correctly. Let me tell you, he is *not* a native speaker of Japanese. It took him a while to get it, but he was so proud of himself when he finally nailed it. The amazing thing to me was he didn't do it for anyone else. I don't think he ever intended to tell you. It was his own private name for you. It's an indication of how reverently he views you and your struggle with your past. One of the things he told me when we had this conversation was how much he admires how well you coped with the hell you lived through without becoming bitter. I think whatever happens between the two of you, you'll always have a cheerleader in Mr. Ashley."

"Wow! Go, Denny!" exclaims Heather. "No wonder Kiera's standards were off the charts high before she met Jeff. He had a lot to live up to. She was a firm believer in Prince Charming, and now I see why."

I debate the wisdom of asking my next question, but then I realize these girls — even though they're younger than me — have been through lifetimes of difficulties, so I take the risk. "I'm not sure how comfortable Kiera is with this idea, so you might not want to share this with her. I need some advice about what's going on. To be honest, I'm a little befuddled."

"Well, you can't go wrong asking the two of us, we're two of the founding members of the Girlfriend Posse, so ask away," Heather prompts, patting my bed in a gesture to invite me to sit down and to make myself comfortable.

Tara nods in agreement. "You may be surprised with what your daughter-in-law is comfortable with too."

"Okay, here goes... You already know I think Dennis Ashley is a very nice man. I've thought that for a long time — pretty much since the first day I met him and he took care of me after the particularly dreadful day with my jerk-wad of an ex-husband. He's been nothing but kind and attentive. Since we met, he's been comfortable being my best hang out buddy. It's been great. Since I met him, I haven't had to go solo to anything. He's been my willing 'plus one' to all sorts of things — and I've been his. I've also got to do all sorts of things I never thought I would be able to do. He even took me to a motorcycle race once. I never thought I would go to one of those. It was loud and chaotic, but lots of fun to be around those screaming fans and loud engines. He says our next stop is a NASCAR race. I'm not sure I'm ready to go quite that far yet. But we'll see."

"So, it sounds like you two are pretty comfortable with each other," Heather remarks.

"We are. I thought things were great," I practically stammer.

"So, what has you so on edge?" Tara asks softly.

"Well, he seems to want to change the rules, and I don't understand why. Things are fabulous between us. It doesn't make sense to change what's working."

"What if something else might work a little better?" Tara asks.

Heather nods. "I don't want to belabor the obvious here — but maybe you're like me. Lord knows, I should be the very last person to speak about this because it took me literally years to see Tyler was head over heels in love with me."

I look back and forth between Tara and Heather with my mouth agape. "Dennis Ashley is in love with me? I don't think so, girls. He's still in love with his former wife. Sure, he flirts a lot. Still, I think he does it to make me feel better. He says he likes to put a smile on my face.

I don't think it's anything beyond a little innocent flirting. He still loves Karen very much."

"Oh, I'm sure he does," concedes Tara. "However, I don't think his love for Karen means he can't find room in his heart for you. I agree with you. He's torn. But I think he wants to explore the idea of moving on from the past. I know with certainty he wants you to be the person he goes exploring with."

"How do you feel about that, Gwendolyn?" Heather asks.

"I'm not sure," I confess honestly.

"Well, then it's a good thing you guys will have miles and miles and miles to talk about it," Tara responds with a mischievous grin on her face. "But, unless you want to go on this trip naked, we better pack you some clothes."

"Me, naked on the back of a motorcycle? Not on your life — not even when I was twenty! I'm adventurous, but not that adventurous," I reply somewhat aghast.

"Oh come on Gwendolyn, I've seen the little hourglass figure you keep hidden under polo shirts and khaki pants. You're pretty hot. I think you could pull anything off," Heather teases.

"Oh hush! You must need to go to the eye doctor or something, Heather."

"I can't believe you got me new riding leathers. How did you even know I'd even like riding motorcycles? I could get in the sidecar and get horribly carsick — Well, I guess it wouldn't technically be carsick, but you know what I mean," I comment as I look down at myself decked out in more gear than Evel Knievel wore.

"You forget I've seen you ride fair rides with Mindy and Becca, I can pretty much bet you a little ride on Betty Boop won't make you sick if you can handle what Mindy dishes out at the state fair," Denny counters.

"Okay, you make a fair point. When I was a kid, I used to be an ice skater and spinning was my favorite. I wanted to be the next Carol Heiss."

"Oh good, I don't have to worry about slowing down on the curves," Denny quips.

"Now, I didn't say that. Perhaps I should've checked your safety record. I was taking it for granted you're a good driver, but now, I'm not sure. Are you a good driver?"

"Of course I'm a great driver. You can't afford to stay in the trucking business long if you're not. So my safety record is exemplary. I knew I had to support Kiera and myself. So, I didn't take any unnecessary risks. The only close call I ever had was when a bridge washed out in front of me. But, it was because the abutment was not structurally sound. It had nothing to do with my driving. But it was enough to give me a heart attack. I was afraid I would not be able to get home to my baby that day. It almost made me quit trucking. Starla, the trucker who I often rode convoy with, reminded me something like that could happen to me in my own neighborhood and I could've had a boring desk job which gave me a cholesterol heart attack just as easily. Quitting the job I enjoyed and which made really good money wouldn't have solved the problem. It was a random fluke."

Before I can engage my brain, an inappropriate question pops out of my mouth. I want to retract the words as soon as they hit the atmosphere. "Did you and this Starla lady have a thing?"

Denny's eyes widen at the forthrightness of my question, but he throws his head back and laughs, "No, but it wasn't for lack of trying on her part. She was real good to Kiera too, but I like my ladies with some class. She could've dropped some dental floss on herself and it would've had more coverage than some of the clothes she wore. Some days, it was stupid dangerous to ride in convoy with her in the lead because guys were nearly crashing their cars when they saw her driving down the road, they were so busy gawking at her goods. It was downright embarrassing."

I can't help myself, and I giggle at his description. I actually had a sorority sister who had a penchant for dressing much the same way. "Did you ever say anything to her?"

"I tried to, but it was a terrible Catch-22. If I said anything to her, she took it as a sign of interest — which started a whole other chain of events I never wanted to be part of. When Kiera became a teenager, it started a whole other bailiwick. I needed Kiera to have the female role model because I don't know anything about female stuff Kiera needed to know about and I didn't have any female relatives left in my life for Kiera to talk to. Heaven knows I didn't want my innocent little daughter to get makeup tips from Starla. Starla was sweet as apple pie, but she looked like she walked right out of Hustler magazine. That's not a look you want on your twelve-year-old daughter. I felt like I was walking on a tight rope the whole summer."

"How did you handle it?" I ask.

"I finally decided to go with the flow. I figured if I threw a hissy fit and told Kiera she couldn't wear makeup, she would want to wear even more makeup. So, I pretended I was completely okay with all of it. Fortunately, my daughter is a brilliant young woman and she took the best of what Starla taught her and toned it down an awful lot and just applied enough to try to fit in with her peers. I, for one, was horrified the girls were wearing make-up at twelve years old; but I was determined not to be a fuddy-duddy about it all."

"I'm sure Kiera was very grateful you made that decision," I reply remembering the struggle Donda felt to fit in.

"She was. She told me it earned me the father of the year award. She made me chocolate chip pancakes for breakfast when I told her she could wear makeup to the father-daughter breakfast."

"That is so adorable, I want to cry."

"How is the headset working out for you, can you hear everything okay?" Denny asks me.

"It sure is. I'm surprised. It actually works better than my cell phone."

"How's your helmet? Is it snug enough or is it too tight?" Denny inquires.

I reach up and touch the hand painted airbrushed helmet covered with flowers and butterflies. "Not only is it beautiful, but it's a perfect fit. I'm not sure how you accomplished it, but it's amazing."

I hear Denny's low chuckle through the headphones. "Did you really think I needed all those precise measurements for a gardening hat?"

His question stymies me for a moment until I remember a conversation we had several months ago. "You ordered this clear back then?" I ask incredulously. "That was the dead of winter."

I can see Denny move slightly as he shrugs his shoulders. "Well, it takes a bit for them to custom make helmets."

"Dennis Allen Ashley! What if I had said no?" I exclaim.

Through the headphones, I hear him expel his breath. "I suppose I would've had a pretty mantelpiece. It never occurred to me you might say no. We've been good friends for so long, this just seemed like a natural extension of our friendship. It doesn't feel like I'm expanding those boundaries very far. Gwendolyn, I promise I won't take things any farther than we're comfortable going. I consider you a really good friend. I won't do anything to jeopardize our relationship. You are too important to me. I cherish you."

"Thank you, Denny, I appreciate that. I like you, too. But I'm confused. You made this seem like it was a last-minute opportunity. Obviously you've been planning this for months and months. I don't understand."

"I guess the easiest way to explain all this is it's a little bit of both. My friends, Eric and Amelia really do own a Dude Ranch. We are going to stay there and there really was a cancellation because some guy had booked his anniversary trip but he got in a bicycle accident and broke his leg. So, we're getting their upgraded cabin. What I didn't tell you was I was planning to take you to Eric's ranch for your birthday anyway. Without a lucky cancellation, our accommodations wouldn't have been nearly as nice. When Eric and his wife Amelia got married, I loaned them my truck and helped them move across the country, so he's returning the favor. I'm sorry if it came across like I wasn't telling the truth. I didn't figure you'd be interested in the whole strange, convoluted back story. If you're interested in all my strange wheeling and dealing across the country, I'll be happy to share those stories with you."

"No, that's fine. I just was confused because you made it sound like this was a last-minute adventure. When I found out you'd been planning it for months, something didn't sound right." I cringe at my tone. I sound like a suspicious, nagging wife. "Look, I'm sorry. I don't have any right to question you. You're the one surprising me for my birthday. I don't know what I was thinking."

"Gwendolyn, I'm not Kevin. If you ever want to ask me anything about any topic, you can feel free. You're right; the way I presented the information was confusing. You have a right to ask questions. It did seem a little shady. If I were in your shoes, I would ask questions too. There is nothing wrong with being curious." Denny looks down at the sidecar and gives me a smile.

"I feel stupid for having to ask about stuff like that. It makes me sound like I don't trust you and I do."

"It might seem odd, but this is one of the parts of being married I miss," Denny says.

I'm confused by the non sequitur. "You miss

pointless misunderstandings and arguments?" I ask, unable to keep the dubious tone out of my voice.

"As strange as it sounds, I guess I do. I always looked at arguments as a true test of our love. It's easy to love each other through the good times when everything is perfect and rosy but it's a little tougher when you don't see eye to eye and when you're bickering. If you can find something you still love about your spouse when they're annoying the heck out of you — that's true love."

"Well, by that definition, Don and I should have been rock solid because we rarely agreed on anything. We were both stubborn people. But, you're right — we loved each other fiercely."

"Karen and I were, too. We were pretty much polar opposites. Whenever we worked through a misunderstanding and fixed it together, I always thought it was like a bricklayer adding mortar to a brick wall. Little by little, every day with each discussion and through each new thing we learned about each other, we were making our marriage stronger."

"I bet you guys had an amazing marriage, Denny."

"We did. I miss being married. Do you?"

I think about it for a bit before I answer, "Well, as you know, being married has been a mixed bag for me. But, if you're talking about my marriage to Donald, yes, I miss it very much. It's the little things I miss the most. The innocuous things often sneak up on you when you least expect it. There are things you think you'll never miss. I miss his god-awful snoring and his silly little cheerful whistling that used to wake me up when I wanted to sleep in on Sunday mornings. Donald used to take out a hand lawnmower and mow the yard. It used to be his grandfather's lawnmower, and he thought if it was good enough for his grandfather, he was determined to use it as well even though he had a perfectly good electric lawnmower in our garage. While he sharpened the lawnmower every week, he would whistle this jaunty little tune — usually slightly sharp and without regard to whether I was still sleeping — I used to be so furious with him. I worked long hours at the bank, and the weekends were the only time I had to relax. But, you know what? After he died, the first week after all the company left my house and I had to face my first Sunday morning without him mowing the lawn, I bawled like a baby."

"I know exactly what you mean. This sounds silly, but one of our traditions was to watch the *Oscars* and *Emmys* together. Karen would pretend she was a fashion commentator for one of the entertainment shows. Then, she would make pithy comments about everyone's clothes and speeches for fun. Little did she know, she was far ahead of her time. Now they have whole networks for that sort of thing. She did it in good-natured fun. The stuff they have on TV nowadays is just mean. Anyway, we would spend hours making up funny jokes about people's clothes or the way they thanked people. It was all very funny. The first one after she died, I held Kiera and wept. Kiera was so confused. She had no idea what she had done to make Daddy so sad. The room was so unbearably silent. I was beside myself. I didn't know what to do. To this day, I can barely stand to watch television. Everything is so silent. Karen had this funny little laugh which squeaked at the end. No laugh track on the planet could replicate her quirky laugh. Without Karen beside me, the whole experience of watching television feels empty."

"Karen sounds like she was one funny lady." I chuckle.

"She was wickedly so. The funny thing was, most of the world didn't know. She was shy and reserved on the outside — I guess you could say she was much like Jeff. With her friends and family, she was a regular comedienne. It was always funny to be around someone who was getting to see her authentic self for the first time. Karen always took great glee in trying to guess how much shock someone would be in when they discovered what her personality was really like."

"Funny you should mention that. As loud and gregarious as Donald was, he was also a quiet, artistic photographer. I think that's where Donda gets a lot of her talent. Don didn't show very many people his talent. He was from a family of tough military guys. Sensitive artist types were viewed as sissies, so he was reticent to let anyone know he even knew how to operate a camera, let alone have the incredible artistic eye he possessed. It was frustrating for me because I wanted to let people know what an amazing gift he had. Yet, he wouldn't hear of it.

I lose myself in the memory of the trips we used to take the Gulf shore and the amazing pictures he took there. I smile as I remember the time we were stranded by a series of road washouts and had to spend three days in a beach bungalow while the kids stayed with their friends.

Denny notices my silence and asks, "Anything

wrong?"

At first, I shake my head but then I remember he can't see me. So, I respond, "No, I was just remembering some of the other things I miss about being married."

"Would it be too forward it me to ask what those might be?" Denny asks hesitantly.

It's an interesting thing about being in helmets with visors and shades, it gives us a degree of privacy to talk about intimate stuff yet, with the headsets and earphones, we can hear each other extremely well, I can even hear changes in his breathing patterns. I don't know if he can hear me quite as well. I'm isolated from the road noise because I'm cocooned in the sidecar and it's well insulated from noise. It's a weird dynamic to say the least. Consequently, I'm feeling a little braver than I would be if I were looking at him face-to-face. "I guess it's only fair for me to share because I'm the one who brought it up, but it's rather personal, so if you aren't comfortable with this, please let me know."

"*Amasa*, I don't think things can get much more personal than the things we've already shared."

"There's some truth in your logic, for sure," I agree. "Donald used too work all hours of the day and night. When we first got married, he had to stay at the firehouse. But as he got promoted, he was able to come home during shift sometimes, but remain on call. He would always take a hot shower — as hot as our hot water heater would possibly allow — and then he would come to bed. No matter what time it was, he would put me on my side and crawl into bed behind me. He would slide his leg between mine and put his arm under mine and cup my breast. Then, he would rest his cheek against my head. He would lay there as if he were absorbing my healing energy. Sometimes, he would do this for a few minutes and other nights, if it were a particularly bad fire, he would not say anything for a couple of hours. He would just whisper in my ear, 'Missed you, Beautiful.' Then, he would fall into the deepest, soundest sleep. I always felt privileged. It almost seemed as if he needed me in his arms to feel anchored and safe in the world so he could rest. I really miss being someone's soft place to land. I liked being held in Don's arms as he fell asleep. I've never forgotten that sensation and I think I'll miss it until the day I die."

It probably should've felt strange for me to share such an intimate confession. Instead I feel liberated and unburdened. I never felt free to share how much I truly missed Donald with the kids because they were so little and having such difficulty dealing with the loss themselves.

"What a beautiful memory."

"When I met Kevin, he wanted me to erase all evidence of Donald from our lives. It should have been my first clue things were amiss. However, I was so flattered a rich, handsome dentist would be interested in the likes of me — a single mom with two kids — that I failed to notice all the warning signs as huge as a bill board on the interstate."

Kevin came into the bank where I worked to get a collateral loan to purchase a new car and expand his portion of the dental practice. He needed to purchase some new machinery to do orthodontia. I thought he was dashing and witty and I was completely taken in by his interest in me and my children. He initially seemed to treat them as if they were his own. He would take them to sporting events where his dental practice had skybox seats, he threw them elaborate birthday parties and Christmas looked like a toy store exploded at our house. "As soon as he persuaded me to marry him, all that changed and he became bitter and resentful toward everything, the kids and my career and my friends. Nothing I ever did was good enough for him and he seemingly hated Jeff on first sight simply because he looked so much like Donald. It was pretty much a no-win situation."

I wait to see what Denny thinks of all of these revelations. Most men don't react very well to hearing a woman waxed poetically about a former love of her life. It will be interesting to see if these disclosures push any hot buttons of Denny's.

Much to my surprise, Denny's response is very atypical. Suddenly, I feel the bike slow as he pulls over to the side of the road. I see some morning glory growing up a fence. He walks around to the sidecar and helps me out. He unbuckles my helmet and gently pulls it off. Abruptly, he envelops me in a huge, but gentle bearhug and murmurs against my temple, "Oh, my sweet *Amasa*, I am so sorry you're lonely. Life isn't fair. A woman like you should never, ever be lonely. If it makes you feel any better, you are my soft spot to land. Why do you think I come up with reasons to stop by and see you at the shop every day? Have you ever noticed sometimes I come in multiple times a day? Do you really think I need that much potting soil? I don't even have all that many plants.

Sometimes, I give my planting soil to my neighbors down the street."

"To be honest, I wondered about that. I've been to your house, and you don't seem like you are much of a green thumb. I mean, your plants are nice and all, but there aren't enough of them to support your potting soil habit. I wondered what was going on. I just didn't know how to ask."

Denny snickers. "I guess Karen isn't the only one with an offbeat sense of humor. The only habit I have is the need to see you."

"What about you? Is there anything else you miss about being married?" I ask rather recklessly, not knowing exactly how he'll answer my question. Sometimes, Denny can be uptight and very circumspect and, other times, the man is a chronic over-sharer and can tell you his whole life story with no filters involved. I'm not sure which Denny will answer my question. I could very well find out more about Dennis Allen Ashley than I ever wanted to know. I'm aware it's a very loaded question.

"Do you want me to be honest?" Denny asks with trepidation.

"As long as you're not gross, be as honest as you're comfortable with."

"I'll give you the same words of caution you gave me. This is personal, so if you want me to stop any time just tell me, okay?"

"All right Denny, I understand. After what I shared with you, I think my threshold for personal detail is pretty high," I assure him. Hopefully, I'll be able to keep my promise. I'm not the type of woman who has had a lot of male friends. I'm not sure what he considers personal details. I suspect workplace stories in the trucking field are a bit different from those in corporate banking. His definition of personal might be different from mine. But a promise is a promise.

"I think I already told you Karen resembled Grace Kelly a great deal. That is not an exaggeration at all. She had this amazing long blonde hair and unlike Kiera and me, her skin was like porcelain. Not a freckle to be found anywhere. From the moment I met her, I always wondered what she was doing with a homely guy like me. She literally could've chosen from any guy on the planet. I'm as confused as the next guy about why she chose me. Whenever I would ask her, she would shrug and answer, 'I just have a feeling.' She never got more specific with me. Karen took her secrets to the grave."

This is a much harder conversation to have with our helmets off. We're leaning up against some old fence posts. Denny gave me some flowers and I'm twirling them between my fingers. "Denny, you have a phenomenal amount of charm. Don't underestimate yourself."

"Umm ... okay." Denny blushes. "Well, anyway .. Karen's hair was a sensory experience all by itself. You know how you said Don would anchor himself to you? I used to do the same with Karen. It was almost an unconscious thing with me. I would weave my fingers through her hair, wrap it around my palm and give her a scalp massage. More often than not, we would fall asleep that way and I loved it. It made me feel connected to her like there was no end to her and beginning of me. I know, it sounds stupid and corny. Still, it felt like we were somehow seamless. When she was gone, it felt as if an extension of me was gone on a molecular level. I swore I still felt the strands of hair wrapped around my wrist like silken handcuffs of grief. I imagine it's a bit like Trevor feels with the phantom pains from his amputation. Although, losing a spouse is not the same as losing a limb through trauma, I think the pain is just as sudden. I don't know if this happens to you, but some mornings if I don't wake up in the right sequence somehow, I still expect Karen to be there beside me."

"Oh my gosh! Isn't that the worst? It's almost as if you want to go back to sleep to recapture the wonderful dream you're having when they were still alive. I notice it happens more often if I'm dreaming Donald is holding me, or dancing with me." I blush deeply as I add, "… or making love to me."

"Thank goodness you said that," Denny says with a heavy sigh, "I've always wondered if those dreams are normal or if I'm a sick weirdo. I don't have the intimate dreams very often anymore, but if I've been thinking about her a lot, or I'm really lonely, it almost seems like she visits me in my dreams. It feels like I can reach out and touch her, run my fingers through her hair and kiss her. It's always such a jolting experience to wake-up and find there is no one in bed with me."

I blush a little. "It's amazing how similar our experiences are." However, as soon as the words leave my mouth, I realize how much I've confessed to him. If his dreams are anything like the ones I have, I've admitted a whole lot.

Chapter Five

Denny

To say this ride with Gwendolyn has been enlightening is the understatement of the century. I've learned a lot of things about her that I would've never guessed in a million years. For one thing, I had always pegged her as conservative, traditional and, quite frankly, a little uptight. Freed from the constraints of her job, she's funny, straightforward, and far more outrageous and open than I would have ever guessed.

The last few days have been game changers for me to say the very least. After my conversation with Gwendolyn about my guilt over betraying Karen, I realized she was right. I never stopped loving Karen. I was rightfully furious with the circumstances which led to Kiera's paralysis. If I'm also honest with myself, I shoulder some of the blame because I let a lot of Karen's symptoms slip right by me. Still, blaming myself isn't going to bring Karen back.

This weekend is about giving myself permission to move on with a magnificent woman — a woman I think

Karen would totally approve of. Had Karen and Gwendolyn met back then, they probably would've been good friends. The more I get to know Gwendolyn, the more I realize their senses of humor are quite similar as are their backgrounds. I don't know if it's coincidence or fate — or perhaps neither.

Although our most recent conversation has made this last leg of the trip uncomfortable to complete on a motorcycle, it has given me incredible insight on things which make Gwendolyn happy. If we are able to move our relationship forward to couple-hood, our discussion has given me some spectacular tools to use to help make our relationship successful. I am having a hard time believing how much we've shared. It is remarkably refreshing. I love her open communication style. It is such a welcome surprise. It reminds me of the way Karen used to hide facets of her self from most of the public.

My thoughts are interrupted by a question over my headset. "Are we expected there at any particular time?" Gwendolyn asks.

"Amelia told me she serves dinner between five o'clock and six-thirty but if we want the good stuff, we need to arrive before five."

"When do you expect to get there?"

"If we don't run into much traffic, it looks like our arrival time is about 4:15-ish."

"That's perfect. It'll give me time to freshen up before dinner."

"Okay, we'll hope for light traffic then," I respond as I weave around a slow car.

Eric and I brush down the horses as the women put the finishing touches on dinner. I tried to help out in the kitchen, but they kicked me out. They told me I can help out with dinner dishes later. Apparently, they have dinner handled.

Eric grins at my dismay. "Got schooled, did ya?" he asks with a chuckle.

I nod. "It appears so. I guess the men don't do much cooking around here."

Eric shrugs. "We do ... we just do it on the campfire or for breakfast. We also sneak some in if we disguise it as barbecue. Otherwise, we stick pretty close to traditional gender roles around here."

"I've been a single dad for so long I'm not even sure I remember what traditional roles look like," I admit.

"Well, then you might find this experience even more jarring than most. What about your wife? What does she think about all this?"

"Gwendolyn? She's not my wife. She's not even my girlfriend. She's my son-in-law's mother," I respond as I take off my baseball cap and re-bend the bill.

"Shut the front door!" Eric exclaims with emphasis, pausing between each word. "You could've fooled me, I thought you guys were here on an anniversary trip. You guys work so well together! You're like an oiled machine. I figured you were here to teach the young-uns a thing or two. Oh my gosh! You are kidding me right? Is this a joke — did Amelia put you up to this?" Erica laughs.

I put my hand on Eric's bicep to get his attention and look him directly in the eye. "Eric, son, look at me. I'm not joking. I'm serious here. Gwendolyn and I are just friends. Now, I'm not denying I'd like to change things between us. However, for right now that's all we are."

"Denny, my man, what are you waiting for? Seriously? You've been single like almost longer than I've been alive. If you don't hurry up, you're going to die before you muster up the courage to ask her out," Eric remarks.

"Eric, you're a cool kid, but that was a line too far. You're not funny," I respond with a frown.

"Oh, shoot you're right. I forgot about your first wife. I'm sorry," Eric apologizes. "I'll ... uh ... have Amelia turn up the ambience around here and see if I can help you out a little."

"I appreciate the offer Eric, but I'm not sure it'll help the situation any."

"I'll be subtle, I promise." Eric winks.

I just shake my head. "I don't think subtlety is within your capability, Eric."

"You know, you might be right about that," Eric concedes as he flushes bright red.

I should have known they had something up their sleeves by the gleam in their eyes when they say there was a change in the evening activities at dinner. They announce there would be an evening square dance instead of the reading of Western tales. Personally, I'm a little disappointed. My legs are feeling like spaghetti after the long motorcycle ride. The bumpiness of the road tends to cause a lot of fatigue. My muscle tone isn't what it used to be. I can't ride as many hours as I used to.

I glance over at Gwendolyn to see how she's reacting to the news. At first, she looks like she's in total shock. I wonder if it's because she likes to dance or if she hates to dance. By the look on her face, I can't really tell. I'm relieved when I hear her mutter under her breath, "I'll be darned, those girls were right. I wonder how they knew? Oh, never mind — Tara probably knew."

When Gwendolyn and I go to check into our cabins, we realize we have keys to the same cabin. When we ask Eric, he explains the duplex suffered a burst water heater. They had to move us to the only remaining cabin. Since Amelia and Eric thought we were married, they didn't anticipate there would be any issue.

Gwendolyn looks at me and then at Eric. "I don't have any problem with it — if Mr. Ashley doesn't mind."

I nod my head. "It's fine with me too."

I hope Gwendolyn misses the shrewd, calculating look on Eric's face. My only thought is, *Burst water heater, my asterisk.*

But I decide to make the best of Eric's blatantly obvious matchmaking efforts and play along. I hold the door open for Gwendolyn. "Shall we?" When we go in, we are confronted with a classic log cabin which could be straight out of any vacation magazine. There is a fireplace on each floor and I can see the footboard of what looks to be two beds. Although from this vantage point, I can't tell the size of the bed on the top floor. One on the bottom looks to be a very large queen-size bed if not a king-size bed.

I turn to her and ask, "Would you like to get ready on the first or second story?"

"Whichever one is closest to the bathroom, please. I don't like running across the room wrapped in a towel."

"I'm guessing in a cabin as opulent is this, both floors will have their own restrooms. So, you may choose whichever floor you prefer. It doesn't matter to me."

"Well, if I pick the second floor, I will have the opportunity to descend the staircase in my dress and you can take pictures."

"You can never underestimate the value of a good entrance. I'll meet you back here in a few. I doubt I'll cleanup quite as well as you do though."

"I don't know, Denny. You may be vastly overestimating the restorative value of a little soap and hot water."

"I've known you for a while now, and one of the things I've learned is that it's not possible to overestimate how beautiful you always look under any circumstances."

Gwendolyn shoots me a skeptical glance. "You're such a polite man, even if you are a big fat fibber."

"I am not a fibber! You just have a hard time taking a compliment."

"Whatever you say, Dennis Ashley ... I've got to go take a shower so you can stand to dance with me," she comments dismissively, but she has a sassy sway to those hips as she walks away.

Generally, I'm a pretty chatty guy, but as I watch Gwendolyn walk down the roughly hewn staircase, I can find absolutely no words to describe what I'm seeing or feeling. I guess the closest comparison would be the first time I was up in a helicopter during Operation Desert Shield. I have the same sense of complete anticipation. I can't seem to catch my breath and my hands are trembling from adrenaline.

Gwendolyn takes one look at the stunned expression on my face and studies me with concern. "Geez, Denny, do I really look so bad? Maybe I should go back up and change. I thought this outfit was cute. I didn't realize it was that far off the mark," she says as she turns to go back up the stairs.

I reach out and grab her hand to stop her as I finally find my voice to say, "*Amasa*, no, that's not it at all. You are absolutely stunning. I love your outfit. You look amazing. In fact, you look so beautiful, it took me a minute to put my brain back in gear."

"Are you sure you're not just saying that?" Gwendolyn asks dubiously.

"Yes, I'm sure. Your lace blouse and denim skirt are perfect for square dancing without being stereotypically touristy for a dude ranch. You look very elegantly casual if that's even a proper description. I love the roses embossed on your leather belt."

"I can't believe you even noticed. One of my neighbor's kids made it. He makes all sorts of leather goods in his garage and sells them for extra money. He made this one especially for me when he found out I am a florist. Isn't it sweet?" Gwendolyn explains.

"He does fine work, I should contact him for some of my restoration work. Sometimes, I need a specific pattern embossed in leather for an upholstery piece or two."

"Oh my gosh, he would love it. He re-finishes old skateboards too. I bet he would think car restoration is a cool hobby."

"Well, let's get to the dance before Eric and Amelia come to hunt us down." I extend my elbow in a gesture of gallantry.

When we enter the main hall, I'm amazed by the transformation, all the big oversized sofas and chairs are gone, as are the ottomans and side tables. It looks nothing like the dining room we left earlier. It's a dance hall now. There are little crystal lights all over the walls and tall tables with candles on them all around the perimeter. Between the tall tables are sideboards with drinks and trays of appetizers. This looks every bit like a social club. One end of the room has a stage area with a little mobile keyboard and a guitar standing there.

Eric steps to the stage area. He is wearing a mobile microphone and much to my surprise, his voice comes from a speaker a few inches above my head on the wall, "Good evening, ladies and gentlemen. Tonight we'll have a little something for everybody. We'll start things off with some George Strait."

This is news to me. I thought it would be square dancing tonight. Still, I think George Strait will work just fine — he writes romantic stuff.

I slide my gaze over to Gwendolyn to see what she thinks of this development. She catches me looking at her and she shrugs. "I prefer Luther Vandross myself, but when in Rome…"

It'll be an interesting night for sure. When I hear the opening strains of *The Chair* I have to chuckle to myself — *So much for subtle, Eric.* The whole premise of this song is one big pickup line. I love this song and it's very sweet, but still how obvious can you get?

Yet, as I place my hands carefully at Gwendolyn's waist, she rests her cheek on my chest and sighs, "I adore this song, it's totally romantic. One of my friends met her husband just like this. They used this song as their first song at their wedding. It was perfect."

Well, what do you know? Score one for Eric. I breathe a sigh of relief as I allow the lyrics of the sappy love song to wash over me. I can only hope our story has an equally positive ending.

Next, Eric calls a square dance. He's remarkably skilled. Even more surprising, Gwendolyn isn't bumbling around trying to follow the steps like I am. Shocked, I asked her, "How do you know how to do this?"

"Well, I have a funny story about that. It involves love, intrigue and betrayal —"

My eyebrows must've shot up to my rapidly receding hairline because Gwendolyn laughs. "Did I say it had to do with *my* love life? You see, I agreed to go to square dancing classes with my friend Mavis. Mavis had her sights set on this guy she met on the Internet, Roy Romple — that name alone should have been a clue. Anyway, she had her heart set on winning this guy.

Apparently, he was big on the square dancing circuit so she figured if she could just learn how to square dance, he would be falling all over himself to date her. So, off to the senior center we went to learn square dancing. After two classes, she quit because she didn't like the fact it made her sweat. But I had already paid for the classes and silly poofy skirt, so I was going to take the whole eight-week class. I'm not poor, but I'm sure as heck not planning to throw money away. Besides, I liked learning something new. Most of the people were respectful. There was one guy who liked to pinch my butt every time he took me for a do-si-do, but otherwise, it was pretty good."

I smile at her description of dance class. I once took a cooking class at Heather's bakery. It had many similarities. Apparently, a man in a cooking class is a hot commodity. "What happened to your friend?" I ask, curious as to where this story was going.

"Another one of Mavis' friends took a picture through one of the big windows of the dance studio and posted it on Facebook thinking it was Mavis. The only problem was Mavis wasn't even at the dance studio that day. So, Roy was busted as the philandering little creep he always had been. The only difference was this time, there was photographic proof and he couldn't talk his way out of it — not that he didn't try. However, Mavis wasn't having any of it. She blocked him and never looked back. A couple of months later, she met the pastor's brother when he visited from out of town, and it was love at first sight. I guess timing is everything."

"As much as we don't understand them, things sorta have a way of working out the way they're supposed to."

"I think we're thinking way too much for two people who are supposed to be on vacation," she murmurs against my chest as Eric starts to play Kenny Chesney's *You Had Me From Hello.*

I meet Eric's gaze over the top of Gwendolyn's head and nod mine in silent salute as I acknowledge the truth in those lyrics.

"You never told me you have hidden skills in limbo," Gwendolyn accuses as she tries to contain the fit of giggles.

"What can I say? The skills necessary to be a trucker are wide and varied." I shrug, but I'm not entirely successful at hiding my grin.

"No, really … how were you able to do that?" Gwendolyn asks.

"You're going to think it's stupid if I tell you. I strained my back a couple of years ago. The physical therapist who treated me was into yoga. He suggested I try it to relieve my back pain. I noticed yoga helped a lot with the pain, so I started going to a lot of different classes. It turned out I was good at it and it increased my flexibility a bunch. So, I sort of became a yoga class junkie. I do a lot of yoga these days. It's funny, on the first day of class, a lot of the women think I'm there to pick them up. It's as if yoga studios are the new form of a singles bar. They are always surprised when they figure out I know what I'm doing. It's fun to shock people."

"I *bet* people are surprised. I took a jazz dance class at the senior center and people reacted much the same way. But, learning routines isn't hard for me because I had done so many of them as a youngster when I was an ice-skater; I picked up the material quickly. People thought I was a professional dancer. They're always quite shocked when I told them I never had any formal dance training — only ice-skating. I still think some of them thought I was lying. But you're right; it is fun to blow people's minds that way and exceed their expectations. Speaking of that, you exceeded my expectations tonight. This is the most fun I've had in I can't remember when."

"Thank you so much for agreeing to come with me. I guess it wasn't only you who needed to live a little on the wild side. I hadn't realized how predictable and stagnant my life has become either. It's fun to break out of the ordinary and do something special with somebody who means something to you." I squeeze her hand good night.

"Denny, I rarely — if ever — say this to anyone, but thank you for bullying me into coming. I really needed this mental health break. Work was becoming incredibly overwhelming. I lost focus and perspective. This was exactly what I needed. I'm having a great time with you."

"Good night, Amasa. Sleep well. I'll see you in the morning. We'd better get some sleep; Amelia said wake-up is at six thirty in the morning. They start things early around here."

Gwendolyn looks indecisive for a few moments before she blurts, "Denny, I hope I'm not ruining our friendship or anything, but our discussion this afternoon reminded me about how lonely I am at night. I wondered if you would mind being my bedmate. I know it sounds presumptuous, but I need you to hold me."

Of all the things I expected her to say tonight, those words were not on my radar. In my fantasies? Sure, maybe. Did I ever think they would ever cross those elegant lips this weekend? Not in my wildest dreams.

I guess it's time to admit a painful truth. I hesitate to say anything because I know doing so will probably be a deal breaker. Yet, it would be dishonest for me not to and I'm too much of a good guy to leave it unsaid. I run my thumb along her jawline and turn her face toward mine.

"*Amasa*, I've been single for a long time and I'm not a big believer in relationships just for the sake of relievin' stress, if you catch my drift. I had a daughter to raise I needed to be a good role model and by the time she was all grown, I was in the habit of being alone," I admit, feeling embarrassed about how pathetic I sound.

Gwendolyn reaches up and puts her hand over my hand, which is still resting on her jaw. "Denny, I'm well aware of your high standards. Your daughter told me years ago how worried she was about your lack of companionship — so to speak."

My mouth drops open in shock. "You're kidding!"

"I'm serious," Gwendolyn replies with a smile. "Now, I don't think she ever envisioned we would become close friends. She was wondering if I had any suitable friends so she could play matchmaker. For now, to avoid any awkward dinner conversation, we might want to keep this weekend between us."

"Oh, I agree. It's never been my practice to discuss

what happens in my bed with my daughter," I answer as I flush bright red. Sometimes I hate my ginger complexion.

"Rest assured, I absolutely don't want talk about it with Jeff and Donda. Donda would probably get me a how-to manual or something," Gwendolyn remarks. I can almost hear the starch in her voice.

I clear my throat. "Anyway, the rest of what I was trying to tell you is I tend to sleep quite deeply and dream quite vividly, so I can't guarantee I'll be able to keep my hands from roaming."

Gwendolyn smiles a bit at my frank admission. "Putting aside my sham of a marriage to the freak-of-nature we like to call my second husband, I've been single about as long as you have. I've already admitted to you one of the things I miss most of all about being married is cuddling in bed. What makes you think I'm any more disciplined in my sleep than you are? Still, I think we are good enough friends to respect our souls are lonely and our bodies crave a connection. I think we are mature enough to separate that from true love. Don't you think so?"

I'm not exactly sure how to answer her question. Will Gwendolyn be my soul mate like Karen was? I don't think so. I think of my relationship with Karen as a once in a lifetime miracle which will never, ever repeat itself. However, there is a strong voice in the back of my head that tells me if I climb into bed with Gwendolyn, I will never be able to go back to being just the affable, good friend, father of her daughter-in-law. I'm not sure if we take this step in our relationship, I'll be able to maintain the same relationship boundaries we've had for the last few years. More frightening, I'm not sure I want them. I've discovered one overwhelming fact over the past few days. I like Gwendolyn Whitaker — not as the mother of my son-in-law, but as a vibrant, sexy woman. The question of the moment is what, pray tell, am I going to do about that?

"Denny, what do you think?" Gwendolyn prompts again leaning her cheek against my palm.

"I-I don't know," I stammer.

Gwendolyn runs her right hand through my hair. "Well, you think about it for a bit while I go get ready for bed, we'll talk about it in a few minutes."

As she leaves the room, I berate myself for my inability to make a decision. It shouldn't be this hard. Why am I so trapped in the past? Karen has been dead for more than a quarter of a century. Why can't I get out of my own head?

While Gwendolyn goes upstairs, I take a moment to change into some flannel pajamas and a T-shirt. It's not the most romantic sleepwear, but then again I didn't have romance in mind when I packed. I thought we were going to be staying in completely different cabins.

When she returns, it appears she has the same issue I do. She's wearing a floor length nightgown covered with candy canes. At my questioning glance, she answers, "I know it's not exactly regulation seduction-wear, but Mindy gave it to me for Christmas and it's very warm."

"Actually, I think it's perfect for you because you're so sweet."

"Would it surprise you to learn I can be quite pithy and cuss like a longshoreman?" Gwendolyn smirks.

"I would be totally stunned; pith does not seem to be in your nature."

"If you had known me before I was married to the Jerk-Wad, you would've seen more of my obstinate behavior. I learned to moderate my true nature to keep from upsetting him because if he was upset with me, he would take it out on the kids. So I became this meek and mellow thing I hardly recognize. I used to be quite sassy."

"What a tragedy. I like the sassy, argumentative side of you. It's fun and energizing," I declare, surprising myself. Although I was happy when Karen and I came through our tiffs relatively unscathed, one thing which attracted me to Karen was her mellow, laid-back attitude.

Gwendolyn came and sat down right beside me which in some ways makes our conversation much more difficult. She smells phenomenal, and it's a bit distracting. I try to breathe deeply through my nose, but my maneuver only compounds the situation.

"Denny, what did you decide about my proposal?" she asks softly.

"What do you think about it?" I counter. "It will probably change the complexion of our friendship forever. Are you prepared to deal with that?"

"I considered all that before I even came along on this trip with you. I anticipated spending all this time with you would probably change things between us. I guess, if I am truly honest with myself: I knew things had changed between us even before I agreed to go on the trip. I knew we had reached a deeper level of friendship when you trusted me with the truth about Karen," she discloses.

"You know, you're right. It even felt monumental when it happened. It sort of felt like a platetonic ground shift in our relationship and things would never be the same. I guess in light of all that, sharing the same bed doesn't seem like such a big deal."

"That's how I hoped you'd see it when I asked. Otherwise, I wouldn't have bothered. It seems I have a rather primal need to have your arms around me right now."

My shock must've been evident in my face because Gwendolyn blushes bright red she gasps and says, "Oh my — that sounded far more sexual than I intended."

"Don't worry about it, Gwen. I think I know what you meant to say. Our discussion today had me feeling nostalgic as well. I hadn't thought about those things for a really long time either but it left me feeling cravings I haven't felt in years," I confess.

"Exactly, that's what I feel. Nostalgic yearnings. In a way, I feel terrible for using you to curb them. In another way I feel like you're the perfect partner in crime. Only you could understand what I'm feeling. It's almost like my heart has an itch only you can scratch."

Abruptly, Gwendolyn stands up and starts to pace in front of the bed. She takes her hair down from the haphazard bun she had placed it in and runs her fingers through it. "Oh my gosh! I'm doing a terrible job of explaining what I need. I sound crazy. I swear I'm not normally this nuts. Usually, I can go a long time without thinking of Donald, but all of this reminiscing of our past loves makes the loss seem like it wasn't nearly three decades ago. I just don't know what's wrong with me. I'm so sorry, Denny, I shouldn't be abusing our friendship this way. I'm going to go upstairs and go to bed now."

As she turns to leave, I capture her by her waist and pull her toward me. I am reminded again how slight she is. I am used to lifting women around. I've done it for Kiera's whole life, but Gwendolyn is substantially smaller than Kiera and as a former competitive swimmer, Kiera is not a big woman by any stretch of the imagination. I spin Gwen around so she's facing me.

"*Amasa*, you didn't wait to hear my answer. I'd like to tell you what I think before you make up your mind, okay?" I watch the panic build in her eyes.

"As long as you don't expect to me to change my opinion to match yours," cautions Gwendolyn.

"Gwendolyn, you have known me long enough to know if you are around me, you are always entitled to your opinion whether I agree with it or not. You know that, right?"

"Yes, you've always made it clear. I'm just nervous right now."

"Honey, the last thing I want to do is make you nervous. Still, I always want to be honest with you. You need to know it was your advice which gave me the courage to come up here this weekend. I wavered often before you gave me permission to forgive myself and move forward. Our conversations about our marriages had much the same effect on me they had on you. For many years, as a survival mechanism, I've been unwilling to look at the happy side of my marriage because I was afraid to feel lonely and sad. I had to put on a happy face for Kiera. I want to thank you for giving me a safe place to have those memories of Karen. For the most part, I had a pretty great marriage with her. Sure, we had our conflicts, but overall, we were happy. I enjoyed being a husband and I need to celebrate that. All these years, I haven't allowed myself to remember the good things. The closest I've come is to present a pretend prettied-up version of marriage to Kiera. In retrospect, that wasn't exactly fair either, but it was the best I could do. You've given me permission to celebrate the real thing. That's even better. The downside is I'm also remembering all the stuff I'm missing."

"I'm sorry I brought the sadness back—" Gwendolyn starts to say. I hold up my hand to stop her as I continue.

"I'd like to take you up on the offer of company in bed tonight. I have a feeling I'm going to need it as much as you do," I admit as I run my fingers through her hair.

"You don't think I'm crazy for asking?"

"After the emotional week we just had? No, of course not. I think as long as we continue to be open and honest with each other about where we stand, we should be okay."

"I think so too."

"My open and honest take is I like you. I like you a lot. I think you are smart and loving and great with your kids and grandkids. I look forward to getting to know you better. That's what I know right at this moment." I gather her into a loose hug.

"I like you far more than I expected to. After the debacle that was Kevin Buckhold, I never thought I would ever be able to stand being in the company of another man again — even casually, let alone contemplating ever getting into bed with one and putting my arms around him. Denny, it speaks to the way you treat me and how much I trust you that I'm even considering this move. Honestly, I can't guarantee you I won't have a meltdown at some point during the middle of the night," Gwendolyn admits with a shy glance.

I give her a small squeeze. "I will tell you what my very wise daughter once told me about progress once. She said, 'Daddy, life isn't like uncooked spaghetti — all neat and straight. It's like cooked spaghetti with tomato sauce and Parmesan cheese. It's messy and gooey, but it's much better that way.' I think we all make progress at whatever speed we make progress and sometimes it's all forward progress and other times we backtrack a little — but eventually it's all good in the end."

Gwendolyn looks up at me in surprise as she chuckles. "Exactly how old was your genius daughter when she gave you this very sage advice?"

I grin. "Oh, about eight."

I fold back the sheets and blankets on the bed and stand beside it waiting for her to get in. "This ought to be interesting; we both sleep on the same side of the bed," she observes.

I wiggle my eyebrows suggestively at her as I tease, "Well, I guess we won't have any trouble cuddling then."

It's an interesting mix of old and new as we settle together. I can tell she's probably having the same struggle.

"Does this feel as odd for you as it does for me?"

she whispers as she carefully shifts in bed.

"Probably, if not more so. Believe it or not, I've never slept with anybody besides Karen."

"In all those years, you never had sex with anybody else?" Gwendolyn asks incredulously.

"No, I can't exactly say that. There were times after Karen's death when Kiera was still in the hospital I hooked up with some pretty young things who, sadly, meant so little to me I can't even remember their names just to have a connection with someone. I'm not proud of that. Those women deserved better than the shell of the man who I was back then and I'm sure they were probably expecting more from me than I could give."

"Denny, you are far too hard on yourself. Those women should have known the score. You wear your feelings for your wife on your sleeve, even all of these years later. I can't imagine how raw your grief would've been back then. If they couldn't see it, they weren't looking. So, cut yourself some slack — it was an incredibly difficult time for you. Who wouldn't seek out comfort where you could find it?"

I don't know how to express this better other than my inner conscience gave a huge sigh of relief. I have always felt incredibly guilty over my actions after Karen's death. As the grandson of a Baptist minister, I knew I should've been making different decisions, yet somehow I seemed incapable of doing so. Gwendolyn's quiet acceptance of my turbulent emotions seems like a gift. I pull her closer and without thinking, I drop a kiss between her shoulder and her neck when her nightgown droops a little.

Gwendolyn shivers and squirms a little as she cuddles a little closer. "Is it me, or is this weird for you too?"

"I'll admit, it is a little different — but it feels nice. You are a tiny thing. I'm afraid I might squish you."

Gwendolyn laughs and the sound is like warm rays of the sun on a beautiful spring day. "Oh, I wouldn't worry. I'm small, but remarkably tough. I am remarkably comfortable as well. I'm a little scared I might find your company strangely addictive. You kind of feel like the world's most comfortable teddy bear. What if I don't want to give you up?"

I smile against Gwendolyn's hair. I know it seems silly because it's dark and she can't see me, but I can't seem to wipe the goofy expression off my face. As I hold her warm, surprisingly lush body in my arms, I am having a hard time seeing the downside to her dilemma. After I hear her snore softly, I whisper under my breath, "Who says you have to?"

Breakfast comes far too early. Last night was a rough one. I spent a long time watching Gwendolyn sleep and marveling over how I found myself in the position to be beside her in the four-poster bed. Then, after about two-and-a-half hours into our little sleepover, Gwendolyn began coughing so violently, it was terrifying. I wondered if I should call the ambulance. However, Gwendolyn assured me her coughing fit wasn't at all unusual and nothing to be concerned about. I *am* concerned. Gwendolyn says except for a few puffs in college when she tried to look cool, she's never been a smoker. I don't care what she tells me, there's nothing normal about her cough.

I learned something about Gwendolyn today. She is not fond of being fawned over even if it's for her own protection and well-being. It's incredibly frustrating for me because I would like to see her get herself checked out at an urgent care clinic. Yet, I'm just a good friend at this point. Apparently, a good friend with very little influence.

At the moment, we're setting out to do something called geocaching to find the key ingredients for dinner. You know what? Call it what you want — it's just a good old-fashioned scavenger hunt like we used to have for treats when I was a kid. It's been re-branded and there are new toys to make it trendy, but it's the same concept. I am so worried about Gwendolyn. It would have been more fun; but she looks a little tired and worn down today, so my anxiety levels are through the roof this morning. Quite frankly, I don't know how she can even move this morning with as violently as she was coughing. I think my ribs would've broken if I'd coughed that hard.

Just as she's coming down the stairs, my cell phone rings. I hold my finger up to indicate I have to take the call. I step outside the cabin to take the phone call. I have no idea who it is because I answered it without looking. Much to my surprise, it's Jeff.

"Morning, Denny," Jeff greets. "How does my mom like the open road?"

"Oh, she seemed fine. She appeared to enjoy the scenery. We went to a dance last night. She laughed all night."

"That's great news; what are you not telling me?" Jeff asks suspiciously.

This seems like exactly the kind of sticky situation Gwendolyn was talking about. I am not sure how much to disclose to Jeff, but this seems important.

"Jeff, have you seen your mom recently?" I ask tentatively.

"Let me guess, you tried to talk her into going to the doctor over her nagging cough?"

"Oh, so you know about it?"

"I am aware of it. Still, I don't think she tells me the whole story," Jeff confirms.

"Why do you think she's avoiding the doctor?" I ask. Originally, I thought perhaps she didn't want to go to the doctor because she didn't want Jeff and Kiera to know about her cough. If they already know, it doesn't make any sense. I'm even more baffled than before.

"I don't know, but it might have something to do with my grandma on Mom's side of the family dying when she was younger."

"Well, that's an interesting thought for sure. It would explain some things."

"I've got to prepare for trial, but I wanted to check in with you to see if you guys were having a good time."

"Hey, Jeff, before you go, I wanted to touch base with you about how you would feel if your mom and I are having a fabulous time and want to keep having a great time beyond this weekend?" I ask.

For a few moments, there is silence on the other end of the phone. My heart drops. I don't know if I would be able to continue this relationship with Gwendolyn if our kids don't approve. I know it would break Gwendolyn's heart if she had to choose between me and her children. I wouldn't want to put her in that type of situation. I hope the silence is not indicative of disapproval. I don't want to be in a no-win situation.

Finally, Jeff clears his throat and begins to speak. I can't believe my palms are sweaty as I await his verdict, however the simple inescapable fact is they are. "Fortunately, I was not blindsided by this development because my wife is pretty intuitive about these things. Apparently she knew this was coming almost from the moment you two met. The idea took a bit of getting used to. I've been the man of the house for a long time now. But, the truth of the matter is I have my own family to look out for now. I'd appreciate some help to look out for my mom. Since I already consider you my surrogate dad, I can't think of a better man for the job. Having said that, I trust you to look out for her in the best way possible. She's lived a nightmare with Kevin Buckhold. I do not want a repeat. If you plan to mistreat her in any way, please just move on. She doesn't need that experience. She's been there and done that. Don't be an asterisk. I'd hate to have to sic William on you," Jeff threatens.

"I wouldn't want to face down William either. He can be quite formidable. Jeff, at this point your mom and I don't even know if we have a formal relationship," I explain. "What we do know is we have a lot of things in common and we enjoy each other's company. If you guys are okay with it, we'd like to explore things a little further and see where things go from here. I promise you I'll never do anything to intentionally hurt your mom. She's too important to me. Besides, I've never really been that kind of guy."

Jeff chuckles. "I know, sir. If you were that kind of guy, you probably wouldn't have raised such an extraordinary daughter. Have fun and enjoy yourself. We'll see you guys tomorrow."

"I'll talk to you later, son," I respond as I hang up the phone, grinning ear to ear. Well, a lot of things this weekend have gone far better than I ever expected. How 'bout about them apples?

Chapter Six

Gwendolyn

"Gwendolyn, how was your trip to the 'wild side', as my dad likes to call it?" Kiera asks as she jumps suddenly. She turns to Madison. "Are your ribs killing you? Nobody told me pregnancy was going to hurt. Between the constant nausea and this little guy's apparent career aspirations as a punter, I don't think my ribs will ever be the same."

Madison laughs. "That was last week's problem. This week, little Lydia has decided to use my bladder as a trampoline. I can tell you there are three hundred and thirty-two tiles in my new bathroom. Fourteen of them are cracked and two of them are faded. That's how much time I spend in there. I've never peed so much in my life."

"It's funny, I'm noticing all that stuff too. I've never paid attention to all the wrecked things in our house. I don't know what's wrong with me. The other day, I was trying to get Jeff to straighten out one of the slats in the blinds. He thought I'd totally lost my marbles. It was driving me nuts. Usually, that kind of stuff doesn't bother me at all. The only thing I totally can't stand are Becca's toys laying all over the house because if I roll over them with my wheelchair, they get broken. I can't tell you how many Barbies I've inadvertently decapitated."

I chuckle. "Well, count yourself lucky you don't have to step on Legos — that's a torture in and of itself."

"I can imagine. I guess there are real perks to being in a wheelchair," Kiera quips. "So, fess up — how did it go with my dad? Was he a total pain?"

I can't hide my blush. "Actually, your dad was quite charming. He's an entertaining guy when he wants to be — although he is a tad focused on NASCAR. He's willing to try almost everything. We did a little dancing and your dad got to help colonize a beehive and identify trees for grafting in the fruit orchards. We went on a refreshing horseback ride at sunset and had a great s'more roast. All in all, it was a very lovely time."

Madison examines me closely. "I get the feeling you're leaving a lot of details out. However, I can respect that since it's your adventure and Kiera is your daughter-in-law. There are probably certain details you'd rather she didn't know. I will put my reporter instincts aside and let it go — as difficult as it might be."

"You do know I am aware my father is a full grown man with needs like every other man in the world?" Kiera chuckles.

"Yes, I know that, but I'm not really sure your dad does. When I tried to tell him, he about had a stroke," I answer.

"That's pretty funny. Didn't Heather tell me Denny gave Jeff condoms as a 'welcome to the family' gift?" Madison asks with a laugh.

"Not exactly, but it was close," Kiera confirms with a giggle. "Don't forget the part of the story where my dad specifically instructed Jeff on the number of grandchildren he wanted." She looks down at her belly and shrugs. "Oops, I guess we messed that one up."

Smiling, I pat her on the shoulder. "As happy as your dad is about having a grandson, I think he'll give you a pass on ignoring his instructions."

I turn to Madison. "What do your parents think of your news? Are they going to be able to make it out to your shower?"

Madison slides her gaze to the floor as she mumbles, "We haven't exactly told them yet."

"Honey, you can't afford to wait too much longer. Aren't you like, seven months along?"

An odd look of understanding crosses Kiera's face. "I'd venture to guess you haven't even told them you and Trevor got engaged, have you?"

Madison looks a little crestfallen. "No, but how did you know?"

"Madison, have you forgotten how long I've been friends with Heather? I've had more than a few run-ins with your parents. I know what they're like. You'll be able to tell them when the time is right, but don't let them steal your sunshine. You and Trevor need to maintain your state of happy as long as possible. If it means excluding the negative people from your life, then that's what you need to do. It's too bad your parents can't be supportive of you guys. They've chosen to be intolerable — that's on them, not you."

"You know, the whole time I was married to Jeff and Donda's dad, I dealt with profoundly negative people. But I also found some unexpected allies in places I never thought I'd find them. People can surprise you. Other people may decide their role in life is to just be a jerk and that's all they'll ever aspire to be. Sometimes you're better off to leave well enough alone."

Kiera laughs out loud. "You know, I have two college degrees related to counseling and I can't top my mother-in-law's advice. You should listen to Gwendolyn."

"Sometimes, the school of hard knocks is a great teacher," I blush at the compliment.

"As is Brown University, Miss Smarty-Pants. I don't know why you never mention it," Kiera adds.

"I guess I've had to downplay it for so many years, I never think about it. This is the second time in a couple weeks I've talked about my degree after not mentioning it for years and years. It's so strange. I just don't think about myself as an intellectual. I think of myself as a blue-collar housewife. I have spent as many years as an unemployed housewife and a small business owner than I ever spent as a college student or a bank executive."

"Well, however you perceive yourself, Kiera and I think you're remarkable. Our baby showers are going to be Hollywood-worthy with all of those beautiful flowers you are providing."

Kiera nods. "I wonder how terrible it would be to let a few of those paparazzi who follow Tara around all the time know about our baby shower so we can have a few extra pictures?"

The idea is so ludicrous and out of character with my daughter-in-law I start to laugh — which of course starts a coughing fit all over again. I am so darn tired of coughing.

Madison and Kiera regard me with twin looks of alarm. "Is that the same cough you had the first time I was in here, Mrs. Whitaker?" Madison asks with concern in her voice.

Kiera nods. "I believe it is, I've seen her every few days when I drop the girls off to play at her house, and she's been coughing every time. Gwendolyn, you ought to go see the doctor. This is getting serious. I don't think it's allergies."

"I don't want to be a bother. You girls shouldn't be under stress. Besides, this is my busy season," I argue.

Kiera looks exasperated. "Mom, don't be silly. Jeff would be happy to take you if you don't want Madison or me to do it."

"Oh, I don't want to bother Jeff. He was just telling me he's involved in two big cases. He doesn't need to be involved in my silly little medical issues. It's a stupid little cough. It's probably allergies."

"What about my dad?" suggests Kiera.

"If there is one view of me your dad does not need to see, it's me in one of those stupid little paper gowns," I quip with a small smile, trying to laugh off the whole issue. "No, seriously, your dad is worried about the whole situation anyway. I don't want to make the situation worse."

"You haven't noticed by now that my dad is an

industrial-strength worrywart?" Kiera asks.

"No actually; I hadn't really paid attention to that side of his personality. He always seems pretty laid-back — well, except for that one time Kevin decided to bring his drama to your house. Other than that, your dad seems like not much ruffles his feathers."

"Oh, a whole lot ruffles my dad's feathers. The more he cares about you, the more upset he gets. If he doesn't think you're getting treated properly or if he thinks you deserve more out of life, you should just step out of the way. The man is quiet and relatively drama free, but he can move mountains in his understated, good-folksy way. When Denny Ashley loves you, he loves you fiercely, with his whole heart. It's a thing to behold."

Her bold pronouncement just sits there because I'm not quite sure what to do with it. Denny is a really good friend, but he definitely isn't in love with me or anything. The silence grows awkward.

Madison comes to the rescue as she claps her hands together in a gesture of dismissal. "Well then, that settles it. If you don't want your kids to take you, your boyfriend to take you, or the pregnant women to take you — that leaves Heather and Tara. Actually, come to think of it, they are probably the ideal combination to escort you to the doctor. Heather is a great distraction. She can tell you a million different stories about any topic under the sun and every single one of them is interesting. She'll have you laughing so hard you'll forget your nerves. But, Tara is so smart and focused; she'll remember to ask the doctor the important questions. It will be perfect."

Kiera nods approvingly at Madison. "Boy! You sure

have all the members of the Girlfriend Posse nailed. I hesitate to think how accurately you have assessed my personality."

"Oh, that's no challenge at all. Given half a chance, you'd be asking Gwendolyn what took her so long to make the decision to go to the doctor in the first place." Madison answers with a smug grin.

I chuckle as I start to cough again. As soon as I'm able to resume speaking, I comment, "She sure has you pegged, Pip." I throw up my hands in frustration. "You know what? Screw it! I'm so tired of coughing I could scream. Kiera, if you have an idea for a good doctor, text me the name and I'll make an appointment for whenever the rest of the Girlfriend Posse can make it. We'll have lunch or something and bring you guys takeout."

Heather, Tara and I are sitting around the cold sterile room. Heather looks up at the walls with the brightly colored photographs.

"Who do you suppose poses for those pictures? Do you think they give them a discount on their bill if they pose? If they do, do they pose for pictures before they get their news or after? If they're patients, why do they look so healthy? Why don't the doctors ever smile that much when they talk to me?" Heather asks in a verbal stream of consciousness.

Tara rolls her eyes at Heather as she mutters, "Heather, I'm sure these aren't real patients. They have stock images for these kinds of things. You just buy the pictures from a service. Those are probably actors who pose for the pictures."

"No, I don't think so. I think I recognize the nurse standing at the nurses station in the picture over there," Heather argues.

The random quibbling between the girls reminds me so much of when Donda and Jeff were young and I used to take them to the doctor for their shots. They used to fight over the magazines with the crossword puzzles in them. Their fights were about as inane as this little argument.

I decide to step in. "Actually, I'll side with Heather on this one. The nurse in that picture looks familiar. But I don't know how they can ethically reimburse them for appearing in the pictures. I bet there are some HIPPA rules and regulations. Whenever the government gets involved, it's a little more complicated. Maybe the staff is real, but the patients aren't. I bet they did something fancy to the pictures with the computer like they do to all those Victoria Secret models."

Heather snorts as she looks at Tara and shrugs. "Looks like we were both right."

Tara shakes her head. "I'm an only child, but something tells me what Gwendolyn just did is a common strategy among moms who have several kids."

I wink at her. "I'll never tell."

Just then a tall, young doctor with glasses comes through the door and extends his hand, "Hello, I'm Dr. Brewer. Sorry to keep you waiting, I got held up on a surgery consult. I had to meet with some nervous parents and it took longer than I anticipated."

"I'm Gwendolyn, but I was expecting to meet Dr. Fontaine," I reply.

"I apologize, but Dr. Fontaine retired last month. What seems to be the problem, Ms. Whitaker?"

I weigh my options. Even though Dr. Brewer appears to be young, he probably is more familiar with recent technology. I take a deep breath and forge ahead, "Well, I've had this stupid cough which won't go away. I've been taking over-the-counter cold medicine, but it doesn't seem to make any difference. A few months ago, I got an inhaler from the urgent care clinic because I have a history of asthma even though it's been years since I've had a problem. I used to be an ice skater when I was much younger. They said vigorous exercise brought on the asthma. However, these days I don't get much exercise unless you count working in my flower shop. That's why I thought this stuff was just allergies. But, it's been months and months and it's still not going away," I trail off as I start to cough.

Dr. Brewer nods as he warms his stethoscope between his hands, "Let me just give your lungs a listen and we'll see what we're dealing with here. The nurse had you blow into a little plastic tool, correct?"

I flush a little as I nod. "Yes, unfortunately, my score was not very high."

Several minutes go by as he listens to my heart and lungs in various different places. I don't know if he's inexperienced or what — but he seems to go back to several spots and re-listen. Trying to regulate my breathing and slow it down so he can listen is making it much more difficult not to cough. Eventually, I dissolve into another round of coughing. Finally, he sits up straight with a grim expression on his face. He writes something on the chart and then looks at me. "Ms. Whitaker, you appear to have diminished breath sounds on at least one side, I would feel much more comfortable if you would consent to some blood work and a chest x-ray. It might be positional, but that's unlikely."

Tara's brow furrows as she grills him, "That doesn't sound good. What do you think is going on?"

Dr. Brewer looks directly at me. "Would you like me to speak to your friends?"

"Yes, I would, thank you very much. They're here to help me. I brought them with me in case I got really nervous and wanted to chicken out today."

"Smart strategy, Ms. Whitaker. We don't know yet if it's good or bad news. There are just enough red flags that we need to check out what's going on."

"I anticipated the news may be awful — that's why I brought some people with me to make sure that I was brave enough to stay. I've been feeling too puny and rotten to have everything come back normal. This isn't normal tiredness. I'm fatigued and beaten down at a cell level. This isn't a simple case of a little flu bug. I am afraid this is something major. I just don't want it to be true. I'm finally getting back on my feet after whatever disaster one could classify my second, so-called marriage. Now to be blindsided by whatever garbage this thing is, it's almost too much irony to comprehend."

Dr. Brewer pats me on the shoulder. "Ms. Whitaker, let's not jump the gun yet. It could be absolutely nothing. It could be simple as the way I had you positioned on the table or some scar tissue or benign cysts. Whatever it is, it needs to wait until we know what's going on inside your body. Once we find out, we'll be in a better position to deal with it. I want you to complete the tests today and then go out to lunch with your friends so you don't pass out from not having breakfast. Try to put it out of your mind because it'll be a few days before lab results are back. We can't do anything until we have more information. Once we have the test results, you can meet with the appropriate people and make decisions. In the meantime, go to a concert or a movie and have fun. Try to forget about today. Dwelling on the most negative potential outcome won't change anything. The bottom line is for today or tomorrow or even this weekend, none of us know what the definitive picture looks like. We may not know for quite some time. Even after this first round of preliminary tests come back, we won't know the full extent for several weeks or even a couple of months. There is no need to put your life on complete hold."

Heather's eyes tear up as she asks in a halting voice, "I know you don't know the answer right at this very moment, but what if she were to find out the worst news? Is it an automatic death sentence?"

"No, lung cancer isn't an absolute death sentence. There are many, many stories of survival after lung cancer, emphysema or COPD. All of those conditions used to be considered almost 100% fatal. But, now the survivability rate is much higher than it used to be." Dr. Brewer looks directly at me. "Hang tight and go get some x-rays and blood work. We'll call you to make a follow up exam to discuss the results."

I am completely numb from head to toe. I seriously

thought the doctor might send me home with some allergy medicine even though I had this nagging fear this was something far more serious. To have my deepest fear voiced out loud is surreal. I want to curl up in a ball and cry. I look over at Heather, and she is actually crying. My heartbeat is echoing so loudly in my ears, I can't even hear what Tara is telling the doctor. I can only see Tara and Dr. Brewer both nodding their heads. My focus is myopic at the moment.

The next thing I know, Tara is escorting me down the hall to have my blood drawn. Mercifully, the nurse is able to stick my vein with one try. Wordlessly, I watch her take four vials of blood. Next, the girls walk me down to the x-ray department. All I can say is it's a good thing they both have an arm around my waist. Otherwise, I would have crumpled on the floor like a discarded Kleenex. Right now, I feel about equally useful. Tara is directing the conversations with medical personnel with military precision and Heather is discreetly undressing me and placing me in a hospital gown so they can take the appropriate chest x-rays. I can't shake the feeling this moment is the beginning of the end. By the time Heather redresses me, I'm shaking so much Tara has to drive my car home.

Heather begs me to call Denny and ask him to stay with me. I plead with her not to involve him. I have visions of becoming a burden to him. I remember him telling me how awful he felt when he couldn't 'fix' Karen's illness. Since I don't know what, if anything is wrong with me yet, I don't want to bring him in on my drama. I'd feel horrible if I brought sadness into his life again. Reluctantly, the girls tuck me into bed after Heather makes me a light supper and Tara waters all of my plants. My shoulders shake silently as I clutch the handkerchief Denny left in my luggage; I wonder what I could have done to the universe to make God so angry at me to take happiness from my grasp not once but twice.

Chapter Seven

Denny

I pull the saddle blanket off of Velvet as Tyler takes the riding bit out of her mouth. "Mindy is so good with her. She hardly needs any supervision at all now," I praise.

Jeff's eyes light up. "I know. She's pushing me to let her jump now. I'm not sure I'm ready to let her go quite that far yet, but you know that girl of mine; she's never met a challenge she doesn't love."

"Gwendolyn is pretty good on horseback too. I was surprised given her urban upbringing," I comment.

"I asked her once," Tyler remarks. "She just said, 'I had a lot of rich friends who owned stables.' She didn't give much of an explanation."

"My mom never explains much of her childhood. It's still mostly a mystery to me too," Jeff replies.

"Speaking of your mom, I had some vintage candleholders to add to her collection and I stopped by her shop to give them to her yesterday but I was surprised to find Isobel was covering for her," I comment. "Do you know where she was?"

"Yeah, Gidget and Tara took her to lunch and to the doctor," Tyler answers with a shrug. "It's about time. She's had that cough forever and a day. I would've thrown in the towel a long time ago. I don't know how she even sleeps."

"She didn't have me take her?" Jeff and I demand simultaneously.

I immediately back off. "No, you're right, as her son, you or Donda should have taken her."

Mindy who has been quietly reading a book in the corner of the barn says, "Papa, Grummy has important reasons for not wanting you to take her to the doctor. Someday, you'll understand, I promise." With that announcement, Mindy puts a colorful bookmark in her book and skips off.

I shake my head as I mutter in Jeff's direction, "I try to understand your daughter and her grand pronouncements, I really do. But sometimes, she's just utterly confounding."

Tyler grins. "I don't know. I don't think it's the most startling announcement Mindy's ever made regarding you and Gwendolyn. There are others you might find a little more shocking. I thought you were in the room for that one, but you might've been elsewhere."

I stop brushing Velvet and look over her back at Tyler, "Look, it's been a long day, cut me some slack and stop talking in riddles. What in the world are you talking about?"

Jeff walks over and puts an arm around my

shoulders as he explains, "Well, Mindy was getting a little punch drunk with her abilities and apparently had a little surge of knowledge on the day Kiera announced her pregnancy. She not only forced Kiera to announce early, she almost spilled the beans on Madison's pregnancy. She also preempted Trevor's intent to pop the question, but not before telling us Madison and Trevor will only get married after you and Gwendolyn get married."

For a moment, I'm stunned into silence. I guess I must've missed something major at the last family dinner. I can't remember what I was doing that was so much more important. The only time I remember being away from the family was when I took Becca for a walk around the ranch, but surely I wasn't gone long. I guess now is as good a time as any to come clean. I have a feeling my daughter probably already knows what my intentions are. Given my last conversation with Jeff, he probably has a good idea as well. It's too bad that Aidan and Trevor aren't here so I can get it all out of the way at once.

I clear my throat nervously. "If I were to do the whole marriage thing again, Gwendolyn is exactly the kind of woman I'd marry. But I don't know if she's even interested in going down that road again. Her last trip with Kevin was pretty bumpy. I'm surprised after the whole mess she is even interested in talking to the likes of me."

Tyler slaps me on the back. "Congratulations! All that courtin' you've been doing has been paying off. I can't think of a better guy for Gwendolyn. You are like the Anti-Jerk-Wad. This is going to be so much fun to watch now that she knows you're actually interested in her. I assume she does know now, right?"

I chuckle at Tyler's question, but I guess it's not so far off base considering I sort of dated her under the radar for several months. "Yes, she is aware I'm interested in her now. Surprisingly, she seems okay with the concept."

Jeff raises an eyebrow at me. "I don't know if this dating thing is off to a great start if you're surprised my mom is a nice woman —"

"Dandelions! I didn't mean to insult your mom, Jeff." I apologize.

"Denny!" Jeff chastises. "Did you lose your sense of humor on the trail ride? I'm just yanking your chain. I know you like and respect my mom. Didn't we already have this conversation? I totally approve of the idea of the two of you together as long as you're not a jerk to her."

Tyler laughs out loud at the two of us. "Why don't you two ever just let out a few choice cuss words?"

The two of us answer in unison again, "Kids!"

"Besides, it's more fun to puzzle people like you with our creativity." I wink.

Tyler nods as he concedes, "I think you have a point. The parking enforcement people were really confused when I started talking about flaming stuffed mushroom soufflés the other day when they refused to rescind a ticket they gave me as I was crossing the street to retrieve my vehicle. It still relieved a little stress to yell all that stuff at them."

Mary Crawford

I carefully dodge a kid on a skateboard as I lift the gift bag out of the way. I was going to save this present for Christmas, but it seems more appropriate right now since Gwendolyn is feeling under the weather. I was thrilled when I found this at the Portland Saturday Market when I made a cake delivery for Heather's bakery. I've never seen a gift quite so perfect for Gwendolyn. It's as if it was custom made for her.

I haven't seen her in about a week. Every time I call her, she complains that she's busy. Finally, I told her if she didn't let me come over, I would have Tyler send his officers over to do a well-check. Reluctantly, she acquiesced and allowed me to come over tonight. I've already called in her favorite Chinese food and rented a movie from Red Box. I figured if I couldn't take her out on a date, I would bring the date to her.

When she opens the door, I'm floored. Frankly, she looks terrible. I haven't seen this version of Gwendolyn since she had a standoff with her miserable excuse for an ex-husband in the middle of Kiera's living room several years ago. I'm immediately alarmed. I set down the movie and gift bag and reach out to place my hand on her forehead. Much to my shock, she shies away. I thought we had moved far beyond that point. Her flinch is soul-crushing. I back away and stuff my hands in my pocket.

For a moment, I just stand there and study her to see if I can gather any clues. Her eyes are dull and rimmed with red. There are deep bluish-purple bruises under her eyes as if she hasn't slept in days. Most concerning of all are the hollows in her cheeks. I notice her wrist bones are even more prominent. Gwendolyn is a thin, petite woman to start with but she has clearly lost even more weight.

I walk toward her to give her a hug and inexplicably she steps backward and crosses her arms over her body. Her body language is abundantly clear. However, I do not understand what's changed between us. The last time I saw her, we warmly embraced, and I gave her a quick kiss goodbye. We talked the next night on the phone and everything seemed normal. We even discussed the possibility of taking a line dancing class together.

I take a stab in the dark. "What did you find out at the doctor? Are you contagious or something? If you are, it's probably too late. We have spent quite a bit of time together in the last couple of weeks. The way I understand germs to work, we've probably already cross-contaminated each other," I joke, trying to unearth her usual smile, which seems to be long gone. I can't read anything into her odd posture. . It's like a weird facsimile of the warm, loving open Gwendolyn I know. When my lame joke doesn't even draw out a hint of a smile, my heart drops to my toes. "*Amasa,* what's going on?" I ask desperately.

Gwendolyn is still standing as stiff as a statue, but a tear slides down her face as she answers, "Dennis Ashley, do yourself a favor and just turn around and walk out that door. Just back off. Go home and forget you've ever met me. I'll avoid the kids' stuff, so it's not awkward for you."

Stunned, I back out the door. I hear her whisper in a hoarse voice, "Take your bag."

I'm surprised I have the presence of mind not to

hurl the flaming gift bag up the street as I stomp to my truck. With shaking hands and a wildly beating heart, I drive my truck a couple blocks away from her house and pull it off onto a side street. For a few moments all I can do is sit and stare blankly out of the window of my truck. Freakishly, the skies break open in a summer rainstorm and the truck is covered in a thick coat of rain. Funny thing is that's exactly what I feel like doing. What the heck? I might as well join Mother Nature. Big tears stream down my face as I try to dissect what just happened.

There is no rhyme or reason to explain her actions. There is no filter through which I can run this to make it make sense. It just doesn't. My girlfriend just broke up with me and I have no idea why. Maybe, she was never my girlfriend to begin with and I just didn't understand. For all I know, I misinterpreted the whole thing. Perhaps I'm just stupid. Am I just too old-fashioned and two dates and a little cuddling doesn't mean what I think it means? I may have put far too much stock in all the time I spent courting her. Perhaps I should take her at her word and back off like she asked me to. Maybe she's just not ready.

A knock at my truck window scares the soufflé out of me. I roll down my window and encounter a police officer. The police officer shines his flashlight in my eyes and says, "Is there a problem here, sir?"

"No, sir," I reply, shielding my eyes from the intrusive light.

"Are you having trouble with your truck?"

I flush with embarrassment. "No, sir. I just had to pull over because I'm having a terrible day. It appears my girlfriend broke up with me. My hands were shaking so badly I needed to pull over."

"Have you been drinking?" replies the police officer.

"Not at all," I respond with a half laugh. "Not in about a quarter of the century, since my wife died. I learned my lesson a long time ago. I stick to pop now. That's about as heavy as it gets for me. I'm just having a terrible day. I thought it would be safer if I pulled off the road. If this is a problem, I'll move."

"Take your time, sir. I wanted to make sure you weren't having car trouble. It's a nasty night out here. Do you need an escort home?" The police officer smiles.

"No sir, I'll be fine, thank you," I respond with a flush and an embarrassed cough.

"Do you mind if I see your license and registration? I'm not going to issue you a ticket or anything. I have to keep track of my contact with the public for statistical purposes. If you ask me, I think it's silly but the politicians want it to look good if you know what I mean," the officer explains with a shrug.

I nod as I open the glove box and dig out my registration. "I understand. Officer Tyler Colton is a good family friend and he works at the Sheriff's office. He says paperwork is the bane of his existence. I used be a long-haul trucker, so I totally sympathize. It always seemed like I did more paperwork than I ever did drivin'."

The young police officer grins. "There is probably some truth in that." He writes down my name and registration number and returns my paperwork. He pats the top of my truck. "You drive safe now. Things will probably look better with your girlfriend in the morning. There's just something weird in the air tonight."

I walk into my house and I'm greeted by the puppy who wandered up on my property a couple of months ago. The vet decided he probably had some Labrador and Newfoundland in him as well as maybe some Spaniel. He's an interesting little mutt, but he's as sweet as they come. I decided to name him Bojangles. He just reminds me of a blues musician. He always has this sad look on his face like he would be playing the piano if he possibly could. Bojangles comes over and puts his food bowl in my lap after I sit down in my chair to mope some more.

"Well, I guess that's pretty clear. You're a good boy," I respond.

His tail wags as if I gave him an Oscar. He follows me over to the food bag. His food is almost gone and I get a twinge in my back as I bend down to get the scoop. I look at him and ask, "Do you expect me to do everything?"

Much to my amusement, he digs in the bottom of the bag in pulls out the scoop and hands it to me. Every other dog I've ever had would stick his head in the bag and just chow down. This dog has some sort of back story. I don't know what it is. The vet says he doesn't have a microchip. Still, this dog has had some serious training. I put ads up all over town, but no one seems to know this dog's story. So, Bojangles has apparently adopted me. Today, I definitely need the comic relief of Bojangles.

When I opened my heart up to Gwendolyn, I never dreamed I might have to fill my bed with a four-legged creature like Bojangles instead. I shoo him away and tell him to go lay down in his bed. However, later, while I'm trying to concentrate on reading the paper instead of what a mess my life has become, Bojangles stealthily sneaks onto the bed and lays his head on my chest — the irony of the switch does not escape me.

Chapter Eight

Gwendolyn

How long does it take for a stupid phone call to come in? I've been waiting for days. Don't they know my life is hanging in the balance? I can't move forward, and I can't move back. Do they even have radiologists and lab technicians working at the hospital? Is it a case of no news is good news or no news is bad news? For a moment, I panic. Would he make an appointment for me in either case? Or is he only going to make an appointment if it's bad news? I can't remember.

I've been having nightmares every single night. I can't sleep worth a darn. If it's not the freaking cough keeping me awake, it's seeing the look of devastation on Denny's face over and over again. In my heart, I know I did the right thing. In the long run, Denny would be completely devastated if I'm terminally ill. I can't explain all that to him right now because he doesn't know what the doctor said. I don't want to tell him because it would destroy him. Yet, not telling him is painful as well. I'm in a no-win situation. If I'm not thinking about Denny, I'm thinking about what it'll be like to receive the awful news from the doctor. Other times when I dream, I dream the doctor tells me nothing is wrong, and it's all a figment of my imagination and it's only bad allergies. On those occasions, I wake up and I feel hopeful like I've imagined the whole thing. Yet, I'm quickly brought back to planet earth when I cough so hard I need to vomit. That happy little side effect is happening with frightening regularity these days.

My cell phone buzzes and I nearly fall down as my anxiety ratchets up. My hands are shaking so violently I practically drop my cell phone. I silently curse my klutziness. The price of cell phones is crazy these days. It's almost like three car payments. I can't afford to drop the blasted thing — not to mention I need to talk to whoever's on the other end.

Breathlessly, I answer, "Hello?"

"Hi, Gwen this is Heather. We're going to come rescue you and take you for some retail therapy at Macy's. They're having a big sale today."

"Oh, hi, Heather. I can't go today. I'm expecting a call from the clinic," I respond.

"Yes, silly, I know. That's why we're going shopping. You'll make yourself sick waiting by the phone. You definitely need some company. Therefore, we, the Girlfriend Posse, are going to take you shopping. Well, half of us. The pregnant half of us won't be there, because you'd bum them out since you're so skinny," Heather explains with a laugh.

"Heather!" I interrupt. "Did you not hear me say I have to wait until the doctors office calls? I can't go anywhere."

"I'm confused. Is your mobile phone not mobile? That's what's really cool about cell phones; you can take them any place you go. You and I have the same kind of phone. I happen to have a spare battery for our phones. You have absolutely no excuse. Throw on some comfortable shoes and get your fanny in gear because I'm coming to get you in an hour."

"Has anyone ever told you that you're one pushy broad?" I throw my hands up in exasperation even though Heather can't see me.

Heather's laughter fills the phone line. "You do remember I'm married, right? I hear those kind of comments almost daily. A woman whom I respect a great deal once told me I remind her of herself when she was younger. I consider that the very highest form of compliment. I'm just helping you find your inner fighter. If today, it requires a few sales racks to find it, so be it."

"Heather Colton, you are too funny ... but I'm glad you're my friend," I respond in a quiet voice.

"Aww, You're so sweet Gwendolyn. I'm glad you're my friend too. I'll see you in a while."

3:03 p.m. over stuffed crust pizza — in the food court.

The beginning of when my world starts falling apart.

Tara, Heather and I are having a snack in the food court when my phone finally rings. Believe it or not, we're having so much fun I'm not braced for the call. Tara is telling us this funny story about one of Aidan's fans. Apparently, he has an ardent fan in her eighties who owns an RV. She is so dedicated she drives from state to state to go to his concerts. She likes to leave a bright orange lipstick ring on his cheek and then see him perform with it on his face. Well, this little routine has started the paparazzi tongues wagging about whether Aidan has a secret lover. Tara thinks it's hysterical because she's met this particular fan several times and thinks she's sweet.

After I answer the call, I have this overwhelming drive to get up and move. I have déjà vu back to the time I was an ice skater. My coaches were always trying to get me to sit still in the kiss-n-cry area. It was the most difficult thing for me. I never could sit still for bad news. My body just wants to flee and run. Consequently, I bolt — leaving everything except my cell phone behind. I make it past about seven stores before I collapse.

Absentmindedly I think to myself, *My goodness, Tara is strong. She's not much heftier than me.* She doesn't even wait for mall security personnel to get there before she scoops me off the floor and onto a nearby bench. Heather catches up to us and shoves a fruit smoothie into my face. "Drink!" she commands.

With shaky hands, I take the sweet concoction from her and sip. Tara studies me carefully and says, "Tell us the news, but take a few deep breaths first."

Five. It takes me five deep breaths before I can even utter a single word. "They need to see me again," I squeeze out, the words barely making it past my closed throat. *When did it become so hard to breathe?*

"Did they say why?" Tara frowns.

"Something about wanting to differentiate findings on the x-ray and confirm abnormalities in my blood work," I answer in a half whisper.

"Oh honey, I'm so sorry. That sounds scary. I have a big anniversary cake to do, but I can pass it off to Piper if you want me there," Heather offers.

"I can be there," Tara announces. "I'll cancel classes for the day. I can put a sign on the door claiming family emergency or have one of my advanced students teach the class."

"This is exactly what I didn't want to happen. I don't want to be a burden on my friends and family. You guys shouldn't have to set aside your whole lives to cater to me," I insist in a panicked voice.

"Gwendolyn, it's not catering to you if we want to be there. We're offering, and we wouldn't do it if we didn't want to. Speaking of that, I'm surprised Denny isn't here. Did he know you were expecting the results? It's unlike him not to be by your side for this. Usually, he's a rock at these kinds of events. I can't remember an announcement of good or bad news where Denny wasn't there supporting someone."

Suddenly, my newly manicured nails become very interesting. "I didn't tell him I went to the doctor or was expecting results."

"You what?" Heather exclaims. "I don't understand. I thought you liked Denny."

"I *do* like Denny. But he doesn't need all this drama in his life. You know what? Come to think of it, I think he knows I went to the doctor. He asked me about it, right before I broke up with him," I reply.

"What do you mean you broke up with Denny?" Tara asks. "Do you realize the man is so far gone for you he's been clandestinely dating you for over a year?"

"Well, now that you've pointed it out, I guess he probably has been. I thought he was being friendly. You know, he isn't exactly shy around anybody. I assumed he was a little extra friendly to me because he was trying to cheer me up from the mind-bend of my alleged marriage to the Jerk-Wad. Perhaps I should've been paying a little closer attention," I concede.

Heather is still shaking her head in befuddlement. "Gwendolyn, help me understand. Obviously, you like Denny a whole a lot. He makes you laugh and smile. Since you guys connected for your special weekend, you were happier than I've seen you since I met you. Even though you've been sick. If the man makes your heart go pitter-patter, why would you push him away?"

"Heather, I'm trying to protect him. He lost a part of himself when he lost Karen, I don't want him to have to do that again. I know he'll never love me as much as he loved Karen. But, even if he loves me just a little, he doesn't deserve to lose someone again. So, if I can save him from loss again, it's my duty. I like and respect him enough to save him from pain."

Tara cups my hands in hers. "Gwendolyn, don't you think it should be his decision? A decision he can make only if he knows all the facts and after some serious soul-searching? If you try to shelter him from all the difficult stuff, you are crippling him emotionally. He has his own pain to work through. He can't get through it and grow, if you try to shelter him from what's going on. The two of you need to grow together as a couple. But you can't if you don't give him all the information he needs. Denny is a strong man who has been through purgatory and back. Something tells me he will, in the end, be able to handle this. Now, I won't tell you there won't be difficult times for the two of you between the beginning and the end. But, it's the journey which makes it worthwhile."

I wipe the tears from my eyes with the back of my sleeve. "What if I'm not up to the journey?"

Heather comes over and hugs me. "The wonderful thing about being in a relationship is that when you feel the weakest, that's often when your partner is feeling strong like Superman. Give Denny a chance to be your superhero for a change, Lord knows you need one."

I relent as I'm enveloped in a group hug, "Okay, you guys have convinced me, I'll give my guy a call. After the way I treated him the other day, I wouldn't blame him if he doesn't bother to come back. Heather, I might need some of your special pie to convince him."

"No worries, Gwendolyn, Denny is especially susceptible to my pie. You decide what kind you want me to make and consider it done," Heather offers.

I'm still on the hunt to try to track Denny down. He's been remarkably difficult to find these last few days. I don't know if it's coincidence or if he's making himself scarce. But when I unlock his front door with the key from its special hiding spot, I am greeted in the kitchen by a very excited Bojangles and a startled Isobel. Isobel is making freshly squeezed lemonade in Denny's kitchen.

Love Seasoned

"Where is everyone?" I ask, looking around.

"Well, they are out on the big mud puddle they call a lake trying to make a big pile of sticks they call the boat seaworthy so they can go fishing in a couple of weeks. William has Denny, Tyler and Jeff and whoever else they can round up trying to help them. If you ask me, it's a recipe for disaster. But, they assure me they're trying to save money. I'll believe it when I see it. Whatever — it keeps them out of our hair. Would you like lemonade?"

I nod and smile at Isobel's description of Denny's outdoor adventures. It sounds like a pretty accurate portrayal of his hunting and fishing acumen. It usually ends up costing him much more than it ends up saving. But he always seems to have a great time. So... I guess it's harmless enough.

As Isobel pours my lemonade, she asks me, "Gwendolyn, are you feeling okay? You look very thin — even for you."

Her words, although they are spoken out of concern, evoke a twin reaction from me. Instantly, my back stiffens at the intrusiveness of her question. Yet, at the same time, my eyes well up with tears. I suppose this is the way it'll be from here on out. The privacy and dignity I'm used to probably will be gone now. I'm going to have medical professionals, nurses, the insurance company and random strangers poking me and prodding me looking me over and questioning every decision I make from here on out for the rest of my life.

The. Rest. Of. My. Life.

How will my life be measured? Is it going to be a matter of days? Weeks? Months? Will I be able to watch

Mindy graduate from high school or get married? What about Becca? Am I even going to live long enough to meet the new grand-baby?

How do I even start to tell Donda? This has the potential to trigger her eating disorder or spur a relapse in her recovery from substance abuse.

As a Kleenex appears in front of my face, I realize tears are freely flowing down my cheeks and Isobel is looking at me with grave sympathy. I am beyond embarrassed. I didn't mean to break down in front of someone I barely know. I mean, I have met Isobel only a few times, and gone over the operation of my store with her when she has taken over for me on occasion. I don't know her well. Denny says she's an amazing person and sings her praises all the time, but it's not like we're close. Here I am having an almost catatonic breakdown in front of her. It's just awkward. I take a few deep breaths in an effort to collect myself, but it's largely ineffective and I cough uncontrollably.

She slides an empty plastic container in front of me and says, "Feel free to use it if you need to. It's okay, I don't mind. I've been there and done that before. There is no shame in it. So, don't be embarrassed; it happens."

"Thanks," I mutter as I'm finally able to bring my breathing and coughing under control.

"I sense there's a little more going on than a debate over whether you'd like a freshly made scone with your lemonade," Isobel remarks with a knowing smile.

"Gee, whatever clued you in?" I ask sarcastically.

Isobel regards me carefully. I half expect her to respond with a joke, but she gazes at me intently before she answers somberly, "I saw the same look in my eyes every time I looked in the mirror right after I got my diagnosis of breast cancer. It's so easy to feel like you've been sentenced to die. But, as you get more information, you'll figure out that there is a big giant support team out there for you, you just need to figure out who your allies are."

"Oh crap! Is it obvious?" I breathe the question under my breath. "I don't know anything yet. I haven't told anybody. Nothing has been decided. I don't want to tell folks what's going on until I know more. If I'm so easy to read, I could get myself into some real trouble. What should I do?" As I ask questions, my voice becomes more and more shrill.

Isobel hands me a cool washcloth as she soothes, "Gwendolyn, take a moment to relax. You don't need to make decisions today, or tomorrow or even next week. If it's anything like what I went through, you have to have more tests, maybe even a biopsy. You'll have to wait for the results of those to come back. So, you've got several days, maybe even a month or so to do research and make some decisions. What kind of diagnosis are they looking at?"

"I don't know exactly, but based on my cough, I would think maybe lung cancer would make the most sense. It was something they found during my chest x-ray. I have to have a follow-up MRI and maybe a biopsy, depending on what they find in the MRI."

"I think those are reasonable assumptions. But I caution against getting ahead of the tests. You never know; it could be something weird like scar tissue or harmless cysts. I wouldn't be making funeral arrangements quite yet. You need to wait and see what they say."

"The waiting is the hardest thing for me. I'm not a patient person by nature. In fact, I'm not a patient person at all. I've been through hell and back with Donda. I know you don't know me very well, but my daughter was very, very sick at one point in her life. She weighed quite close to eighty pounds, and we were on a deathwatch with her. She barely had a heartbeat and her organs were all shutting down. They told us to pick out a casket for her. She was so small at that point, we could have buried her in a child's casket. It was the most emotionally excruciating time in our lives. Consequently, I am in no way looking forward to the endless wait for medical exams and tests. The sight of a hospital parking lot is enough to make me throw up."

"I understand what you're saying. We've had our own nightmares," she replies.

"So, tell me this? Why am I the one who might have cancer instead of some jerk like my ex husband? Why can't I have a second chance at real love? It doesn't seem fair, does it?"

"Gwendolyn, every time I look down at my disfigured chest and my artificial nipples, I think the same thing. However, I have come to the conclusion cancer is rarely fair. If cancer were fair, kids would never get cancer. Women would never lose their breasts or ovaries to cancer and men would never have testicular cancer. Singers would never lose their vocal cords and athletes would never lose their limbs. Yet, as we all know, that's not the way it really works. Cancer doesn't care who you are or what you do for a living. Cancer kills without discrimination."

"What am I going to do, Isobel?" I plead, in a hoarse whisper.

"The first thing you're going to do is eat. I know you don't feel like eating. Nerves will do that to you. Your body needs fuel to fight. You can't fight if you're too weak. You need the strongest weapon you can have. So, have Heather cook you some of her amazing food. Your daughter-in-law and granddaughter are phenomenal cooks too. Put them to work for you. Secondly, get some sleep. If you need to get medication from your doctor, do it. Don't be ashamed to ask. Again, you can't fight the battle if you're too tired to go to war. Do whatever it takes to get some sleep."

I blush. "It's too bad I kicked Denny out of my bed, he is the best teddy bear ever. I sleep so well when he's beside me."

"I'm not sure I should hear this since Denny and William have been friends since childhood. It might violate some pinky-swearing they did back in the day," Isobel responds with a scandalized giggle.

I scoff. "Oh, whatever. What the guys don't know won't hurt them. Besides, they're probably out there gossiping about us too."

"We're out where, Mom?" Jeff asks as he traipses through the kitchen carrying a bucket of fish with all the guys trailing behind.

"Oh, I was telling Isobel I thought you guys were outside somewhere," I cover quickly.

Mary Crawford

"No, Amasa, I don't think that's what I heard it all," Denny counters. "I thought I heard a whole different discussion going on —"

Chapter Nine

Denny

The startled look on Gwendolyn's face is priceless. I'm not sure what she thinks I overheard, but it must've been good, because she's bright red. It's funny how intertwined she's become in my life. It's only been a couple of weeks, but I miss her something fierce. I still don't know what happened, so I don't know how long she'll allow me to stay here and stare at her like a child who covets birthday cake.

Finally, Gwendolyn breaks the silence. "Denny, it's great to see you. I'm sorry for the other night; I don't know what got into me. It's been a rough month. I don't feel well, and it's affecting my mood. Again, I apologize. I should've never treated you that way."

Isobel clears her throat lightly as she interrupts, "Denny, it's been … um … great to see you. Thank you for allowing me to use your stove and thanks for entertaining my husband for a while. We'll talk to you next time. Take care of yourself and Gwendolyn — you guys should come out to the house for dinner. I'm going to get out of your way so you guys can talk," Isobel comes over and hugs me. As she does, she murmurs in Gwendolyn's ear, "Don't be afraid. If you are, call me."

Gwen sinks down into one of my large leather chairs and she watches with trepidation as Isobel walks out the door. I wonder why she looks like she's lost her last friend on the planet. Isobel is the wife of my best friend and very nice, but as far as I know the women are not close friends.

I notice Gwendolyn is looking down at the ground in what appears to be shame. I hope she isn't still feeling bad about the other day. Everyone has an off day every now and then. It's not the end of the world.

I'm more than a little frustrated by the growing distance between us. I walk over and hunch down in a squat in front of her. I look directly into her eyes as I study her. "Amasa, why do you look so broken?"

"Denny, I'm not even sure there are enough words in the English language to answer that question," she whispers as she buries her face in my neck.

In all fairness, perhaps I should've been prepared for what she told me, but I just wasn't. It's as simple as that. Gwendolyn's spirit seems invincible. She's overcome so much in her life she seems totally unstoppable. It's part of the reason I call her Amasa. She has managed to stay sweet regardless of all the crap her life has thrown her. The death of her first husband, the sexual assault and subsequent eating disorder and drug addiction of her daughter, the physical, mental and emotional abuse by her second husband — even starting over after her divorce, it doesn't matter. Gwendolyn always beats the odds.

Yet, now it seems the odds might be stacked against her. I am blindsided by the news. It seems stupid to say. I know she's been sick for months. I'm one of many who've been nagging her to go to the doctor. Now, I'm kicking myself because I should've tried harder to flat out make her go. I should have physically taken her there myself. Why didn't I do more? Maybe she wouldn't be so sick. What if they had caught it sooner? I don't know. I feel like I felt before. I'm so damned helpless. Fake cuss words aren't enough. This calls for real cuss words. What in the hell was God thinking? This woman doesn't deserve any more pain. She's had far too much. It's my job to take pain away from her, not add more misery to her life.

Knowing what a phenomenal person she is, now, her behavior the other day makes so much more sense. She would be the type to preemptively break up with me so I wouldn't feel obligated to take care of her or something.

It's an interesting dilemma — do I save myself the pain of doing this all again? I'll be honest: the temptation is there. But as soon as I have that thought — the realization hits me there is no way on God's-green-earth that walking away is even an option. Gwendolyn is in my life, whether I want her to be or not. She is the mother of my son-in-law. I'm going to see her at every family event for the next twenty years. So, unless I want my daughter to get divorced, Gwendolyn is in my life — just as a practical matter.

Yet, beyond that, I like this woman — I like her a lot. I think back to the discussion I was having with her son and Tyler in the barn. I was talking about a real future — not scratching some temporary need. Does my feelings all go away because she's sick? That's an offensive thought all by itself. I'm not that kind of person. If I had been that man, I would've ditched Karen the moment she threw my daughter down the basement stairs and permanently injured her. It's not consistent with my moral fiber to abandon someone when they need my help.

Which begs the question: am I strong enough to love another person through their death? I simply don't know. It just about gutted me the last time I undertook the task. I don't know if I have enough reserves left to do it again. My circle of friends and family is a little bigger now. I've got Kiera and Jeff and the girls and the new grand-baby on the way. If Mindy's correct, it's a little boy. Now, I've got all those people to worry about in addition to Gwendolyn. Yet, all of those people are people who love Gwendolyn too. So they'll be grieving as well. We have to be able to support each other. It's going to be a complicated situation. We're all going to be grieving and fighting for Gwendolyn together. I think almost every person involved in our lives is a friend of both of us.

Fear threatens to overtake me as if it's a physical being. It's been three days since Gwendolyn told me the news. I have yet to have a moment of peaceful sleep. My dreams are tormented by memories of Karen's last days — of the doctors coming to me with the paperwork and telling me I needed to take her off of life support because she had no discernible brain function and her final act of defiance in passing away before I could say my final goodbyes. I was stuck in a stupid traffic jam between Kiera's Children's Hospital and Karen's rehabilitation center. The irony of that haunted me for years. Me — the professional truck driver, couldn't navigate my way through an idiotic traffic jam caused by nothing more than rubberneckers so I couldn't say my final goodbyes to my wife. I haven't thought about that moment for years. But, the stress of this week has caused it to replay incessantly in my head like some sick movie trailer.

I am ashamed to admit I don't know if I am strong enough to relive this nightmare.

As I try to rinse the taste of my sour stomach out of my mouth with some mouthwash, my cell phone rings. Who in the world could be calling this early? It's not Gwendolyn's ring tone. My heart sinks to the pit of my stomach.

"Hello?" I answer, my voice scratchy.

"Hey Denny, ready to go? I'll be there in ten," Tyler announces cheerfully.

"Be where?" I ask, befuddled.

"Did you forget about the Judge's epic fishing trip today?" Tyler asks.

I run my fingers through my unruly hair. "Yeah, I guess I did. I haven't been sleeping very well. I forgot what day it is."

"Trust me, I understand. Before I met Heather, I didn't sleep worth beans. I bet this news about Gwendolyn has stirred up all sorts of bad crap for you," Tyler guesses.

For once, I don't even bother to try to correct his language, because he's so spot on.

"You guys know?" I probe, surprised at the revelation. I didn't think that Gwendolyn was telling people quite yet.

"Yeah, Heather and Tara were there when she got the call from radiology. Heather said it scared the snot out of her. I guess Gwendolyn went nearly unconscious in the middle of the mall. If Tara hadn't been there to pick her up, I don't know what would've happened."

"Oh geez, Gwendolyn didn't say anything," I mutter.

"Did you expect her to? Your lady-love is pretty tough. She's not used to trusting people to take care of her. It'll take some convincing on your part for her to let you in. You know that, right?"

"What if I'm not up to the job?" I ask almost involuntarily. Gwendolyn is not the only person who hates to expose her weaknesses.

"Denny, my dad lives a good ways away. Over the past few years, I've learned to rely on you as a sort of substitute. You are a phenomenal man who raised a daughter almost all on your own. If anyone's up to the job, it's you. I'm not too worried about your ability to step up to the plate. If you need a hand, let us know."

I collapse against the edge of the tub as his emotional words hit me.

Tyler adds a quiet instruction, "Just a little something I've learned the hard way during my time as a commander — don't forget to take care of the caretaker."

I have to clear my voice of tears before I can answer, "Thank you, son. Your words mean a lot."

I don't know why am always surprised; I've been friends with William ever since we first traded baseball cards and stuck them in our bicycle spokes, but the man can never seem to do anything in a small way. I thought we were going to go out in his little dilapidated fishing skiff, but instead, he chartered a boat to go trout fishing up on the mouth of the McKenzie. I send Gwendolyn a text message to let her know about the change in plans and to tell her I may not be reachable by cell.

Once we're finally settled and have our lines in the water, William turns and asks me how Gwendolyn is coping with her news. Again, I am surprised William is aware of what's going on. He shrugs. "She just happened to be in the right place at the right time, and Gwendolyn needed to talk that day. I don't know if you remember but Isobel is a breast cancer survivor She was able to share her experiences with Gwendolyn and I think Gwendolyn found them helpful."

I look at William as if he's lost his marbles. "Of course I remember Isobel had breast cancer. I helped you guys rearrange the house so her bed could be downstairs after her surgery, remember? I only hung out at your house all the time. Geez, William, it's not like she's not my friend too." I chuck a Cheeto at him.

"Okay, I didn't mean to offend you. The whole time is a bit of a blur. I went from one doctor's appointment to another, to yet another. I think at the beginning, I kept hoping the diagnosis would be different. Then, I thought that maybe I could study the diagnosis away as if it were a complicated legal case. If I could only find enough studies that found one thing, it would outweigh any negative test results and make them go away. Unfortunately, medical test results aren't like that. They can't simply be overruled by the body of medical evidence. They have to be treated. It took me a while to adjust my thinking and embrace my new reality. The new reality was my wife had breast cancer and if we didn't aggressively treat it, she was going to die. It wasn't something I could hope away by the preponderance of the evidence, she had to treat it by having a bilateral mastectomy with radiation and chemotherapy."

"How did you deal with the fear that eats you alive?" I wonder as I search his face for answers.

"I hate to tell you, Den — you don't. You simply manage fear like a circus trainer manages an exotic cat. You train it into a semblance of what you'd like it to look like, and then you manage the flare-ups. You hope and pray it doesn't go crazy and show its true colors in front of people you care about. But, your fear is never totally contained. Fear always has a wild side which threatens to break free. There are certain stressors you know are going to aggravate it. A new test, a new doctor, a new treatment measurement, a news story promising hope. A fever, or bizarrely enough a lack of a fever — all that can lessen your tenuous control on this amorphous thing called fear."

"William, I don't know if I can do this again. I barely survived it the last time." I shift my sunglasses to wipe away tears.

Tyler puts his hand on my shoulder. "I am sorry this happened, Denny. Yet, I don't see that you have a choice. After all, this is Gwendolyn we're talking about."

I nod. "My heart already knows what my head is taking a while to accept."

Once again, I am standing outside of Gwendolyn's front door. I don't know how it's possible, but my hands are shaking even more than they were last time. I'm almost afraid to drop the heavy knocker shaped like a watering can. There is so much at stake, it's like opening Pandora's box. Yet doing nothing is not an option either; time is going to move forward either way. So, I shift the somewhat wilted gift bag to my other hand and knock on her stained oak door. As she swings it open, I can already tell this is going to be a better day; she looks much spunkier today than she did the last time I was here. She's obviously not one hundred percent back to her perfect perky self, but neither does she look like she's gone twelve rounds with Mohammed Ali during his prime.

Gwendolyn looks at the bag in my hand and frowns. "Oh, Denny. I was so awful the last time you were here. Can you ever forgive me?"

"*Amasa*, it's already forgotten. At first, I'll admit, it stung a lot. But I understand what happened now. You're entitled to a crappy day — even if I might not comprehend what's going on at the time. It's part of being human. If anybody has an excuse to have a crappy day, it's you."

Gwendolyn gives me a watery smile. "Thank you, I

appreciate your patience. I still shouldn't have taken it out on you. It wasn't fair. You did nothing to deserve that."

"Gwendolyn, may I come in?" I ask as I wipe my feet on her mat.

She flushes. "Of course, I don't know where my manners went." She takes my coat and hangs it up and then carries the gift bag into the living room and sits down on the couch. "May I open this?" she asks, as she fingers the gift tag on the beautiful bag.

"Of course, that's why I got it for you," I tease. "Most people are all about getting gifts, but I like giving them. I love finding the perfect gift for people. I should be one of those professional gift shoppers. Or maybe I should go into the antiques business or something. It's cool to go on treasure hunts. I'm like a kid who never grew up."

"Somehow, that doesn't surprise me about you. I see the way you restore antiques. You don't do what a lot of people do and shop for random parts on eBay and hope they match. You track down specific serial numbers and make sure the materials are authentic. It doesn't surprise me you are a very careful, meticulous gift finder. I for one, wouldn't think anything was amiss if I found you in the gift department of a store. I would think you were buying an anniversary gift for your wife or a wedding gift for your daughter. It would be even better if you were buying cookware you could use to make your somebody special a gourmet meal. The world is full of Renaissance men these days."

I laugh at her comparison of me to a Renaissance man. "I can hold my own in the kitchen, but not like Jeff or Aidan. Actually, it's a good thing Aidan knows his way around the kitchen. Tara is helpless when it comes to the kitchen."

Gingerly, she takes the gift tag off of the bag and removes the wrapping paper. She folds it and sets it aside. When she sees the tea pot and teacups formed like origami cranes, she gasps with delight. "Oh my gosh! These are exquisite. Look! There are teeny-tiny butterflies and cherry blossoms painted on them. I love them! Thank you so much."

"I thought of you when I chose these, you are strong and artistic but fragile and flexible at the same time," I explain bashfully. It's funny; my fanciful ideas didn't sound so silly when I thought about them in my head. Yet, when I say them out loud, they sound lame. I sound like some cheesy descriptive catalog somewhere. I swear that's not what it felt like when I was choosing something to get for Gwendolyn. She really is one of the most remarkable women I've ever met in my whole life. I thought that several months ago when I first chose this set.

Gwendolyn gently sets it down on her mantle. Then she deliberately walks over and threads her arms around my neck. She carefully kisses me directly on the lips. For a moment, I'm stunned, because we've talked at length about her cultural reluctance to make the first move. For Gwendolyn it's bold. It's an especially assertive move if you consider how we last parted ways. Finally my libido has the good sense to tell my brain to quiet down so I can enjoy myself and for the first time since I can remember, I melt into the simple enjoyment of a kiss.

I would've been more than happy to stay right in that pleasure zone for the rest of the night. Unfortunately, real life has other plans for us. An alarm goes off on Gwendolyn's phone. I pull away and look at her with a question on my face. She shrugs. "It's an alarm to remind me to eat a small meal. Isobel set it up for me. I've been coughing so hard nausea is becoming a real problem for me. I've been vomiting a lot. Isobel tells me this is a serious problem — I will need all the strength I can get. She has me on a body-replenishing regimen to help build me up. I will need to help fight whatever this is."

"I'm not sure Isobel should be giving you any medical advice," I caution.

"Oh, you misunderstood. Isobel isn't giving me any medication or anything drastic. She's just helping me choose healthy foods. It's nothing weird — just dairy, organic vegetables and meats. It's probably the same type of thing the hospital dietitian would put me on if I were already under their care. Isobel is giving me a jump start because she's already been through all of this. She's concerned because I've already lost some weight. She doesn't want me to be behind the curve where I might have to start from a deficit."

"To be honest, I've been a little concerned too. I didn't know if you were one of those body conscious women just trying to lose weight on purpose —" I admit.

"Geez, of course not Denny, I work with dirt and bugs all day. Do I look like I'm one of the *Real Housewives*? I don't have time to keep up with my appearance like that. Besides, I think all the plastic surgery and stuff is creepy.

Kevin had all these rich friends who kept trying to outdo each other with plastic surgery. It was weird — they looked like walking skeletons with big butts and big boobs. They looked stranger than Becca's Barbie dolls. When I walked away from Kevin, I gladly left behind that whole lifestyle."

"I'm so relieved. I didn't think it sounded like you. You weren't talking to me. I really wish you would've told me what was going on. I could've been a better support system for you."

"Denny, is that what you really want? It will be one of the hardest things you'll face."

"Gwendolyn, if anyone knows how hard it'll be, it's me."

"Denny, that's exactly why I didn't want to tell you what was going on. I don't want to be like Karen . . round two," she comments with a heavy sigh.

Chapter Ten

Gwendolyn

Well crap! I seem to be incapable of having a single conversation with Denny Ashley where I don't inflict some sort of pain on the poor man. As soon as those words of comparison flew out of my mouth, I knew it was absolutely the wrong thing to say. I know Karen and I were not the same. He looked like I physically punched him. He tried to pretend it didn't bother him, but the rest of the night he was more reserved and less open with me.

I tried to reestablish the moment we had had when I thanked him for the beautiful tea set, but I just couldn't get it back. I guess it's a positive sign he is here today. We've spent about an hour talking about how frightened we both are about what today might bring. He insists since he is mostly retired — he should be the one to take me to my medical appointments. Isobel will continue to watch the flower shop. She's done some remarkable things with my displays. I'm quite happy with her work.

We have, however, come to a stalemate in our discussions. Denny wants to be named as a contact person on my medical records so he can speak to the doctors about my condition. I am hesitant to do this. I don't think Denny will do anything nefarious with my medical records. I just don't want him to feel like he needs to be burdened with my care. Aside from our little weekend romp, we haven't even been officially on any dates. I know the whole family thinks he's been courting me for over a year, but I'm not sure if I've seen any overt evidence of his intent. Yes, we've been hanging out. But Denny hangs out with lots of people. So, while I don't think he's been out dating half the town, I'm not entirely sure he's been courting me. We do lots of friendly things, but I'm not sure that counts as formal dating. If we are dating, I'm not sure it should make him responsible for my medical care. During our long ride to Hood River, we talked in-depth about his excruciating decision to take Karen off of life support. He said it was the most difficult decision he's ever had to make. What if he was in charge of my medical care and had to make that kind of decision for me? I don't think he knows me well enough. It doesn't make any sense for me to put him on my medical records as a decision-maker even though he requested it. I know he thinks he's being helpful. But I don't want him to harm himself in the process of being a friend. Someone has to watch out for Denny in this process. Right now, because he's being so kindhearted, I have to protect him.

Denny seems to be hurt by my decision. I don't want him to be hurt by my choices. After all, I have a very talented attorney for a son. Doesn't it make sense to have Jeff be my primary medical and legal decision maker? I don't want this simple thing to come between us. Yet, it seems it has — it seems like such a stupid little fight.

Still, I remember what Denny said about two grown adults in love having a fight and the cracks between them being filled with love and respect. Maybe that's what's happening between us. But, are we even at the point in our relationship to be even thinking in terms of the L word? I'm not even sure. It's all so confusing between us. Nothing is normal or typical.

As I lie here on the cold mat, I decide this is entirely the wrong environment to try to make relationship decisions. Suddenly, I hear a disembodied voice say, "Ms. Whitaker take a deep breath and do not move; we are going to begin the test now. This portion of the test will take approximately two minutes. You will hear some noise, do not be alarmed."

Soon the whole MRI tube is filled with earsplitting sound. The earplugs they provided are not sufficient. Some noise, my butt! I try to remain still, but every cell of my body wants to get up and escape the brain numbing sound. The vibration of the tube around me makes me want to cough. I coughed during the last sequence of pictures and they made me redo them. So, I'm trying desperately not to cough any more. To be in this contraption one-second longer than necessary would be unbearable. It seemed like I was in the blasted machine for hours as they kept repeating little segments a few minutes at a time. Finally, the same disembodied voice informs me the test is complete and they would be in after a few moments to help me get up. It would not be ladylike for me to repeat the words I mutter under my breath.

Love Seasoned

An overly perky technician comes in and informs me I need to go back over to phlebotomy to have more follow-up blood work done. Oh great... my arm is still bruised from the last time.

When I'm finished, Denny holds my jacket and helps me get my sore arm into the sleeve. If I'm not imagining things, he holds me in his arms a second longer than is necessary to be polite.

As we enter the parking garage, I don't see Denny's rust bucket of a truck. I look up at him in horror as I exclaim, "I can't believe it! Someone actually stole that thing?"

Much to my shock, he chuckles. "I always told you it was a collector's item, but you would never believe me."

"No, seriously — we were parked in B14 right by the elevators. It was funny because it sounded like a bingo number. I'm sure I remember where we parked. It's not here! Somebody parked this nice sedate looking family car here. It's nice, but it's totally not your style," I urgently point out.

"*Amasa*, do you like the color?" Denny asks.

"Why does it matter if I like the color of a stranger's car?" I ask with exasperation. "Denny, someone stole your truck. You should call Tyler or something. I know it's probably not valuable or anything but you might have paperwork or something in there."

"Gwendolyn, honey!" Denny interrupts my tirade. "Just answer my question. Are you fond of the color?"

I stop for a second and take a close look at the sparkly blue gray color of the car and its clean lines and sputter an answer, "Yes, I like it very much. It reminds me of your eyes. But, I ask again, why does it matter what color a stranger's car is?"

Denny smiles mysteriously. "What if I told you this is my car?"

I am quiet for a moment as I blink slowly. "I'd ask where the candid camera is," I answer honestly. "What are you talking about?"

"Well, I've been doing a little Internet research," Denny starts as he blushes a bit.

"Isobel told me to stay away from the computer."

He shrugs. "What can I say? I'm a fixer —"

I look at him with alarm. "You know, Denny, if what they suspect is wrong with me turns out to be true, you won't be able to fix it. Perhaps no one can."

A stricken look crosses Denny's face again and I curse myself for bringing up the potential terminal nature of my presumed condition again. I don't know why I can't be all Pollyanna about this. I wish I could. However, I just can't. As I look at Denny's face, I feel like I've kicked a puppy.

With sorrow in his voice, Denny adds, "I had the dealership drop this off here today while you were having your MRI. I thought it would be a happy surprise. I know you've always disliked my truck. I figured this was more in line with what you're accustomed to traveling in. If the results come back as less than what we've hoped and prayed for, something like this will be more comfortable for you to ride in and get in and out of —" Denny's speech trails off as he moves to take a sticker off of the windshield. "Anyway, I thought you might like it."

The simple generosity of the gesture is overwhelming. I lean up against the car and cry.

Denny slowly walks up and stands in front of me. He opens his arms wide in an unspoken invitation. I don't need to be asked twice. I walk into those arms and lay my head on his chest as gut wrenching sobs wrack my body.

I feel Denny kiss the top of my head as he murmurs against my temple, "Come on, *Amasa*, let's get you home. Mr. Bojangles is waiting for us."

The young medical tech carefully wipes my arm down with antiseptic cleanser as I look at the medical tray in shock. "Denny, can I tell you how much I absolutely hate needles? This is insane. How are they going to put that in me? Sheer panic makes me nearly hyperventilate.

"Gwendolyn, you'll be all right. You are the same woman who gave birth to two amazing babies. Didn't you tell me Jeff was almost ten pounds when he was born?"

I nod as hysterical tears roll down my face. "Yeah, my little stinker wouldn't stop growing. I should probably warn Kiera what she's in for, but I don't want to scar the poor woman for life," I comment.

"Well, each pregnancy is different. She could have a little one like her. The doctors kept warning Karen she was gonna have a gargantuan size baby because I was a large baby and so was my brother. But Kiera came into the world at slightly less than five pounds. I used to tell her I had squeaks in my air brakes which weighed more than she did — hence the name 'Pipsqueak'."

"That's funny!" I snort unattractively. "I bet she didn't appreciate the nickname so much in junior high school."

"She didn't much mind. She decided being a nerd was cool, so she embraced being weird — or, who knows maybe she didn't and told me she did so I didn't feel bad. Kiera always played stuff close to the vest. She was always sensitive to what other people felt. My daughter never wanted me to know how she felt about things because she didn't ever want to upset me. She was always respectful because I was doing the whole parenting thing by myself. She always felt like she needed to be like a daughter and a half. I think it was a good thing Karen and I decided to wait awhile to have kids so I wasn't tempted to fall into the 'my kid is my best friend and I don't need to be a real parent' trap. It would have been easy to do because we hung out so much on the road."

"Oh, I know what you mean. After Kevin dropped his whole 'I'm going to be the world's most charming dad routine' and became a monster, the kids and I tried to band together to protect each other. Sometimes, it was more effective than others because Kevin tried to split us up and play us off each other," I admit, feeling ashamed to say it out loud.

"I've helped out with some domestic violence classes Kiera and Tyler have taught for the county, it's a common strategy among abusers. You can't feel bad for being a victim," Denny advises.

The technician operating the fluoroscope machine nods in agreement, but says nothing.

A tear leaks down my face. "Thank you so much for

saying that, but I think I'll feel guilty for as long as I live. I don't think I'll ever stop feeling responsible."

"Take a deep breath," the technician says as he studies a Fluoroscope machine. "Little pinch here," he warns. "But it shouldn't be much because we numbed the area up pretty well."

I grip Denny's hand so hard I'm afraid I hurt something. A moment too late, I remember Denny has severe arthritis in his fingers, but he doesn't complain. Hopefully, I didn't hurt him as horribly as I think I might have. However, the anticipation of the test is more painful than the actual thing. I feel pressure as the needle goes in, but I don't feel any severe pain. It's weird because I can watch the needle be threaded through my ribs on the fluoroscope machine and go into my lungs. I can see a little hook come out from the big needle and take a little piece of tissue out of my lungs. Then I watch the needle be pulled out of my lungs. I don't want to see the more bloody part, so I look away and watch Denny observe my face. I'm a little surprised by the complete look of adoration and admiration on his face. He, for lack of a better term, seems to be completely focused on my well being, as if he's willing me to be better and to not have the big C word.

I waver back-and-forth about whether I want to know everything about it or pretend like I've never heard of cancer. Today, for my sanity, I'm pretending I've never heard of the word cancer. Aside from this little field trip to the radiology lab, Denny and I are merely on an outing in town. I have to be fasting for this test in case something goes dramatically wrong and they have to go in and aspirate me or something. After we're done here,

Denny and I are going to go out for lunch at my favorite little bistro. I plan to have French onion soup, which is my absolute favorite when it's made from scratch. If they make it from canned au jus, it's disgusting. But if it's made correctly like Heather makes it — it's amazing.

After lunch, we're going to go visit a bookstore. I might pick up a few novels and maybe a couple new cookbooks. Isobel said I should get a pretty journal to write in. I think she's crazy. I don't know why I would want to remember any of this nightmare. She insisted I will want to remember all of this a few years down the road. I guess, if this turns out to be something really nasty like cancer, the medicine will make my brain fuzzy and I won't remember any of the treatments. But, if I write them down, later if I want to remember what it was like to go through all of this, I'll be able to remember it all in living color. It all sounds crazy. I don't know why I would want to remember losing my hair and throwing up. Yet, both Isobel and Gracie assure me sometimes, it's helpful to remember the darkest days. Even Tara, who has been through her own traumas in life, told me that later when things are better I might be grateful when I look back and remember how bad it really was.

Right now, I can't imagine having that much perspective. I feel like I am drowning in information, data and decisions. I'm trying to avoid it all because Isobel warned me not to freak myself out on the internet.

Even though I'm not actively looking for information, it feels like it's everywhere. It's on the news, on billboards, Twitter, Facebook, Pinterest. Everywhere I look, somebody has advice for me about cancer. How to live with it, how to live without it, how to avoid it, how to die with dignity from it. I feel like I have to make a decision about my life with cancer every second of every day. The ironic thing is I don't even know for sure if I have cancer yet. I'm just guessing.

I look around the sterile room without a growing thing in sight and I wonder if this will be my future from now on.

Denny strokes the inside of my wrist with his thumb. "What are you thinking about, Amasa?"

"All sorts of nothing and everything all at once, why?" I am confused by his question.

"Well, your pulse rate went through the roof, and there's no smile on your face. I have to conclude you're not thinking about us. Or, at least I hope you're not — you look absolutely terrified. All I can think is you must be pondering worst-case scenarios. Today is not a day for thinking about what might happen because we just don't have enough information, remember? Today is for information gathering. That's all — there's no need to panic."

The technician who was assisting with the biopsy sticks his head into the room.

"Oh good, you're dressed now. You are free to go. The doctor will call you with results either way. About the other thing you were talking about — I want to share my story. I was a star athlete on the basketball team in high school and had a scholarship to play in college. I thought I was pretty smart and savvy. Yet, my status didn't stop me from getting involved with a woman who liked to abuse me. It started small, but it ended with her holding a broken beer bottle to my jugular vein because I couldn't travel out of town to go to her birthday party. Domestic violence is scary and insidious no matter who you are. No one ever expects it to touch your life and until it does, no one can understand what it's like to walk in your shoes."

I have to blink tears away and swallow a couple times before I answer, "Thank you for sharing. I know you didn't have to, but I appreciate what it took for you to say something."

"No problem Ms. Whitaker, I suspect there are far more of us out there than people are willing to admit. I hope you have negative results on your needle biopsy. God speed." With that, he closes the door leaving us in complete silence.

After a few moments, Denny turns to me. "What an extraordinary young man."

"I agree. It reminds me I'm not the only person in the world with a difficult life."

"Wow, those are some strange pictures on the wall," Denny observes, looking around at the cheesy grins.

Something about the fact that his comment is almost identical to what Heather said a few months ago strikes me as hysterically funny. I start to laugh. I don't giggle politely — no, I engage in full on side-splitting laughter.

Denny reacts like I've completely lost my marbles —probably, rightfully so. "What's so funny?" he asks with alarm.

"Nothing really — other than I've already had this

conversation once with Heather and Tara. They said nearly exactly the same thing. We had a long philosophical discussion about whether the people in the pictures are patients of this clinic. After that, I found out I probably didn't have allergies and I more than likely have lung cancer. Today, I'm having the same conversation and I'm here to have the diagnosis confirmed. It's too bizarre."

Denny still looks confused. "Okay, I'll admit it's a little strange, but I don't see how they're going to put you in reruns on Comedy Central or anything."

"I didn't say it would be funny to anyone else, and it probably wouldn't be amusing if I could get any sleep. Since I got the call a couple weeks ago from the radiology department, I haven't slept well."

"Gwendolyn, I know you haven't gotten any sleep. I sleep next to you, remember? You move around more than a bucking bronco."

"Denny, you should've said something. I can go sleep in the spare room. That's not a problem. I'll move tonight. Just because I can't sleep, doesn't mean you shouldn't be able to."

Denny finds his arm around my waist and loops his finger through my belt loop on my jeans. "Gwendolyn, don't you dare go anywhere. I like you right where you are. I don't care if you have to sit up all night and watch television or read a book. I like having you in my bed."

Just then, Dr. Brewer knocks softly at the door. He smiles as he shares, "I love when I have couples your age who are still sharing a bed. It gives me hope for my own marriage."

Denny beams. "Thank you, I treasure every second

with her."

"Well sir, I'm glad. Those moments will become even more important because I'm sad to say the results of the blood work, chest x-ray, MRI and needle biopsy are all consistent with a finding of adenocarcinoma in your lungs. Now, the good news is it looks like we've caught it relatively early and it's the least lethal kind of lung cancer and the survival rates for this particular kind of lung cancer are good."

"But, I'm not a smoker. My parents weren't smokers. My ex-husband used to smoke, but he usually smoked at his social club and I was almost never invited. I don't understand. I don't have any risk factors. I don't even eat much red meat. I mean, look at me. I'm not overweight ..." my voice trails off in a sob.

Dr. Brewer silently hands me a tissue.

"I'm so sorry, Ms. Whitaker. If there's one thing I've learned over many years of being a physician, cancer can sometimes be very random. Although there are risk factors for many kinds of cancer, like smoking or working around asbestos, sometimes it just happens."

"With all due respect Dr. Brewer, you look about fourteen. How many years of medical experience could you possibly have?" Denny challenges.

"More than you might think," Dr. Brewer answers succinctly. "First, I'm older than I look — by quite a bit. Secondly, my little sister died of brain cancer when she was nine. So, I've been interested in medicine for an absurdly long time. I can tell you unequivocally from first-hand experience I've seen cancer be cured many times. I've also cried with patients and family members when the battle has been lost. It doesn't matter how you slice it: cancer sucks. I won't lie to you, sugarcoat it, or tell you anything I don't know. How is that for honesty from the medical profession?" Dr. Brewer says with a heavy sigh.

Denny salutes him. "My daughter has a spinal cord injury caused by my wife who was acting out because she had a brain tumor in her frontal lobe. You gave me the single most honest answer I've heard from a medical professional in thirty years. I can't tell you how much I appreciate it. However, I know enough about how all of this works to know you won't be able to keep Gwendolyn as a patient. Tell me if Gwendolyn was your wife or your mother, which oncologist would you send her to?"

Thank goodness Denny is with me. My brain is still ruminating over the fact that I have lung cancer and I don't engage in any risk behavior to deserve it. Yet, even as my brain is trying to sort through the information. No one — no one on the planet deserves cancer — well, maybe sick pedophiles like my ex-husband — but no sane person deserves cancer. Why should I be so special?

I watch as Dr. Brewer hands Denny a piece of paper and instructs, "Take your wife here, I'd trust her with my life. I've sent other patients her way and seen her speak at medical conferences. I only wish she had been practicing when my sister was alive."

I am so grateful when Denny places his big leather jacket around my shoulders because suddenly, I am freezing cold. I think I may never warm-up again.

Chapter Eleven

Denny

I knew it was coming. I tried to prepare myself, and I actually thought I was ready. All the signs were there. This time, there had been some warning. Gwendolyn has been coughing incessantly and no medicine seems to relieve her symptoms. She is worn down and losing weight. Each medical test she has had pointed to negative results. So, why do I still feel like somebody sucker-punched me?

I wanted to argue with that young upstart of a doctor and tell him he had no idea what he was talking about. He couldn't possibly have learned enough in the fancy-schmancy schools these days with their slick diplomas and their electronic classrooms to even get an idea what wreckage he was causing in our lives. Yet, as I looked at him man-to-man and sized him up, I knew better. When I looked into his be-speckled eyes and saw it was like looking in a mirror at my younger self, I knew he understood all too well what he was telling us. The young man is not a doctor who takes his job lightly. It was then I knew my every nightmare was happening again.

Love Seasoned

I think back to the days when I used to sit in my grandfather's church; he used to tell us God would never give us more than we can handle. Well, I would like to know why God thinks I can handle so much because right now I would like to respectfully disagree with my God. I don't think I'm up to handling this.

I no more than think that thought before a chime in my car sounds. It takes me a moment to realize it's an indication I've received a phone call. I push a button on my steering wheel to answer it. It's amazing how far cell phones have come since I first started driving my truck and we used CB radios. I'm almost afraid to answer the phone for fear it's another call from the hospital. I look over at Gwendolyn and she is sound asleep against the door support. "Hello?" I answer as quietly as I can.

"Hi Papa, it's Mindy," her melodic voice is magically piped through my speakers, thanks to the guys at the car dealership.

I breathe a sigh of relief. I'm not sure how she knew my spirits can use a lift today, but she's exactly what my bruised soul needs.

"Aunt Tara said I can only tell people things if it's a matter of life and death. Since you feel like you're dying inside, I figure this counts. So, I called to tell you God trusts you to love Grummy through this because he knows you won't let her down. She needs to have someone to believe in again. I've gotta go, Papa, Tara needs me to line up the little kids in tap class. Love you, Papa. Bye," Mindy finishes in a rush.

I click the off button on the steering wheel and lean my head back against the headrest and a tear leaks out of the corner of my eye. Well, it wouldn't be the first time I've thought my granddaughter has a special connection with God.

At least this doctor's office isn't as cheesy as the last one and it's not as sterile either. It kind of reminds me of an expensive hotel — the kind we stay at when we travel with Aidan. The cynical side of me can't help but think, of course this office space is nicer because Oncologists make a whole heck of a lot of money from patients like us. It's why insurance companies don't like to pay for treatment. I try to remind myself that my first impression was a sense of peace and home which is probably why they've tried to improve the environment.

For the first time in a long time, Gwendolyn has a smile on her face as she is walking around the perimeter of the room looking at all the beautiful greenery. Not to sound stereotypical or anything, but she is ooh-ing and ahh-ing over each one. She turns and says, "This is remarkable. Every single plant is perfectly watered, I'm not even sure I could accomplish it and I've been around plants for years. It's extraordinary!"

Just then, a tall woman wearing a white coat enters from a side entrance. She extends her hand and says, "Oh, my Aunt Josephine would be so happy to hear it, even though I grew up working in the nursery, she never quite trusted me with her babies. Hi, I'm Dr. Susan Churchfield, I'll be your pulmonary oncologist."

"So, how do we get rid of this? I don't want to die. I've got a grand baby on the way," Gwendolyn asks as she sits down in the chair beside me.

"I don't want you to die either. Let's come up with a plan to stop it from happening. In a certain percentage of cases, it doesn't matter what we do — the cancer cells seem to take over your body and they win. However, judging by your MRI and chest x-ray, and studying your biopsy results and your blood work — your adenocarcinoma is probably very early. It looks like a stage two and seems very contained and looks like it can be easily removed."

I lean forward in my seat. "Well, then let's get it out. It seems to me you guys have spent a mighty long time trying to figure out what-ever-the Hershey's-bars is wrong with her. So, why are you still dragging your feet? If you can take it out, why don't you?"

The young doctor, who looks an awful lot like Donda, gives me an indulgent smile. "Well, Mr. Whitaker, it's not so simple. I wish it were as simple as cutting around the seeds on a watermelon but there are many more risks I have to discuss with you. This is major life-changing surgery, especially at your age."

"It's bad enough I'm sick, but do you have to call me old, too?" snaps Gwendolyn.

"Unfortunately, as uncouth as it might seem — yes I have to talk about your age as a factor. The human body just doesn't heal as fast as we age. I wish everybody healed as quickly as the fifteen-year-olds I have coming in here. But unfortunately that's not how it works. You're also at higher risk of complications from pneumonia, MRSA and just the good old-fashioned flu."

"Before we talk about carving me up like a

Thanksgiving turkey, are there other options? I don't heal well from broken bones, I broke my wrist when I was an ice skater, and even though I was only seventeen, it took a while for my bone to heal. I don't know if it's because I'm so fine boned, but the doctors were amazed it took me so long to mend. So, I'm scared about breaking myself open from stem to stern," Gwendolyn declares.

She is holding my hand and I can feel her fingers trembling against mine. This is disconcerting for me because she has been so stoic about this. I have tried to talk with her a bit about the research I've done about lung cancer, but she refuses to listen. I can't say I blame her because there's a lot of misinformation out there. But after years of taking care of Kiera and the research I did about Karen's condition, I'm pretty good at sorting the junk science out from the real stuff. However, I guess Gwendolyn doesn't have any basis to know. I always forget on many levels, we don't know each other well yet. Our relationship is a strange mixture of intense intimacy and polite distance. It's devastatingly confusing to my heart. Yet, it seems inappropriate and rude to expect Gwendolyn to sort all that out when she's in the middle of fighting for her life.

The doctor pops up some large films from Gwendolyn's MRIs and chest x-rays. This isn't the first time I've come face-to-face with those little innocuous blobs. It's just been a quarter of a century since I've had to stare down cancer's ugly face. It's funny; those strange little shapes don't look so devastating. If you haven't had them pointed out to you before, you probably wouldn't even notice them against the blurry blotches and swirls on the MRI. But having studied so many of Karen's films before, my eyes are immediately drawn to the troubling areas. Suddenly, I'm finding it hard to breathe. I've been doing research for weeks now and I've been looking at pictures like this online for weeks. I've been doing a good job of staying objective and scientific about it all. However, seeing Gwen's lungs spread out on the huge computer monitors and seeing those familiar blobs and ghostly-web looking shadows makes my heart physically hurt in a way I had forgotten was possible.

Dr. Churchfield looks at me with alarm and asks, "Mr. Whitaker, you look pale, are you all right? Do you need to lie down?"

"No Ma'am, I'll be fine. It hit me a little harder than I expected," I answer, swallowing hard. I suddenly feel like I've been on a four-day bender. "I mean, I knew Gwendolyn was sick. On one level, I have accepted that she has cancer. I'm no doctor, but my first wife died of cancer so I have a good idea of what I'm looking at in front of me and I can see Gwendolyn is very, very sick. I guess I didn't expect it to be this bad."

"Well, I'm not in the business of lying to my patients by promising things will be a walk in the park. But, they may not be as bad as you are projecting, Mr. Whitaker. There are worse kinds of cancers to have and as far as lung cancer goes, your wife has the most treatable kind. Although, this looks overwhelming, you guys caught it very early and it's in a very treatable stage."

"I appreciate your candor, I really do. But you need to understand this woman is critically important to me. She puts a smile on my face every single day. I've already lost one love of my life. I'm not sure I could handle losing another. Please don't ask me to do that. Just tell us what we need to do and I'll make it happen, I promise. I learned a lot going through what I did with Karen. I'll do things better this time and maybe you can save Gwendolyn," I plead.

"Mr. Whitaker, you can't be blaming yourself for who cancer decides to take. It's a ruthless monster. It doesn't care who the person is or who loves them, it just creates mutant cells and goes from there. But it's the job of doctors like me and scientists around the world to fight back. We have more tools now than we used to. I don't know how long ago your first wife passed away, but the science has come amazingly far in treating cancer, we can fight it on a gene level now. It's quite astonishing how much progress we've made in just a few short years. From what I can tell from the lab results and the imaging, Gwendolyn has a reasonable chance of recovering fully from this," Dr. Churchfield replies calmly.

Gwendolyn pats me gently on the bicep. "Denny, this was what I was trying to explain the other day when I messed up the conversation so terribly and hurt your feelings. I don't want to be another burden to you. I know I'm bringing back all sorts of nightmares for you and dredging up all the worst times you had with Karen. It's probably threatening to drown out all the good memories you have with her. I don't want the time you spend with me to tarnish the memories you have with your wife. It's not fair of me. I can't help but wonder if maybe it would be better for you to choose to part ways with me at this point. This is not going to be a nice path and I'm not sure it's fair of me to ask you to travel it with me. After all, it's not like you signed up for this just because you're my friend."

The doctor glances at me in total surprise. "You mean you're not her husband?"

Guiltily, I shake my head because I know I allowed her assumption to stand uncorrected through several misidentifying remarks. But honestly it doesn't bother me to be called Mr. Whitaker — or anything else that attaches me to Gwendolyn.

Dr. Churchfield looks back at Gwendolyn and says, "Ms. Whitaker, this complicates things a little. I'm assuming you don't mind if we discuss your medical issues in front of Mr.—" she pauses for me to identify myself.

"Dennis Ashley," I supply.

The corner of Gwendolyn's mouth hitches up into a little half smile. "I'm not sure Mr. Ashley here cares much if we're formally married or not. As the young ones say these days we are 'friends with benefits' — although we are still deciding what those benefits are. It's a little complicated given the family dynamics. We are practically related because our children are married."

I flush a little as I sputter, "Gwendolyn, I'm not sure she needs to know all that. I think she just needs us to sign the HIPAA release."

Dr. Churchfield just laughs. "Don't worry about it, Mr. Ashley. This would probably be a good time for me to remind you everything said in this room is completely confidential. The only exception to that is if you are planning to do harm to yourself or others. In that case, I would need to pull in some outside help. Mr. Ashley guessed my intent. In order for me to continue speaking to Mr. Ashley, I need you to sign a release. Would you like Mr. Ashley to be able to make medical decisions for you in case you are unable to?"

I hold my breath. The doctor has no way of knowing she has just opened a huge can of worms. This topic has been a bone of contention between the two of us for weeks. I still don't know what Gwendolyn has decided. It's a touchy subject. She is in a no-win situation. Donda is her oldest child, but not the one she feels would be emotionally the most stable of her children and capable of dealing with the situation. Gwendolyn has concerns about adding more responsibility to Jeff's plate. Intellectually, she knows Jeff, being an attorney and Kiera as a social worker would be the most responsible family members able to take over this particular duty. But their lives are completely chaotic at the moment. Therefore, she doesn't want to burden them any more than they already are. She doesn't want to alienate Donda anymore from the family than she already is. Donda has always felt a bit like the outsider because of her past addiction and health problems. If Gwendolyn does not choose her as the medical decision-maker, Donda could feel even more ostracized. Gwendolyn doesn't want to open up any more old wounds. She's feeling paralyzed into inaction. Even now, as the time to make a decision is clearly upon her, she doesn't know what to do.

I'm trying not to be hurt one way or the other. I know even though I feel very attached to Gwendolyn, she might not return my feelings quite so intensely. She's right, although she's not formally my wife, it feels very much like she is. I don't ever foresee myself dating anyone else. I don't feel like I am some hot senior bachelor playing the field. I feel like Gwendolyn is pretty much my de facto fiancé. It's as if we're just waiting for the appropriate time for our relationship to mature into the more traditional kind.

Gwendolyn starts having a violent coughing fit. Recently, I've taken to carrying re-sealable storage bags in my jacket pocket. I silently hand her one, in case she needs to throw up. She waves me off as she struggles to catch her breath. I pass her some of her ginger honey tea. She sips it as she whispers, "Thank you, Denny. I don't know what I would do without you."

Gwendolyn turns to the doctor. "I've been agonizing over this decision for weeks now. I've decided there is no way to make the decision be between my two children without offending one of them. Since Mr. Ashley here has decided he would like to be in those shoes, I'm going to let him do this. For the life of me I can't understand why he wants to wear them."

"Amasa, I volunteered to put myself in those shoes because I love you. It's simple," I caress her cheek.

"Denny, love is for the young and hopeful. Loving me will cause you a great deal of hurt. Are you sure you're up for it?" Gwendolyn looks at me with large tears rolling down her face.

"The thing about love is you never know how strong it is until your love has been seasoned by a few tears," Denny murmurs as he tucks my hair behind my ear and kisses away the tracks of my tears. "We may not be young, but our love has been seasoned by time, experience and a few tears. We know how to weather the tough stuff and get through it together. I know better than most this won't be an easy fight, but I want to be in this fight together with you. Let's go kick cancer's asterisk, shall we?"

When I turn around and face Dr. Churchfield, I notice she is wiping away a few tears as she clears her throat and says, "Well, I'm glad we have it all settled. I will add the paperwork so it's official and in the file." She turns to Gwendolyn. "Gwendolyn, my recommendation for you is to have the lower right lobe of your lung removed completely. There is also a spot on the left side - I won't have to remove the whole lobe to get that spot because it's much smaller. In order to completely eradicate the cancer, removal is your safest choice. You could do chemotherapy and radiation, but your chances of survival are not as high as if you completely remove this tissue."

"But what about my slow healing fracture when I was a teenager?" Gwendolyn asks.

"I don't know what to say. Your blood work does not come back as anemic or lacking in calcium so there shouldn't be any reason your bones wouldn't heal," Dr. Churchfield answers. "I'll have you meet with a dietitian to boost your nutrition to help with healing. I'll give you some materials to study and I'll give you the number for the scheduling department. You can let them know whether you want to schedule chemotherapy and radiation or surgery. I have to reiterate my professional opinion; I can't recommend the surgery strongly enough."

I watch as Gwendolyn swallows hard and struggles to take a breath. I can tell all this information is overwhelming to her. I remember feeling the same way when the doctors approached me about my wife.

Karen wasn't really aware enough about her surroundings to fully grasp what was happening to her. She was drifting in and out of reality. We were young and felt so invincible in those days, we never took the time to think about any of those decisions. In retrospect, it seems pretty silly considering I was a long-haul trucker who routinely drove from one end of the country to the other. I spent many long hours on the road and anything could've happened to me. Nothing was ever going to happen to either one of us. So, why plan ahead for our eventual demise? It didn't make any sense to us. I watched Karen slip away from me blink by vacant blink until there was nothing left of the sweet, vivacious, wickedly funny young woman I fell in love with. Life ceased being breezy, lighthearted and fun the day my daughter learned basement steps were scary for reasons other than silly ghost stories and I learned ultrasounds can find more than flashing heartbeats of tiny babies.

I remember balancing a very sleepy Kiera on my shoulder as I wrote a handwritten will and — I guess they call it a living will now — instructions to the hospital about what I would want if the same thing happened to me. Poor William came to visit me that day to check up on me. He brought me a bacon lettuce and tomato sandwich from the local deli. The mere sight of it made me collapse into tears.

William persuaded Isobel to babysit Kiera and took me to the local Irish pub. At first, he couldn't figure out why a simple sandwich would cause me to turn into a blubbering pile of snot. After I started explaining the type of questions the doctors were asking me regarding Karen, he quickly understood why the sight of my favorite sandwich would push me over the edge. I shoved my paperwork into his hands and told him since he was an associate at some fancy law firm, he was now responsible for taking care of whatever needed to be done to make sure those documents would go into effect. Up until this drama came up surrounding Gwendolyn, that was pretty much the last time I thought about those papers. I just trusted William to take care of the situation. Gwendolyn is right, this thing is dredging up some haunting memories I'd rather not remember.

I'm jolted back to the present when I see Gwendolyn sway a little as she stands. Trying not to embarrass her, I step right next to her and pull her close to my body as I help her put her jacket on. I slide my arm around her waist. I try not to cringe as I can feel her hipbone under my palm. I wonder how much more weight she'll lose. I'm relieved Gwendolyn's not doing this to herself on purpose, but I'm still concerned. I reach out to shake Dr. Churchfield's hand. "It was nice to meet you. We'll be in touch. I'm going to take Gwendolyn out for some lunch. I was a little nervous to eat this morning so I'm starving now."

Dr. Churchfield smiles at me. "You do that, Mr. Ashley. I wish I had the time to go out to eat. Somehow, I managed to get behind on my paperwork. I'll be buried for the next couple months, I think. My office manager threatened to kidnap me and keep me in the office until I finish."

I place my hand in the small of Gwendolyn's back as we head out the door. We get almost all the way to the car and I hit the beeper to open the lock. Gwendolyn exclaims abruptly, "Stop! I need to go back in there."

"Right now?" I ask, puzzled.

"Yes, right now. I need to speak to Dr. Churchfield. It's really important."

"Okay, I'll see what I can do, *Amasa*," I assure her.

She places her arm around my waist as she stands beside me and places her head on my shoulder as she says so quietly I have to strain to hear her, "Thank you for doing this, Denny. By the way, I love you too. It's a different kind of love than I had before. But, it's love all the same."

For a moment, I'm stunned into total silence. Part of my spirit completely soars with joy. But the other part of me is concerned that perhaps she is just saying it out of obligation. I freely confess I'm one of "those guys". You know, those silly romantic guys who they make Hallmark commercials about? I'm the kind of guy the jewelry stores in the kiosks at the mall love. I love to do things with romantic gestures, big and small. The fact that we've professed our love to each other in a doctor's office and the dingy parking lot of a hospital is somewhat heartbreaking for me. I had much bigger plans for this moment.

I look down at Gwendolyn. "I completely understand what you're saying, Gwendolyn. The love I had for Karen was like a special first time only love I don't think will ever be replicated. It was young, stupid love. It was reckless and full speed ahead. I don't think I'm capable of falling in love the same way again. Life has taught me too many lessons about caution and pain for me to be free-spirited anymore. But those same life lessons have taught me to be so much more appreciative of what I have in my life. I am capable of so much more depth when I love now. I have much more faith in my ability to make you happy and provide the things you need in a relationship than I would've ever been able to provide all those years ago."

"Well, unfortunately you've been around for a few of my lessons. I guess what I've learned since I lost Donald is that I need to love and accept myself first before I can expect someone else to. I had a lot of confidence in myself when I was with Donald, but somehow I lost my way after he passed away. Even with Donald, it was easier to take a backseat to his giant personality. He was gregarious and outgoing while I was content to live in the shadows. This was especially true after the kids were born. I was never as successful as I had hoped to be in the business world, so I was just as happy to be the model stay-at-home mom to my adorable children. It became easy to become a pretend version of what I thought should be the perfect mom, behind his bright, shiny personality. I almost forgot who I was — a sassy, smart girl with moxie. After he died, my life became so much more difficult than I anticipated. It became far too easy to fall for the first guy who didn't seem to mind I had two children and was older. I fell for his garbage hook, line and sinker. I don't know how I could've been so stupid. Yet, somehow I was. At first, he was everything I dreamed he would be and then he was every nightmare I had ever been warned about."

As I open the clinic doors, I brush a kiss against her temple. "I'm sorry, Amasa, no one deserves that."

"I think I'm finally in a place in my life where I can fully embrace that I didn't deserve any of it. Kevin Buckhold is one sick, twisted miserable excuse for a human being who preyed on my vulnerabilities and I did not deserve what he did to me or my children. But more importantly, I can't let what he did rob me of happiness for the rest of my life — whether that will be a few months, a few years, or for many decades."

"There you go, Gwendolyn. That's one thing love seasoned teaches us. We've got hard-earned perspective," I point out resting my hand on her shoulder.

"I wish your theory didn't involve quite so many tears and it would be nice if the perspective would be a little less hard-earned. I think I might like to trade some of it for the easy breezy naïveté I once had. I'm getting a little tired of the tough stuff," Gwendolyn complains.

"*Amasa*, I would give anything on the planet to be able to take some of your pain away," I offer.

"I totally believe you would," Gwendolyn expresses as she squeezes my hand.

We have to wait a few minutes before we're ushered back to see Dr. Churchfield. This time, we are escorted back to her office instead of an exam room. Much to my surprise, it is much less lavishly decorated. In fact, it looks a lot like Kiera's dorm room during her first couple of years of graduate school before she moved off campus. There are brightly colored finger paintings hung from nearly every surface and on Dr. Churchfield's desk there is a picture of an adorable little girl with her two front teeth missing.

Dr. Churchfield looks up from her desk and says, "Sorry about the mess, but I don't like to eat in the patient rooms and I haven't had a chance to eat lunch yet."

Gwendolyn replies, "Oh, don't worry about it. We're the ones interrupting you. Is that your daughter? She's so cute."

Dr. Churchfield smiles. "Yes, that's my Anna Grace. She was a surprise in more ways than one. I didn't exactly meet the criteria for a high risk pregnancy for Down syndrome, yet here she is. She's doing amazingly well."

I can't help myself, the corners of my mouth turn up in a smile as I tease, "Well, Doc, you know what they say — you can't always trust what those doctors tell ya."

Initially, she looks at me with an expression of surprise on her face, but then she throws back her head and laughs out loud. "Ain't that the truth!"

Even Gwendolyn who hasn't been doing much laughing recently, giggles.

"I know you guys had bigger plans than sharing a peanut butter and jelly sandwich with me. So, what can I help you guys with?"

I don't know why Gwendolyn dragged us back in here, so I can't begin to answer this question. I glance over at Gwendolyn to see if I can derive any answers from her body language but I simply can't. She looks nervous but her discomfort could be attributed to anything.

Gwendolyn twists the tissue she took out of her pocket between her fingers as she abruptly blurts, "I want to have surgery. Now — today, if possible. I'm tired of weighing options and second guessing myself and trying to think things through. I'm tired of feeling like my ribs are about to shatter every time I move. I am exhausted because I can't sleep. The thoughts of the unknown haunt me. The known evil has to be better than what I imagine."

"While I appreciate your decisiveness Ms. Whitaker, I am not sure even I can get the ball rolling quite that fast. I'll do my best though. I understand Dr. Brewer gave you a pretty clear indication during his initial visit with you this is where he thought things may be headed so you've had a bit to get used to the possibility. Is that correct?"

"Yes, I always knew from the expression on his face as he was listening to my lungs, he was not happy with what he heard. But he took a very cautious approach and took great care not to alarm me before he had real test results."

"I'll call scheduling and see where we are in the process. I can certainly understand wanting to have it all resolved. For now, hold off on your plans until we have more information."

A few minutes later, I knock on Dr. Churchfield's door again while Gwendolyn is in the restroom.

"Hey Doc, do you have a couple minutes? I'll be quick, I promise. Gwendolyn will need me soon anyway," I promise in a rush.

She looks up from her desk, takes off her reading glasses and rubs the bridge of her nose. "Of course. At this point, I'll take any excuse to get away from my paperwork. I swear it multiplies at night when no one is looking. How can I help you?"

I have to clear my throat and take a drink of my water before I can muster up the courage to ask my question. There isn't a good way to approach this subject without sounding like a complete loser, but helping Gwendolyn is far more important than not sounding like a wuss in front of the oncologist, so I guess I'll give it a whirl.

"I know you don't know anything about my background but, I lost my Karen to a brain tumor. The brain tumor caused my wife to throw my daughter down the stairs — rendering her an incomplete paraplegic. Unfortunately, they weren't able to save Karen because I wasn't observant enough to notice the changes in Karen in time to get a diagnosis which would've saved her life. Regretfully, I didn't push Gwendolyn harder to come to the doctor sooner. I tried, but we didn't yet have that kind of friendship. We're getting there, but it's been slow going because of people who have burned her in the past."

Dr. Churchfield interrupts me. "Mr. Ashley, you probably couldn't have obtained a diagnosis for Gwendolyn sooner than you did. It would not have shown up on the tests very much earlier — besides, it's our responsibility not yours."

"I guess what I'm saying is I didn't do such a great job last time. What if I fail this time too? Gwendolyn's life is in balance. I love her too much to play Russian roulette with her life. Perhaps she deserves someone stronger than I am. What if I'm not up to the task?" I worry, my voice shaking with emotion. I'm embarrassed because I wanted to be much more objective in this discussion but my emotions are betraying me.

Dr. Churchfield pins me with a direct stare and doesn't look away. "Mr. Ashley, the very fact that you are here with Gwendolyn when you are under no obligation to be speaks volumes to me. I've seen couples who have been married for many years whose spouses never bother to come with them to any of the visits — not for the consultations, surgeries post-ops or the day they are released. It is the saddest, most lonely thing I've ever seen in my life. I've been known to send flowers to those patients under the names of the spouses just so these clients don't feel like they've been completely abandoned."

I shake my head in dismay at the thought of someone being completely alone through the fight of their lives. But, a sense of shame washes over me as I remember how precariously close I came to leaving Karen in exactly the same situation. Those very thoughts crossed my mind at one point. I guess I can't sit here in pious judgment of someone else because I don't know what it was like to walk in their shoes.

"I'm a big believer in love and romance and for love and romance to thrive, there has to be communication. Obviously, you and Gwendolyn communicate openly and often about her current situation and how each of you would handle it. It's a beautiful thing to see. I don't see it very often and the fact you were willing to state so openly and honestly you are willing to put yourself on the line for her is wonderful. I hope you don't lose your ability to do that throughout this process."

"That's one of my biggest fears. Sometimes,

Gwendolyn closes up and doesn't want to talk at all," I confess.

"I know this will be extremely difficult for you given that you've lost one love to cancer, but there's something extremely satisfying about standing by your partner's side as they beat back the monster called cancer. If the two of you can conquer this together, you can conquer anything. I think with the two of you standing side-by-side, there isn't much you can't do I don't have any doubts you'll be strong enough to do this."

Dr. Churchfield starts to dig through some paperwork in a file drawer next to her desk as she continues, "However, if you need some help, there are many support groups for both cancer survivors and their families as well as support groups for caregivers of people with medical needs all around town and specifically for patients of this hospital. You might want to look into those if you're interested."

She stands up and walks over to me and hands me some pamphlets. "I tell all my patients you can't forget to take care of yourself throughout this process."

"What if I'm too weak to be strong enough for her? I don't want her to be disappointed in me. She has had enough disappointments in her life."

Dr. Churchfield smiles softly at me. "Welcome to the twenty-first century, where someone is perpetually disappointed about something." She laughs slightly before she adds, "Seriously, Mr. Ashley, the fact that you are here supporting her at all during this stage is unusual. You clearly are invested in what happens to her and making sure she has the best information and access to care puts you leaps and bounds ahead of most guys who come in here. To top it all off, you're polite to everyone you interact with — that puts you in your own special class of people. I think you'll do just fine."

I chuckle as I remember the guy who was dressing down the janitor for getting a few drops of glass spray on his briefcase. She probably has a point.

"I won't kid you and say it won't be painful and bring back some terrible memories you may wish would've stayed suppressed forever. Unfortunately, there's nothing that I, or anyone else can do to stop it from happening. It's the unfortunate side of having a compassionate, loving relationship with a couple of great women. When they disappear from your life or they're hurting, it impacts you greatly. It's like a concussion to your heart and soul — it takes time to heal. If the injury is dramatic enough, you will always suffer an impact from it. I wish I had better news for you, but I don't."

"Thanks for not pulling any punches, Doc. I was hoping you had some magical advice I hadn't already thought of, but I guess there isn't an easy way through this." I get up to leave

"If your behavior in the exam room today was anything to go by, I think you performed remarkably well, and I don't have any complaints about how well you did under the circumstances. I wish I had someone as supportive as you in my life."

"Well, don't give up hope. You never know, my daughter found the love of her life when she went pedal boating with a bunch of her friends and dove off the boat. Because she had the good fortune to do that, I'm having a second chance to find love in mine. It's funny how all these things work out," I reflect.

Chapter Twelve

Gwendolyn

"Denny, are you sure we made the right decision?" I ask as I settle down into the rich down comforter, which has been placed on the hotel's huge king-size bed.

"Yes, *Amasa*, it makes perfect sense to stay here. Dr. Churchfield said you could eat until midnight. It seemed silly to drive all the way home fighting rush hour traffic only to turn around and come back fighting morning traffic just to check into the hospital. This way, we were able to register at the hospital this afternoon and get all your paperwork out of the way so you'll be able to sleep in the morning in this nice comfortable bed and not have to worry about traffic."

"What about breaking the news to the kids? I haven't even fully told them what's going on. Kiera knows I went to the doctor because she gave me the name of Dr. Fontaine, but she doesn't know all of what's happened. Heather may have told her, but I don't think Heather and Tara would break my confidence unless I gave them permission to."

"Gwendolyn, what time is it?" Denny asks as he hangs his clothes up in the little closet.

"It's 4:27, why?" I ask, but then another thought occurs to me, "Dennis Ashley, how long are we planning to stay at this hotel? Do you even know how much it costs?"

Denny grins at me. "Yes, I'm aware of how much this hotel costs. I am a member of the Gold Club. You've forgotten how much time I used to spend on the road. In my younger days, I could spend most of it in the cab of my truck. But, as age set in, spending time in the cramped quarters of my truck even with its nice cushy bed in the back became a hassle, so I spent more nights in a hotel than I'm proud to admit as a hardened, tough-guy truck driver. I became quite familiar with this hotel chain. I have tons of reward points stacked up — I'm going to use them to stay here while you're in the hospital. They are thrilled to see me. Didn't you notice the upgraded room?"

"I wondered about that," I admit. "It seems rather nice for a run-of-the-mill hotel room for killing time. So, why did you ask me what time it is?"

"Oh, Becca's at a sleepover with one of her school friends, so the kids are gonna drive up and have dinner with us. Mindy is tickled pink because we're going to go to PF Chang's. It's her first grown-up dinner date and she's about beside herself," Denny answers.

"Denny, do you think Mindy is old enough for this news? It's an awful lot to lay on a child who's not quite twelve years old."

Denny nods. "Normally, I'd be concerned, but this is Mindy. Mouse has probably known far longer than even the doctors. Being included in the discussion will probably make her feel more at ease with what's going on."

"You have a good point. That child carries entirely too much weight on her shoulders. I hope it doesn't become too much for her. It's really surprising how normal she is, considering how much knowledge she carries around in her head. It must feel awful to know as much bad news as she does," I reply as I think about how sad and reflective my granddaughter often appears.

"That's true, but remember she also knows good news — like when people are falling in love or expecting a family or getting new puppies for Christmas. In a way, I think it might all balance out. Yet, it has to be stressful to not know when she should tell people things and when to keep it a secret. I guess Tara has been working with her. I notice she's been much more circumspect about keeping other people's secrets to herself. I kind of miss the days when she used to blurt everybody's business like she was the town crier. It made for some interesting family meals."

I smile at the memories of some recent dinners. I've been so tense lately the expression feels odd on my face. A random thought occurs to me and I ask Denny, "Who do you think will take the news the hardest?"

"Strangely enough, I don't think it will be Mindy. Mindy is philosophical about it all and has a good sense there will be a positive outcome. Tyler was telling me Heather is torn up about even the possibility of you being ill because you've become a real mentor and surrogate mother to her since her mother, for all intents and purposes, has disowned her. I think Kiera might struggle with it for many of the same reasons. Between the two of your kids, it'll be a close call. At one point, you and Donda may have had a strained relationship, but you seem to be repairing those broken bonds every single day. She might take it harder than you anticipate," Denny responds as he helps me get off the bed "Do you want to wear your red dress or the teal one?"

"When did you pack dresses for me?" I ask with shock in my voice. "In fact, I didn't even know you packed *any* clothes."

"I honestly didn't know what would happen today. I've been told Tara is a magician at packing so I told her to pack a bag with a bit of everything in it to cover all of our bases."

"I guess since we're going to PF Chang's, I might as well go in style and wear the red one. I don't get to wear it very often any more. Has anybody told you lately you're a really good man, Denny Ashley?"

"Well, I don't have anybody around to tell me and I feel pretty silly giving myself life affirmations in the mirror — although I had one yoga teacher who swore by the practice. I'm trying to make life a little easier for you. The kids will meet us at the restaurant at around six fifteen. So, go do whatever mysterious thing women do. I'll clean up when you're done."

"I'm still worried about how Donda and Jeff will take all this," I say as I grab my makeup case out of the suitcase.

"Something tells me Donda has gotten used to rolling with the punches in life. She seems to be in a pretty healthy place right now — especially since Kevin has been held accountable for his crimes. So, she might consider this one more example of life kicking everybody when they're down. It seems like she's sort of begun to expect bad things to happen."

To hear him so accurately sum up my daughter's outlook on life makes me sad and I have to wipe away a tear. "Sadly, I think you might be right. I wish she expected things to be happy and perfect and then was disappointed. But unfortunately, that's not the way she looks at the world."

"It's funny, I get exactly the opposite impression of Jeff. He likes to give the impression he's logical and down to earth, but I think at heart he's a total optimist. That's even more true since he married my daughter. I almost bawled like a baby when I heard their wedding vows. When your son vowed to love my daughter until the stars fall from the sky I knew God designed their pairing because my daughter has been obsessed with stars since she was old enough to pronounce the word. She loves the beauty, science, mythology, symbolism, and the mystery of them. The family folklore Jeff shared about your family was perfect for my daughter's romantic heart."

"It is a special and unique thing for them to share, that's for sure," I muse.

Denny runs his fingers through his hair making it stand up in all directions. "I think it's this unique mixture of personality traits which makes it more likely your illness will be the toughest on Jeff. The orderly side of Jeff who likes to see things neat, clean and controlled is going to not react well to the chaos of not being able to control cancer. It'll frustrate the heck out of him that he won't be able to predict what will happen next. He can't direct it, control it, cajole it or persuade it. Cancer just is. It controls you, you don't control it. On the other hand, the emotional side of him is going to react in a personal and visceral way and it'll be difficult for him to hide what he's feeling. When you add the fact he's going to want to cover up his feelings to spare his children, it'll be a delicate tight rope for him to walk."

By the time I'm done listening to Denny wax philosophical about my children's personalities, I am openly weeping. I can't even almost cover-up my reaction to his casual words. When Denny finally looks up and notices my expression, he looks crestfallen. I try to escape to the bathroom. But he catches my arm and pulls me back against his chest as he envelops me in a huge bear hug.

"*Amasa*, I didn't say all those things to hurt you. I would never do that in a million years. I did it to prepare you for the reactions you might get," Denny murmurs against my temple as he carefully gathers my hair and tucks it behind my ears.

"How do you even know all this? You might just be guessing. Kiera is the one with the psychology degree, you don't have a degree," I accuse defensively.

Denny sighs heavily as he scrubs his hand down his face and shakes his head as if trying to dislodge a bad picture from his memory. "No, you're right. I don't have a psychology degree. In fact, I tried everything I could to run away from home. I joined the military not once, but twice. I've driven countless miles, millions over my lifetime across this nation trying to find peace, to outrun sadness; yet it always seems to follow me."

"Something besides Karen? Well, Karen and now me —" I ask quietly.

Denny nods somberly as he sinks down on the bed. "I was a little bit younger than Mindy when I was on the receiving end of one of these conversations we're about to have with your kids. I never dreamed I would somehow become the expert in conducting them. Yet, it seems to be my role now."

"What do you mean? I got the impression from Kiera she was a child when your parents passed," I ask, seeking clarification.

"It seems like such a lifetime ago, you hardly hear of it anymore but remember I told you my brother was a big baby like me? At one point, I did have a brother. But, when I was around ten years old, he died of polio. He spent weeks in the hospital in an iron lung. For a while, it looked like he would be able to fight it off, but in the end it was too much for him and he couldn't fight any longer."

My eyes tear up as I sit down beside Denny on the bed and lay my head on his shoulder. "I'm sorry Denny, I had no idea."

He tilts his head so it's laying on top of mine and replies, "It's okay, Amasa, you couldn't know what I didn't tell you. I didn't tell you so you could feel sorry for me, I told you so you would understand that I know a little about how these conversations go. Your kids aren't going to know what to think at first. There will be a thousand thoughts going through their heads. They may say a bunch or not much at all. It's totally normal."

I nod as tears roll down my face.

"There is no right or wrong way to process all of this. Just when I think I'm done figuring it all out, I discover I'm not. Even now, over fifty years later, something will strike me and I will miss Roger. The other day, a wave of sadness hit me out of the blue. It was triggered by the most benign thing you could ever think of. Mindy was playing with Becca on my front porch. They were building a Lincoln Log tower and Becca stood on her tippy toes and tried to place a log in place. She looked up at Mindy and said, 'Help, I'm too l'il, I can't reach.' For a moment, she sounded so much like Roger, I had to do a double take. It was like I was transported back to my childhood. Roger had been sick so much of his life, he was a tiny little thing and he was forever asking me to reach things for him. I remember being so annoyed by it as a kid, I wanted to play my own games. I didn't want my brother tagging along. What I wouldn't give to have my little brother tagging along in my life right now. After he died, I felt so guilty for having those thoughts. I remember thinking if only I hadn't felt that way he might still be alive — maybe I was the reason he passed away."

I splay my fingers across his chest. I feel his strongly beating heart under my palm as I tease, "So, what you're telling me is that this huge heart and abnormally strong feelings of guilt are not a new phenomenon for you?"

Denny shifts his position so he can cup my chin with his large hand. He brushes my cheek with a kiss. "Go take a shower, Ms. Sassy-Pants, before I decide to put those sassy lips to better use."

Since I feel like I'm about ready to face a firing

squad, I have to think about his suggestion a few seconds before I reluctantly get up and head to the bathroom to take a shower.

I used to love coming to this restaurant. It has delicious food. Like everything Kevin Buckhold touched, he sucked all the joy out of it for me. Although I'm trying hard not to remember the time he put me on display for his partners to drool over, the memories sneak back into my brain. I'll never forget that day for as long as I live. It was probably one of the most vicious beatings I've ever received.

It started out normally enough. In fact, I was excited about the prospect of coming to such a fancy place. It was supposed to be a corporate get-together for Christmas. All the wives were attending; it was supposed to be a family-friendly event — or so I thought. Jeff was out of town at a cross country meet and Donda had a drill team competition. So, I thought it would be a romantic weekend away for just Kevin and me. We hadn't had very many of those since we got married. I thought I would treat it like a mini-honeymoon getaway. I treated myself to a spa treatment and got a new hairstyle and had my fingernails and toenails painted. Of course, in those days we were still using tanning beds, so I appropriately roasted myself.

Kevin misinterpreted what I was planning and was sure I must've been sleeping with some unknown guy. So, instead of the beautiful clothes I planned to wear to this fancy corporate event, Kevin made me go to a thrift store and buy clothes which were several sizes too small and totally inappropriate for the dinner. He paid a makeup artist to come over to the house and do a "makeover" on me. It was cringe worthy. After we got to the restaurant, he paraded me around to all the other tables where his other partners were sitting and loudly announced that since his wife was a whore, my services would be available free of charge for the evening.

Kevin certainly accomplished whatever sick goal he had in mind. Most of the men in the room lost all respect for me, if they ever had any. Their wives hated me on sight. There were a couple who were probably in relationships much like mine who understood the power games, but for the most part, I was labeled a piranha and no one wanted anything to do with me.

This was not how I had envisioned being part of the upper crust. I thought my education and upbringing would've prepared me for life as a dentist's wife. But nothing, and I mean nothing I had ever gone through, including the death of my husband, would have ever prepared me for the humiliation of being Kevin Buckhold's spouse.

I involuntarily shiver as Denny opens the door. He misinterprets my response and says, "Oh, I know they serve sushi here but you don't have to eat it. They have all sorts of other great food."

Donda meets me in the lobby and uncharacteristically gives me a warm hug and as she pulls back from me she asks, "Mom, are you going to be okay? Isn't this 'the place' where 'the thing' went down 'that night'?"

I nod as the hostess motions for us to follow her.

Love Seasoned

She seats us in a very secluded back corner of the restaurant, which has privacy partitions around it. I look around for Jeff and Kiera. It's unusual for them to be late because one of Jeff's big claims to fame is his punctuality.

Donda sees my quizzical look. "He sent me a text and said they were stuck behind a jackknifed truck and held up. He says Kiera says to tell Denny the driver is okay — it was just low-quality retreads."

Denny smiles. "My daughter knows me all too well; I would've been worried all night about whether it was one of my colleagues."

Donda says, "Speaking of worrying — Mom, why here? Of all the restaurants in town —"

"Denny doesn't know about it, okay? He probably chose it because they have some of the best Asian food around and he knows I love Chinese food," I explain.

"I don't know about what?" Denny asks, trying to follow the conversation.

"My sick, perverted stepfather humiliated my mom in front of a restaurant full of his colleagues and their wives and tried to get her to perform blow jobs on all the men in public in *this restaurant*. When she refused, he beat her so bad she probably fractured a rib and peed blood for a week."

"You knew about that? I must have gone through a hundred dollars worth of concealer that week trying to cover up the bruises. I didn't think you knew since you and Jeff were gone when it happened. Kevin said if I told anybody that he would use you guys as punching bags next. I was so afraid that you guys would find out. I didn't dare breathe a word to anyone."

"Mom, were you aware the narcissistic sicko would tell me what he did to you? He would threaten to do the same to Jeff if I didn't do what he wanted me to do. I knew what he was doing to me was bad enough, I couldn't imagine the torture he was inflicting on you and I couldn't let him do that to my little brother. I knew he probably wasn't making empty threats because I played basketball and I was on dance team. I knew what rib injuries look like—I wasn't stupid. I just wanted it all to end. I prayed every single, effing — sorry Denny — night someone would notice what was going on and stop it. Still, no one ever did. God knows I tried. But with my history of eating disorders and drug and alcohol use, everybody thought I was crazy or making stuff up. No one ever wanted to believe me. So, I was helpless. To make matters worse, whenever I started feeling better, Kevin would doctor my food or drink to put me back in crisis mode so I no longer sounded lucid or sane. Toward the end, I felt crazy. I didn't know whether to trust myself or anyone else."

I'm trying hard not to pass out right now. Donda and I have never talked about this period of her life. For many years when she was undergoing treatment for her eating disorder, we were estranged because she felt like I was interfering with her relationship with food. She really resented me — or, at least at the time that's what I thought the issue was. As things have unfolded, I realize the eating disorder was only the tip of the iceberg. It will be nearly impossible for me to pile even more devastating news on top of the awful subjects we've been discussing tonight. I don't know how I'm going to gather the strength.

While I'm turning those ideas over in my head, I realize Donda is still speaking. "I didn't know who to believe, I tried to turn to you. Yet, you were sinking as much as I was. You were so busy trying to pretend everything was fine, I didn't know if you didn't know it wasn't fine or you didn't dare look around to see it was awful. I didn't know if he was drugging or brainwashing you too. I wanted to turn to Jeff, but I didn't know if Jeff was in as much danger as I was. He was my little brother. How could I put him in harms way?"

I sway a little as I feel her words hit me as if they are a sucker punch to my gut. I don't have any coherent excuses for my behavior. I should have been a better mother. I should have never let that man cross the threshold of my home. In retrospect, I know that now. I can't explain why I let a guy like him walk all over me. I'm a smart woman, or at least I used to be. I don't know what happened. "I'm so very sorry, Donda, I was a failure and there is no excuse," I whisper in a hoarse voice as tears roll down my face.

Denny comes to my rescue as he hands me a cotton handkerchief. He pulls me tight to his chest as he says softly, "*Amasa*, would you like to eat somewhere else? There are probably ten thousand restaurants in this town. We don't need to eat here. This evening will be difficult enough without adding to your stress."

I shake my head and finally find my voice. "No, I *won't* leave. I've already given the Jerk-Wad control of enough things in my life. He's not going to get custody of my favorite restaurant."

"Good girl!" Denny exclaims with approval. "Go

ahead and order whatever you want off the menu. Even things the Jerk-Wad thought you would never be brave enough to try."

Donda tearfully laughs. "Go for it, Mom! You should eat Oysters Rockefeller just for spite. Remember the time he was yelling at the TV when you were watching the Food Network saying women should never eat seafood because it turns them into sick nymphomaniacs?"

Despite my tears, I can't help but giggle at her suggestion.

"Oh, and by the way, Mom, you so do not have the market cornered on choosing losers. Remember Gabriel's dad? The guy I thought had it all together with a good job and a future who turned out to be a drug dealer? There are guys who put on amazing disguises. Kevin even had me fooled in the beginning, remember? He took me to all those basketball games and sent me to basketball camp. He had me convinced he knew one of the managers of the WNBA teams. I bought his stories hook, line and sinker — just like you did. He had his con game raised to an epic level."

"I can't say I'm a super religious person and go to church on a regular basis, but if I did, I'm not sure the minister would approve of what I pray every day happens to your former step-dad," Denny interjects.

"You and me both Denny, you and me both. Even if God answered our prayers, it would be too good for him," Donda asserts emphatically.

Love Seasoned

After the waitresses deliver several trays of food to our table, Jeff finally has reached the end of his patience.

"Okay, do you want to tell me why we're all here and Tyler and Heather are babysitting Bojangles? I'm aware something serious is going on. Mindy's been acting like she's sitting on a case of TNT for a few months now and I think it has more to do with Mom than it does with Kiera's pregnancy. Tara won't even look me in the eye. Can we finally let everybody off the hook and be truly honest?"

"Daddy, before you blow a gasket. You need to know Grummy will be okay. Did you pay attention to what I said a long time ago? 'Member, I said Papa and Grummy are going to get married before Madison and Trevor. It's still true, I promise."

Donda ruffles Mindy's hair. "Are you sure you're not angling for a new pair of high-heeled shoes?"

"That'd be cool, Aunt Donda, but that's not why I'm saying this. Trust me, it's important."

Jeff turns his gaze to me and stares at me until I feel compelled to answer him. My palms are sweaty and my mouth is dry. I quickly take a sip of tea. "Are you sure you don't want to eat first? The food might get cold," I try to stall.

Donda and Jeff both exclaim, "Mom!"

Mindy leaves her chair and stands beside me. She holds my hand as she softly says, "Grummy, it'll be okay. Just tell them. If you don't know the big words, I'll help you. I looked them up."

As I grip my granddaughter's hand, I say the words out loud I have been rehearsing in my head over and over for the past couple of months, "I'm afraid I don't have great news. You know the nagging cough I've had for several months? Well, the doctors have found the cause of my cough. Unfortunately, the cause is lung cancer. I have a specific type of lung cancer called adenocarcinoma in situ. They say it is the most treatable kind of cancer and I've caught it early."

"Son of a bit — !" exclaims Donda under her breath. Then she catches herself, looks around the table and apologizes with the look of chagrin on her face.

Mindy pats her hand. "It's all right, Aunt Donda, under these circumstances I don't think my mom will enforce the swear jar. As my dad says, 'These are exigent circumstances.'"

My son cracks a tense smile. "Yes, indeed they are. Somehow I knew teaching you all those legal words was going to haunt me someday."

"It's a good thing you taught me all the doctor words too, huh? Now I can talk to Grummy's doctors and understand what they say. That was good thinking, Dad."

Jeff shakes his head as he looks at me. "Mom, did you by any chance ever wish I would grow up and have a child just like me? Because if you did, your wish came true in spades. My child is too smart for her own good. Anyway as you were saying... you received a diagnosis of lung cancer. What are they planning to do about it?"

Mindy raises her hand, "I know the answer to this. Can I answer?"

Kiera lays her hand on Mindy's arm. "Mindy, I think

maybe you should give Grummy a chance to answer this one first. After all, it is her news."

As usual, Mindy's unbridled excitement makes me smile. "To be honest, Mindy probably knows more about it than I do. But, I'm going in for surgery tomorrow to have portions of my lungs removed. Dr. Churchfield says this is the most effective treatment for the type of cancer I have. After they remove the affected portions of my lungs, I'll have to get some chemotherapy to cleanup any additional cancer cells which may have been left behind. If they don't get clean margins on my removed tissue, they may have to get more aggressive and do radiation treatments. But based on where my cancer is, they fully expect they'll be able to get clean margins. So, the doctor is not anticipating I'll need to do any radiation treatments."

"Mom, have you even bothered to get more than one opinion?" Jeff asks sharply.

Mindy looks at her dad with alarm and reprimands him, "Dad, were you not paying attention to me? I told you not to blow a gasket. Don't be mean to Grummy. She actually saw three doctors and had a bunch of tests. They stuck her with a needle and Grummy hates needles. Her doctor is super-duper nice and looks like she could be Aunt Donda's sister — except she doesn't have funny colored hair."

I have to remember to close my mouth because at the moment my jaw is open wide enough my chin could be laying on the table.

Denny shakes his head in a small gesture as he addresses our granddaughter, "Mindy, I understand you're upset but, you don't get to talk to your dad that way. Remember he doesn't see the same things you see. So, he has to ask questions to get more information. All of this news comes as a surprise to most of us. Everybody processes it differently."

"I'm sorry, Daddy, I'm just frustrated. You were being awfully hard on Grummy, considering this is a very sad day for her too," Mindy responds with big tears welling up in her eyes.

Jeff comes and collects Mindy from my side as he pulls her onto his knee and kisses the top of her head and soothes, "Princess Mindy, you're right, I was being selfish with my questions. Although I don't appreciate your tone, you had a good point to make."

Denny speaks up, sounding a bit like a professor, "To answer your question, Jeff, I've done tons of research about this. As you are aware, Kiera's mom died of brain cancer because we found it far too late to intervene. Your mom is fortunate in a sense — the cancer cells seem to be clustered into two main areas. Gwendolyn has a larger area of bad cells on the right, so they are planning to do a lobectomy from that side. The area on the left is smaller so they feel they can get away with a wedge resection and segmentectomy."

I swing my head around to look at him in total shock. I was at the appointment with him and I don't remember Dr. Churchfield going into so much detail. "How do you know so much about the specifics?"

Mindy's hand shoots in the air. Denny smiles. "Yes, Princess?"

"Papa, I know exactly why it's awesome news

Grummy's bad side is the right side. I looked it up on You Tube. By the way, you should never, ever smoke. Have you seen what cigarettes do to your lungs? Anyway did you guys know even though our lungs look like they are the same size the right side has three lobes? Isn't that weird?"

"Wow! You have been looking up some interesting stuff, Min," Kiera comments.

"I had to make sure Grummy's new doctors know their stuff. But, Dr. Sue does. So, I'm not worried any more. Besides her daughter is disabled sort of like Mom, but different, because she goes to special classes."

"Mindy Jo Whitaker, were you snooping around on these poor folks?" Jeff demands.

Mindy shakes her head vehemently. "No, sir! That's creepy. I was just clicking medical information. I swear. The rest of it is just me being weird I guess. I think I'm supposed to watch out for the girl. It's not clear yet. I'm not sure it's still kind of fuzzy. I've been thinking on it, but I can't figure it out."

Mindy's distress level concerns me. She is an extraordinarily compassionate child and I worry about the price she pays for empathy. "Mindy, please try not to worry about me quite so much. I've got lots of doctors and nurses who have that job. If they happen to slack off at the job, your Papa's got them all covered. Remember what your dad said your only jobs are right now?"

Mindy smiles and nods. "Yep. I'm supposed to study hard and have fun."

"As much as I appreciate you checking out the credentials of my doctors, does that really sound like it fits in to your job description, Mindy Mouse?" I inquire gently.

"But, Grummy I had to know. I don't want you to die. I already lost one family, I don't want to lose another," Mindy replies, her voice breaking with emotion.

It takes everything in me to keep it together and not break down crying in front of my granddaughter. I know sobbing in public won't help the situation. I take a deep breath and pull on every reserve I've ever developed over the years. For once, I'm grateful for the fact that I lost Donald and had to rebuild my shattered soul piece by piece and learned to put on a polite front even when inside I felt as if I was broken into a million little slivers of broken glass. "Mindy, you were one of the first people to tell me I'll come through this with flying colors. I'm going to hold on to hope. Every doctor I've spoken to about this has told me things look very promising. Apparently, if you're going to get cancer, this is the very best kind to get. The recovery rate for this cancer is relatively good. Since I have great family members around like you, Tara and Heather, I went to the doctor and they found the cancer early. Most people don't find their cancer this quickly. It's the easiest kind to treat — not to mention I'm not a smoker — all that works in my favor. You're right, Dr. Churchfield is one of the best and after my consultation with her, I'm feeling much better about the outcome. The best way you can help me is to focus on being a kid. Just be a big sister to Becca and Charlie Dennis."

Mindy hops off of Jeff's knee and runs over and gives me a big hug as she whispers, "Okay, Grummy, it's a deal. I'll work on that stuff, if you work on getting better."

I stick my pinky finger out and say, "I'll try my very best, okay? Deal."

Chapter Thirteen

Denny

I watch as Gwendolyn dozes in the corner of the car. Tonight's dinner went about as well as could be expected. Still, I was completely blindsided by the stories about her ex-husband. Just when I think I can't find out anything more horrific about him, something else surfaces.

Both Tyler and Kiera work with victims of domestic violence and have taught special classes for victims and their families. I've helped out with their presentations several times. Intellectually, I thought I understood the concept. Yet, to see the dynamics play out in front of me from the inside of a family is a whole different experience. There aren't enough apologies on the planet to heal the pain Kevin Buckhold caused his family. Apologies don't undo the harm and they don't make the memories go away. I'm not sure anything will ever persuade Gwendolyn to forgive herself. I am at a loss about how to help.

I'm proud of the way Gwendolyn held up tonight. She stood her ground on many fronts. Obviously, she is still a warrior at heart.

After pulling into the parking spot, I gently shake her awake. "Come on, Sleeping Beauty, it's time for me to escort you to your bedchambers so you can get some sleep. You have a date with destiny tomorrow. We want you nice and refreshed."

"Aren't you my Prince Charming?" Gwendolyn observes sleepily as she cuddles up against my side.

Once again, I am struck by how naturally we've come to fit together. At first, it felt different because she wasn't Karen, but we've quickly adapted to each other, and now it feels like we've spent a lifetime together instead of just the last few months. She lays her head on my shoulder and sighs softly as she mumbles, "This feels so nice; I wish we could stay like this forever. I've missed this so much."

Her honest, open sleepy mumbles stir desires in me I thought were so long buried that they'd never resurface. I guess I shouldn't be surprised. We've been flirting around the edges of this moment for several weeks now. At first, sharing a bed with her was merely a comfort measure for both of us, but it's evolved into something more. It has become, at least for me, something I eagerly anticipate, almost crave.

There have been only a few times my cravings have felt decidedly sexual. Tonight when she was putting her earrings in, all I could think of was how stunningly beautiful she is. I still find it hard to believe in a matter of a few hours, this woman will be having surgery, which will mark the start of the battle to save her life. From the outside, aside from the weight loss, you would never guess. She looks as elegant and beautiful as the day I met her.

I set the keys down on the bedside table and turn down the bed sheets. I walk over to the large window and shut the drapes. After I grab a pair of pajamas from the dresser, I go to the restroom to get ready for bed. When I emerge, I find Gwendolyn sitting on the edge of the bed still wearing her red dress in her bare feet.

She looks up at me with tears on her lashes. "I need help with the zipper."

I've known Gwendolyn long enough to know she's not crying over a stuck zipper, but I don't know how hard to push, given the emotional roller coaster she's been on tonight. Quietly, I walk over and slowly pull her zipper down. I'm a little confused because it's not even stuck.

I've been introducing Gwendolyn to some beginning yoga poses in the morning when we get up. Apparently, at one point her creep of an ex-husband decided to kick her in the knee as punishment for some imaginary infraction and she has had trouble with it ever since. It tends to bother her on rainy mornings, so I showed her some techniques the physical therapist showed me to deal with my sore joints. She is so flexible I started teasing her and calling her 'My Little Gumby'. Therefore, I'm a little puzzled as to why she's asking me to help her with a zipper that's not broken.

Suddenly, her intent becomes clear as Gwendolyn shifts in my arms holding the front of her dress up. She looks into my eyes and pleads, "For tonight, help me remember what it's like to be a real woman. Every time you look at me, I feel like the most beautiful woman in the world. Soon, even more scars will mark up this old body of mine. I want to erase the reality from my mind for tonight. I want to see myself through your eyes. I want to forget the way the monster saw me. I want to stop being damaged goods. I never was the whore he thought I was. Unfortunately, his hands are the last man's hands ever placed on me. I don't want that to be my legacy. If, God forbid, something were to happen to me tomorrow, I want to be able to say I died in the arms of the man I love who cherishes me beyond measure."

I take a moment to absorb all of what Gwendolyn said. Even when I do, I have to unravel it and put it back together a couple of different ways to completely understand the meaning of her words. After I do, I have to process it before I respond. I have to tamp down my visceral reaction to her words and try to understand the meaning behind what she said. I decide to be truthful and share my gut-level response. I'm not sure she'll completely understand, but I think I'll give it a shot. "Honestly, as much as I would love to have the chance to make a love to you and completely erase all of your bad memories of that poor excuse for DNA, I'm not sure how I feel about being used as a tool to exorcise the ghost of your ex-husband. If I did, I'm afraid it would cheapen what we have together. I think the two of us together are worth more. Our love story deserves better," I explain with a shrug.

"Denny, I didn't mean to suggest anything less. It just turns out to be really rotten timing that's all. I didn't expect all this garbage with Kevin to come up. I've wanted to take this step in our relationship for a little while now, but I didn't know how to approach it. I'm not used to being the one making the moves. So, I didn't do a good job of explaining how I feel. I have to be honest and say tonight's dinner has my emotions all messed up. That doesn't change the fact this really is where I wanted to be all along. I just didn't realize I would be in a tailspin when I got here."

"Well, I have to admit hearing the things I heard tonight put me into a bit of an unexpected emotional spiral too. Where were your friends and your family through all of this? Didn't they know what was going on? Why didn't they step up to help all of you?" I try to focus the thoughts which are bouncing around my head like ping pong balls.

"I had gotten so good at hiding, I don't even know at this point who knew and who didn't. I lived a pretend life for so long I am no longer willing to be anybody other than who I really am. The person I am right now is Gwendolyn Whitaker, girlfriend of Dennis Allen Ashley. I'd like to take a moment to be happy about it before I have to be scared — as scared as I've ever been in my whole life. Can we do that?"

Her honest request — stripped-down, bare and raw — is both awe inspiring and frightening as all get out. I hope I can live up to her hopes and dreams.

"I can try, but I may be a little out of practice," I confess as my face grows hot with embarrassment.

For the first time in a while, I see a genuine smile on Gwendolyn's face. "Well, you know what they say about practice?"

I raise my eyebrow quizzically.

She smirks as she answers, "You have to keep trying

until you get it right."

"Something tells me I'm gonna like this a lot more than the cello lessons I had as a kid," I joke with a wink.

After what seems like hours and hours, I'm finally in the family waiting room wearing a goofy little band with, ironically enough, yellow smiley faces identifying me as an approved family member. Kiera is sitting next to me wearing an identical band.

Kiera hands me a stack of new magazines about antique automobile collecting. "Dad, you might as well sit down. The doctor said it would be several hours. I still don't understand how you got in here so fast. Are you sure you're telling me everything? When my friend had breast cancer, the surgeon was booked out four weeks."

"Yes, we've told you everything. We wouldn't lie to you. This happened to be a fluke because one of Dr. Churchfield's patients who was already scheduled, developed a fever and couldn't go through with surgery. Gwendolyn was fortunate enough to be able to take their spot on the schedule. Gwendolyn was tired of not knowing the outcome of things and wanted to get it over with. The treatment course was pretty much determined by the results of her x-rays, so there wasn't much debate about what needs to be done. Gwendolyn wanted to get it out of the way so she could stop coughing and get well. The cough has debilitated her and made it hard for her to work at the flower shop. She decided that knowing was better than not knowing even if what she found out was bad news."

"Dad, I know I was really little when mom died, but I remember you being sad a lot of my childhood. I know you tried to hide it from me. Even so, there were times I found you out in your wood shop alone and crying. What if the outcome with Gwendolyn is not what you hope? Are you prepared?"

"I have to believe it'll be okay."

"I know everybody puts a lot of stock in what Mindy says. I'm not sure we should be so complacent in this situation. This isn't like choosing clothes for the baby. It could simply be that Mindy wants it to be true so much it's what she's chosen to predict. I just don't know. Even though I've been friends with Tara for so long, I'm not sure how their gift works. Don't get me wrong. I do very much want them to be correct. However, I want to prepare you in case something more serious comes up. Our family hasn't had the best of luck medically, if you know what I mean."

"Pip, trust me. Every single one of those thoughts has been tumbling around in my head like old ball bearings. I've turned this problem over and over in my brain like those silly Rubik's Cube toys you used to play with when you were a kid. I've done so much research my brain hurts. All we can do right now is pray and hope for the best. I took Gwendolyn to three different doctors and they all seem to say the same thing. I even talked into a holistic doctor who doesn't believe in surgery or chemotherapy. He confirmed the diagnosis, but didn't want to do any traditional treatment. Gwendolyn and I decided it wasn't the route for her. Even that doctor agreed on the severity and the location of her cancer. I'm pretty confident her cancer isn't any worse than the tests show. Still, I'll be relieved when she's out of surgery and they do fancy testing on the tissue samples."

Kiera pats my shoulder. "Me too, Daddy."

"Did I tell you they're taking the wedge out of her left lung using a robotic arm with a camera on it? I guess it's supposed to be less invasive and more precise. It's a newfangled way to do surgery. I saw a video about it online. It looks high-tech and futuristic. I guess they've had good success and there'll be a lot less trauma to her lung and much less bleeding. Hopefully, she'll heal faster."

"I'm impressed Dad, I guess you really have done your research."

I take a drink of lukewarm root beer and reply, "Pip, more than you can possibly imagine and more than I can explain in a lifetime. I should probably change my major at the community college from criminal justice to nursing based on all the research I've been doing."

"Dad, are you taking care of yourself?" Kiera asks, and tosses me a pear. "These are from Madison and Trevor's tree in their front yard. You look exhausted. I'm worried about you."

On one level, I totally understand I am a single adult who's been a widower for several decades, this is America and I have the right to have a girlfriend. On the other hand, this is my daughter I'm talking to. My body responds accordingly and I blush bright red like a stop sign. Since Kiera has the same propensity, this reaction does not escape her notice.

I have a feeling my good-natured teasing when I left Kiera and Jeff a lovely little greeting card with a string of prophylactics inside may come back to haunt me at any time. The peal of giggles from my daughter confirms my fears. She elbows me in the knee as she teases, "Hey, Dad, if you need Jeff to take you to the drugstore or anything, he'd probably be happy to do so. We've been married long enough now he's kind of an expert at it."

I smirk as I reach out and pat her belly. "My dear Pip, all evidence to the contrary. I should tell your Boy Scout he wasn't quite prepared enough."

Kiera snorts with laughter as she exclaims, "Good Lord, Dad! Do you want my husband never, ever to speak to you again? We've been married close to five years now and my husband still calls you 'sir'. If you said something like that to him, he may never leave the house. I was the one who messed up on the birth control anyway. If the Honorary Boy Scout had been in charge, the girls wouldn't be getting a little brother. It never occurred to me to watch out for medication interactions. But, I guess I'm not the only one. I've got Madison to keep me company."

"Speaking of your husband, what does he really think about Gwendolyn and I dating?" I ask, curious about whether my daughter has any insight into her husband's real attitude about the situation. Outwardly, Jeff has been supportive. However, in light of the conversation last night at dinner, I wonder if there may be more going on behind the scenes. I wonder how much he was privy to about the situation that went on with Kevin.

Kiera shrugs. "I know he doesn't have strong feelings one way or the other, Dad. He was young when Donald died. Once he figured out it wasn't his fault, he was able to process his dad's death pretty well. He doesn't have a lot of memories of Donald. Obviously, Donda has many more memories since she's quite a bit older than Jeff. Most of Jeff's good memories of Donald have been supplanted by horrific memories of Kevin. He's still working through the rage. I think as long as you treat his mom with love and respect, he'll be okay with your relationship. If I were you, I wouldn't brag about your sex life with his mom with him. I think those kind of conversations would make him highly uncomfortable. Beyond the intimate details of your relationship, I think Jeff supports it as a general rule."

"That's kinda the feeling I got from him, too. In fact it's almost verbatim what he told me. He told me if I planned to treat his mom poorly I might as well take a walk right now. I told him his mom was important to me and I had no such plans. So, I guess the best thing I can do for everyone, Gwendolyn included, is to just continue to follow through with my plans. From what I can tell right now, this is the real deal for me. I know it sounds like a weird plot from a soap opera — I get a second chance at love with my son-in-law's mother, but I guess you find love where you find it. I've definitely found love with Gwendolyn."

Kiera grins. "Way to go, Dad! Your high standards paid off. Gwendolyn is one classy lady."

"The weird thing about it is I think your mom would've approved of Gwendolyn for me. In some strange way, their personalities are quite a bit alike. Gwendolyn is a lot more outgoing than Karen in some ways but in other ways, not so much. I guess you could say Gwendolyn has done a better job of learning how to put on a public mask to hide her inner reserve and shyness. They're both pretty stoic about hiding their true self and passions from the world. But, they both have this infectious love of life and generous spirit they don't put on display a lot. So it's a curious puzzle that intrigues me."

"I know what you mean about Gwendolyn. She has a very different public and private side. When I first met her, I was really intimidated by her public persona but I quickly learned it's only a defense mechanism. Who she is under all of those protective barriers of the social grace is an amazingly warm, caring human being. I'm glad you fell in love with her, Daddy, I think you two make a great pair."

I'll be darned if I didn't blush again when my daughter gave me that compliment. I'm glad she thinks we are good together — because I totally agree. It seems as if we, like a lost key and lock, found each other in some great antique store somewhere by happenstance. It's amazing if you think about it. Neither one of us ever thought we would find love again. We both thought we'd had our one and only chance at love.

"I don't care what anyone else thinks. I think it's wonderful, Dad," Kiera asserts firmly.

I clear the tears from my voice. "Thank you, I'm glad you think so. It breaks my heart when I think of all she had to go through to learn to put on her public mask. Amasa had to come through a lot of hard times to learn to put on her battle gear and learn to smile gracefully through it. I wouldn't wish that hell she's been through on my worst enemy."

"Oh Daddy, I understand. Still, maybe in some

weird way all she's been through has toughened her spirit for the fight she's got ahead of her. You've been through hell and back too. The two of you know what it's like to come through on the other side victorious. Together, you two will make a formidable team against cancer, because you know what it's like to fight for something with everything you've got. I know you might not think so because of the way things turned out with Mom, but Gwendolyn is so lucky you love her. I know this because you fought beside me and you helped me come back from what could've been a fatal injury. I think you forget because I recovered so well, but in those early days, Grandma told me it was touch and go for a long time."

Just then the nurse calls me back into a consultation room. Kiera comes with me for moral support and much to our relief, Dr. Churchfield comes out and says, "Mr. Ashley, Ms. Whitaker tolerated the surgery amazingly well. She was on the heart bypass machine longer than we would've liked, but we encountered more scar tissue than we had anticipated. Apparently, Ms. Whitaker had a series of rib and collarbone fractures which were not treated properly over the years. But with a little time and patience, we were able to work around those limitations and get everything in place. She'll be sore for a while and she'll have a raw throat because of all the machines. But hopefully her recovery won't take too long."

I practically run down the hall to Gwendolyn's room. The nurse has to jog to catch up with me, but I'm so intent on seeing Gwendolyn I barely process her words of caution. I have been so focused on Gwen's long-term survival, I forgot to take into account the toll that all of this would take on her poor body in the short term. I have to catch myself on the doorjamb and sink into a nearby wheelchair when I see my beloved Amasa wrapped in a tangle of tubes, wires and cords. The cacophony of beeping machines is deafening. The sense of déjà vu is heartbreaking. Once again, as tears are streaming down my face, I ask God why he thinks I can shoulder so much pain. My only answer is the rhythmic, hypnotic whoosh of Gwendolyn's breathing machine.

Chapter Fourteen

Gwendolyn

"Gwendolyn? Is that you?" A stranger with sad eyes asks me. Something about him is vaguely familiar, but I'm too tired to figure it out. I try to pretend I don't hear him. I'm really not up to speaking with anyone today. I was throwing up nearly all last night. It's amazing that I didn't rip out every single stitch in my whole wretched body. Pardon the pun, but I feel like death warmed over.

Unfortunately, Denny, the ever-friendly one, who has never met a stranger in his life, doesn't understand I'm trying to imitate a hermit crab today and taps me on the shoulder. "Honey, your friend is trying to say hello."

I know it's wrong and kind of a selfish thing to do, but I can't seem to stop myself. I look up at the man without shielding the raw pain in my face. Considering I was just released from the hospital four days ago and I'm here for an obligatory incision check, I'm in an insane amount of pain. That's a lot of garbage to unleash on an unsuspecting stranger. Yet, somehow it feels cathartic in a way.

Don't get me wrong — Denny has been amazing in ways I could not have even predicted. On some level, I always knew he would be because I've watched him with Kiera and the grandkids and he has always been nothing short of phenomenal but it's a different experience to be on the other end of all that love and attention. I almost feel like I need to shelter Denny from some of the bad. I know intellectually it makes little sense. He has been through some of the worst of the worst in life and I know he can handle it— but part of me thinks he shouldn't have to. I often tell him I am feeling better than I do because I don't want him to worry about me. It's a bit of relief to show the full extent of my pain to someone, even if it's someone who I don't know. Holding up a brave face is more exhausting than I expected.

I immediately regret my actions as the stranger's eyes widen and he frowns in dismay. "I'm so sorry to bother you — obviously, I'm intruding," he stammers as he backs away.

"Oh nonsense," Denny dismisses his statement. "These doctors' offices are so boring. The magazines are decades old. It's nice to have somebody to talk to. Obviously, you know Gwendolyn, so you should sit down and talk," Denny offers as he picks up our bags from the seat next to us.

"Are you sure Gwendolyn doesn't mind? She looks like she might prefer to be alone," the stranger observes, eyeing me carefully.

I guess I don't blame him. My reaction was rather psychotic there for a moment. I must've looked like a scary creature from a strange horror movie for a few seconds. I bury my pain — again — and gingerly shrug as I tilt my head toward the vacant seat. "Help yourself," I croak. I still find it hard to maintain the right amount of breath control — not to mention my ribs are killing me with every single millimeter of movement.

Denny smiles up at the guy. "Isn't she doing great? She's a trooper. The respiratory therapist said she might not be able to talk for several weeks. But I can hear her just fine. She's doing amazin'."

What does that even mean? "Like a trooper?" Right now, the only trooper I feel like is a paratrooper who's fallen out of the plane without a parachute. I don't know I've ever felt so beat up in my entire life and that includes the days I was actually getting beaten up. My vision is getting fuzzy at the edges again and the world is starting to spin so, I take a drink of Denny's sports drink and try to steady myself.

"What happened? Did she get in a car accident?" the gentleman asks, looking at me with concern.

"No, my Gwendolyn is beating the pants off of lung cancer. They took big old chunks out of her lungs. But, the folks down at the lab said it all looks good — her margins came back clean. They tell me it's the best possible result. She has to do a little chemotherapy to make sure she cleans up any stray cancer cells, but other than that things look great."

The gentleman swings his gaze back at me." "Gwendolyn, I'm glad you are doing better. It will be so much better for Donda's recovery to not lose a parent."

Now, I'm confused. I'm not even sure who the heck this is and I'm pretty sure he doesn't have the right to comment on my life. Sure, it's great for Donda that I'm not dead but right now, I sort of wish I was. Wait, that's not true. I feel like I've survived death. The time I spend on the breathing machine at the hospital has made my throat sore, my ribs hurt so bad I can't move, even going to the restroom hurts. What do you do when the basic act of breathing makes you feel like you've been turned inside out? This is all just crazy.

The guy takes in the sudden rage on my face and remarks with a sense of embarrassment, "Oh, I'm sorry you must not remember me. I'm Bill. We used to attend the … umm…" he shoots Denny a sideways look, scrubs his hand down his face and continues on, "… parent support group at Whispering Willow before my daughter lost her battle."

I want to disappear into my seat as the puzzle pieces fell into place. Instantly I feel guilty for the thoughts I just had. This is a man who has lived the nightmare I was so casually contemplating. But then another thought occurs to me. "How is Tina?" I force myself to ask.

A truly bleak expression crosses Bill's face as he answers, "The combination of multiple sclerosis and the grief from the loss of Trina finally caught up with her so she's gone, too. It's just me now."

"Bill, I'm so sorry. I don't even know what to say." I struggle not to breathe deeply or cough because those things are so painful.

Bill leans over and pats me on the shoulder as he shares, "I can't say I'll ever understand how my child could've ever starved herself to death. Her mama's passing was a long time coming and needed to happen. I have to trust the good Lord knows what he's doing and there's some plan at work I just can't see. If I didn't believe that, I would go crazy." He grabs a tissue off of the little table and noisily blows his nose. He turns to Denny and advises, "You should take care of this one, she's special. She has a good heart." He turns back to me. "It is clear your husband loves you, so fight hard for him. It hurts to be the one left behind. Anyway, it was great to see you. I hope the next time I see you, we'll both be in a much better place in our lives."

"I hope so too, Bill; I hope so too," I croak with tears in my eyes as a perky nurse calls us back.

Mindy is arranging cookies on the beautiful tea tray Denny bought me to go with the origami teapot and teacups. Apparently, it's Kiera's turn to babysit me today. I know I shouldn't look at it that way, but in the month since my surgery, I feel like I haven't had a moment to myself.

Mindy stops to look at all the pictures on the coffee table. "Grummy, do you love everybody in your family the same?"

"What do you mean, Princess?" I ask, puzzled by the question.

"Well, you have two kids, do you love them just the same?"

"I don't think it works that way, Mindy. Every child is different. You love different things about each child. I guess you love each child a little differently."

"So, do you love one kid less?" Mindy prods.

"No, I don't think so. Different doesn't necessarily mean less, it means you recognize each child has unique talents and gifts," I clarify.

Mindy picks up the cookie and nibbles on it. "What about Papa? Do you love him differently than you loved Daddy's other dad — you know the one who died?"

I let out a small puff of air, a deep sigh is out of the question these days, my ribs are still far too sore to take in a deep breath, but I'm working on it. "Mindy, you know your friends Sarah and Abi, from dance class?"

Mindy nods.

"You consider them both to be your best friends, right? If I asked you to choose a favorite, could you?"

Mindy's eyebrows draw together as she thinks, "No, I guess you're right. That would be hard. Sarah's funny and tells great jokes. But Abi is a good listener and we have great fun drawing pictures together. I really wouldn't be able to choose because I like them both."

"That's the way it is with my family. I love everyone, but I love everyone for different reasons. It's not like I line everyone up and give everyone a 'love grade' like a teacher. Why are you asking, Mindy?"

"Well, somebody at school told me Mom and Dad will love Charlie Dennis more than Becca and me because he'll be their real kid and we're not really theirs."

"Mindy Jo Whitaker, first of all, whoever that child is needs to mind their own business. Secondly, they are entirely wrong. Every child is a miracle regardless of how they come into your family. Your brother is going to develop his own collection of stories just like you have yours and your mom and dad have theirs. Some of the stories will be shared stories like the Pippi Longstocking books. I read those books to your dad, you read them to Becca and now both you and Becca can read them to little Charlie."

"But Mom doesn't have any stories of me when I was a baby," Mindy laments.

I motion for Mindy to stand closer to the couch as I run my fingers through her long curly blonde locks. "That's true, she doesn't. On the other hand, your brother will never have the story of rescuing his baby sister and saving her from a potential kidnapper. At the time, you were too little to understand this, but you saved me that day too. Watching your bravery gave me the courage to follow through with my plans to divorce my ex-husband who was hurting me. In my book, your help is way better than a few baby pictures."

Mindy looks doubtful. "I still wish I looked a little more like Mom and Dad."

"Sweetie, you may not look like your parents, but you've got your mom's attitude and your dad's smarts. You fit into this family like it was tailor-made for you. I don't think you have a thing to worry about," I assure her as I gingerly hug her.

The nurse is putting a bandage over the PICC line. Strangely enough, after only my third chemotherapy treatment, it's all become very routine. I am stuffing my crocheting into my tote bag when my phone rings. It's not Denny's ring tone so I am a little baffled by who would be calling me here.

I answer the phone but before I can even say hello, I am met by a barrage of words. As nearly as I can tell, it's Madison and she sounds completely stressed out.

"Oh my Gosh, Gwendolyn, you tried to tell me I would want my mom here, but I didn't believe you. Now I don't know what to do! It's too late. Heather's not even here. Do you know what my sister is doing? She is cutting wedding cake for a movie star who's so famous that she can't even tell me who it's for — right now, at this moment — it's some friend of Aidan's. It shouldn't be a big deal, right? Nobody thought it would be a big deal. Except Little Princess Lydia here has decided to come into the world two weeks early. Guess where my husband is?"

It's so bad of me, but to hear the normally calm and composed investigative reporter so frazzled strikes me as funny. I have to stifle a laugh. I'm tempted to put the phone call on speakerphone to amuse the rest of my friends. Over the last few weeks, I've met several nice people here who are also in the fight of their life. Many of them could use a laugh. Unfortunately, I've also discovered Madison has a tendency to salt a few of her conversations with cuss words just like me. So, the conversations may not stay PG and I'm not sure what my neighbors would think of her embellishments. "Madison, take a deep breath. Now, where did you say Trevor is?" I ask, struggling to be the grown-up I am — besides, laughing still hurts my ribs.

"My husband is over in Idaho!" she exclaims. "Do you hear me? *Idaho!* He can go over there and help horses and cows give birth, but is not here for the birth of his own daughter? What is this world coming to?"

Okay, I can't help it now. I do snicker out loud as I remind her, "Madison, I have met your fiancé. He is one of the most conscientious, duty-bound men I have ever known in my life. I'm one hundred percent certain Trevor did not do this on purpose. One of the interesting things about childbirth is you can never plan what happens."

"I know that!" Madison snaps. "I'm just frustrated with the timing of it all. Tara and Aidan are with Heather and Tyler is on call. Kiera has the flu and they won't let her come near the maternity ward for obvious reasons."

"Madison, honey — you still haven't told me what you need," I prompt.

"Gwendolyn! My water broke. It looks like I peed my pants. I'm standing in the middle of the optometrist's office. Can you believe that? What in the heck am I going to do?"

My expression sobers as the seriousness of the situation sinks in.

"Lucky for you, Denny has been studying up for Kiera's delivery and he has extensive military training. So, you're in good hands. I've got a few hours before the nausea from the chemo hits. I don't like taking the Zofran to combat the nausea because it makes me sleepy, but in this case I'll make an exception."

"How in the world do I track down Denny?" Madison asks anxiously.

"Well, according to the text message he sent me — he is down in the parking garage at the hospital."

"Wait? You guys are at the hospital?" she asks with surprise.

"Yes, I'm having my afternoon lunch date paired with chemotherapy, remember?" I tease. "I guess the universe decided my social schedule wasn't packed enough before."

"Oh geez, Gwendolyn, I completely forgot about that. I should totally leave you alone. You probably don't feel like helping me," she frets.

"Hush, child! It's been a while, but I remember that they've got couches, chairs and dishpans to puke in on the delivery ward too. So, I can watch bad TV and toss my cookies while I keep you company just as well as I can on my own couch. In fact, it will distract me from my own problems for a while. It'll be a win-win for both of us."

"Are you sure, Gwendolyn?" Madison asks skeptically. "I have a feeling I might not be a very nice person when I'm in labor."

"Honey, if my husband wasn't a saint, he would've had grounds for divorce based on the things I said during labor. Don't worry about it, not only have I heard them all — I've *said* them all."

"But what about Denny?" Madison's worries are reflected in her voice. "You are aware the man still uses pretend cuss words?"

"Yes, I am aware. Isn't it charming? However, it doesn't mean he isn't well versed in a wide variety of other words in the English language. After all, the man was a truck driver."

Just then, I hear a long low pitched whine from Madison followed by a terse suggestion, "I think you guys need to get to Dr. Hu's office soon."

"Madison, why in the world do you have a filing cabinet worth of work files in your to-go bag?" I demand as I look through her bag for a pen to write a list of things she still needs to get before she goes home.

She grimaces and pants before explaining, "I don't know. Viewers kept writing in and telling me they were in labor for a hundred and twelve hours. I figured I might have time to work on some stuff."

Denny massages her shoulders. "Madison, women's labor stories are kind of like men's fishing stories, they tend to get a tad exaggerated. If someone had been in labor for a hundred and twelve hours, it would've put the baby at risk. The doctors would've intervened. They were probably having Braxton Hicks."

"So you're saying I won't be facing Armageddon, after all?" Madison asks as she grips the rubber stress ball Denny gave her.

"Honey, I can't lie to you and tell you it won't hurt. The simple truth is it does. But, the funny thing is — once you see your daughter's face, all your pain will fade into the background. It'll all be worth it, I promise. The doctor said you were already at five centimeters so that's good," I explain.

Madison gives a yelp of pain as she mutters, "Well, I'll tell you something, at this point our little romp in the woods — even as fun as it was — wasn't worth all this.

How long have we been here? Like three days, right?"

Denny shrugs. "Oh, I'd guess about six hours based on the number of times Gwendolyn has thrown up." He chuckles as he adds, "I don't know what happens to you wonderful ladies in these rooms, but when Karen had Kiera, she called me the spawn of Satan and told me she was never going to let me touch any part of her body ever again. She kept her word for about six months, too."

"Dennis Ashley, you might want to tread carefully or you may find yourself banned from this room. Speaking as a man who's never been pregnant, or had your ankles be the size of watermelons, you don't know what it's like," I caution.

"Okay, shutting up now. I can take a hint," Denny quips as he hands Madison a cup of ice chips.

Madison gasps and cringes. When she can catch her breath again, she praises Denny, "I see you have one of the smart ones, Gwendolyn."

"I don't know… if he keeps making fun of my vomiting prowess I might not aim so carefully next time," I threaten as I stick my tongue out at Denny.

"I'm so glad to see such a strong bond between the two of you. It gives me hope for Trevor and me," Madison comments.

"Madison, do you have your car seat and diapers all lined up?" I ask.

"Yes, we have a ton of diapers and Tyler took a child safety seat class through his work at the Sheriff's office. He's all up to date on the latest technology in child restraint systems so he wanted to be the one to choose the car seats for Kiera and me. Trust me, we have the Cadillac of all child seats. He had the instructor of the class install the seats for us. Becca even got a brand-new booster seat."

"That sounds just like Tyler. On the surface, he seems all casual like he belongs in some video promoting cowboy hats and blue jeans but under all his good old boy casualness, lies a ruthless strategist," Denny points out.

"I think I'm all set. The only thing I might need is premie clothes because I wasn't expecting her to be early," Madison replies with a sigh as she rubs her neck.

I hear a knock at the door as Trevor enters and says, "Obviously, neither was I. If I had known, I would never left town. Sweetheart, why didn't you say something?"

"Trevor! How in the world did you get here? It's like a fourteen hour trip," she mumbles into Trevor's shirt.

He pulls back from her and wipes the tears from her face with the pads of his thumbs. "Mad… think about it. Who did you call?"

"Oh… Aidan strikes again," Madison concludes as she shakes her head in wonderment.

Just then, Tara peeks her head around the corner, "You know Aidan well enough to know he wouldn't let Trevor miss this. I had to talk him out of flying your parents and Trevor's parents in for the occasion. I figured it might be a little overwhelming since no one had planned a family reunion. Madison, you need to take a big cleansing breath. Trevor, if you haven't already done so, you need to wash your hands." Tara looks up at me. "Gwendolyn, you're looking a little tired, this is going to take a bit. Why don't you take a break? We'll keep you up-to-date about what's going on. We can take over from here."

Not surprisingly, it turns out Tara is right and a huge contraction overtakes Madison. Trevor blanches a little as he sees how much pain Madison is in.

After the pain passes, Madison squeezes my hand and says, "Gwendolyn, thank you for stepping in as my mom and coach. I really appreciate it. I don't know what I would've done if you hadn't been there to keep it all together for me."

"Madison, you didn't lose it. You just had a moment of panic. There's a big difference. You'll be an excellent mom. The only thing you need to remember is that it's all worth it in the end and the guy whose hand you're holding loves you more than you can possibly imagine. Other than that, nothing much else in life matters."

Chapter Fifteen

Denny

"Papa and Grummy! will you guys hurry up? Aunt Madison told the nurses I could help with the diaper changing because I haven't been home since Mom got the flu. I was staying at Abi's house and nobody is sick over there. Tara convinced the nurses I knew all about babies because I used to take care of Becca. So, I get to be one of the first people to change Lydia's diaper. I'm so excited," Mindy babbles in a rush without taking a breath.

"That's neat, Mindy Mouse, but you need to calm down or you could hurt Lydia. She's going to be even smaller than Becca was."

"I know. I just have a good old-fashioned case of the wiggles because I'm so excited. Did my dad tell you I'm thinking about being a neonatologist because I like babies so much?"

I smile. "Well, it makes perfect sense because you are incredibly smart. I bet you would make a great doctor."

As we reach the nurses, they wave at Mindy.

Apparently, she is a frequent visitor here. She shows them the electronic bracelet we've been issued as visitors so they can scan it. They offer to allow us in the nursery as well so we present our wrists to be scanned. It's amazing how high tech the nurseries have become since Kiera was born.

It takes no time at all to locate Lydia in the nursery. She is the spitting image of Madison. The only hint of Trevor is her hair has a little tinge of copper in it and it's on the curly side. I know every mother says their child is the cutest ever. However, Madison might have some valid arguments. Lydia looks like a porcelain doll. For the moment, her eyes are clear blue, but I don't know if they'll stay that way. It's hard to tell with Trevor having blue eyes and Madison's being a rich, beautiful brown.

True to her word, Mindy is fearlessly changing Lydia's diaper like a pro. Belatedly, it occurs to me I probably should've been filming the whole encounter. It would've been cute to show Jeffrey and Kiera. The whole time Mindy is changing the diaper, she's providing a running commentary to Lydia about who all the family members are and how we are all interrelated. She is telling elaborate stories about how we all met. She sounds like she's hosting an odd version of *So This is Your Life*. Lydia seems completely mesmerized by the encounter. She is watching Mindy with wide, alert eyes and trying hard to maneuver her fist into her mouth.

When Mindy is finished, one of the nurses comments, "I'm impressed. You certainly have the magic touch. That's the calmest she's been all night. When you are old enough to get a work permit, please come back and volunteer as a candy striper so you can work in the nursery. We could use someone like you."

Gwendolyn and I tiptoe as quietly as we can with Mindy into Madison's room. Madison is sound asleep and Trevor is absently stroking her hair until a nurse brings in the baby from the nursery. He immediately stands up and walks over to the isolette. A look of awe softens his face as he asks the nurse in a quiet whisper, "May I?"

The nurse smiles. "Of course."

Trevor grins as he strips off his sweatshirt and watch and lays them down on a nearby table. He picks up one of the brightly colored receiving blankets Madison received from Mindy and puts it over his shoulder. Gently he scoops up Lydia from the Plexiglas bassinet and cuddles her against his chest as he walks over to the rocking chair. I watched this with fascination because, as far as I know, Trevor doesn't have any siblings or other experience with babies, but he looks like he's done this his whole life.

Apparently, the nurse thinks so too because she praises, "You're a natural at this. I didn't even have to tell you to support her head."

"Well, I actually don't have a lot of experience. I'm just the honorary uncle to a bunch of families. I'm usually present at births. I tend to be the person people dump their babies with when they get tired of holding them. I like being a baby cuddler. There isn't anything better on the planet. Well, I like holding puppies too, but I think babies are great. It's going to be wonderful to have one of my own. I can't get over how beautiful she is. I guess I shouldn't be surprised since her mom is perfect in my eyes. But, to see a miniature version of Madison is a little astonishing. I always thought babies pretty much looked alike until I saw Lydia. I can see Madison's beautiful eyes and the shape of her lips in Lydia's face. It's pretty miraculous."

"I don't know, son. I see a lot of you in your little girl too. When Mindy was changing her diaper, she gave a hint of a smile, and I swore I saw your dimples and cheeks. I don't think she's all Madison by any stretch of imagination. The two of you created a beautiful child," I remark.

It's funny; there were never any doubts about whether Kiera was mine. She is essentially the female version of me. With our flaming red hair and freckles, it is hard to ignore the resemblance. Her resemblance to Karen was more in mannerisms and personality. I'm sure she absolutely hated the freckles and the red hair at some point, but genetics can be tricky. It looks like little Lydia got the best of both worlds. Everyone is absolutely correct: she is a stunning little baby. She could have a future in television commercials if she ever wanted one. However, I'm sure her parents will keep her well grounded. It wouldn't surprise me if she turns out to be a little ninja prodigy between Madison's influence and Trevor's. I could see Madison enrolling her in all of Tara's martial arts training class.

Trevor gently rocks Lydia and curls her hair around his pinky. When she starts to suck on her fist, he looks up at me in awe. "I don't know how you did this by yourself. I can't even imagine."

I chuckle softly as I answer, "Well, Pip wasn't quite that little when Karen passed away. Although, it seemed like she was. She was already walking and jabbering a mile a minute when she was hurt. So, we had already established a bit of a relationship — she knew I was her Daddy. I was fortunate. Even though I was on the road, Kiera and I were always buddies. Whenever I was in town, she always followed me around. If I was working on a project around the house, she wanted to be right there handing me the tools or helping me clean up. I remember she had this goofy little mop and bucket set. She used to have a little measuring cup Karen gave her. She would pull her step-stool around to the bathroom and put water in it. She would follow me to wherever I was and dump it on the floor so she could mop it up — just so she could 'help' me. When she got her first wheelchair, she was so mad she couldn't reach the sink anymore. I had to add a spigot to the laundry room so she could still mop."

"You make it seem so easy. I guess I didn't expect her to seem so fragile. I don't know what I was expecting exactly. It sounds kind of stupid for me to say it out loud. Madison is not exactly gargantuan or anything, and I've been afraid all along Madison's extreme nausea would create problems. Lydia's just so little."

Gwendolyn walks over and pats him on the shoulder. "Trevor, what did the pediatrician say? I don't think they would allow her out of the nursery if there was a real problem. It doesn't seem like they have her breathing any special air or anything. She's not even under those special lights. When Donda was born, they had her under all these medical lights and she had to stay in the nursery all the time. They barely even let me hold her. I was so sad because she was my firstborn and everything, I felt like a real failure as a mom."

"They told us her lungs were fine. So far, knock on wood, her liver functions are fine and she doesn't need to be under the bilirubin lights."

"The fact that she's not in the NICU or anything even though she was born a tad early, means she's not struggling too much." Gwendolyn shrugs.

"I agree," I chime in as I look at Lydia more closely. "If I remember correctly, your little munchkin is a bit bigger than mine was at that age."

"How much did she weigh, Trevor?" Gwendolyn asks as she covers the two of them with a blanket.

"Well, it turns out that my daughter has some interesting timing. Just as the nurse was getting ready to put her on the scale, Lydia peed down her arm. The nurse said if she hadn't peed, she would have been six pounds, five ounces."

Gwendolyn laughs out loud. "It must be something about this group. When Jeff was a baby, he peed in the pediatrician's eye. The pediatrician criticized me like it was something I taught him to do. I stared right back and asked him, 'Does this look like a David Letterman skit? I can't make my baby pee on command.' Needless to say, I quickly found another pediatrician."

I jump when I hear Madison's voice behind me, "Well, if he was a jerk, I'm glad Jeff had good aim. I'm almost jealous because girls can't do that."

"Oh, cute little princess babies are not without their own weapons — baby poop has a wonderful way of seeping through the legs of the cutest outfits. It can take the most pious of know-it-alls off guard," Gwendolyn remembers with a mischievous grin.

Lydia makes her presence known with an insistent cry. Madison's eyes widen as she realizes, "Umm, I guess I'm being paged."

I walk over to Madison and kiss her on the cheek as I praise, "You did a great job. Grandma Lydia would've been proud of you. We're going to give you guys a chance to bond as a family and we'll see you later."

I'm in the middle of buttering Gwendolyn's bread because one of the side effects of her chemotherapy causes her fingers to hurt. She has a hard time holding the knife especially when her hands are cold. I look up at her and ask, "*Amasa*, do you want jam on this?"

She grimaces at me. "Eww, are you trying to make me throw up again? I'm dipping those in my chicken soup. That would be disgusting."

"Oh, I'm sorry. I forgot my daughter has turned you into a soup fanatic. I don't know what it is about this place. She started with Heather, then she got Tara, I think she's probably moved on to Madison. She's even got the guys eating soup and sandwiches."

"Don't forget, they make excellent bagels and cookies too."

"I agree, I think we should take a few back to the hotel tonight. What did you think of Madison's little one?"

"Well, of course she's stunningly gorgeous. Still, I'm sad I wasn't there for the birth. I can't believe you let me sleep through it."

"I didn't have much choice. From what Trevor said, once things started happening, they happened in a hurry. She went from eight centimeters to 'hurry up and get the doctor in here quick' in no time flat. He didn't even have time to call me until it was all over."

"To be honest, today's visit scared me to death," Gwendolyn reveals with a sigh.

"Why in the world would it scare you?" I ask, befuddled by her response. "I thought Mindy was amazing with her and Madison and Trevor seem like they were born to be parents. You would never guess they were taken by surprise by the pregnancy."

"No, that's not it at all. It's not about them. My reaction is about me and what I stand to lose. All those memories of when my kids were babies came rushing back. On one hand, it seems like it was just yesterday I was in the hospital with Donda under all those lights. But, then I remember that I'm over seventy-one years old and I have a terminal illness."

"Gwendolyn, as far as I'm concerned you *had* a terminal illness. You stopped being terminally ill the day they cut those pieces out of your lungs. The chemotherapy is a safeguard to make sure there aren't any stray cells around. You heard the doctor, she didn't expect there to be any. It was done out of an abundance of caution, remember? Those were the exact words she used. They're being super cautious. All your margins came back clean. There's no need to think you still have cancer. All the cancer you had in your body was thrown away in those red trash bags. We have to believe — *you* have to believe. It's important for your recovery to view yourself as a cancer free patient."

"I wish I was as optimistic as you are. I really don't know. I mean, look how sick I was, and I chose to ignore my body. I didn't get help in time. If I was so wrong about that, how can I even trust my own judgment?"

"Gwendolyn, it was like you were saying. You're not the typical cancer patient because you don't have the risk factors for lung cancer, you don't smoke, you weren't raised around smokers and you didn't work around asbestos. There wasn't any reason for you to look for cancer. It made more sense for it to be allergies, especially since you work around all those flowers. You can't beat yourself up over not thinking about cancer. That's just silly. We have to believe in the positive now because all the tests they've done seem to indicate it's not likely to be cancer anymore, because when you had the PET scan there were no other signs of cancer in your body. So, that's where I'm placing my bets."

"Denny, I hope you're right. But I can't help but be nervous for tomorrow's appointment. What if she says I've suddenly gotten worse? Is the transplant list next? I'm too old for a transplant! I would die waiting."

"Remember what Dr. Brewer said about getting ahead of test results. You can't do that to yourself, Gwen."

I catch the eye of the young girl standing behind the counter and nod. She grins and brings over an elaborately wrapped to go box and sets it in front of Gwendolyn.

"What in the world? Dennis Allen Ashley, what have you done now?" she demands with a laugh.

"I don't know… it seems like a silly convention, but where I'm from, when we get presents, we say, 'Thanks' and tear right into them — but that's just me," I tease in an effort not to let my nerves show. The last time I gave her a gift, it didn't go so well.

She blushes. "You are too good to me, you know that, right? Don't think I don't notice all those gift credits on my Amazon account either. I should have never given you my email address. You are like a sneaky fairy Godmother of Books or something."

"Says the person who snuck VIP tickets to the Model-T Auto Show in Portland under my pillow — that sucker has been sold out for a while. I don't know how you pulled it off."

Just then, a young customer from a nearby table says, "Open your present already! I've got class soon and I want to see what he got you."

Gwendolyn laughs. "Oh, then by all means, let me proceed. I didn't realize you have a fan club Denny — although I guess I shouldn't be surprised. You seem to collect friends everywhere we go."

She sets down her tea and slowly unwraps the box, one ribbon at a time — taking time to admire each one. Normally, I would think her behavior is cute. Right now, I'm annoyed. I just want her to open the box. Finally, she opens the lid with excruciating slowness.

The crowd breaks out in a quiet murmur of disappointment when they see the contents. "I wasn't expecting so much build up over a cookie to be honest," Gwendolyn remarks with a smirk.

"Amasa, look at what type of cookie it is," I suggest.

"Oh, you're right it's a giant fortune cookie. I love fortune cookies. Isn't it cute how they dipped the edges in chocolate?"

"Gwendolyn, I love you to pieces, but you are driving me nuts here —" I admit.

"Us too," the kids from the table next to us chime in.

"My goodness, can't a lady savor the joy of getting a present?"

"Only if you hurry. I have class, remember?" quips the young man.

Gwendolyn chuckles. "Oh all right, I did promise after all. I would feel bad if you were distracted in class." She picks up her soup spoon and cracks the cookie wide open. A collective gasp goes up from the crowd when a little wad of polka-dotted tissue paper falls out of the cookie and escapes on to the plate.

"Dennis Allen Ashley, tell me this isn't what I think it is!" she whispers in a shocked voice. "How could you? You don't even know if I'll get a clean bill of health tomorrow. She could be essentially signing you up for a death watch again."

"Amasa, that was kind of my point of asking you today. I want you to know I love you regardless of what happens. Do understand? It doesn't matter what the outcome is tomorrow. Whether God grants me thirty minutes, thirty days or thirty years with you, I will be by your side, Gwendolyn, will you be next to mine? Will you marry me?"

I swear, every single, solitary noise in the restaurant

stops as everyone seems to hold their collective breath for her answer.

A single tear trickles down the side of Gwendolyn's face. "I'm beginning to understand why Jeff was a goner the moment he first saw your daughter, you Ashleys are irresistible."

Not wanting to leave anything to chance, I clarify, "So, is that a yes?"

"Denny, you always said I needed to live on the wild side. I'd say accepting a marriage proposal when I'm not even sure if I'll live long enough to see the ceremony definitely qualifies as living on the edge. If you're brave enough to take the gamble, so am I. Dennis Allen Ashley, I would be honored to be your wife."

Chapter Sixteen

Gwendolyn

"Girlie, you are blinding me with your new rock," Trudie Lee Temple exclaims with a wink. "I may just miss with this needle. I don't know how you can even lift your hand to crochet with that on."

"Oh hush, Trudie, you're jealous because your boyfriend got your ring out of the claw-machine," Eleanor teases.

"Ms. Eleanor, you were supposed to be too sleepy to remember my goofy story," Trudie scolds.

"Oh, just because this old body of mine has decided it's seen better days, doesn't mean my mind doesn't work fine. I wasn't a math professor for nothing."

"Did being a math professor teach you to play possum in the middle of a room?" the oncology nurse asks with a grin.

Eleanor snickers. "Oh, you'd be surprised. How do you think I caught those wily college students cheating on my exams?"

Trudie gives her a mock salute. "Well, here's to hidden talents then."

"Speaking of hidden talents, did you have any idea your beau was planning to surprise you?" Eleanor asks me.

"My first instinct is to tell you no, I had no idea Denny was going to do anything, but I guess it's not really true. Lord knows the man has been dropping boulder-size hints for a while. It's been confusing to say the least. For a long time, I thought he was being friendly. I guess he's wanted to be more than friends for quite a while. It happened so gradually I didn't even notice when we changed the boundaries. I guess, it's probably better it happened that way, given my past issues. If he had come in and made some sort of grand announcement in the beginning, I would've probably run in the other direction so fast, the only thing he would've ever seen of me would have been trails of dust behind me."

"Pardon me for saying this, but you don't seem to be the type of girl who would take well to being claimed like you're some sort of bag of treats in the vending machine to be fought over," Eleanor observes.

"You're right. Maybe, he even knew that about me. For whatever reason, he elected to take the safe approach or maybe I'll never know what spurred him to take the first year of our relationship so glacially slow. Yet, I'm so glad he did. We got to know each other as friends first. I was able to learn to trust him, conversation by conversation and inch by inch. Before I knew it, I had a man as one of my best friends. Just a few years ago, I could have never imagined that in my wildest dreams, but it is so true. Dennis Ashley has become my very best friend."

Eleanor takes a deep breath and sighs as she professes, "I'm really happy for you, but I'm sad for me. I probably won't live long enough to find myself a second love like you found with your Denny. Of all people, I think I'm well-qualified enough to know my odds of surviving the cancer this time are infinitesimal. So, I've done what I can. I've taken time to say goodbye to my adult children. It was the hardest thing I have ever done in my life. I've run out of time to fall in love again. If God or the universe has given you the chance to fall again, don't question it. Embrace it."

"Eleanor, you've become such a great friend, I wish things were different for you," I cry, practically choking on my tears.

"Gwen, the time for tears for me is long past, they won't change anything. Do me a favor, go have your second chance. I'm not going to get one, but I want you to celebrate yours like there's no tomorrow."

"Eleanor, if you're so sure this won't work, why are you putting yourself through all of this?" I ask as a metallic taste travels through the back of my throat.

"Oh, the answer is really simple, I promised my kids I wouldn't give up until I could no longer tolerate it. This, although uncomfortable, is still tolerable. So, I keep fighting even though I know I probably won't win. The mathematician in me can see there may be an outside chance that I'll win — although it's increasingly unlikely I will," Eleanor admits.

"How do you find the courage to get out of bed

every day?" I ask before I can help myself. I regret the question as soon as it leaves my lips. I can't seem to stop my intrusiveness, but I don't know who else to ask. When I go to my cancer support group, I'm considered one of the courageous, victorious ones so it's hard to hide my real fears there. Immediately, I apologize, "I'm sorry, that was rude. I shouldn't have asked. It's none of my business."

Eleanor laughs out loud until she coughs. "Look, if we can't talk about this stuff with each other, who would we talk about it with? I mean, it's not exactly like we can talk about it with our kids, right? If we talk about it with the doctors, they mark it down in our files like we're one conversation away from the loony bin. Lord knows it's not appropriate conversational fare for getting your haircut."

I start to laugh too. "I thought I was the only one who felt that way. Even though I have all these people hanging around me almost constantly, I don't think I have ever felt so alone in my life. I feel like I have to protect everyone from knowing how I really feel because they want me to be okay. Some days, I don't feel okay — some days, I feel like crap."

"Well, to answer your question, some days, I don't get out of bed. But things have been better lately. I went and adopted a dog from the Humane Society. Now I get out of bed whether I want to or not because Smokey wants to go for a walk. Having him depend on me to be up and around has made a bit of a difference. I can't get lost in my own self-pity when he sticks his cold, wet nose in my ribs every morning."

"Oh, that's sweet — you have your own version of Denny," I joke.

"Well, I guess in a way I do. I have to feel better because he counts on me. You have to feel better because you don't want to disappoint your fiancé," she remarks. "I suppose it's pretty much the same."

That word takes me off guard. When I think of the word 'fiancé', I think of the person I was before I married Donald, not the person I am now at seventy-one. Who would've thought I would go back to being a fiancé? I can't get over how strange life is. But her comment brings back all my insecurities, which started this conversation.

"Eleanor, isn't it my responsibility to stop Denny from making a huge mistake? What if this is all a mistake, and the doctor gives me terrible news this afternoon?"

"Okay, suppose she does? What happens then? Don't you want Denny by your side?" Eleanor counters as she studies my reaction.

"Well, course I do. But that's not fair to ask of him," I insist as I throw my hands up in the air causing my pulse oximeter to beep.

Eleanor looks at me steadily as she asks quietly, "Gwendolyn Whitaker, who in the hell ever told you cancer was fair?"

I look at my friend with her colorful headscarf, sunken face and frail body as I tearfully whisper, "Nobody."

"Then, stop expecting there to be good choices. There aren't any great choices for you to make throughout this process. You make the most informed choice you can make under the circumstances and hope for the best. There aren't any optimal choices — I'm just telling you. Stop trying to make it make sense, because cancer never, ever makes sense. My only advice to you is to go live like there's no tomorrow — because there might not be."

"Still —" I start to argue.

"Gwendolyn, did Denny give you the ring knowing you have cancer?"

"Yes, of course—"

"Does he know what Dr. Churchfield is going to say this afternoon?"

"No, as far as I know, he hasn't spoken with Dr. Churchfield since our last appointment, why?"

"Think about this logically. Your fiancé doesn't know whether you are going to live or die, yet he still asked you to marry him. Obviously, he loves you either way. So, I don't know what you're so worried about. It seems Denny is in this for the long haul. He'll fight right along with you, however long it takes. I don't think you have to worry about him abandoning you if the times get tough and I think you don't have to worry about sheltering Denny from whatever you're feeling. He's a tough guy who's used to hearing bad news."

"It seems unfair. I shouldn't pile more worries on Denny's plate. He's had a lifetime of things to worry about. I hate to be just one more thing."

"There's that word again. I've learned 'fair' doesn't have a place in relationships. Relationships are give and take. One person is strong and the other person is weak;

one person is healthy and the other person is sick. Relationships are a matter of timing and luck. Sometimes it works out, other times, it doesn't. It's almost like a giant game of Jenga — everything can look great on paper, but until you start building it three dimensionally in your life, you never know what forces from the outside can sweep in and destroy your best laid plans."

"So, what you're saying is I'm supposed to go forward in my relationship with Denny as if nothing is wrong in our lives? Are we supposed to pretend like everything is hunky-dory and normal? I don't know if I can. This cancer diagnosis has shaken me to the core. It's fundamentally changed who I am I don't know if I can go back to being the person I once was."

Eleanor smiles weakly at me as she reminisces, "Did you ever think you'd see the day we wouldn't ever be finished growing up? I remember thinking as a kid 'I'll be so glad when I'm a grown up'. I never thought I would still be changing and growing when I was our age. I think I would have been totally horrified at the thought if I would've known back then I wouldn't have it all figured out by the time I was sixty-two years old. I think my inner eight-year-old would've thought sixty-two was unbearably old. Now, I think of all the years I wish I still had left to live. I want to sit my inner eight-year-old down and give her a lecture about how not to take those years I took for granted thinking I would be invincible and live forever. I'm learning I'm not so invincible. I may not have the chance to live the long, fulfilling, charmed life I thought I would live. I'm rather disappointed in my younger self now. If I had only known time would be so precious, there are many years during my twenties I would've lived completely differently. I would've not squandered so many of those days being so self-absorbed and unkind to people."

"Oh, I know what you mean. If I had known I would be facing mortality so quickly, I would've skipped my entire second marriage. Well, there are a boat load of other reasons I should've skipped my second marriage, but I cringe when I think how many unhappy years I spent with that jerk. I could've been spending them with a wonderful man like Denny."

"So, celebrate your wonderful engagement and try to put the cancer out of your mind," she advises. "The doctors have given you no hint it'll be bad news, so you need to assume it's good news. You just got engaged, that's wonderful news in any language, in any setting, at any age. Do the world a favor and go have yourself a good time."

"Denny, you have me completely baffled about where we are going. The girls assure me I'm dressed completely appropriately, but rarely do I pair Levi jeans with my diamond earrings and a pair of boots to go out to eat."

"The girls are right on the mark. You look perfect. I love the new short haircut. It looks very sassy."

"You really think so? The medicine I'm taking makes my face swell up so much, I hardly recognize myself. Anyway, I noticed some extra hair in the bottom of the shower the other day. So I figured I might as well get ahead of the curve if I'm going to lose all my hair to chemotherapy. Apparently, this new drug is kind of hit or miss about whether it will cause me to lose all of my hair or just part of it. I guess I'd better be prepared."

"Gwen, do you understand it doesn't matter? I would love you if you were bald as a billiard ball. In fact, if you went bald, it would give me an excuse to shave my head, too. Then I would get rid of all these strange curls that keep popping up all over my head," Denny offers.

"You probably would because you're such a goofball. You didn't answer my question about where we're going today."

"Now, *Amasa*, have I ever steered you wrong on a date?" he asks.

"Well, there was that one unfortunate food poisoning incident," I counter.

"Okay, I grant you that, but it wasn't my fault. The restaurant had good reviews. It should have been spectacular," Denny replies.

"Okay, you're right. As a general rule your dates are amazing — even the ones I didn't know were dates," I concede.

"I think you'll find this one to be just as spectacular," Denny brags as he pulls into the parking lot.

I look around dubiously. Quite frankly, the building looks like a tin storage shed that's seen better days. There are neon beer signs plastered around the outside of the building providing an eerie cast of light. I can hear a rhythmic beat coming from the inside of the restaurant.

I shake my head as I mumble, "Do I even want to know what I've gotten myself into?"

Denny grins at me. "Only the adventure of a

lifetime. You promised, remember?" He holds up my hand with the engagement ring on it and kisses my knuckles. "By the way, thank you. I thank the good Lord every day you said yes. I can't imagine my life being any more perfect."

I can think of a lot of things I wish were different right now, but I don't want to ruin Denny's evening, so I keep my thoughts to myself. He helps me navigate a bumpy spot in the parking lot. As he opens the door, I notice Jeff and Kiera waiting right inside the doorway. More precisely, they are making out. It must be a kid-free date night. Rather than act embarrassed at having caught them, Denny shrugs and says, "You know, your son has the right idea." He takes his cowboy hat and hangs it on a nearby coat rack. He tunnels his fingers through my newly shorn locks. It's all I can do not purr when I feel his strong fingers against my scalp. He thoroughly kisses me, not caring there are other patrons in the restaurant.

Just then, a host in cowboy boots and a cowboy hat with a red, checkered shirt says, "Whitaker, party of eleven?"

My eyes shoot wide open as I pull away from Denny and mouth, "Eleven?"

Before he can answer me, Kiera rolls past her dad and gives him a high five as she inexplicably says, "Way to go! Just remember, my Boy Scout can take you to the drugstore anytime, Dad."

"Pip, you do remember I know where you hid all of your diaries when you were young, right? Don't make me divulge that knowledge," Denny threatens with a wink.

"Ooh, pulling out the big guns. I admire your

tenacity. But, you forget your granddaughter has become the town crier. So, if I ever had any secrets, she's probably already spilled them to her dad. You forgot I led the most boring childhood ever. However, I do give you points for trying," Kiera replies laughing.

Jeff and I look at each other and shrug, clearly we are both lost. The host is leading us back to what appears to be another building not visible from the outside. It seems to be a banquet room with a dance floor. When my eyes get acclimated to the light, I notice Aidan is in the corner with some other musicians. Yet, he doesn't seem to have his usual band-mates with him. One of them looks familiar. I think she's one of the fellow contestants from the TV show.

I glance around the room and notice Tara and Heather are gathered around a cake.

As I'm still trying to untangle it all in my brain, Isobel comes up behind me and gives me a gentle hug. "Gwendolyn, it is so wonderful to see you. You look much better."

"Thank you, Isobel, I am feeling better. In large part it's because of your advice. The dietitian I worked with was very impressed with the changes you had made to my diet. She said I was the easiest client she ever worked with because I was already doing most of the things she was planning to recommend for me. Although, she did have the doctor prescribe me some milkshakes to help me gain weight. Let me tell you, those things are nasty! I much prefer the recipe for smoothies you gave me."

"The coconut-peanut butter ones are phenomenal, aren't they? I got rather addicted to those," Isobel concedes.

"Those sound luscious, maybe you should tell me about them?" I whirl around when I hear Eleanor's voice.

"Eleanor, what are you doing here?" I ask, unable to disguise my surprise.

"Oh dear, maybe I wasn't supposed to say anything, but your fiancé invited me to a party. I decided I should probably come since nobody thinks I'm any fun anymore since I got diagnosed with the big C."

Isobel nods vigorously. "Oh my gosh! Isn't that the truth? I remember how it felt. It was like my life stopped outside of going to doctor visits. I was so frustrated because it wasn't like my whole identity was being a patient who threw up all the time. After my reconstructive surgery and chemotherapy were over, I pretty much went back to normal after a few months, but everybody treated me like I was still a sick woman. For a long time, I was confused about who I was. Inside, I felt one way. But everyone acted like I was completely different. It made me second-guess whether I was feeling as good as I was. It was very strange."

"Exactly! And if you talk to other cancer survivors, and you tell them you're doing well, and if they are not, then you feel guilty. On the other hand, if you're feeling crappy and they're doing well, you feel guilty about bringing them down. It's almost as if there is really no safe place to share how you're really feeling. It's a bizarre place to be. If you share on social media, there are people who want to know more details, and then there are people who want to know no details at all because they consider it vulgar and unseemly for you to tell what it's actually like. But, if you don't tell what it's like then you'll have other people saying you're sugarcoating the situation. There's really no winning in this situation."

"Gwendolyn, Denny told us you have a degree from Brown University. Did you take any writing classes or journalism classes?"

"No, not really. I wasn't a creative arts major, I had my sights set on taking over the business world. I was planning to conquer Wall Street back in the day. That was back when I was single. I still believed I could be the super modern girl back — super wife, mom and corporate CEO. For me, the dream didn't work out. Maybe for other women it did, but my timing was never right and I could never juggle all the balls in the air at the same time. So, I became a stay home mom to my kids until I was widowed. I was unbearably lonely, so I married the biggest narcissistic jerk there ever was and was essentially held captive in my home for several years before I was finally set free from him. Then I started the flower business, and finally I got cancer."

"Don't forget, somewhere in there, my husband's best friend fell head over heels in love with you."

I smile widely at Isobel. "Oh yes, that's the best part of the story. Why do you ask?"

"Well, it seems to me if we're willing to talk about stuff that other people aren't. Maybe we should write a book," Isobel suggests.

Eleanor laughs. "How about I survive one challenge at a time first?"

From across the room, I see a tall African-American woman, but it doesn't look like Donda. She's missing

Donda's characteristic streak of color. I wonder who it is because I thought Donda had a job interview at an upscale design company this week.

When she turns around, I'm startled to find it's Dr. Churchfield.

Now, I'm puzzled. What in the world is she doing here? I thought Denny and I were going out to dinner. What is Denny up to? He always confuses me.

As if my brain isn't spinning fast enough, Gabriel, my other grandson, and Mindy come traipsing across the dance floor with Dr. Churchfield's daughter skipping between them. I recognize Mindy's work as a 'makeup artist' on this little girl. I hope Dr. Churchfield is not upset. Sometimes, Mindy's makeup can tend to be on the theatrical side. I run over to Dr. Churchfield in case I need to offer my apologies, but when I get there, I'm pleasantly surprised by her reaction, "Anna Grace, you look so beautiful! Who did your make up?" she gushes.

Dr. Churchfield interprets her daughter's signs and repeats, "A Princess did your makeup?"

Her forehead creases in confusion as she looks at me in question, but before I can answer her, Mindy clarifies, "Anna heard my Aunt Donda call me 'Princess Mindy' so she thinks Princess is my name. I'm okay with that because Princess Mindy is my nickname, which is kind of like my name so it's no big deal. I'll let her call me Princess Mindy, it's fine."

"Do you always talk this fast, Mindy?" Dr. Churchfield asks with a grin.

Mindy thinks about it for a second before answering, "Nope. Sometimes I talk even faster. My mouth has a hard time keeping up with my brain."

Dr. Churchfield nods as she signs, "Fair enough. I've been there a few times myself." She turns to Gabriel and says, "What does Anna Grace call you?"

"I can't really tell. Her name sign for me seems to have something to do with my curly hair, but I don't know what it is. I've never seen it before," Gabriel replies with a shrug.

"Oh, you guys know about name signs?" the doctor asks curiously.

"Our uncle is deaf so we know all sorts of signs," Gabriel explains.

"Well, what is your usual name sign so I can teach Anna Grace?"

Gabriel demonstrates his usual name sign of an artist's palette and the G that Aidan and all the kids at the climbing school Aidan runs use with him. "I like to draw a little," he explains.

I catch Dr. Churchfield's eye as I correct, "'Draw a little' is a vast understatement of his skill."

I hear glasses clink together as Denny announces, "Great! Now that everybody is here, we can begin."

I look around and notice while I've been talking to my grandkids, the whole room has pretty much filled up with my friends and family. It is absolutely astonishing. I don't know how Denny pulled this off, but then again, I never know how he does any of the stuff he accomplishes without me being aware of what's going on. Clearly this is a surprise party of some sort. I know it's not my birthday, so I don't know what he's up to.

Mindy is tugging on my jeans as she orders, "Look at what Gabriel designed for you!" She points to a banner that's been unfurled over the cake Tara and Heather were obscuring earlier. I have to laugh when I see what it says. It says, "Congratulations on Kicking Cancer in the Asterisk!"

The cake is almost an exact replica of the origami tea set Denny gave me, complete with the tiny cherry blossoms. It is simply breathtaking.

Denny jogs over and takes the microphone from Aidan's stand and starts to make a speech. "We, or at least I, wanted to make a really big deal out of this a while ago. In fact, most of you who know me well know I've been in love with this gal for quite some time. My first plan was to take it slow and easy until she was ready to notice me. But, as we all know, the minute we mere mortals make plans, God laughs."

A soft smattering of laughter travels through the audience.

"So life and a few cancer cells got in the way of my 'take it slow and easy' plan. A little while ago, I asked this wonderful woman to marry me and much to my shock and amazement, she said yes. But the treatment of cancer got in the way of us celebrating it properly. Tonight, Gwendolyn is on a little break from chemotherapy before she has to go back for one more month. So tonight, we are going to celebrate the fact that everything looks A-Okay and I'm engaged to the prettiest girl in the Pacific Northwest."

One would think at my age, I would've lost my ability to blush — but unfortunately, that's not the case. I can feel my cheeks grow hot under his effusive compliments. Eventually, I find my voice and answer, "Well, it was easy to fall in love with one of the nicest guys I've ever met."

Much to my amusement, now it's Denny's turn to turn bright red as he proposes, "Why thank you, Gwendolyn, but I wasn't fishing for compliments. I hope you're feeling up to a dance or two tonight."

I pretend to think about it for a moment before I walk over and kiss him gently. "Oh, that's right, you promised to teach me some of your fancy line dancing steps. I don't know. I'm a little skeptical. I think you might have been exaggerating a little," I tease with a wink. The audience hoots and hollers for a minute before I hear Kiera comment from the back of the room, "Gwendolyn, normally it's all about the power of the Girlfriend Posse, but you may have bitten off more than you can chew here. My dad is pretty darn good."

"Who's to say I'm not better?" I challenge with a wink.

Chapter Seventeen

Denny

My body sags with relief when I see Gwendolyn is smiling, laughing, and having a good time. It has been quite a few months since I have seen unbridled joy on her face. My fiancé looks as if she feels strong. She doesn't seem to have any trouble catching her breath or having regular conversation. For a long time after her surgery, even maintaining the proper level of breath support required to carry on a regular conversation was difficult for Gwendolyn. It was very frustrating for her to be so chronically fatigued. Even that seems to be abated as long as she isn't feeling the side effects of chemotherapy. Right now she's on a little mini break until she has to go in for her last few weeks. For now, the doctor has given us the all clear. Of course, she won't be completely considered cancer free until she's gone her full five years without having any signs of relapse. But, I feel confident the doctor has removed it all. Every sign points to positive news; so that's my story and I'm sticking to it.

She looks positively radiant today. All color is back

in her face and there's a bright sparkle in her eyes. You wouldn't even guess anything was ever wrong with her. Gwendolyn is having so much fun and I am thrilled.

For the moment, we have switched partners and Tyler is dancing with Gwen. I'm dancing with Kiera. Jeff is dancing with Eleanor and Eleanor is having the time of her life. Jeff is used to dancing with Kiera's wheelchair so he doesn't have any trouble including Eleanor in the dance. Eleanor is absolutely delighted to be part of the activities.

As I turn my attention back to Kiera, I am concerned by an expression I see cross her face. She doesn't notice my attention at first and her pain is absolutely palpable. Once she notices she's being watched, a filter comes over her and she appears warm and happy. I know her move too well. She's pulled it on me a million times. But I know better. I know there's something wrong with Kiera. I just don't know what it is. When the song is finished, I call Jeff over to my side and tell him quietly, "There's something going on with Kiera and I don't know what it is. You might want to investigate further. I know she won't tell me because she's protecting me. She's hidden stuff from me before. I don't know if she does something similar to you. She thinks she's protecting me from something dangerous. Maybe she treats you differently because you've been a paramedic. I hope to God she does because with the baby on the way, it could be something serious. I hope not. Good luck." I pat him on the shoulder. I walk over to Gwendolyn and ask, "How was the dance with Tyler?"

She flexes up onto the balls of her feet. "A little painful. You can't say the boy lacks for enthusiasm. I just don't think dancing is his gift. Is Kiera all right, she looks like she's hurting somewhere."

"That's what I'm trying to figure out. Jeff is talking to her right now. Maybe he'll be able to find something out," I answer as I look over at my daughter.

Madison comes up behind me. "Oh, I know that grimace. Denny, are you ready to be a Grandpa again? I think this is probably it for Kiera. It's a good thing Becca is already at the sitter's house. I have a feeling she might be there for a while. Is Kiera planning to have Mindy at the delivery?"

"I don't think so. She has to have surgery."

"It's a little out of your way since we live in Sisters now, but Mindy can come home with us if you want her to," Madison offers.

"That's okay, I think Kiera made contingency plans with Tara or Heather. If I know Mindy, she'll want to stay close to the action. She won't want to miss a single moment she doesn't have to with her baby brother. I think she probably has an itinerary set for him for the first seven or eight years of his life."

Madison grins as she tucks a little blanket around Lydia who is sleeping in the front carrier on her chest. "Only the first seven or eight years? She's already decided Lydia is going to be in Tara's ballet class and star in the Nutcracker when she turns thirteen."

When Jeff rejoins our conversation, he's pushing Kiera's chair in a hurry and it appears he's only barely hanging on to his composure. "I think it's best if we head on over to the hospital now. It seems my wife has been keeping a secret from me. She's been having contractions for quite some time. I'll call you when I know more."

"Relax, I've been timing my contractions. They are only four minutes apart. I have plenty of time. I didn't want to disrupt the party."

"Pip!" Jeff roars with exasperation. "Didn't you learn anything from Madison? Everything went really fast with her after she got started. I don't think Dr. Ross wanted you to even go into labor. It could trigger an episode of your dysreflexia."

"Aside from feeling as big as a house, I feel fine," Kiera assures Jeff as she reaches up and pats his forearm. She looks at Gwendolyn and me. "Bye, Daddy. Congratulations you guys, I couldn't be happier. Now, I have to go have a baby before my husband has a conniption fit."

Before I can decide what to do next, Aidan hops on stage, grabs the mic. "Remember what Denny said about God laughing in our face when we make plans? Well, it seems to have happened again tonight. Instead of having a big, long celebration, we seem to be on baby watch tonight. I guess little Charlie Dennis didn't want to share the limelight. So, we're going to cut this shindig short and go home and get some rest."

Mindy scampers up on stage and pulls on Aidan's belt loop as she says in a loud stage whisper, "Uncle Aidan, I think you forgot something important."

Aidan looks down at Mindy with a look of surprise. "You know what, Mindy Mouse, I was distracted but you're right. We can't close out our set without doing your number. Do you want to join us on stage?"

Aidan pulls the stool up into the spotlight. Mindy

hooks her heel into the rung on the stool as Aidan hands her the guitar he gave her last Christmas.

Aidan grabs the mic and announces to the crowd, "Denny, you may want to dance with your fiancé on this one. I hadn't planned for this to be last dance of the night, but in many ways, it's quite fitting. I am pleased my friend, Tasha Keely has joined us tonight. Tasha and Mindy Whitaker have been working on a special number. I'm going to go back to my first love and play piano on this one and let them work their magic."

Suddenly, the noise level in the room disappears and it seems as if everyone is holding their breath. As far as I know, this is the first time Mindy has played her instruments in public. She's played for me privately in my living room, so I'm not particularly worried because I know like everything else Mindy does, it'll be spectacular, but I guess not everyone knows.

I place my arm around Gwendolyn's waist and escort her to the middle of the dance floor. I place my other arm on her shoulder and gather her close. I kiss her forehead. "I'm so glad you said yes."

She tears up. "I'm glad I said yes, too. Thank you for tonight. I needed something to celebrate." She rests her cheek on my chest as we wait for the music to start.

Mindy adjusts the mic and says, "Grummy, this song is for you because I know you love music and sometimes your heart has a hard time hearing what Papa means when he says he loves you."

When Gwendolyn hears those words, tears leak from her eyes and travel down her cheeks. I wipe them away with my knuckles as I respond with a whisper, "It's okay, *Amasa*, I know you know I love you, even if sometimes it's hard to understand why."

I thought I knew what to expect from Aidan's friend because I watched her every week when Aidan was competing on that television show he was on. She was good then, but she's probably better now. But, I'm not prepared for the emotional impact of the opening strains of Martina McBride's song *I'll Love You Through It*. The impact of her soft husky voice singing Martina McBride's lyrics about a woman being diagnosed with cancer is enough to bring me to my knees. It's as if whoever wrote this song has crawled into my brain and pulled the lyrics right from my thoughts. It's true. It doesn't matter what happens to Gwendolyn or whatever toll cancer takes on her body, I will still love her until she takes her last breath.

Gwendolyn buries her face in my neck as a deep shudder passes through her body. I hear her sob before she asks, "Denny, are you sure we'll make it through this?"

"Yes, *Amasa*, I've never been more certain of anything in my life."

I look up toward the stage as Mindy plays the last haunting notes of the song and tearfully smile as I declare, "That was perfect, Princess Pumpkin."

The atmosphere in the car is heavy with emotion. You can almost hear thoughts turning in our heads. Finally, the silence becomes oppressive and I have to say something, "I'm sorry Gwendolyn. Everything didn't turn out exactly like I had planned."

"Denny, I'll admit I'm worried for the kids, but other than that it was perfect. I was really surprised. I can't believe you thought to invite Eleanor. That was an inspired touch."

"She seemed to enjoy herself. I'm glad she could come. Still, I'm sorry it ended so soon — I was looking forward to dancing the night away with you."

"Me too, but there will be other nights, I'm sure," Gwendolyn reasons as her phone buzzes. After she checks the message, she adds, "That was Heather, she says Kiera's temp is up a bit so they feel safer doing a C-Section rather than labor and an epidural. So, they are keeping her under close observation to make sure there aren't any complications. If all those little pictures in the text message are anything to go by, I'd say Heather's frustrated by the doctor's decision. I think she had planned to be Kiera's personal cheerleader. If I know my son, he can get a bit tense in these situations; he'll probably be arguing with the doctor about how to properly care for Kiera."

"It is true, Jeff is a fierce advocate. If they don't do right by her, there will be heck to pay. I guess we should go home and sleep while we can. Things could get dramatic later."

Gwendolyn shrugs. "Well, that wasn't exactly what I had in mind, but if a nap is what floats your boat —"

I'm sure I look like a Jerry Lewis comedy sketch as I give her classic double take. "Plans can be changed. I'm a flexible man."

Gwendolyn smiles mischievously. "Oh good, I would hate to have gotten all gussied up for nothing."

Chapter Eighteen

Gwendolyn

As I sit in front of my vanity mirror and remove my jewelry, I examine the damage the years of living have done to my once beautiful skin and I try to tamp down the panic which is slowly rising from my gut. I was never the most beautiful woman in the room. I was more the girl next door type; I guess you could say. If I were cast on a show like Gilligan's Island, I would be the Mary Ann character, not Ginger. I had pretty good skin, but my hair was nothing to write home about — it used to be dark blonde and I have blue eyes. Not anything poets would write sonnets about or anything — they're plain blue. Now my brown hair is white with age and my once smooth porcelain skin is wrinkled with age spots. Whatever skin Kevin Buckhold left unscarred has now been marred by cancer and its aftermath. Although Denny has made it perfectly clear he finds every part of me beautiful, it is hard for me to shed the doubts Kevin has planted deep in my soul.

Just as I am about to cave to my inner doubts,

Denny comes out of the restroom with my favorite lotion. He spins me around on the little roll around chair I use at the vanity and starts to unbutton my shirt.

Denny smiles when he encounters my lacy camisole. I don't want to shatter his illusions or anything, but my reasons for wearing it aren't entirely sensual. If I wear a bra, it rubs in the spot where one of my incisions developed scar tissue and it bothers me. So it's easier for me to wear these camisoles. However, if Denny wants to think I dressed sexy for him, I won't disabuse him of the fantasy.

I struggle to keep my mind on what I have now, instead of what I lost. It's incredibly difficult. It seems everything in my current relationship is fighting with the past. It's either colored by the ghosts of my first marriage or my nightmare of a relationship with Kevin or by my cancer, I can't seem to separate the happy of now and concentrate on my joy. It's so frustrating.

Denny seems to understand my hesitation as he pulls the camisole over my head and then spins the chair back around. He methodically heats the lotion in his hands before he massages my neck at the base of my skull and works his way down my neck in long even strokes. I'm a sucker for touch. I always have been. When I had long hair, before my mom died, she used to spend hours brushing it and it was my favorite time of the day.

It would be easy to be lulled into complacency with the comfortable nature of his touch, but as he strokes down the curve of my back, I look up into the mirror and happen to catch the look of open desire on his face. It's something I've come to appreciate about Denny. I don't have to guess or try to interpret what he's feeling; he wears his emotions on his face like it's a movie projector. There's no artifice or disguise. It's all out there, good or bad. In this case, though it's a little disconcerting, it's also very reassuring. In fact, it gives me a boost of bravery I might not have otherwise.

Denny catches my eye in the mirror. "*Amasa*, I have seen a lot of things in my lifetime, but I've never seen anything more beautiful than what I'm looking at right here. Tell me you see what I see."

I stare at the sensual image for a few more moments. It's surreal — like watching a movie of someone else's life, someone who's not me, someone beautiful, graceful and sexy. As I feel the roughness of Denny's palm against my body, I cannot deny the image I see reflected back at me. It takes a second before I can catch my breath and form the words to say, "Thank you for giving me the courage to see beautiful again."

My stomach growls as I smell sausage and coffee. It's such an odd sensation to be hungry again. For many, many months, I feared I might never feel the sensation of hunger again. For a long time, the thought of food repulsed me. I had to force myself to eat. After the breathing tube came out, food was a painful proposition. I didn't even want to think about putting anything in my mouth; even liquids hurt to swallow. I never thought I would enjoy food again. Eating seemed like an unnecessary luxury. I am so glad for the simple pleasure of a rumbly tummy in the morning.

A sound drifts up from downstairs. I can't wipe the silly grin off my face when I realize the origin of the sound. It's been years since I've heard it, but the sound is the happy, contented whistle of a well-loved man. I can't help the swell of pride that comes with the thought I am the woman who put the whistle on those lips. There's a really good reason there's a smile on my face too. For two people who haven't done this in a while, it hasn't taken us long to get into the swing of things.

It's hard not to play the comparison game because I'm at such a different place in my life than I was when Donald and I were together. With Don, our love was all fireworks and passion. It was hot and intense, but rarely patient. My relationship with Denny is much different. Although I am very attracted to Denny, my attraction grew in many layers so it built like a slow burn. Our lovemaking is that way too. It's not rushed like it was with Don. Since I don't count the nightmare I went through with Kevin as lovemaking, I don't have a lot of experience so I don't know if the difference is my maturity level or just because the men are different. But it adds a whole new dimension I must confess I like.

As Denny comes into the room carrying a tray, I smile in greeting. When he looks disappointed, I ask, "Is something wrong?"

As a look of chagrin crosses his face, he answers, "Oh, nothing's wrong. I was hoping to surprise you."

"Trust me, I *am* surprised. I don't get a gourmet breakfast in bed very often."

An odd look crosses Denny's face as he mumbles, "Just humor me, I'm an old sentimental guy and I'm into the grand gesture. So, close your eyes, please."

I can't help myself, I giggle like a schoolgirl as I dutifully close my eyes and pretend I don't see him in his old gray sweatpants and Dale Earnhardt, Sr. T-shirt with an apron which says **Hot Guys Cook**. I rollover and turn my back to him and pretend to be asleep. I hear him set the tray down on the bed and I hear some random rustling as he arranges things. He kisses me on the shoulder. "Good morning, *Amasa*; it's time to rise and shine. I suspect we might have a grandson by now."

I roll back over and put the bed into a sitting position. Denny was so funny when we started staying together at his house. When it became clear I needed a place to recover, he completely remade the master suite for us. He installed a vanity for me and put in adjustable beds — he claimed it was so he could use his computer in bed to research antique sales, but I know better.

Finally, I can't contain my curiosity any longer and I look at the tray he's prepared for me and my heart melts a little more.

Denny has taken an old Mason jar and tied a ribbon around it and taken some of the flowers from the bouquet Isobel made and placed them in the jar. On the tray he had tucked a vintage Valentine inside a folded napkin. As I fold back the napkin, I can see instead of writing on the Valentine, he stuck a note on the back in his own distinctive writing. As a collector himself, he knows I take my collections seriously. Since he found out I collect vintage Valentine's Day cards and photographs, he's been contributing to my collection regularly. It's a beautiful piece. It looks like it's from the early 1900s. I hesitate to even guess how much it cost him because it looks to be in mint condition.

Before I can explore much further, my stomach makes its presence known as it growls quite loudly and unattractively.

"Gwendolyn, honey you need to eat. We didn't get much sleep last night and then we got rather — distracted — I guess you could say," Denny teases, as he opens the carafe. "Do you want coffee or tea this morning?"

Much to my dismay, I blush at his remark as I remember all the distractions of last night. Fortunately, his attention is elsewhere and he doesn't seem to notice. I stretch and yawn. "I think today feels like a coffee day for sure. Maybe I'll have some tea later, but I need to start with coffee."

"Okay, coffee it is. Go ahead and eat your breakfast before it gets cold," he instructs.

"Aren't you going to eat?" I ask as I suddenly notice there aren't two plates on the tray.

Denny grins at me as he shrugs. "Well, I guess you could say I ate. I couldn't exactly trust Bojangles' opinion on quality control so I had to try a few things myself. I wanted to make sure I got your eggs just right and my first few tries weren't exactly spectacular. So, somebody had to eat the evidence," he admits.

"You're so silly! I'm not that picky," I insist. "I would've eaten whatever you brought me."

"I know you would've, but you shouldn't have to. I wanted to make it perfect for you. You made last night so perfect for me I wanted to return the favor. Before you came into my life, I didn't realize I had been merely existing from day to day. You took out the loneliness and replaced it with light, beauty and love. I will forever be grateful. If I can bring a few of your favorite things into your life, I want to. If it means eating a few of my messed up broken eggs, I'm more than happy to do that. Besides, Bojangles thought he hit the breakfast lottery this morning. I mean usually he's ecstatic to get his kibble, but this morning he was over the moon," Denny replies.

His disjointed confession of affection is heartbreakingly honest and I feel the need to share my own feelings. I take a deep breath and share things I've been feeling but not necessarily sharing with him because I have trouble finding the words. "Denny, I'm the one who's lucky to have you. I don't know how you were still single and available for me because you are truly one of the most generous souls I've ever met in my life. I would've never made it through my ordeal had it not been for your support. I don't just mean the fact that you took care of me. You believed I could beat the odds, and you were strong on the days I couldn't be. You have given me more gifts than you can imagine and more than I could ever explain in words. I don't even know how to tell you other than to say you gave me back me. Through your eyes I see glimpses of the fighter I used to be. You've given me permission to be strong and feisty, tough and sassy and as odd as it might seem at my age, sensual and sexy. I've missed having all those sides of myself. It's been surprisingly fun — and sometimes hard work to discover who I am again. For those reasons and so many others, Dennis Allen Ashley I will love you until the day I die," I declare, tears breaking my voice.

Chapter Nineteen

Denny

"Here we are racing to the hospital again. I wonder how many more times we'll do this in the near future?" I ask Gwendolyn as I clasp her hand. We're stuck in traffic on the way to the hospital to see Kiera, having finally gotten the all clear from Jeff.

"I don't know; it's conceivable we could do this a few more times. There's Heather and Tara or perhaps Donda might have another one. Something tells me Mindy won't be too many years behind the rest of the crew."

"Oh my! Do me a favor don't mention Mindy to your son. Unless you want to give him a heart attack right in the maternity ward. He's not fond of the idea of Mindy growing up at all. The idea of is daughter having her own child would give the poor man a coronary for sure."

"That's true, he probably wouldn't like the idea much. But, it would be amusing to see his expression. It's true though if I have ever seen a natural-born mom-to-be, it's Mindy. So, I don't know if he'll be able to counter

Mother Nature though — even if he wants to. The only thing which might save him from that fate is she wants to go to school to be a doctor. She might put her plans for motherhood aside long enough to pursue a career. But I don't know if she'll be able to fight her biological clock long enough."

"Yeah, the one thing I've learned along the way is we make plans and then life happens and those plans get changed. I always thought I'd have three or four kids and they'd all probably be baseball-playing boys. It didn't happen. But, I am grateful now things turned out the way they did. If they hadn't, I would've never met you. Since I am head over heels in love with you, I can't regret the way it all happened even though I went through a great deal of pain along the way," I reply philosophically.

Gwendolyn looks down at the ground abruptly, and I wonder if I've touched a nerve. Finally, she looks up at me nervously. "Do you ever feel guilty?"

"Guilty about what, Honey?"

"This is going to sound silly because Donald has been dead for years and I wasn't even there when he died, but sometimes when I think about how happy I am with you, I wonder what would've happened if Donald would have lived and our paths might have crossed. Would we have still been attracted to each other? If I had to choose between the two of you, which one would I choose?"

If Gwendolyn didn't look so distressed, I probably would have laughed out loud. In part because the idea is utterly silly, but also because I had similar ideas when I first became interested in Gwendolyn. I had never seriously dated anyone since Karen died so I had to adopt a new mindset before I was ready to take the leap. I can honestly relate to her fears because I had similar ones. I do my best to reassure her. "*Amasa*, I think nothing catastrophic would've happened if you would've still been with Donald and our kids would've met and fell in love. You would have probably thought I'm a weird old man who works on ancient rust buckets and has a strange obsession with NASCAR. For the most part, I think our hearts are only open to falling in love when we're ready. Your heart would've been so full of love for Donald you would've had no room for thoughts of me."

"Do you really think so? I worry somehow I'm being dishonest and disloyal to the memory of Donald by falling in love with another man," Gwendolyn frets.

I squeeze her hand gently. "Having never met the man, I can't speak for him entirely, but from what you've told me, I don't think Donald would want you hiding away from the world. I think he would want you to fall in love and recapture the person you were when you met him. You said one of his favorite things about you was your moxie and sassiness. He would be devastated to know someone systematically beat that out of you physically and emotionally. He would be thrilled to know you've rediscovered the spunky side of yourself."

"I hope that's what he would've wanted for me. We didn't have time to talk about it because we were busy raising a family and it never occurred to us we would run out of time, which was ridiculously presumptive of us considering the fact that Donald was a firefighter. Of all couples, we should have had this conversation long before he ever passed. After he passed away, I could never figure out why we never talked about matters of life and death. But knowing Donald the way I did, he probably figured if he talked about death, it would be like inviting it to happen in his life and he never wanted to give death a foothold in his mind."

"The only couple I know who have had that discussion are William and Isobel. When she got breast cancer, she point-blank told William if she didn't make it, she wanted him to go find someone to love. When she first told him, he was angrier than a bull at a bullfight, but after he had time to think about it, he realized what a true gift she had given him.

"You know, come to think of it, I think our kids have had a similar conversation because of Kiera's condition. As I recall, Jeff's response was much like William's. He did not cope well at first. But he came to accept what Kiera was offering. Ironically, it wasn't too many weeks after they had that conversation, Jeff was handling a case in family court and one of the defendants on the other side pulled a knife in court and made it frighteningly close to Jeff's side of the table. It just underscored the idea it's not only Kiera who's in danger on any particular day."

"Wow! My daughter didn't happen to mention it," I grumble.

Gwendolyn laughs. "No, I don't suppose she did. Your daughter is protective of you. Kiera doesn't seem to have any issues about us dating."

"No, she doesn't. She wanted me to start dating a while ago. She's always been worried about me being alone, especially as she got ready to graduate from high school. She always insisted no sane wife would ever want to die and leave her husband all alone in the world. I suspect she's probably right. I think if Karen and I'd had the foresight to talk about all of this stuff, she would've not only given me her implicit permission to move on, she would've strongly urged me to do it. In fact, she would've probably made me promise to move on. It's likely she would have left me step-by-step instructions and a list of her single friends to start dating — she was that kind of person. In an odd way, I think you guys would've been good friends if you would have known each other. I know that sounds as creepy as Hershey's bars, but I don't mean it to be," I trail off as I run out of words to explain my thoughts.

"No, I understand exactly what you mean. You're a lot like Donald's friend who perished with him in the accident. It's kind of spooky actually how much you two resemble each other, not only physically, but in your personalities. I suspect if you had known Donald, the two of you would've probably hit it off as well. So, it's a small, spooky world isn't it?"

As I pull into the parking garage of the hospital, I kiss her knuckles and say, "Are you ready to go meet our grandson? From what I understand from Jeff, little Charlie Dennis has some big shoes to fill. I guess Jeff's grandfather was a legendary figure in his life."

"That's true enough, I suppose. But I think Kiera is levelheaded enough that she'll allow Charlie to establish his own legacy. And even if she weren't, I think Mindy is enough of an influence that he'll have his own path and identity in life regardless of what his parents decide. Life with Mindy is unusual any way you slice it."

When we arrive on Kiera's floor, Mindy meets us at the elevator. "Com'ere guys, I have something to show you," she greets us enthusiastically as she practically drags me to the room. Gwendolyn has to run to keep up with us. When we reach the doorway, Mindy starts to chatter excitedly, "I don't know what I was worried about. Charlie looks a lot like Becca n'me. See his hair is curly like ours and he's got a dimple like us. Look at this mark behind his ear, Becca has one too. The nurse says they're called stork bites. Mom says they're angel kisses, kinda like autographs from God. My Nana used to say it was the mark of the devil and it showed where the devil entered Rebecca's body and because there weren't any on her feet, it meant the devil was still in there."

I have to shake my head at the garbage her birth family tried to fill this child's head with. I've never heard such craziness in my life and the fact that they tried to use it to harm children is beyond me.

Mindy continues on as she explains, "I knew it wasn't true because Becca was just a baby and the devil wouldn't go into Becca's body when she was little. It was silly. I knew it had to be a birthmark or something. But Nana wouldn't listen. She washed my mouth out with soap and told me I was the devil's child, too. She said she knew because I had one behind my ear too. I tried to look in the mirror for it, but I couldn't see it. I don't know she if was telling me the truth. It's hard to tell. Nana lied to me about all sorts of stuff. So, I never knew what to believe. Anyway, Becca and Charlie have matching Angel kisses from God. I think it's kinda cool that even though we're adopted, we match Charlie. I guess you're right, Grummy, we do match in this family. Isn't that amazing?"

"Princess Pumpkin, that's really nifty, but I'm not surprised. I think God designed it so that you would be part of our family since your family didn't have the good sense to keep you. But it's neat you have something in common with your brother. By the way, I think your brother is adorable. Did everybody still decide to keep his name as Charlie Dennis?" I ask.

"Yes, Papa, he has an important name because he has important things to do in his life. He's going to make great changes in the world when he grows up. He can't be named after just anybody. He has to be named after important people with smart brains and big hearts," Mindy announces.

"Well, I'm glad I could lend my name to the cause. But, I'm not sure my name holds much weight," I comment.

Mindy *tsks* me, "You need to have a better sense of your family history. Besides, I think your heart is amazing."

"Dad? Are you coming in or are you just going to stand in the doorway?" Kiera asks from inside the room.

"I would come in but your daughter is giving me a verbal description of her brother before I even get a chance to see him. I get the feeling she's quite proud of the miracle you've produced."

"That she is, you would almost think Mindy gave birth to him herself. For as invested as she has been in this pregnancy, she might as well have. She watched my diet more carefully than I did. I think she probably checked in with my obstetrician more frequently than any of us. She had a detailed list of questions for every visit.

My OB said she would make an extremely astute student."

"Mom, you can't go into this unprepared. If you don't ask questions, you can't figure out what's going on. Since you didn't give birth to Becca and me, you didn't go through this before; it was all new to you. So, someone had to ask the questions. We needed to make sure Charlie Dennis was healthy."

"You're right, Mindy, I did appreciate the help. You did ask some important questions."

Gwendolyn walks over and kisses Kiera on the cheek. "My important question today is 'How are you feeling?'"

"I'm tired and for once, I'm glad for my level of injury because it means I can't feel my C-section incision. Although, Jeff keeps checking the bandage for seepage every few minutes and it's driving me nuts. I'm sure the doctors knew what they were doing when they sewed it up and it's probably not going to break wide-open. It seems to be his overwhelming fear for some reason."

"Give your poor Boy Scout a break, you knew he was a worrywart when you married him. He's not likely to change right when you've just given birth in a high risk pregnancy with a potentially life-threatening condition," I tease.

"Thank you for the vote of confidence, sir… I mean Mr. Ashl… I mean Denny," Jeff stammers correcting himself each step of the way.

Chuckling, I add, "Jeff, call me whatever you're comfortable with. At this point, it doesn't matter. I know you're my son-in-law and you know I'm your father-in-law. Trying to get you to conform to whatever anyone else calls me obviously isn't working very well."

Jeff sags in relief. "Thank you, sir, I'll keep it in mind. It might be a little easier if I don't have to consciously think about it. The pressure to remember sometimes causes me to flub up. Would you like to hold your grandson?" Jeff offers as he picks Charlie up from Kiera's arms and walks over toward me.

Mindy skips over to stand beside me; she is practically vibrating with excitement as she announces things like a color commentator on a sports broadcast, "At first, I chose a different outfit for him thinking he was going to be tiny like Lydia, but he was already too big for it so, we're going to give it to the women's shelter so someone else can use it. He doesn't like things to go over his head, but his neck is ticklish. You have to be careful when you put a diaper on or he will pee on you if you're not fast enough. He peed on Dad's shirt last night when Dad forgot. Mom missed it because she was sleeping. Charlie has little baby snores like Dad's big snores. Sometimes he wakes himself up. See what I mean about how much he looks like Becca? But he is way bigger than Lydia. Daddy says he might be a football player like Uncle Tyler but I told him football is probably not a good idea because there are new studies that say football is not a very safe sport."

I look at Gwendolyn in total disbelief. I'm not exactly sure how to respond to all the information my precocious granddaughter just dumped on me. Before I can respond, Mindy continues her monologue.

"What? I'm not wrong. That's the same look Dad

gave me before he told me that I need to get off the computer and stop researching things so much. But how am I supposed to learn? I was just trying to figure out something I heard on the news. They were talking about a football player who committed suicide and they used a medical term I hadn't heard before so I went to look it up on the Internet. That's where I read the story about high school athletes and football."

"No, Mindy, you're not wrong. But what I think your dad is trying to say is we're concerned you might be worrying about things you don't need to be at this point. Your brother is still very tiny. It will be years and years before he is eligible to play football. By the time Charlie is ready for football, there might be something invented which will prevent the head injuries that cause all the problems with football at the moment. It's not something you need to stress out about at this point. Besides, your brother could be totally uninterested in athletics. Right now, it's a wild guess."

"But what if it's not just a guess with me?" Mindy asks.

"It's true that you may have some inside information, but his choices affect the outcome. Think about all the things you've wanted to be in the time I've known you. At one point, you wanted to be a musician and join One Direction, another time you wanted to be a lifeguard like your dad, still another time, you wanted to be a fireman and a trucker like me. Our plans change a lot as we grow and change. I wouldn't go around planning all of Charlie's life based on how he looks at this very second; you might want to wait until he grows up a bit and can tell you what he likes."

"But what if he makes the wrong choices?" Mindy asks solemnly.

"Mindy, that's a tough position for any sibling to be in and it'll be even tougher for you given all you can perceive. One of the ways Becca and Charlie will learn best is through their own mistakes and you have to allow them to make them. We can't stop them from making mistakes, we can only be there to help them make the right choices and to comfort them when they make the wrong ones," Gwendolyn advises. "I don't think I ever stopped worrying about my brother."

"Being a big sister and loving people is scary stuff." Mindy sticks her hand close to Charlie's and allows him to grasp her pinky finger.

Jeff leans over Kiera, drops a kiss on her lips and then walks over to Mindy and kisses the top of her head before he kisses his son's cheek. As he stands up, I notice his eyes are welled up with tears. "You're absolutely right Mindy, it is really scary, but the benefits are out of this world. If I didn't have your mom, your sister, your brother and you in my life, I don't know what I would do. You guys are my definition of happy."

Chapter Twenty

Gwendolyn

I try not to flinch as Trudie Lee Temple removes my PICC line. It has become such a part of me, it's hard for me to believe it's actually coming out.

"Look at you! It's graduation day. What are you going to do — go to Disneyland?" she teases.

"I'll probably do the usual and puke my guts out for a few hours while I pretend not to notice my fiancé pretending not to notice."

Eleanor pipes up, "I think it's so funny he does that for you. When my daughter comes to take care of me, she can't even be in the same house as me when I'm throwing up or she throws up too. If she can even almost hear me throw up, then both of us are doing it. Trust me, it's not a pretty sight. I'm almost better off by myself. But since the incident when I threw up way too much and passed out from dehydration, the doctors don't want me to be alone. So now, I'm in a terrible catch-twenty-two. I can't afford to have somebody stay with me, but I can't be alone either. None of my family wants to do it because they're tired of me being sick. It's not happy times at my house. I wish I would hurry up and die or get better. This halfway-in-between garbage sucks."

"Weren't you telling me your blood work was looking better?" I ask, trying to boost her spirits.

"It's marginally better, but not enough to save my life. I think it's the lab's way of trying to give me some hope to get up in the morning. But I doubt it's anything other than a statistical blip," Eleanor explains with a shrug.

"Eleanor, I know you are as smart as they come, but in this case, I hope you're totally wrong. I pray this is the turnaround you've been looking for. I want you to be well enough to dance at my wedding. As far as I know, no one else is pregnant so we shouldn't have any more babies arriving at my reception," I encourage as I pat her knee on the way by.

"I hope you're right, Gwendolyn, I really do. I'm sure you'll make a beautiful bride," Eleanor predicts with a teary smile.

"I'll come back and visit soon," I promise.

Eleanor gives me a stern look. "Don't you dare. I want you out there living your life, not back here on this floor. You can text Trudie with your updates. But I don't want to see your butt on this floor ever again, do you hear me?"

"Yes ma'am," I confirm with a sharp salute as Trudy Lee Temple wheels the rickety hospital wheelchair outside the chemotherapy wing for the last time.

Love Seasoned

As I hang Bojangles' leash on the hook by the back door, I hear Heather and Tara discussing something in my bedroom. Curious, I go to investigate what's going on. I wasn't expecting them to come over. I thought Tara had to teach classes at her art center today. As I round the corner, I hear Heather say, "I think she should take this along with her just in case."

Tara responds with, "Normally I would agree, but this is Denny, and he likes to dress down. I think she can get away with less formal stuff."

At this point, I cough gently and step all the way into my room. It's all I can do not to gasp out loud as I see huge piles of clothes on every surface of my room. I can't stop myself from exclaiming, "What's going on?" I didn't mean to sound disapproving, but my surprise made my voice sound more harsh than I intended.

Tara and Heather jump like two junior high school kids caught painting graffiti on the girls' bathroom walls. Tara is the first one to regain her composure. As she gracefully stands up from her position sitting cross-legged on my bed, she brushes nonexistent wrinkles out of her wool skirt.

"Uh ... we're packing," Tara answers vaguely.

"I can see, but why? The only trip I have planned is to Michael's to pick up more crochet yarn. The only thing I have planned is a bunch of sappy Hallmark movies."

"Well, I guess I could pull out one of Madison's lines and say, 'I'm not at liberty to disclose the specific parameters of my assignment'."

"You can, I suppose, but keeping a secret would be cruel and unusual punishment and you wouldn't want to do that to one of your good friends now would you?"

Heather looks in real pain, "No, we don't want to, but we're under strict orders of secrecy."

"Can you tell me anything?" I plead.

Both women shake their heads no as Heather confirms, "Pretty much that's a big no. We can ask you what colors you like though."

"Will I need to kill Denny when this is all finished?" I ask, my frustration level growing by the minute.

This time, the women give different answers. Heather shakes her head and speculates, "No, I don't think so. I think this is a win-win for everyone. You'll just have to be patient."

Yet, at the same time Heather is saying this, Tara is nodding. "Yes, I would definitely need an arrest warrant made out in my name. I would kill Aidan if he pulled this. Trust me, left to his own devices, this is totally something Aidan would do."

Now I'm terrified — there is a wide range of things Denny could do which could be Heather approved and Tara disapproved. Those two girls can be thick as thieves, but polar opposites.

Tara turns to Heather and asks, "Did he say if he was going to take Betty Boop or the sedan?"

Heather shrugs. "He didn't make it clear, but I suppose it depends on the weather. It can be nasty out this time of year."

"So, we're going on another road trip?" I guess

tentatively, hoping they'll give me some clues.

Heather smirks as she looks around the room at the devastation they've wrought upon my once orderly living space. "Well, Gwendolyn, I think it's safe to say you're going *somewhere*. If you don't want to take Betty Boop, you should probably speak up and Tara and I can lobby Denny and see if we can preemptively change his mind before he makes it."

I laugh out loud at her comment. "Oh, I see you're settling into married life just fine. You seem to be figuring out the finer points of marital negotiation right up front," I tease.

Heather winks at me. "As I tell my husband, I may be blonde but I am *not* a bimbo. It didn't take me very long to figure out if I could get him to make the decision I wanted him to make up front, it was easier than getting him to change his mind after the fact."

"Very true. I'm so sick of being cooped up and stuck in bed. If I have the option of riding the motorcycle — that's what I'd rather do. I'm afraid of freezing to death. It isn't the middle of summer anymore."

"I have clothes Aidan got me for rock climbing — they wick away moisture but they keep you very warm. They'll be a little long on you, but we can work around that," Tara offers.

"That would be great. I don't even know how to begin to tell you how trapped I've felt. I mean, I feel ungrateful because people have been really supportive and tried to keep me company, but what I wanted to do was be out and about. I wanted my normal routine back.

It would've been great to go to the flower shop or work in the flower garden or even go to church. I was too physically weak and immunocompromised to even think about it. I always wanted to view myself as a calm serene person, but cancer has taught me to think differently about myself. I'm not calm and serene at all. I am impatient, pushy and fidgety. I'm also grumpy when I'm bored. It's amazing Denny decided to even stay with me after all I put him through. If I were him, I would've left a long time ago. It has not been a pleasant few months."

Heather chuckles. "Oh Gwendolyn, I'm sure you weren't so bad. You always were nice to me when I came over. You even tried to teach me how to crochet and that wasn't an easy task considering I have the attention span of a goldfish. Even Mindy gave up when she tried to teach me how to make a rug using yarn and hook because I couldn't count the squares."

Heather studies me scientifically for a moment before she says, "Oh, I see the problem now. You have passed the threshold."

"The threshold?" I ask, befuddled.

"The threshold — you know, the one where they see the real you — where they figure out girls poop and we don't come prepackaged with beautiful eyelashes, perfect lipstick and breasts which stay perfectly perky?"

Something about the way she described that strikes me as funny and I laugh as hard as I've laughed in months, fortunately for me, it doesn't hurt quite as bad as it used to. My ribs are finally healing some. Eventually, I catch my breath and explain my sudden hilarity. "Heather, sweetie — have you taken a good look at me recently? I am old enough to be your great grandmother. I am old and wrinkled in places where my wrinkles have wrinkles. My breasts haven't seen perky in decades — that was before I got cancer and I was sliced open like a Thanksgiving turkey. Denny and I are so far over 'the threshold' we don't even remember it. Not only does Denny know I poop, the man has had to clean it off of me, along with vomit, spit, blood and pee. Why the man hasn't gone running for the hills, I have no earthly idea "

"He doesn't go running for the hills for the same reason Aidan, Jeff, Tyler and Trevor don't go running for the hills. Our men love us regardless of our flaws. It's simple. Remember, we also love them and they aren't perfect either. It's a balance," Tara reminds me.

"It feels out of balance to me. I don't know what I contribute to this," I confess.

"You gave something to Denny he hadn't had in many years either. You love Denny without trying to change him. You let him tinker, fiddle with things and be exacting without making him feel like he's wasting his time. You allow him to be a natural nurturer without making him feel like it makes him less of a man. In case you haven't noticed, Denny likes to take care of people — all people. It doesn't matter who those people are. He has adopted everyone into his world from the kid who delivers his papers to the barber who cuts his hair. In big and small ways, he has adopted us all into Denny's world. A lot of people might think his all-encompassing compassion might make him a soft man, but you have given him permission to make that his strength and be proud of his empathy and compassion. Your gift to Denny is priceless."

I take a long drink of my iced tea as I think about our time together. I realize Tara's advice is spot on. From the way Denny has mentored Jeff and Tyler to the way he stood up for Eduardo at the restaurant, caring for other people is definitely part of Denny's personality.

"Tara, do you think that's the reason he's in love with me? Does he only love me because I need a caretaker?" I fret.

"No, I absolutely do not. I was there when Denny met you for the first time. We were all kinds of distracted. I was not so distracted that I didn't notice him be completely besotted by you. Denny had eyes for you the moment you walked through the door. Now, he tried to play it cool, he really did. I could tell his reaction to you was different from any person I had ever seen him meet. I've been friends with Kiera for a long time. I have seen Denny meet a wide variety of people. The man has never met a stranger, you know this. He was introduced to lots of people when we were at college and through Kiera's work and through Heather's work and neither one of us have ever seen anything like Denny's reaction to you."

Heather nods as she agrees, "It's true. If the two of you were cartoon characters from Looney Tunes, he would've had hearts coming out of his eyeballs and his heart pounding out of his chest when he saw you. Although Denny is very helpful to other people, it's not like him to put his heart on the line like he did with you. In all the time I've known Kiera, I have never seen him date anyone, let alone set out to woo someone like he did you."

"If you remember correctly, he started all the

courting before anyone had any idea you were sick," Tara interjects. "I hate to break it to you, Gwendolyn but I think he likes you just because you're smart, funny, hot, and sexy."

I grimace. "Um-hmm, whatever you say."

"It sounds like you may need more convincing," Heather accuses with a grin.

I groan. "This is going to involve a mall, isn't it?"

"Absolutely!" Heather responds enthusiastically. "When you've crossed the threshold and you're feeling less than spiffy, there isn't a better recipe for getting your mojo back than some retail therapy. We need to get you ready for a nice romantic evening away so you two can remember what it was like to be lovers instead of patient and caretaker. Personally, I don't think Denny has ever forgotten the lover part of it. However, you should play it on the safe side and surprise him. When was the last time you had a nice manicure and pedicure?"

I try to slam my brain shut against all the negative associations I have with those words after the debacle with Kevin because I used to love the process of getting manicures and pedicures. I swallow hard before I answer, "It's been a good long while — longer than I care to admit, actually."

"Well, let's go get you beautified and find you a beautiful dress so you can show off those stunning legs of yours. I swear you could be a dancer in Tara's company. I'm jealous of you guys and your long legs. I feel like a midget next to you guys," Heather whines wistfully.

I look around the chaos in my room and decide the

mall seems like a better option. "You're right, shopping does sound like more fun than packing right now and wearing Tara's thermal underwear two feet too long probably won't win me any points for looking ravishing. I suppose I should find my own — not that long underwear could ever be considered lingerie."

"You never know, some of that stuff can be rather skintight. On your little hourglass figure, it could be quite alluring."

"It's much more likely I would look like Denny's old fishing poles he covers with dusty sweat socks," I counter.

Heather turns to Tara, "Remind me to special order some kick-butt self-esteem for Ms. Whitaker over here. She seems to have misplaced hers."

I have to admit, the Girlfriend Posse is an unlikely support group, but that's what they've turned out to be. Madison and Lydia ended up joining us for our impromptu shopping trip. Trevor had business to do with Aidan's record company in Portland, so they met us at the outlet mall for some industrial-strength shopping. Let me tell you, when Heather says she's going shopping, she means it. As much as I protested the trip I had a great time.

Interestingly enough, even though Madison and Heather are sisters, it wasn't the two of them who fought like siblings. That honor was reserved for Heather and Tara. For two best friends, they don't seem to agree on much. It was a good thing Madison was there to play peacekeeper between the two of them. If she hadn't been there, I would've been put in a very awkward situation.

When we finally located 'the' dress for me, there was universal agreement among all parties. Although I have no idea where Denny could take me where a dress this formal would be appropriate, I found the loveliest pale lavender dress I've ever seen in my life. I feel as glamorous as Audrey Hepburn in it. Tara found me some handcrafted earrings made from seashells which complement the dress perfectly. The finishing touch was my manicure and pedicure done as a French tip with lavender sparkles throughout. I have to give credit where credit is due, by the time I was done being pampered, I felt like the most beautiful woman in the world. I think maybe Heather was right, I had let cancer take too much of my identity as a woman. It's time for me to take some of my identity back.

Madison's contribution to the trip was invaluable; because of her experience on the frigid East Coast, she knew all the best places to get discount winter wear. She found me the cutest winter jacket and vest. I'm getting excited about this mystery trip, but no matter how much I pry, the girls assure me everything will be taken care of. They won't spill a single detail — so much for the loyalty of the Girlfriend Posse. I'm regretting that Mindy isn't with us. She is usually more forthcoming — whether she intends to be or not.

When Heather and Tara drop me off, Heather keeps the dress. Heather claims she needs to hem a spot in the dress. It's funny, I didn't notice anything wrong when I tried it on — but then again, I was pretty distracted by everyone's shenanigans. I may very well have missed something.

Denny meets me by the car. He kisses me on the cheek. "Wow! You look nice. Is there a special occasion I missed?"

"No, not really. The girls took me out for a tune-up to celebrate the end of chemotherapy. I guess they thought I was looking a little ragged."

"Well, I always think you look great. But, you look especially spiffy today so it's a good thing I can take you to dinner at the Italian place. One of the waitresses told me Eduardo is graduating early from high school so I thought I would make sure he got a good tip tonight. I guess he wants to go to culinary school at the community college and needs to buy books."

"That's so sweet of you. Hey, Isobel called me and I guess William is going to some legal conference and she doesn't want to go. She says they're boring; but she doesn't want to hang around the house all day either, so she volunteered to cover the shop for a few days for me so we can have a few days together. Are you free?"

Denny grins from ear to ear. "As a matter of fact, I am. It turns out were supposed to be having a warming trend over the next few days. I mean, it's not Florida or anything, but it's not supposed to be pouring down rain either — what do you say we hop on Betty Boop and take a little road trip?"

Chapter Twenty-One

Denny

I hope my plan doesn't come back to bite me in the butt. Everyone involved seems to think it's a great idea, including Jeff and Donda. From what I understand, to get the two of them to agree on anything is almost an impossible feat. So far — knock on wood — everything seems to be going smoothly. The only glitch in the plan is finding someone to cover the flower shop because Isobel can't be in two places at once.

    I look down at Gwendolyn riding in the sidecar. She looks like she's snug and comfortable. I found an aftermarket part which collects heat from the engine manifold and pipes it into the sidecar so she's probably pretty warm in there. I was worried about her getting chilled, but it's likely as warm in there as it would've been in the car. I'm so relieved she's excited to go on this trip. I wasn't sure how she would react to the prospect of going on a trip or what her tolerance level would be after being so confined for several months. She appears to be having a great time. I'm a little concerned about how she'll react to my huge surprise. All of her friends seem to think she'll be fine rolling with the punches. I hope her friends and family have read the situation correctly. It will be catastrophic if they're wrong.

I turn up the volume in my headset. "Amasa, how are you feeling?"

"This is great, I'm a little sad we didn't come sooner. We missed most of the fall leaves but it's still beautiful out here. If you had told me I would fall absolutely in love with motorcycle riding, I would have thought you were nuts. But I love being this close to nature and the rush of adrenaline."

"I'm so glad. What do you think about getting your own bike?"

"Do you really think I could handle one? I'm not very heavy; it would seem like the bike would pull me right over."

"That's a good point. Maybe you should just ride tandem with me," I suggest.

I can hear her chuckle through the headset. "Well, I can think of worse fates than having to snuggle up next to you for hours on end."

"Come to think of it, it may be the best idea I've had in a long time. Gwendolyn, on a scale of one to ten how adventurous are you feeling on this trip?" I toss the question out, trying to sound casual. She has no idea how much is riding on her answer to one simple question. I try desperately hard to concentrate on the road as I come up on a convoy of logging trucks and have to navigate around a few blind curves, but all I can think about is how long it's taking her to answer my question. In reality, it's probably only been a few seconds. But in my mind, it seems to take for-ev-er.

Finally I hear her blow out a breath into the microphone as she says almost to herself, "You know what? I spent so many years living the safe life and doing what was expected of me and it didn't bring me anything but pain and suffering and a horrifically lonely life. So for once, I'm going to throw caution to the wind and live the lessons I've learned over the past few months. Life is too short to live according to how you think others might want you to live. You have to follow your own heart. So, Denny Ashley, I will follow you wherever this wild road takes us. On a scale of one to ten, I guess I'm probably about one hundred. I'm tired of living my life safe. As the kids say, I'm over it."

All I can say is it's a really good thing I have the bike to keep me upright; if I didn't, I would be in a puddle of shock on the asphalt. I was not expecting her to say anything of the sort. The relief coursing through my body is a tangible thing. I take a couple minutes to calm the thoughts in my head enough to be able to talk. Gwendolyn must've noticed my silence because I hear her in my ear piece calling my name, "Denny, is everything okay? Can you hear me?"

"Yes, Amasa, I can hear you fine. I'm just trying to process what you said. We've come so far in a few months. It's not just you who's becoming bolder and braver, it's me too. I think we bring the courage out in each other," I respond, trying to sound neutral. I don't want Gwendolyn to hear how close to the edge I really am. These last few months have been incredibly difficult for me. There were times I was worried she might not make it. I couldn't let her know because I had to be strong for her. But to see how far she's come both physically and emotionally since the day we met is mind-boggling.

As I pull off the highway onto a curvy road, Gwendolyn notices the marker to the state park. She practically squeals with delight. "Are you serious? We're going to Silver Creek Falls? I haven't been here since the kids were small. I love this place. It's like a fantasy land here; I could spend hours looking at all the plants and trees."

I make a mental note to send Donda lots and lots of chocolate and tickets to go see her favorite basketball team. She made my whole day.

"I aim to please. This is just one portion of your wild adventure today. So, fasten your seatbelt. It'll be an adrenaline rush like you've never had."

"If this is the start of the adventure, I can't wait to see the rest," Gwendolyn practically bounces out of the sidecar with excitement. I only hope her attitude stays the same as the rest of my plans unfold for the day.

Given the time of the year, Silver Creek Falls is quiet and peaceful. It's not like it is during the peak of the summer. I walk her to a quiet secluded grove of trees with a rock wall and a seating area. I think she can sense my stress as she places her hand on my knee and voices, "Denny, is there something wrong? It's not like you to be this pensive. Usually, you are a chatterbox talking a million miles an hour about anything and everything. Talking to you is usually a bit like talking to Mindy or Heather. Often, I can't get a word in edgewise. But today you've been uncommonly quiet. I'm almost worried you have devastating health news this time. Have you been keeping something from me?"

I squeeze her hand. "Yes, Gwendolyn, I have been keeping things from you but not in the way you think. It's nothing bad. Do you remember when we had the long conversation about how we were frustrated about not being able to move our lives forward because the cancer got in the way of us?"

"Dennis Allen Ashley, if you brought me out here to my favorite place on the planet to give me the brushoff, I'm going to be royally pissed off at you!" Gwendolyn warns with fire in her eyes.

"Oh, my — I must be doing a terrible job of explaining what's going on. That's not what's happening at all. In fact, it's the opposite of what's happening. I brought you out here today to marry you," I reveal as I scrub my hand on my face in frustration.

The look of total shock on Gwendolyn's face was exactly what I feared. I don't know if this will end well. She opens and closes her mouth a few times as if she's gulping for air. She shakes her head as if she's trying to clear her thoughts. "Excuse me? I think I must've misheard you," she sputters abruptly.

"Amasa, you didn't mishear me. That ring on your finger says we planned to get married, so I just chose today as the day," I explain as if it's the most logical decision in the world.

"Dennis Allen Ashley!" Gwendolyn exclaims. "I thought you were setting land-speed records with planning Kiera and Jeff's wedding in a week. Have you gone 'round the bend? I know speedy weddings are your thing, but usually the bride is consulted." She looks down at her cable knit sweater, jeans and biker boots. "Do you realize how insane this is? I don't even have a dress."

"If I were to venture a guess, I would say the Girlfriend Posse has you covered on all sides. Whatever they don't have covered, Jeff probably does."

"What do you mean Jeff has me covered? He has a brand-new baby to worry about," Gwendolyn protests.

"Oh, come on Gwendolyn. You know Jeff has this parenting thing down to a science. He could do it with one hand tied behind his back. Plus, Mindy is doing eighty percent of the work for him whether he wants her to or not. Did he tell you she's already researching preschools for him? Charlie isn't even close to his first birthday. Yet, she's already evaluating school curriculum." I chuckle.

"See, he's got more than enough stuff on his plate, he doesn't need to be worrying about me," Gwendolyn counters.

"Honey, I've got news for you. He's Jeff — he'll worry about you whether you tell him to or not. So, you might as well let him in on the fun," I point out. "So, what do you say Ms. Whitaker? Are you ready to be adventurous and become Mrs. Ashley today?"

Gwendolyn crosses her arms and glares at me. "If I know anything about you, the engagement party was small potatoes compared to what you've got planned for today, right?"

I blush. "Well, the guest list is smaller, but I'm hoping the emotional impact is right up there."

She chews on her bottom lip. "You've already spent

weeks or months planning and talked to dozens of people, correct?"

"Longer than you might imagine, actually. The idea first came to me the day in your flower shop when you told me I should be a wedding planner. I sat in your little grotto in the store and imagined what your ideal wedding environment might look like and decided you wouldn't want an inside wedding. This place was the closest match I could come up with. Donda helped me get reservations."

Gwendolyn's jaw is slack. "Denny, how is that even possible? We weren't even officially dating back then. Sure, we were friends, but you're friends with a lot of people. How could you have possibly known we would fall in love and get married?"

"Gwendolyn, I had my eye on you for a really long time before I ever let it slip that I actually — for lack of a better term — had a crush on you like a schoolboy. I was so afraid you'd find out we were more than casual acquaintances before you had a chance to find out I was a decent man. You were so skittish I was afraid you might give up on our friendship before you could find out men were not all evil, terrible creatures. I didn't know how else to approach it. I wanted to get to know the real woman underneath all of this fear. You were that important to me."

I watch as all the anger and suspicion seems to melt out of Gwendolyn. "Denny, you know one of my hot button issues is being handled and told what to do. But I guess that's not what's happening here. You're just trying to recover from life interrupted even though it's in the clumsiest way I can imagine from a woman's perspective. But that's probably what makes our relationship work so well: we see things from such different points of view. There's one thing to be said about us. We will never be boring or conventional. People will never know what to expect from us. We will always be beating the odds and doing the unexpected. When it comes right down to it, I kind of like that about us. It has come to define who we are and I'm all right with that."

I open my arms wide and Gwendolyn walks into them as I envelop her in an all-encompassing hug as I try to pour all of my emotions into the one gesture because suddenly, I'm incapable of speech. Until this moment, I hadn't given myself permission to think about how much I feared the prospect she might actually say no. I'm not sure I could survive if I had to go back to a world without Gwendolyn in it. She has become as essential to me as oxygen and water. I honestly can't remember what my life was like before I met her. Well, I guess technically I can, but I don't really want to.

Chapter Twenty-Two

Gwendolyn

"You guys are terribly sneaky, you know that? I can't believe you took me shopping for this dress without telling me what it was for." I look in the mirror, at Tara who is putting in my earrings.

"Hey, I'm not going to cross Denny. He keeps my car running in tip-top shape. I don't want to tick him off. He swore me to secrecy," Tara admits with a small grin.

Heather shakes her head. "Nope, me either. He's the only one who can get my wood-burning oven at the bakery to work halfway decently. Besides, he's like my dad. So that makes you like my mom. I treated this like a giant surprise birthday party. I'm getting much better at keeping secrets. Being married to a Sheriff's Officer has improved my skills a bunch."

I narrow my eyes at my daughter who's doing my hair as I complain, "Was it too much to ask for some solidarity from you?"

Donda smiles mysteriously at me. "Mom, I was acting in your best interest. If you'd had months to think about this and get cold feet, you would have come up with a dozen reasons why you couldn't, shouldn't, or wouldn't marry Denny and none of them would be valid. They would all relate back to the garbage Kevin shoved in your brain for years. So this surprise wedding just short-circuits all the bad. You can be happy and in the moment without having to deal with your past."

It's quite scary how well my daughter understands me and what makes me tick. I wonder if it's because we're so similar or so dissimilar. Whichever is true, the bottom line is: she's absolutely correct. Had I had time to ruminate and think about our situation, my panic would've taken over and I would've talked myself out of the best thing to ever happen to me. I have to give Denny credit as well. He has the best instincts in our relationship right now. He knew in order to let go of the past, I needed to be able to grab onto the present with both hands.

Donda hugs me from behind. "Mom, I've never seen you look so beautiful. I'm so proud of your courage. Someday, I hope I find the courage to pick up the pieces of my life and find someone who loves me as much as Denny loves you."

"Gwendolyn, I have to agree with her, love looks good on you. Now, go rescue your man." Kiera says. "Dad's about fit to be tied with nerves."

There's something fitting about the fact that we're standing in front of a fireplace to get married. Since it's a small family affair, we skipped the whole processional.

Mindy was less than thrilled about this decision because she has been practicing her runway walk in her newly minted grown-up shoes. She does look very mature indeed. I feel very sorry for my son. He looks like he's seen the ghost of Christmas future and does not like what he's seen. Unfortunately, I know the feeling all too well. But as parents, there's not much we can do to stop the march of time. Kiera is trying her best to console him and reassure him even if Mindy grows up, she will always need her dad, but it seems to be having very little effect.

William takes his place in front of the room. He is in a simple pullover sweater and dress shirt instead of his customary robe.

Denny takes note of his attire. "Gee, Will, I'm so glad you could dress up for the occasion."

"First of all, I'm on vacation. Secondly, this is *your* wedding. Quite frankly, I'm surprised we're not all in racing T-shirts and coveralls. I would've expected the dress code from you. It's obvious being with Gwendolyn has improved your life greatly."

"Very funny; you forget I was in *your* wedding. I happen to remember a mustard yellow tuxedo with a plaid tie. Do you really want to compare fashion tips?"

"Don't remind me of the debacle. He's lucky I still married him," mutters Isobel from the audience.

Everybody laughs in understanding.

"I've actually become fond of racing T-shirts and coveralls. Although, I never thought I'd see the day I would say it out loud," I tease.

"Ladies and gentlemen, now that's true love," quips

William as he opens his wedding notebook on the podium. Suddenly, he seems to change his mind as he closes it back up. "I don't even know why I'm bothering with this today because this wedding is going to be unlike any other I've ever performed. Not because it's any less solemn or important, because it's not. It's probably more sacred than most. Because these two people have been through more pain and tears than many couples ever see — they've faced pain separately as individuals and they faced it together. Perhaps one of the most important lessons from their love story is to never fear the new and unknown."

Mindy is watching William with spellbound attention; it is adorable to watch. I do believe she has a case of hero worship going on.

William continues. "I can't pretend that I'm unbiased about this love story. I'm simply not. Denny has been my friend — perhaps my best friend — since I could tie my shoelaces. We were each other's best man when we first fell in love and got married. Sadly, I also was by Denny's side as he had to bury his wife when she passed away from cancer. I also had the privilege of watching Denny raise an amazing daughter all on his own. Kiera grew into a beautiful young woman who not surprisingly won the heart of a phenomenal young lawyer, Jeff Whitaker. That in itself would please any father, but Denny didn't expect that Jeff's mother would take his breath away."

All eyes turn to me and I blush at the compliment. Denny looks at me and squeezes my hand as he mouths, "It's true."

"Denny resisted at first, he had been in love with Karen for so many years, he wasn't sure how to deal with his feelings. Not to mention it felt odd to be in love with the mother of his son-in-law. But his feelings couldn't be denied. I knew there was something special there. His face would light up every time he talked about her. There was a special reverence in his voice any time he mentioned her name. He admired her fighting spirit and her willingness to deal with the pain and suffering in her life and her ability to rebuild after the chaos which happened to her. He was fascinated by every single word she ever uttered. It was funny, it reminded me of the days when he was in high school and had a crush on the pastor's daughter, but this was so much more intense. I was watching my friend fall in love again after more than a quarter of a century of being alone. I was absolutely thrilled. It couldn't have happened to a kinder, nicer soul."

I can't help but nod at William's heartfelt sentiments.

"I'm equally happy for Gwendolyn. I know Gwendolyn because she is the mother-in-law for my goddaughter. As I mentioned, Kiera has never had a mother figure, but Gwendolyn has gladly stepped up and fulfilled that role for Kiera since she met Jeff. Gwendolyn has been gracious and loving to Kiera and they have formed a close, loving, supportive bond. I have to give Gwendolyn a lot of credit. I can't tell you how many cases I've seen in my courtroom where the in-laws are at war with the family over petty issues. But Gwendolyn never saw Kiera as competition for Jeff. They've formed a partnership to help support Jeff, and it's encouraging to see their family become stronger with the addition of the kids. It's what you hope for when you get married and have a family."

I flush at the unnecessary compliment.

"Gwendolyn, I want to say, I'm sorry the justice system didn't do more for you far earlier in your struggles with your former ex-husband. I'm monumentally sorry your first husband was killed. Because you made my best friend so happy, I can't be sorry you have found each other. I'm sorry it took so much pain in both of your lives for you to find each other."

Kiera hands me a Kleenex and I wipe my eyes before I reassure him, "It's okay, William, I think we've come to a place of peace around our pasts."

"I've said my piece. Now, Denny and Gwendolyn have a few things to say to each other," William announces.

I look at him in shock. "Actually, William, I don't. I didn't even know I was getting married today. I just figured we were going on a motorcycle ride. If I were to guess this morning, I thought we were going to go to the orchards of Mount Hood like we did before to see how the flowering trees were progressing. I had no idea I'd be expected to come up with vows and exchange them with Denny. I have no idea what to say. I would have to make them up as I go along and I tend to be a rambler. Can you tell?" I say all in one breath.

Jeff comes over and kisses me on the top of my head. "Mom, take a deep breath. We won't leave you stranded. I promise. Aidan is singing a song while you catch your breath. Kiera has notes for you. You may want to take a look at them. The bottom line is we all know you all love each other. The words dress it up and make it pretty, but the love is there in every glance, gesture and word you guys share. Don't worry about getting it perfect. The very fact that you are strong enough to stand here in front of all of us is testament of your willingness to fight for this marriage and your love together."

Jeff hugs me before he returns to his appointed position. Once again, I am struck by what an extraordinary human being I somehow raised amongst all the chaos of my second marriage.

As Aidan positions himself with the guitar, I take a moment to examine the piece of paper Jeff shoved in my hands. Much to my surprise, it's a bunch of quotes from me about my relationship with Denny. I think back to the conversations it refers to and realize it took place several months ago. Kiera and I had met before I went to the doctor about my cough. She wanted me to come over to give me the referral list. Somehow, the conversation had drifted to all the things I thought were sweet and funny about her dad, and we compared notes on all the things we loved about Denny. I remembered ribbing him a bit about all of his quirky habits, but I guess I hadn't realized how many things I had mentioned that I completely adore. I also hadn't realized how obvious my intentions were or how open I had been with Kiera. I thought I had been more circumspect. Yet, as I read these quotes, my feelings were raw and on the surface. It doesn't take much reading between the lines to understand even back then I was completely and fully in love with Dennis Allen Ashley.

My eyes tear up as I listen to Aidan cover Kenny

Chesney's classic *You Had Me From Hello*. When I hear an additional strain of guitar added, I realize Mindy has quietly joined Aidan on stage. I can't help but marvel over how much she has changed since she burst into my son's life with her sad eyes and pigtails. She has grown into a smart, confident, beautiful girl on the cusp of becoming a great beauty with talents which would baffle most adults. I'm barely hanging onto my composure until I make the mistake of looking over at Denny. His eyes are welled up with huge tears. Seeing him openly emotional is the last straw for me and it pushes me over the edge and I start to cry.

My tears are startling. I spent so many years hiding my emotions or disguising them as something else, shedding tears publicly would have been considered an unthinkable sin a few years ago. I've become so free Denny and I are standing here openly weeping. When I escaped from Kevin, I couldn't imagine this day would ever come. I quietly reach out and interlace my fingers with Denny's as we absorb the love of our friends and family on this sacred day.

As Mindy sets down her guitar and returns to her seat, she stops to give me a brief hug. She stands on her tiptoes to whisper in my ear, "Grummy, I believe in you, and now you believe in you. You can do this. You're finally strong and you're ready. Trust what your heart says."

I return the hug as I whisper, "I think I can handle it now. Thank you for the pep talk though."

William returns to the podium. He looks at us. "Are you ready to say your vows now? Who would like to go first?"

Denny gestures toward me and offers, "Ladies first—"

I wave him off and acquiesce, "Oh, you go ahead … I'm still collecting my thoughts."

Denny looks up at William and says, "I hope you don't have to be anywhere in a hurry because this'll take a while."

Williams shrugs. "What else is new? You've always been the slowest talker around. It takes you forever to get to the point. I'm used to it by now. Isobel and I planned to be gone three days. You plan to take longer than that?" he teases.

"I don't know," Denny answers with a wink. "I love my Gwendolyn an awful lot. It's hard to quantify."

William sighs. "Oh, all right if you insist. I could rearrange some stuff on my docket. But it would be hard to explain on the record."

Denny laughs. "With all due respect, Justice Gardner, the only docket you need to rearrange is your fishing schedule. You're retired now in case nobody bothered to remind you."

Isabel's snickers. "Oh good, I'm glad I'm not the only person who has to point it out to you, dear husband-of-mine."

William blushes slightly. "Okay, it's conceivable I miss work a tad more than I anticipated."

From the audience, Mindy clears her throat. "Are we ever going to have a normal wedding in this family?"

About four people answer her in unison, "Probably

not."

Mindy shrugs. "Okay, just checking. I haven't seen a normal one like they have on TV yet. I wonder if they're real."

William laughs. "I've been officiating for a long time and the one thing I can tell you is everyone's ceremony is different. I have never done two exactly the same. Although, I do have to admit this family does tend to stretch the boundaries a bit farther than most. Anyway, as I was saying — Denny, would you like to proceed? I think I may have a seat over here, these dress shoes are hurting my feet — the way you can wax poetically about Gwendolyn, we could be here for weeks on end," William teases.

"It's true. I could," Denny concedes. "But in the beginning I wasn't sure it was going to be that way. When you first entered our lives, my overwhelming emotion was anger."

Of all the things I expected Denny to say in this setting — that was not it. I can't keep the expression of shock off my face, and I suspect I'm not the only one. I hear a gasp travel through the audience.

Denny hears the reaction and hastens to explain. "I didn't say my anger was justified, I just said I had it. Some of it was justified because I was furious at your ex-husband for the way he treated you and my daughter. He came into Kiera's house and disrespected her and everything she stood for. After I got over the shock, I was completely enraged over the disrespect he showed you and your children. Then I was scared. I was scared for what his rage meant for you and Donda. My suspicions alone made me sick to my stomach."

Instantly, my thoughts traveled back to the intensity of his reaction that day, I knew it wasn't typical, but back then, I didn't know how atypical it was.

Denny straightens his tie and swallows hard as he continues, "The more I thought about how deeply your dilemma affected me, the angrier I became at myself. Once I got over my anger about the disruption your very presence in the universe caused in my life, I had to decide what to do with you. My heart had one idea, and my head had another. I had to decide whether I was brave enough to follow my heart or my head. You were so supportive of me during this process. Whether you knew it or not at the time, you loved me when I wasn't sure I loved myself. Your faith in me meant the world to me."

"What else was I supposed to do? Above all else, Denny, you deserve to be loved. You are an amazing human being," I whisper.

Denny caresses my cheek. "You can see why I call you *Amasa* — you're pure sweetness inside and out. Your faith in me is unshakable. It didn't matter what I told you, you always believed the best about me in any situation. That kind of belief is priceless."

From the back of the room Tyler says, "Amen to that!"

Mindy just rolls her eyes. "Uncle Tyler, this isn't like church. God doesn't care if you say 'Amen'."

Madison mutters, "God might not care, but Kiera and I might not talk to you for a while if you wake up our babies during the ceremony. Do us all a favor and put a lid on it."

Denny clears his throat and pauses for a moment. "Gwendolyn and I thought we had dealt with the tough stuff when we talked about our past loves and the people we had lost in our lives but it turns out it was only a taste of what was to come. Those difficult conversations were a sort of trial run for what we would soon face. Little did I know I would soon face my worst nightmare again."

It's so hard for me to see the despair on Denny's face as he relives those moments. I cannot even imagine the pain he was in when it happened. It's difficult to watch him relive the memories. I remove a Kleenex from the tissue holder and dab at Denny's cheek as a tear escapes the corner of his eye. He leans down so I can reach it better. I mouth the words, "I'm so sorry."

"Amasa, it's not your fault you got cancer. Cancer doesn't care who you are or who you love. It destroys lives like the tornado of death and destruction that it is. But, as strange as it may seem, good things happened as a result of this awful disease," Denny declares.

My eyebrows shoot up in surprise at his unorthodox analysis of the worst few months of my life. Denny looks at my face and chuckle slightly. "No, I'm not crazy — really. Hear me out here —"

"I'm thinking this might be the type of conversation that's rather time-limited, Denny. You might want to get to the heart of your argument pretty fast here, buddy. I'm sensing this might be a losing proposition for you."

"I think you guys are jumping to all the wrong conclusions, it's really not all bad, I promise," Denny protests.

"I think I'll reserve judgment until I hear the whole story from Denny." I turn to him. "You were saying?"

"Gwendolyn, your health made me face my fears in a way I probably never would have it if you had never gotten cancer."

"You were shouldering way too much," I murmur.

Denny grabs my hands and holds them tightly as he explains, "The cancer made us strip away the things which weren't important in our relationship and pay razor-sharp attention to everything else. I think it has made us much closer as a couple and stronger together than we would have been if we would've done the typical things a couple does together when they first started dating. There's nothing like waiting to hear whether the person you know you want to spend the rest of your life with will live or die to clarify what's important in your life. That's a reality I don't want to ever have to live through again. I wanted to do everything in my power to make sure you were beside me for as long as humanly possible. I waited nearly thirty years to find love again and since I've found you, I'm not willing to let go. I hope you're okay with that."

I nod mutely as I stare into his earnest, emotional expressive face.

"I love you, Gwendolyn. Although our love might be seasoned with tears along the way, it is strong and tested and I believe it will last forever," he proclaims.

I take a drink from the bottle of water sitting on the table. I vamp it up a bit because Denny looks a bit shaken, but mostly I do it in an effort to buy time until I can reign in my own emotions and speak coherently.

I pretend to wipe sweat off my forehead as I begin, "Well, I'm glad I don't have to pretend to be succinct and organized after all of that. Thank you so much for taking the expectation right off the table for me, Sweetheart."

Everyone in the room roars with laughter as Denny blushes.

I clear my throat lightly before I begin speaking from my heart, "Since I wasn't expecting to get married today, I should have a perfectly legitimate excuse not to have any ideas in mind about what to say. But my lovely daughter-in-law took care of that for me and for reasons which are not entirely clear to me, she has notes from a conversation we had months ago before we knew I had cancer."

Mindy leans forward; I can feel her practically willing me to find the strength to get through this.

"Talking with Kiera reminded me of the first time I met you. You did something for me that hadn't happened for me ever — well, not since I was a small child."

I swallow hard before I can continue. "What was this amazing, miraculous feat that captured my attention?"

Denny smiles at me in a silent gesture of support.

"Dennis Allen Ashley, you protected me. That's it. Without question, without doubt, without wanting anything in return, you stepped up and stood by my side and offered to stand with me against the personification of evil."

I shudder at the memory of Kevin Buckhold's

spittle flying in my face as he screamed vile things at me. I take a deep breath so I can continue speaking.

"Little by little you changed not only what I believed about men, but what I believed about myself. A funny thing happened when I wasn't paying attention. I fell for you. It happened gradually. It wasn't like it was back in high school when I wrote my beau's name all over my notebook or inside my locker. This is a much quieter love. This is the kind of love rooted deep in my heart and stays. It's the quiet contentment of knowing the other person is always thinking about me and putting my well-being first — like you are with them. I think everybody in this room knows the type of love I'm talking about. The little things matter. It's choosing to buy a different laundry detergent because it's the type they prefer or putting up with a marathon of television programming because they been waiting for it for weeks when you would rather watch grass grow but you gladly do it because it puts a smile on their face. It's not fireworks, flashy cars and fancy clothes, but it's the kind of love that makes for happy families and contented Sundays doing crossword puzzles."

I have to stop to wipe away tears before I continue, "I had a lot of the same issues Denny had to work through. I had a pretty great first marriage that also ended in a tragic death. Unlike Denny, I followed my great marriage with the terrible one. I didn't trust anybody to take care of me."

"That's like the understatement of the millennium," Donda mutters under her breath.

"I wasn't interested in romance ever again," I

continue. "Denny had some serious convincing to do. Denny didn't try to persuade me to do anything. Denny just became my friend. Somehow my heart knew the right thing to do."

Denny places his arm around my waist and gives it a gentle squeeze. As I take a steadying breath, my voice shakes. "I guess it was obvious to anyone who knew me I was head over heels in love with you before I could ever say those words out loud."

William clears his throat before he pauses to take a drink of water. Isobel quietly walks up to the front of the church and hands him a box of tissue. I hear her quietly assure him, "You can do this, Bill."

William kisses her hand and takes a tissue from the box and wipes his glasses and surreptitiously clears tears from his eyes before he looks at me and declares, "After Karen died, I was worried Denny might never find someone worthy of his generous spirit again. But I see God has chosen to provide his perfect match. I'm so glad you have found each other, Gwendolyn."

Denny regards William with a look of bemusement. "If you think you're relieved, how you think I feel? I don't even know what to say. I'm at a loss for words."

"Well, lucky for you it's not your turn to speak right now. I have to say a few words to make this ceremony all official." William's smiles. "Please join your hands and repeat after me. Denny, we'll start with you."

"I, Dennis Allen Ashley take you Gwendolyn Faith Whitaker to be my wife, my partner in life and my true love. I will cherish our friendship and love you today, tomorrow, and forever.

I will trust you and honor you

I will laugh with you and cry with you.

Through the best and the worst,

Through the difficult and the easy.

Whatever may come I will always be there.

As I have given you my hand to hold,

I give you my life to keep."

Denny's eyes never leave mine as he solemnly repeats the vows. I know he means every single word. It's hard for me not to cringe when William mentions the worst and the difficult. I pray with every fiber of my being that we've put the difficult behind us and we've only got the best and the easy ahead of us.

William nods at me and in a shaky voice, I repeat the same vows, "I, Gwendolyn Faith Whitaker, take you Dennis Allen Ashley to be my husband, my partner in life and my true love. I will cherish our friendship and love you today, tomorrow and forever.

I will trust you and honor you.

I will laugh with you and cry with you.

Through the best and the worst,

Through the difficult and the easy.

Whatever may come I will always be there.

As I have given you my hand to hold,

I give you my life to keep."

I'm proud of myself for holding it together with the emotionally charged environment in this room. Well,

I'm holding it together until I make the mistake of raising my eyes and looking at Denny. Here is the man I love, who has weathered the worst of storms with me, standing before me with huge tears rolling down his cheeks. It's almost too much to bear.

I pull a Kleenex from my little pack and dab his face. "Please don't cry. You'll make me ruin my makeup and my daughter will never forgive me. Hopefully, we're through the worst now, and we have only the best ahead."

"I hope so too, but *Amasa* — it wouldn't matter because I'll love you through it all."

"I know you will. It took a long time for me to believe in love again, but you made it safe for me to believe. I know these vows are not a prison but represent my freedom," I declare quietly.

Denny swallows hard as he turns to William and says, "I hope you don't mind, but I might need a second to catch my breath. This is emotional stuff for a guy like me."

William takes a bottle of water from underneath the podium and uncaps it before handing it to Denny. "Don't worry about it. I think all of us need a minute or two."

Denny gulps down the water like he hasn't had anything to drink in a week.

After Denny sets down the water bottle, William looks at me and asks, "Are you ready to exchange rings?"

The question strikes me as funny given the unusual nature of our wedding, so I laugh out loud. "No, of course I'm not ready. I didn't know I was going to get married today. Nonetheless, something tells me someone probably has this aspect of the ceremony covered."

William chuckles. "I'll give you a moment to confer with your wedding party."

I wasn't aware I had a formal wedding party but Donda steps forward and hands me a ring box. She pulls me into a tight hug as she murmurs, "I'm so damn happy for you." Apparently she forgot William is wired for sound because her quietly uttered sentiment was broadcast for the whole audience to hear.

Mindy clasps her hand over her mouth before she corrects, "Sorry, Papa. I'm sure she meant to say dandelions."

Denny looks back at her and grins before he remarks, "I think it's probably okay today. I don't think your mom has the swear jar."

"I'm sorry, Mindy's right. I shouldn't have sworn. I'm genuinely thrilled you two found each other. I hope I can find someone like you someday, Denny," Donda admits softly.

I meet William's gaze. "I guess I'm ready now."

"I've been ready for longer than I'd care to admit," Denny answers with a self-deprecating smile.

William chuckles. "Okay, I'll try to wrap this ceremony up sometime in the next decade or so. Although I've seen many fads come and go over my years of officiating, I thought the two of you might appreciate a traditional ring ceremony. I hope you don't mind that I chose a traditional script."

"Of course I don't mind. William, you know me better than anyone else on the planet. I trust your judgment," Denny remarks.

William looks down at the floor and seems to flick away tears as he clears his throat and says, "These ceremonies are always meaningful, but this one is especially touching for me. Denny, as you place the ring on Gwendolyn's finger, please repeat after me:

On this day…

I marry my best friend…

The one who shares my life, my love and my dreams.

Gwendolyn, I give you this ring

As a symbol of my love and devotion

I offer you my heart, my hand, and my love

I join my life with yours

To cherish and protect you as my wife

With all that I am…

With all that I have…

I honor you as my wife until the end of time."

I struggle to hold my hand still as Denny slides the beautiful Black Hills gold ring on my finger. I notice he's added a gold band to my engagement ring with its beautiful leaf and vine pattern running throughout it. I guess if I had been paying closer attention, I should have been suspicious something was up. A couple of weeks ago Denny was insistent that I get my ring cleaned and resized. Since it really wasn't loose, I couldn't figure out why he was so insistent on me getting it done right that very second. Now, it makes so much more sense. The ring was beautiful before, but modified it's absolutely stunning. I want to stand here and stare at it all day, but as I hear William clear his throat impatiently, I realize this might not be the best time.

"Are you ready to proceed, Gwendolyn?" William asks.

I fumble with the ring box and remove the Black Hills gold band we chose for Denny. "Yes, I guess I've got it under control now," I answer.

Williams smiles at me as he instructs, "Gwendolyn, as you place the ring on Denny's finger, please repeat after me:

On this day…

I marry my best friend…

The one who shares my life, my love and my dreams.

Denny, I give you this ring

As a symbol of my love and devotion

I offer you my heart, my hand, and my love

I join my life with yours

To cherish and protect you as my husband

With all that I am…

With all that I have…

I honor you as my husband until the end of time."

Much to my relief, the ring slides onto Denny's hand like it was custom made. I still have no idea how anyone knew which rings Denny and I had been window shopping for all those months ago.

Denny looks at our clasped hands and kisses my left hand.

"Hey, what did I tell you about getting ahead of me?" William teases.

"Well, hurry up and get to the good part then!"

"Oh, all right if you insist," William teases before continuing in a solemn voice. "Denny and Gwendolyn you have consented together in matrimony before God in this beautiful setting with your friends present, have pledged your vows to each other, and have exchanged rings as tokens of your love and commitment to each other. In accordance with the laws of the state of Oregon, with great joy, I now pronounce you husband and wife."

"It's about time," responds Denny.

He doesn't even wait for William to give us formal permission to kiss before he theatrically scoops me up into his arms and gives me a surprisingly sensual kiss. Denny doesn't even pay Jeff, Tyler, Trevor and Aidan any mind when they approach us with water bottles and threaten to hose us down.

I look up at the young men and raise my eyebrow as I declare, "Can't you see I'm a little busy here? Don't you all have wives who could use love and attention?"

Chapter Twenty-Three

Denny

"I'm not sure if I should be all sorts of concerned about how sneaky you are, my dear husband. On the other hand, how in the world are you going to top yourself for our anniversary?" Gwendolyn challenges me as she picks birdseed out of her hair.

"That was an epic surprise, wasn't it? I'm pretty good at this stuff, but I even impressed myself with this one. Although, I have to give credit where credit is due I wouldn't have been able to pull off half of it if your kids hadn't been on board helping me. Donda is a very impressive young woman."

"I'm not sure how you did it, but I'm so glad you did. I can't believe you arranged for us to come back to the Dude Ranch. I thought Eric and Amelia closed it for the season."

"They usually do, but once they heard about our wedding, they wanted us to come honeymoon here because they feel responsible for our romance."

"I guess, in a way they sort of pushed us along a bit.

If it hadn't been for their clever maneuvering, I probably wouldn't have danced with you or played limbo. I'm relatively certain I would've never let my guard down enough to share a bed with you that night. I think my decision changed the foundation of our relationship. We built some serious trust on our first trip here."

"That night changed my life too. It was the start of me forgiving myself for my shortcomings in the past and remembering to live."

"Well, what are we waiting for, Mr. Ashley?" she teases. She looks down at the thermal underwear she is wearing under her jeans and riding leathers and mutters to herself, "I really wish I would've known what was going on, I would have planned a lot better. This is the third time I've been with you in a romantic environment and had absolutely nothing sexy to wear. Not that you could even remotely guess this by anything you've seen me wear to bed recently, but one of my secret guilty pleasures is silk nightgowns. Now, I don't even get to wear one on my wedding night. There's so much irony there I can't even begin to tell you."

"Gwendolyn, I'm sure I've told you this a million times, and I'll tell you a million more; it doesn't matter what you wear or if you wear anything at all," I remind her as I gently kiss her neck. "Having said that, I do believe my daughter and her friends have played the role of fairy godmother quite nicely. I'll go grab us a bite to eat before the diner closes. That will give you time to do whatever magic happens when us guys aren't looking."

Gwen giggles and turns around as she exclaims, "You're so silly! After all we've been through, there isn't any part of me you don't know far too well — inside or out. I heard you tell the radiologist the other day he was looking at the wrong films because the shape of my ribs was wrong."

I blush. "Well, it was true. He was looking at somebody else's x-rays. Anyway, if getting all gussied up and pampered makes you happy, it makes me happy too."

"Okay, I guess I'll go see what the girls picked out for me. This could be scary. Heather thinks I'm a little more adventurous than I actually am and I understand Madison reads some very interesting books." Gwendolyn winks and sashays toward the restroom.

I can't believe it took so long to get food. Every logger, construction worker and trucker from every county for five hundred miles around must've been in the diner tonight. Most days, I would've been content to sit and chat with everybody, but I have better things to do tonight. The funny thing is, Gwendolyn probably thinks I'm actually sitting around chatting. For I'm not. It was just an overworked cook whose assistant never bothered to show up. I almost volunteer to pitch in and help. It can't be much different from KP duty in the military. But, I figure they might be a little offended if I did.

As I'm trying to balance the boxes of food, Gwendolyn opens the door to the cabin. She is covered head to toe in a heavy fleece robe with a bright geometric pattern on it. It looks a bit like an Indian blanket you see in all the touristy places. I suspect this is one of Kiera's purchases. This looks like something she would have picked up somewhere.

"Oh, thank God you're okay. I was wondering if you had gotten in an accident with Betty Boop. Haven't you ever heard of using your cell phone?" she chastises as she takes the boxes of food from me and sets them on the table.

I look over at the nightstand where my cell phone is dutifully wearing its hunter orange case so I won't leave it behind. I cringe as I apologize, "I'm sorry. I left it behind again. If my head weren't attached, I'd probably lose that too. The diner was overrun with customers tonight. There must be a heavy machinery conference in town or something. I've been up here several times before, and I've never seen so many people," I explained. "If I had known there would be so many folks up here, we could've rented a yurt or something down at Silver Creek Falls."

"Oh, here is just fine. I'm not sure I would've wanted to spend my honeymoon in the middle of a tent at the end of November. That sounds fun in August, but not so much fun in the dead of winter," Gwendolyn maintains as she pretends to shiver.

"As your husband, isn't it my job to keep you warm now?" I tease. I kick off my riding boots and shed my clothes.

"Well, one would think. Yet I found myself all alone watching infomercials on my wedding night. There is something seriously wrong with this picture," she replies with a sigh as she sits down on the bed and files her nails. As she shifts to make herself more comfortable, her heavy robe parts revealing her shapely leg all the way to her lace covered hip. My heart speeds up and my mouth goes dry as I take a second to drink in the sight before me.

Gwen looks up from her nails and reads the look of open desire on my face I don't even bother to hide. Her eyes widen and she draws in a quick breath as she whispers, "Denny —"

Any thoughts of eating dinner fly out of my head the moment I hear my name on her lips. "Mrs. Ashley," I reply, trying to keep my voice steady.

With a look of awe, she runs her hand down my chest. "I never dreamed I would get married again at my age. But I have to admit I like the sound of it. I'm rather attached to the idea that you're mine. I know it sounds terribly old fashioned and archaic, but that's the way I feel," she confesses shyly.

I climb into bed behind her and kiss the nape of her neck before I reply, "It's a two way street, believe me. I am so honored to call you my missus, I have to pinch myself to make sure you're real."

Gwendolyn looks up at the large mirror across from the bed and meets my gaze. "I can't believe how nervous I am. We've gone to bed together every night for months. It's silly if you think about it." She slowly unties the knot of her robe and lets it fall from her shoulders. I can tell from the way she's holding the robe at her midsection, she's still anxious, but I know with Gwendolyn sometimes I need to show her what I'm feeling. I run my hands down her neck, over her shoulders and down the contour of her gently curved waist.

Once again Gwendolyn amazes me with her agility as she suddenly flips over. She hovers over me and leans down to plant a sensual kiss on my lips. My surprise must have been written all over my face because Gwen giggles. "What's wrong, Denny? Did you think I forgot all about the perks of being a wife?"

I mutely shake my head as she gingerly removes my watch and sets it aside. She kisses my palm and works her way up my arm as she declares, "I can tell you, I haven't and after months of sharing a bed with you, I've developed quite a long list of things I'd like to practice."

"I love you, Mr. Ashley. Count me in," my wife responds with a sexy smile.

Epilogue

Gwendolyn

I close the scrapbook containing Eleanor's obituary. It turned out she was right. Her cancer got the best of her in the end. But not before she patched things up with her kids and go to one of Aidan's classical music concerts at his special invitation. Since becoming a big pop star, Aidan hadn't played classical music in quite some time. But for Eleanor, he briefly came out of "retirement" from the field and played a little mini concert for her. He recorded the concert and gave the proceeds to the American Lung Association at Eleanor's request. She said it was her way of spitting in the face of cancer.

I glance up and see Denny come into the office. I can tell he's been working with mums today because he's got small petals sticking to the front of his apron. We're both wearing holiday themed aprons with hearts and butterflies on them in honor of Valentine's Day. "Sochi, the mail guy came. He said this was too large to drop through the slot," he explains, holding up a large oversized card. I'm instantly curious. I don't know who would send a card to the shop. It's addressed to Denny and I both. I don't think it would have anything to do with our wedding since it was a few months ago. I don't know who would send us a Valentine's Day card. Jeff and Donda are still local.

"Amasa, are you going to sit there and stare at it or are you going to open it?" Denny teases.

I grab a letter opener from the desk and carefully tear it open. Much to my surprise, two tickets to Aidan's show in Vegas land in my lap. It's kind of a big deal because this is some televised thing. We were all surprised when Aidan decided to do it after his last television debacle. It was for one of his favorite charitable causes so he went ahead and took the risk, but the venue is so limited there weren't very many tickets available. They sold out within minutes and Aidan had spoken to us all via Skype, to tell us we wouldn't be able to attend.

I must be grinning from ear to ear because Denny taps me on the shoulder and says, "Are you going to share the news or am I supposed to guess?"

I show him the tickets and his first response is "Love it! It's too bad it's February. The bikes get a little cold in this kind of weather."

"You crazy man. I'm not going to ride across Oregon on a bike in the middle of February. Lucky for you, Aidan knows you well enough to nix the idea. He gave us a private airline escort to get there. He wants us to arrive in style."

Denny shakes his head. "That young man burns money like it's kindling. I've never seen anything like it."

I pat my worry-wart husband on the forearm as I

assure him, "Well, from what I understand, 'that young man' had three of the top ten slots on iTunes last week. I think he'll be doing okay for a while."

As I look around the studio made over to be an old-fashioned supper club, I thought I glimpsed Kiera — but the more I think about it, I must be mistaken. Surely, Aidan would have us all travel together if that were the case, wouldn't he?

Aidan lays it all on the line and has an amazing show. He and the band outdo themselves. They have about three encores before he finally gives his final bow. Denny and I wait in our seats until Aidan is completely finished with his band and whatever he needs to do backstage. Tara comes over and joins us. We are chatting about her dance school when the house lights suddenly come up and the full extent of Aidan's surprise is revealed. The whole gang is here, including my grandchildren.

Tyler is the first to find his voice and ask, "Aidan, you know I've always appreciated your flair for the dramatic, but this goes above and beyond. Would you care to explain what's happening here?"

"I would, but this isn't my surprise. I'm just the facilitator. If you want details, you're going to have to talk to Trevor," Aidan explains with a shrug.

Trevor smiles and steps up to the mic. "Apparently all the men in this family have set the bar incredibly high for a guy to impress his lady, so I had to pull out the big guns and offer to have a destination wedding. But, you know my Madison. She doesn't really care where she gets married or what environment it's in. She would get married in the middle of a big box store for all she cares. In fact, she saw something like that on the news one day and thought it sounded like a pretty clever idea. So, I'm lucky we aren't getting married in the middle of Walmart somewhere."

"You mean you guys are getting married today?" Mindy asks, her voice heavy with shock. "How did I not know this? I usually know everything —"

Tara rushes over to Mindy and envelops her in a hug. "Remember when I told you about the small glitches? They occur every once in a while. This may be one of those cases. Maybe you're too close to this one to be accurate — it sometimes happens."

Madison comes over and kneels down in front of Mindy. "Perhaps I can shed some light on the situation. Trevor and I have decided since you have very definite ideas about how weddings should go, we're putting you in charge of running our ceremony today. It's all about you. You can make it short and sweet or very elaborate; it is your choice."

Mindy frowns at Madison. "You do remember I'm still a kid, right? They might decide it's just pretend."

From the stage, Aidan says, "I took care of that, Mindy Mouse. Shirley and Vern are here from Rings and Things Mobile Wedding Service. My security team checked them all out and they're keeping things on the up and up for us. The floor is all yours."

"Where's Judge Gardner? Is he okay with this?" Mindy demands.

Jeff chuckles. "I'm sorry, Mindy. William wasn't able to get out of a speaking engagement he had scheduled. Otherwise, he would have been here. He said to tell you it is perfectly okay as long as the paperwork is signed by the right people."

Mindy ponders the situation for a few seconds before she asks, "So, is everybody going to listen to me, for real?"

From the stage, Trevor responds to Mindy, "We wouldn't have asked you to do this if we didn't trust you to do it right. We know you take weddings very seriously and you've always wanted one to go your way. So, here's your chance to play conductor."

Mindy searches the room for the professional wedding officiates. When she spots Shirley, she asks, "Do you have a Bible or something I can study?"

Shirley smiles at her. "Honey, I have everything you need in this handy notebook. Come with me while the bride gets all gussied up. I'll make you a pro in no time."

Mindy follows Shirley out of the room and as she does, she looks over her shoulder. "You guys are lucky I decided to dress up today and I've had a lifetime of practicing pretend marriages between my Barbie and Ken dolls."

The change in the stage over just a few minutes time span is remarkable. Jude, Aidan's new equipment manager is something of a magician. He completely rearranged everything and magically made wedding paraphernalia appear from thin air. Soon, there was a graceful arched gazebo graced with wildflowers.

Mindy solemnly walks out on stage carrying the notebook. She walks up to the music stand serving as the lectern. She carefully sets the notebook down and adjusts the microphone. She nods to Aidan. Aidan plays an elaborate version of the wedding march on the piano. As we stand, I marvel at how much strength I have gotten back in just a few months. I'm stronger now than I was even before the surgery. It's cute to see how attached Denny has become to Madison and Trevor. He is snapping pictures with his cell phone as if he is a proud dad.

Madison looks stunning as Carlton proudly escorts her down the aisle. She stops to kiss Lydia who is currently dozing in Donda's arms. Trevor wipes away a tear as Madison approaches and he joins her and shakes Carlton's hand.

Mindy clears her throat as she announces dramatically, "Ladies and gentlemen, we are gathered here today to join Uncle Trevor and Aunt Madison in marriage — I mean Trevor Black and Madison LaBianca in marriage. If you know of any reason they can't, speak now or forever hold your peace."

The seconds tick by as Mindy looks around. She lets out a long breath. "Whew! I was kinda sweating that one. I thought maybe this might be one of those weird TV shows where they play practical jokes on people."

Madison smiles indulgently at Mindy as she reassures her, "I think we're in the clear."

"Okay let's begin by sharing a bit of your love story. But please don't be like Papa and Grummy. I still have a big test I need to study for on Monday. Aunt Madison, how did you know Uncle Trevor was the guy for you?"

Madison turns toward Trevor and studies his face with a tender smile as she grips his hands. "Trevor Black makes my world safe — not just by catching the evil people who were tormenting me. He allowed me to find peace with the darkest part of my past. He makes it safe for me to believe in love again. He helps believe in myself and a future so bright I have to pinch myself every morning to remind myself it's real."

Mindy addresses Trevor, "Uncle Trevor, when did you know Aunt Maddie was your forever?"

A ghost of a smile crosses Trevor's face as he pulls up memories. "It's funny you would phrase it that way. Before I met Madison, I had a hard time focusing on tomorrow, let alone forever, because I was so mired down in my past. I couldn't look beyond my own failures and see a future filled with love and laughter. You gave me something to fight for and cherish. You restored my dreams in faith, family and love. Lydia is perfect and I love our little family beyond measure."

Mindy swallows hard and blinks away tears. "That was just perfect. I hope someday I find love like yours." She looks down at the notebook in front of her and then continues, "Trevor do you take Madison to be your wife?"

"Absolutely, I do," he vows with a wide smile.

Mindy grins as she declares, "Cool beans! Madison do you take Trevor to be your husband?"

"Of course I do," Madison replies as she wipes away a tear.

"Great! Do you guys have rings?" Mindy asks.

Aidan pulls rings out of his jacket pocket and hands them to Trevor and Madison.

Mindy holds the microphone in front of Madison's face and instructs, "Repeat after me."

Trevor makes a show of loosening his tie and the audience laughs.

"Trevor, with this ring, I thee wed." The audience laughs when the ring appears to get caught on Trevor's knuckle and won't go on correctly.

"Geez, Trev someone may think *you* had a baby or something —" Madison teases.

"Well, since I don't have to do compulsory marching anymore, I may have put on a few pounds," Trevor admits.

"That's okay, I love you anyway," Madison responds with a wink.

Mindy blows her bangs out of her eyes in exasperation as she scolds, "Come on guys, can we stay on script here please? We're so close to being done."

Madison and Trevor straighten up as if they had been threatened with a visit to the principal's office.

Mindy continues, "Uncle Trevor, repeat after me: Madison, with this ring, I thee wed."

I can see Madison's hands shaking as Trevor puts the ring on her finger. Madison can't seem to contain her joy as she throws her arms around Trevor and gives him an all-encompassing hug.

Mindy giggles. "Okay, hold your horses. I now

pronounce you two husband and wife, under someone's authority, I guess — though I'm not real sure whose."

Trevor places his arms around Madison's waist and a loose embrace as he waits for Mindy's instructions.

"Congratulations, you may kiss each other, but don't make it too gross."

"Mindy Mouse, you might want to turn around. I make no guarantees where this guy is concerned. He's pretty mushy," Madison cautions before Trevor captures her lips in a decidedly hot kiss.

Denny leans over and whispers, "No use wasting a perfectly good idea," before he gives me a rather spicy kiss himself.

There's something to be said for having your wedding reception at a concert hall. The professional sound system and lighting definitely lend something to the party atmosphere.

While Aidan's band is taking a well deserved break, someone plugs in their MP3 player with Billy Ray Cyrus into the sound system and *Achy Breaky Heart* blares over the speakers. Denny laughs with glee as he drags me onto the dance floor. "Gwendolyn Ashley, you have run out of excuses now. It's time to show me what you've got. You said you could keep up with me in a line dance, now prove it."

For a moment, I panic. It's been a while since I've danced but as my body reacts to the beat of the music, the steps start to instinctively come back to me. "Oh, I beg to differ my dear husband, I think it's you who needs to worry about keeping up with me," I counter as I throw in a complicated turn.

Denny looks at me in shock. "Where in the world did you learn to do that?"

"A woman has to keep her mysteries every once in a while. I'll never tell," I tease.

By the time the song is finished, we're both breathless. We pause to eat some hors d'oeuvres and grab something to drink. As the members of Aidan's band return to their places, Denny escorts me into the center of the dance floor and holds me tight.

"Well, I think I've finally managed to do it," Denny murmurs against my temple.

"Do what?" I ask, unable to follow his train of thought.

"I've not only managed to capture the attention of the prettiest woman in the room, I got to entertain her all evening at a spectacular party and I get the extra special honor of being able to call you my wife in the process while I slow dance with you. In my book, it doesn't get any better than that."

Just then, Aidan starts to sing *Unchained Melody* and chills race up my spine and my arms are instantly covered with goose bumps. Denny looks at me with concern. "Are you all right, *Amasa*?" he asks. I watch in total fascination as a single white feather floats in from nowhere and lands on Denny's shoulder. I bury my face in his chest for a moment while I collect myself so I can answer him. I carefully pick the white feather off of his shoulder and show it to him as I explain, "I get a little emotional when I hear this song. It was the first dance for Donald and I at our wedding,"

Denny draws in a sudden breath. "I don't know if I should be in awe or completely freaked out by the fact that it was our first song as well. Karen loved the Righteous Brothers. Where did you find that feather? White doves were Karen's favorite bird."

"Denny, it fell on your shoulder when the song started," I explain softly.

"I think they might be trying to tell us something," Denny remarks.

"Well, I'll take it as an omen meaning they approve of our new found love." I snuggle up closer and lay my head on his chest as we continue to sway to the music.

Denny gently kisses the top of my head. "Me too *Amasa*, me too."

Acknowledgments

I would like to acknowledge all the people in my life who have shown me what true love really looks like and the people who have shared with me how difficult it is to start over again after you've lost someone.

I'd also like to say a word of thanks to all the care providers in my life, past and present, who make it possible for me to get up every day and do this job. I know it's a tough job and I appreciate everything you do.

It's a special, scary challenge to love someone with health issues, yet my amazing husband has done it for more than twenty-eight years, and has been with me every step of the way on this crazy journey—twenty-seven of them as my beloved husband—Happy Anniversary to my most ardent fan.

I'd be remiss if I didn't mention the other members of my core support team: my book trailer maker, Rachel Bostwick, my beta readers, Linda Lloyd and Heather Truett, and my editor, Lacie Redding. Thank you all. I could not do this without you.

Thanks to the fans who support my work and my vision to change the world of romance — one book at time. If you liked this book, please tell someone (or a bunch of someones).

Note from the Author

Dear Reader:

Thank you for reading *Love Seasoned*. I hope you enjoyed this out of the ordinary romance. You can read more about Denny and Gwendolyn in *Love Claimed*. Gwendolyn and Denny cheer Donda on as she makes her claim on love.

When she meets him — the one she's destined to be with — the world moved under her feet.

Okay, maybe that's not what really happened, but that's how Donda feels when she meets Jaxson Shepherd.

Too bad he's a doctor. There are few people in the world she trusts less.

To make matters worse, her teenage son seems to think Dr. Jaxson Shepherd walks on water.

Donda has made enough mistakes in her life. She doesn't need to compound the situation by falling in love with a doctor who is too handsome for his own good.

Can Donda and Jaxson make their claim on love or is it too late?

You'll love this family-centered love story with unexpected twists and turns.

Claim your copy of *Love Claimed* in paperback, e-book, or read for free with Kindle Unlimited now.

~Mary

Because love matters, differences don't.

About the Author

I have been lucky enough to live my own version of a romance novel. I married the guy who kissed me at summer camp. He told me on the night we met that he was going to marry me and be the father of my children.

Eventually, I stopped giggling when he said it, and we've been married for more than thirty years. We have two children. The oldest is a Doctor of Osteopathy. He is across the United States completing his residency, but when he's done, he is going to come back to Oregon and practice Family Medicine. Our youngest son is now tackling high school, where he is an honor student. He is interested in becoming an EMT.

I write full time now. I have published more than thirty books and have several more underway. I volunteer my time to a variety of causes. I have worked as a Civil Rights Attorney and diversity advocate. I spent several years working for various social service agencies before becoming an attorney.

Mary Crawford

In my spare time, I love to cook, decorate cakes and, of course, I obsessively, compulsively read.

I would be honored if you would take a few moments out of your busy day to check out my website, MaryCrawfordAuthor.com. While you're there, you can sign up for my newsletter and get a free book. I will be announcing my upcoming books and giving sneak peeks as well as sponsoring giveaways and giving you information about other interesting events.

If you have questions or comments, please E-mail me at Mary@MaryCrawfordAuthor.com or find me on the following social networks:

Facebook: www.facebook.com/authormarycrawford

Website: MaryCrawfordAuthor.com

Twitter: www.twitter.com/MaryCrawfordAut

Resources

If you need help immediately, call 911.

National Domestic Violence Hotline:
800-799-SAFE (7233) or 800-787-3224 (TDD)

National Sexual Assault Hotline:
1-800-656-HOPE (4673)

Domestic Shelters.org— A tool that enables you to find a domestic violence shelter in your area by ZIP Code or address. You can search by the specific service you need. There are also informative articles about how to help someone who may be a victim of domestic violence or sexual abuse.

RAINN (Rape, Abuse, Incest National Network) — The nation's largest anti-sexual assault organization. RAINN operates the National Sexual Assault Hotline at 1.800.656.HOPE and the National Sexual Assault Online Hotline at rainn.org, and publicizes the hotline's free, confidential services; educates the public about sexual assault; and leads national efforts to prevent sexual assault, improve services to victims and ensure that rapists are brought to justice.

Take Back The Night—Media links, literature and other information about surviving and preventing date rape. Many of these resources are beneficial for helping survivors as well as their family and friends through the healing process.

When Georgia Smiled—A Foundation created by Robin McGraw to create and advance programs that help victims of domestic violence and sexual assault live healthy, safe and joy-filled lives. Initiatives include a phone app that helps create a safety plan for use in domestic violence date rape situations, education initiatives for use in high school and college settings and support programs for women.

American Lung Association—A comprehensive resource for finding information about lung cancer and other lung ailments. There are also extensive research and education programs available.

Family Caregiver Alliance—Family Caregiver Alliance supports and sustains the important work of families nationwide caring for loved ones with chronic, disabling health conditions

CPSIA information can be obtained
at www.ICGtesting.com
Printed in the USA
LVHW031723110321
681234LV00001BA/100